"When Greene writes as splendidly as he does here, we are reminded that he has no equivalent."
—*Kirkus Reviews*

"An exciting and moving work, his best in many years."
—*Chicago Sun-Times*

"Superb in every way...."
—*Milwaukee Journal*

"THE HONORARY CONSUL is...as vivid, alive, and unmistakably uniquely his own as *Brighton Rock*, *The Confidential Agent*, and *The Power and the Glory*."
—*Atlantic Monthly*

"A major new novel from the hand of a master craftsman...the premier writer working today in the English language."
—*Chicago Tribune*

"A perfection few significant novelists ever attain."
—*Newsweek*

"It is vintage Graham Greene. What higher recommendation need a book carry?"
—*Detroit News*

THE HONORARY CONSUL—Over 25 weeks on national best-seller lists.

Books by Graham Greene

Novels

The Confidential Agent
The End of the Affair
England Made Me
  (Also published as
  The Shipwrecked)
The Honorary Consul
Our Man in Havana
This Gun for Hire (Original
  British title: A Gun for Sale)

Short Stories

Twenty-One Stories

Autobiography

A Sort of Life

Published by POCKET BOOKS

THE
HONORARY
CONSUL

GRAHAM GREENE

A KANGAROO BOOK
PUBLISHED BY POCKET BOOKS NEW YORK

POCKET BOOKS, a Simon & Schuster division of
GULF & WESTERN CORPORATION
1230 Avenue of the Americas, New York, N.Y. 10020

First Pocket Books printing September, 1974

6th printing

Trademarks registered in the United States and other countries.

Printed in the U.S.A.

Not one of the characters in this book is based on a living character, from the British Ambassador to the old man José. The province and the city in Argentina where the scene is principally set bear, of course, resemblance to a real city and a real province. I have left them nameless because I wished to take certain liberties and not to be tied down to the street plan of a particular city or the map of a particular province.

For Victoria Ocampo with love,
and in memory of the many happy weeks
I have passed at San Isidro
and Mar del Plata

All things merge in one another—good into evil, generosity into justice, religion into politics . . .

—Thomas Hardy

PART
ONE

1

Doctor Eduardo Plarr stood in the small port on the Paraná, among the rails and yellow cranes, watching where a horizontal plume of smoke stretched over the Chaco. It lay between the red bars of sunset like a stripe on a national flag. Doctor Plarr found himself alone at that hour except for the one sailor who was on guard outside the maritime building. It was an evening which, by some mysterious combination of failing light and the smell of an unrecognized plant, brings back to some men the sense of childhood and of future hope and to others the sense of something which has been lost and nearly forgotten.

The rails, the cranes, the maritime building—these had been what Doctor Plarr first saw of his adopted country. The years had changed nothing except by adding the line of smoke which when he arrived here first had not yet been hung out along the horizon on the far side of the Paraná. The factory that produced it had not been built when he came down from the northern republic with his mother more than twenty years before on the weekly service from Paraguay. He remembered his father as he stood on the quay at Asunción beside the short gangway of the small river boat, tall and gray and hollow-chested, and promised with a mechanical optimism that he would join them soon. In a month —or perhaps three—hope creaked in his throat like a piece of rusty machinery.

It seemed in no way strange to the fourteen-year-old boy, though perhaps a little foreign, that his father kissed his wife on her forehead with a sort of reverence,

2

as though she were a mother more than a bedmate. Doctor Plarr had considered himself in those days quite as Spanish as his mother, while his father was very noticeably English-born. His father belonged by right, and not simply by a passport, to the legendary island of snow and fog, the country of Dickens and of Conan Doyle, even though he had probably retained few genuine memories of the land he had left at the age of ten. A picture book, which had been bought for him at the last moment before embarkation by *his* parents, had survived—*London Panorama*—and Henry Plarr used often to turn over for his small son Eduardo the pages of flat gray photographs showing Buckingham Palace, the Tower of London, and a vista of Oxford Street filled with hansoms and horse-drawn cabs and ladies who clutched long skirts. His father, as Doctor Plarr realized much later, was an exile, and this was a continent of exiles—of Italians, of Czechs, of Poles, of Welsh, of English. When Doctor Plarr as a boy read a novel of Dickens he read it as a foreigner might do, taking it all for contemporary truth for want of any other evidence, like a Russian who believes that the bailiff and the coffinmaker still follow their unchanged vocations in a world where Oliver Twist is somewhere imprisoned in a London cellar asking for more.

At fourteen he could not understand the motives which had made his father stay behind on the quay of the old capital on the river. It took more than a few years of life in Buenos Aires before he began to realize that the existence of an exile did not make for simplicity —so many documents, so many visits to government offices. Simplicity belonged by right to those who were native-born, those who could take the conditions of life, however bizarre, for granted. The Spanish language was Roman by origin, and the Romans were a simple people. *Machismo*—the sense of masculine pride —was the Spanish equivalent of *virtus*. It had little to do with English courage or a stiff upper lip. Perhaps his father in his foreign way was trying to imitate *machismo* when he chose to face alone the daily increasing dangers on the other side of the Paraguayan border, but it was only the stiff lip which showed upon the quay.

The young Plarr and his mother reached the river port at almost this hour of the evening on their way to the great noisy capital of the republic in the south (their departure having been delayed some hours by a political demonstration), and something in the scene—the old colonial houses, a crumble of stucco in the street behind the waterfront—two lovers embracing on a bench—a moonstruck statue of a naked woman and the bust of an admiral with a homely Irish name—the electric light globes like great ripe fruit above a soft-drink stand—became lodged in the young Plarr's mind as a symbol of unaccustomed peace, so that, at long last, when he felt an urgent need to escape somewhere from the skyscrapers, the traffic blocks, the sirens of police cars and ambulances, the heroic statues of liberators on horseback, he chose to come back to this small northern city to work, with all the prestige of a qualified doctor from Buenos Aires. Not one of his friends in the capital or his coffeehouse acquaintances came near to understanding his motive: he would find a hot humid unhealthy climate in the north, they all assured him of that, and a town where nothing ever happened, not even violence.

"Perhaps it's unhealthy enough for me to build a better practice," he would reply with a smile which was quite as unmeaning—or false—as his father's expression of hope.

In Buenos Aires, during the long years of separation, they had received one letter only from his father. It was addressed on the envelope to both of them, *Señora e hijo*. The letter had not come through the post. They found it stuck under the door of their apartment on a

Sunday evening about four years after their arrival when they returned from the cinema where they had watched *Gone with the Wind* for the third time. His mother never missed a revival, perhaps because the old film and the old stars made civil war seem for a few hours something static and undangerous. Clark Gable and Vivien Leigh bobbed up again through the years in spite of all the bullets.

The envelope was very dirty and scrumpled and it was marked "By Hand," but they were never to learn by whose hand. It was not written on their old notepaper, which had been elegantly stamped in Gothic type with the name of the *estancia,* but on the lined leaves of a cheap notebook. The letter was full, as the voice on the quay had been, of pretended hope—"things," his father wrote, were bound to settle down soon; it was undated, so perhaps the "hope" had been exhausted for a long time before the letter arrived. They never heard from his father again; not even a report or a rumor reached them either of his imprisonment or of his death. He had concluded the letter with Spanish formality, "It is my great comfort that the two whom I love best in the world are both in safety, your affectionate husband and father, Henry Plarr."

Doctor Plarr could not measure himself exactly how much he had been influenced to return to the small river port by the sense that here he would be living near the border of the country where he had been born and where his father was buried—whether in a prison or a patch of ground he would probably never know. He had only to drive a few kilometers northeast and look across the curve of the river. He had only like the smugglers to take a canoe . . . He felt sometimes like a watchman waiting for a signal. There was of course a more immediate motive. Once to a mistress he had said, "I left Buenos Aires to get away as far as possible from my mother." It was true she had mislaid her beauty and become querulous over her lost *estancia* as she lived on into middle age in the great sprawling muddled capital with its *fantástica arquitectura* of skyscrapers in mean streets rising haphazardly and covered for twenty floors by Pepsi-Cola advertisements.

Doctor Plarr turned his back on the port and continued his evening promenade along the bank of the river. The sky was dark by now so that he could no longer distinguish the plume of smoke or see the line of the opposite bank. The lamps of the ferry which linked the city to the Chaco approached like an illuminated pencil at a slow-drawn wavering diagonal as it fought through the current moving heavily south. The Three Marys hung in the sky like all that was left of a broken rosary chain—the cross lay where it had fallen elsewhere. Doctor Plarr, who every ten years, without quite knowing why, renewed his English passport, felt a sudden desire for company which was not Spanish.

There were only two other Englishmen, so far as he was aware, in the city, an old English teacher who had adopted the title of doctor without ever having seen the inside of a university, and Charley Fortnum, the Honorary Consul. Since the morning months ago when he had begun sleeping with Charley Fortnum's wife, Doctor Plarr found he was ill at ease in the Consul's company; perhaps he was plagued by primitive sensations of guilt; perhaps he was irritated by the complacency of Charley Fortnum who appeared so modestly confident of his wife's fidelity. He talked with pride rather than anxiety of his wife's troubles in her early pregnancy as though they were a kind of compliment to his prowess until Doctor Plarr was almost ready to exclaim, "But who do you suppose is the father?"

There remained Doctor Humphries . . . though it was still too early to go and find the old man where he lived at the Hotel Bolívar.

Doctor Plarr found a seat under one of the white

globes which lit the river front and took a book out of his pocket. From where he sat he could keep his eye on his car parked by the Coca-Cola stall. The book Doctor Plarr carried with him was a novel written by one of his patients, Jorge Julio Saavedra. Saavedra, too, bore the title of doctor, but it was an authentic title, for twenty years ago he had been awarded an honorary degree in the capital. The novel, which had been Doctor Saavedra's first and most successful, was called *The Taciturn Heart,* and it was written in a heavily loaded melancholy style, full of the spirit of *machismo.*

Doctor Plarr found it hard to read more than a few pages at a time. These noble and uncommunicative characters in Latin-American literature seemed to him too simple and too heroic ever to have had living models. Rousseau and Chateaubriand were a greater influence in South America than Freud—there was even a city in Brazil named after Benjamin Constant. He read: "Julio Moreno would sit for hours in silence, on those days when the wind blew continuously from the sea and salted their few hectares of dry earth, shriveling the rare plants which had survived the last wind, his chin in his hands, his eyes closed as though he wished to live only in some hidden corridor of his nature from which his wife was excluded. He never complained. She would stand beside him for long minutes, holding the maté gourd in her left hand, and when he opened his eyes Julio Moreno would take it from her without a word spoken. Only a relaxation of the muscles around the stern and unbeaten mouth appeared to her like an expression of thanks."

Doctor Plarr, who had been brought up by his father on the works of Dickens and Conan Doyle, found the novels of Doctor Jorge Julio Saavedra hard to read, but he regarded the effort as part of his medical duties. In a few days he would have to take one of his regular dinners with Doctor Saavedra at the Hotel Nacional and he must be ready to make some comment on the book which Doctor Saavedra had so warmly inscribed "To my friend and counselor Doctor Eduardo Plarr, this my first book to show him I have not always been a political novelist and to disclose, as I can only do to a close friend, the first fruit of my inspiration." Doctor Saavedra was in fact far from taciturn, but Doctor Plarr suspected he regarded himself as a Moreno *manqué*. Perhaps it was significant that he had given Moreno one of his own Christian names . . .

Doctor Plarr had never caught anyone else reading in the whole city. When he dined out he saw only books imprisoned behind glass to guard them from humidity. He never met anyone unawares reading by the river or even in one of the city squares—except occasionally *El Litoral,* the local paper. There were sometimes lovers on the benches or tired women with shopping baskets, or tramps, but never readers. A tramp would proudly occupy a whole bench. No one cared to share the bench with a tramp, so unlike the rest of the world he could stretch at full length.

Perhaps reading in the open air was a habit he had acquired from his father who always took a book with him when he went farming, and in the orange-scented air of his abandoned country Doctor Plarr had got through all the works of Dickens except *Christmas Tales*. People when they first saw him sitting on a bench with an open book had looked at him with keen curiosity. Perhaps they thought it was a custom peculiar to foreign doctors. It was not exactly unmanly, but it was certainly foreign. The men here preferred to stand at street corners and talk, or sit drinking cups of coffee and talk, or lean out of a window and talk. And all the time, while they talked, they touched each other to emphasize a point or just from friendship. In public Doctor Plarr touched nobody, only his book. It was a sign, like his English passport, that he would always remain a stranger: he would never be properly assimilated.

He began to read again. "She herself worked in an unbroken silence, accepting the hard toil, like the bad seasons, as a law of nature."

Doctor Saavedra had enjoyed a period of critical and popular success in the capital. When he began to feel himself neglected by the reviewers—and still worse by the hostesses and the newspaper reporters—he had come to the north where his great-grandfather had been governor and where he was shown the proper respect due to a famous novelist from the capital, even though there were probably few people who actually read his books. Strangely enough the mental geography of his novels remained unaltered. Wherever he might choose to live now, he had found his mythical region once and forever as a young man, the result of a holiday which he had taken in a small town by the sea, in the far south near Trelew. He had never encountered a Moreno, but he had imagined him very clearly one evening in the bar of a small hotel, where a man sat in melancholy silence over a drink.

Doctor Plarr had learned all this in the capital from an old friend and jealous enemy of the novelist, and he found the knowledge of Saavedra's background of some value when he came to treat his patient who suffered from bouts of voluble manic-depression. The same character appeared again and again in all his books, his history changed a little, but never his strong sad silence. The friend and enemy, who had accompanied the young Saavedra on that voyage of discovery, had exclaimed scornfully, "And do you know who the man was? He was a Welshman, a Welshman. Who has ever heard of a Welshman with *machismo?* There are a lot of Welshmen in those parts. He was drunk, that was all. His weekly drunk when he came in from the country."

A ferry left for the invisible shore of scrub and

swamp, and later the same ferry returned. Doctor Plarr found it difficult to concentrate on the taciturnity of Julio Moreno's heart. Moreno's wife left him at last with a casual laborer on his land who had youth and good looks and some facility in talking, but she was unhappy in the city by the sea where her lover remained unemployed. He soon became habitually drunk in bars and garrulous in bed, and she felt a nostalgia for the long silences and the dry salt ruined earth. So back she came to Moreno, who made room for her without a word at the table where he had prepared a meager dinner, and afterward he sat mutely in his customary chair with his chin in his hands while she stood beside him holding his maté gourd. There were still another hundred pages to come, though the story, it seemed to Doctor Plarr, might well have ended there. However Julio Moreno's *machismo* had not yet found full expression, and when he indicated to his wife, in the fewest possible words, his decision to visit the city of Trelew, Doctor Plarr felt quite certain of what would happen there. Julio Moreno would encounter the laborer in a bar of the city and then there would be a fight with knives, won of course by the younger man. Hadn't his wife, when he left, seen in Moreno's eyes "the expression of an exhausted swimmer who surrenders to the dark tide of his ineluctable destiny"?

It could not be said that Doctor Saavedra wrote badly. There was a heavy music in his style, the drumbeats of destiny were never very far away, but Doctor Plarr sometimes had a longing to exclaim to his melancholy patient, "Life isn't like that. Life isn't noble or dignified. Even Latin-American life. Nothing is ineluctable. Life has surprises. Life is absurd. Because it's absurd there is always hope. Why, one day we may even discover a cure for cancer and the common cold." He turned to the last page. Sure enough Julio Moreno's life blood was draining away between the broken tiles on the floor of the Trelew bar and his wife (how had she got there so quickly?) stood by his side, though for once she was not holding a maté gourd. "A relaxation of the muscles around the hard unbeaten mouth told her, before the eyes closed on the immense weariness of existence, that he found her presence welcome."

Doctor Plarr closed the book with a bang of irritation. The Southern Cross lay on its crosspiece in a night which was full of stars. No towns or television masts or lighted windows broke the flat horizon. If he went home might there still be the danger of a telephone call?

When the time had come to leave his last patient, the finance secretary's wife who was suffering from a touch of fever, he was determined not to go home before the early morning. He wanted to keep away from the telephone until it was too late for any unprofessional call. There was one particular possibility, at this hour on this day, of being troubled. Charley Fortnum, he knew, was dining with the Governor who needed an interpreter for his guest of honor, the American Ambassador. Clara, now she had overcome her fear of using the telephone, might easily call him and demand his company, with her husband out of the way, and he had no wish to see her on this Tuesday night of all nights. His sexual feeling was anesthetized by anxiety. He knew how likely it was that Charley would return unexpectedly early; for the dinner would certainly, sooner or later, be canceled for a reason he had no right to know in advance.

Doctor Plarr decided that it was better to keep out of the way until midnight. The Governor's party would have surely dispersed by that time, and Charley Fortnum would be well on his way home. I am not a man with *machismo*, Doctor Plarr reflected ruefully, though he could hardly imagine Charley Fortnum coming at him with a knife. He got up from the bench. The hour was late enough for the professor of English.

He did not find Doctor Humphries, as he expected, at the Hotel Bolívar. Doctor Humphries had a small room with a shower on the ground floor with a window opening on the patio which contained one dusty palm and a dead fountain. He had left his door unlocked and this perhaps showed his confidence in stability. Doctor Plarr remembered how at night his father in Paraguay would lock even the internal doors of his house, the bedrooms, the lavatories, the unused guest rooms, not against robbers but against the police, the military and the official assassins, though they would certainly not have been deterred long by locked doors.

In Doctor Humphries' room there was hardly space for a bed, a dressing table, two chairs, a basin and the shower. You had to fight your way through them as though they were passengers in a crowded subway. Doctor Plarr saw that Doctor Humphries had pasted a new picture on the wall, from the Spanish edition of *Life,* showing the Queen perched on a horse at Trooping the Color. The choice was not necessarily a mark of patriotism or nostalgia: patches of damp were continually appearing on the plaster of the room and Doctor Humphries covered them with the nearest picture which came to hand. Perhaps however his choice did show a certain preference for wakening with the Queen's face rather than Mr. Nixon's on the wall. (Mr. Nixon's face would surely have appeared somewhere in the same number of *Life.*) Inside the small room it was cool, but even the coolness was humid. The shower behind the plastic curtain had a faulty washer and dripped upon the tiles. The narrow bed was pulled together rather than made—the bumpy sheet might have been hastily drawn over a corpse, and a mosquito net hung bundled above it like a gray cloud threatening rain. Doctor Plarr was sorry for the self-styled doctor of letters: it was not the kind of surroundings in which any one with free will—if such a man existed—would

12

have chosen to await death. My father, he thought with disquiet, must be about the same age as Humphries now, and perhaps he survives in even worse surroundings.

A scrap of paper was inserted in the frame of Humphries' looking glass—"Gone to the Italian Club." Perhaps he had been expecting a pupil and that was the reason why he had left his door unlocked. The Italian Club was in a once-impressive colonial building across the road. There was a bust of somebody, perhaps of Cavour or Mazzini, but the stone was pockmarked and the inscription no longer readable; it stood between the house, which had a stone garland of flowers over every tall window, and the street. Once there had been a great number of Italians living in the city, but now all that was left of the club was the name, the bust, the imposing façade which bore a nineteenth-century date in Roman numerals. There were a few tables where you could eat cheaply without paying a subscription, and only one Italian was left, the solitary waiter who had been born in Naples. The cook was of Hungarian origin and served little else but goulash, a dish in which he could easily disguise the quality of the ingredients, a wise thing to do since the best beef went down the river to the capital, more than eight hundred kilometers away.

Doctor Humphries was seated at a table close to an open window with a napkin tucked into his frayed collar. However hot the day he was always dressed in a suit with a tie and a waistcoat like a Victorian man of letters living in Florence. He wore steel-rimmed spectacles; probably the prescription had not been revised for years, for he bent very low over the goulash to see what he was eating. His white hair was streaked the color of youth by nicotine, and there were smears of nearly the same color on his napkin from the goulash. Doctor Plarr said, "Good evening, Doctor Humphries."

"Ah, you found my note?"

"I'd have looked in here anyway. How did you know I was coming to your room?"

"I didn't, Doctor Plarr. But I thought somebody might look in, somebody . . ."

"I had been going to suggest we have dinner at the National," Doctor Plarr explained. He looked around the restaurant for the waiter without any anticipation of pleasure. They were the only clients.

"Very kind of you," Doctor Humphries said. "Another day, if you'll let me have what I believe the Yankees call a raincheck. The goulash here is not so bad, one grows a little tired of it, but at least it's filling." He was a very thin old man. He gave the impression of someone who had worked a long while at eating in the hopeless hope of filling an inexhaustible cavity.

For want of anything better Doctor Plarr, too, ordered goulash. Doctor Humphries said, "I am surprised to see you. I would have thought the Governor might have invited you . . . he must need someone who speaks English for his dinner tonight."

Doctor Plarr realized why the message had been stuck into the looking glass. There could have been a last-minute slip in the Governor's arrangements. It had happened once, and Doctor Humphries had been summoned . . . After all there were only three Englishmen who were available. He said, "He has invited Charley Fortnum."

"Oh yes, of course," Doctor Humphries said, "our Honorary Consul." He underlined the adjective in a tone of embittered denigration. "This is a diplomatic dinner. I suppose the Honorary Consul's wife could not appear for reasons of health?"

"The American Ambassador is unmarried, Doctor Humphries. It's informal—a stag party."

"A very suitable occasion one might have thought for inviting Mrs. Fortnum to entertain the guests. She must be accustomed to stag parties. But why does the Governor not invite you or me?"

"Be fair, doctor. You and I have no official position here."

"But we know a lot more about the Jesuit ruins than Charley Fortnum does. According to *El Litoral* the Ambassador has come here to see the ruins, not the tea or the maté crop, though that hardly seems likely. American ambassadors are usually men of business."

"The new Ambassador wants to create a good impression," Doctor Plarr said. "Art and history. He can't be suspected of a take-over bid there. He wants to show a scholarly interest in our province, not a commercial one. The secretary of finance has not been invited, even though he speaks a little English. Otherwise a loan might have been suspected."

"And the Ambassador—doesn't he speak enough Spanish for a polite toast and a few platitudes?"

"They say he is making rapid progress."

"What a lot you always seem to know about everything, Plarr. I only know what we read in *El Litoral*. He's off to the ruins tomorrow, isn't he?"

"No, he went there today. Tonight he returns to B.A. by air."

"The paper's wrong then?"

"The official program was a little inaccurate. I suppose the Governor didn't want any incidents."

"Incidents here? What an idea! I haven't seen an incident in this province in twenty years. Incidents only happen in Córdoba. The goulash isn't so very bad, is it?" he asked hopefully.

"I've eaten worse," Doctor Plarr said without trying to remember on what occasion.

"I see you've been reading one of Saavedra's books. What do you think of it?"

"Very talented," Doctor Plarr said. Like the Governor he didn't want any incidents, and he recognized

15

the malice which remained alive and kicking in the old man long after discretion had died from a lifetime's neglect.

"You can really read that stuff? You believe in all that *machismo?*"

"While I read it," Doctor Plarr said with care, "I can suspend my disbelief."

"These Argentinians—they all believe their grandfathers rode with the gauchos. Saavedra has about as much *machismo* as Charley Fortnum. Is it true Charley's having a baby?"

"Yes."

"Who's the lucky father?"

"Why not Charley?"

"An old man and a drunk? You're her doctor, Plarr. Tell me a little bit of the truth. I don't ask for a very big bit."

"Why do you always want the truth?"

"Contrary to common belief the truth is nearly always funny. It's only tragedy which people bother to imagine or invent. If you really knew what went into this goulash you'd laugh."

"Do you know?"

"No. People always conspire to keep the truth from me. Even you lie to me, Plarr."

"Me?"

"You lie to me about Saavedra's novel and Charley Fortnum's baby. Let's hope, for his sake, it's a girl."

"Why?"

"It's so much more difficult to detect the father from the features." Doctor Humphries began to wipe his plate clean with a piece of bread. "Can you tell me why I'm always hungry, doctor? I don't eat *well,* and yet I eat an awful lot of what they call nourishing food."

"If you really wanted the truth I would have to examine you, take an x-ray . . ."

16

"Oh no, no. I only want the truth about other people. It's always other people who are funny."

"Then why ask me?"

"A conversational gambit," the old man said, "to hide my embarrassment while I help myself to the last piece of bread."

"Do they grudge us bread here?" Doctor Plarr called across a waste of empty tables, "Waiter, some more bread."

The only Italian came shuffling toward them. He carried a bread basket with three pieces of bread and he watched with black anxiety when the number was reduced to one. He might have been a junior member of the Mafia who had disobeyed the order of his chief.

"Did you see the sign he made?" Doctor Humphries asked.

"No."

"He put out two of his fingers. Against the evil eye. He thinks I have the evil eye."

"Why?"

"I once made a disrespectful remark about the Madonna of Pompeii."

"What about a game of chess when you have finished?" Doctor Plarr asked. He had to pass the time somehow, away from his apartment and the telephone by the bed.

"I've finished now."

They went back to the little over-lived-in room in the Hotel Bolívar. The manager was reading *El Litoral* in the patio with his fly open for coolness. He said, "Someone was asking for you on the telephone, doctor."

"For me?" Humphries exclaimed with excitement. "Who was it? What did you tell them?"

"No, it was for Doctor Plarr, professor. A woman. She thought the doctor might be with you."

"If she rings again," Plarr said, "don't say that I am here."

"Have you no curiosity?" Doctor Humphries asked.

"Oh, I can guess who it is."

"Not a patient, eh?"

"Yes, a patient. There's no urgency. Nothing to worry about."

Doctor Plarr found himself checkmated in under twenty moves, and he began impatiently to set the pieces out again.

"Whatever you may say you are worried about something," the old man said.

"It's that damn shower. Drip drip drip. Why don't you have it mended?"

"What harm does it do? It's soothing. It sings me to sleep."

Doctor Humphries began with a king's pawn opening. "KP_4," he said. "Even the great Capablanca would sometimes begin as simply as that. Charley Fortnum," he added, "has got his new Cadillac."

"Yes."

"How old's your home-grown Fiat?"

"Four—five years old."

"It pays to be a Consul, doesn't it? Permission to import a car every two years. I suppose he's got a general lined up in the capital to buy it as soon as he's run it in."

"Probably. It's your move."

"If he got his wife made a Consul, too, they could import a car a year between them. A fortune. Is there any sexual discrimination in the consular service?"

"I don't know the rules."

"How much did he pay to get appointed, do you suppose?"

"That's a canard, Humphries. He paid nothing. It's not the way our Foreign Office works. Some very important visitors wanted to see the ruins. They had no

18

Spanish. Charley Fortnum gave them a good time. It was as simple as that. And lucky for him. He wasn't doing very well with his maté crop, but a Cadillac every two years makes a lot of difference."

"Yes, you could say he married on his Cadillac. But I'm surprised that woman of his needed the price of a Cadillac. Surely a Morris Minor would have done."

"I'm being unfair," Doctor Plarr said. "It wasn't only because he looked after royalty. There were quite a number of Englishmen in the province in those days —you know that better than I do. And there was one who got into a mess over the border—the time when the guerrillas went across—and Fortnum knew the local ropes. He saved the Ambassador a lot of trouble. All the same he was lucky—some ambassadors are more grateful than others."

"So now if we are in a spot of trouble we have to depend on Charley Fortnum. Check."

Doctor Plarr had to exchange his queen for a bishop. He said, "There are worse people than Charley Fortnum."

"You are in bad trouble now and he can't save you."

Doctor Plarr looked quickly up from the board, but the old man was only referring to the game. "Check again," he said. "And mate." He added, "That shower has been out of order for six months. You don't always lose to me as easily as that."

"Your game's improved."

2

Doctor Plarr refused a third game and drove home. He lived on the top floor of a block of yellow flats which faced the Paraná. The block was one of the eyesores of the old colonial city, but the yellow was fading a little year by year, and anyway he couldn't afford a house while his mother was alive. It was extraordinary how much a woman could spend on sweet cakes in the capital.

As Doctor Plarr closed his shutters the last ferry was approaching across the river, and after he got into bed he heard the heavy thunder of a plane which was making a slow turn overhead: it sounded very low, as though it had lifted off the ground only a few minutes before. It was certainly not a long-distance jet overflying the city on the way to Buenos Aires or Asunción —in any case the hour was too late for a commercial flight. It might, Plarr thought, be the American Ambassador's plane, but he had never expected to hear that. He turned off the light and lay in the dark thinking of all the things that could so easily have gone wrong as the noise of the engine faded, beating south, carrying whom? He wanted to lift the receiver and dial Charley Fortnum, but there was no excuse he could think of for disturbing him at that hour. He could hardly ask: did the Ambassador enjoy the ruins? Did the dinner pass off well? I suppose at the Governor's you must have had some decent steaks? It wasn't his habit to gossip with Charley Fortnum at that hour—Charley was an uxorious man.

He turned his light on again—better to read than

worry, and as he knew now what the ending would be without any possibility of mistake, Doctor Saavedra's book proved a good sedative. There was little traffic along the river front; once a police car went by with the sirens screaming, but Plarr soon fell asleep with the light still burning.

He was awakened by the telephone. His watch stood at exactly two in the morning. He knew of no patient likely to ring him at that hour.

"Yes," he asked, "who are you?"

A voice he didn't recognize replied, with elaborate caution, "Our entertainment was a success."

Plarr said, "Who are you? Why tell me that? What entertainment? I'm not interested." He spoke with the irritation of fear.

"We are worried about one of the cast. He was taken ill."

"I don't know what you are talking about."

"We are afraid the strain of his part may have been too great."

Never before had they telephoned him so openly and at such a suspect hour. There was no reason to believe that his line was tapped, but they had no right to take the smallest risk. Refugees from the north were often kept under a certain loose surveillance in the border region since the days of the guerrilla fighting, if only for their own protection: there were cases of men who had been dragged home to Paraguay across the Paraná to die. There had been an exiled doctor in Posadas . . . Because he was a man of the same profession the doctor's example had been present often in Plarr's mind since the plans for the entertainment were first disclosed to him. This telephone call to his apartment could not be justified except in a case of great urgency. One death among the entertainers—by the rules they had set themselves—was to be expected and justified nothing.

He said, "I don't know what you are talking about.

21

You have the wrong number." He replaced the receiver and lay looking at the telephone as though it were a black and venomous object which would certainly strike again. It did two minutes later, and he had to listen—it might be an ordinary patient's call.

"Yes—who are you?"

The same voice said, "You have to come. He may be dying."

Doctor Plarr asked with resignation, "What do you want me to do?"

"We'll pick you up in the street in exactly five minutes. If we are not there, then in ten minutes. After that be ready every five minutes."

"What does your watch say?"

"Six minutes past two."

The doctor put on a pair of trousers and a shirt; then he packed a briefcase with what might be required (a bullet wound seemed the most likely trouble) and ran lightly down the stairs in his socks. He knew the noise of the lift was audible through the thin walls of every flat. By two ten he was standing outside the block and at two twelve he went in again and shut the door. At two sixteen he was watching a second time in the street and a two eighteen he was back inside. Fear made him furious. His liberty, perhaps his life, seemed to lie in hopelessly incompetent hands. He knew only two members of the group—they had been at school with him in Asunción—and those who share one's childhood never seem to grow up. He had no more belief in their efficiency than he had when they were students; the organization they had once belonged to in Paraguay, the Juventud Febrerista, had effected little except the death of most of the other members in an ill-advised and ill-led guerrilla action.

Indeed it was that very sense of amateurism which had persuaded him to become involved. He hadn't believed in their plans, and to listen to them was only a mark of friendship. When he questioned them about what they would do in certain eventualities the ruthlessness of their replies seemed to him a form of play acting. (They had all three taken minor parts in a school performance of *Macbeth*—the prose translation did not make the play more plausible.)

Now, as he stood in the dark hall, watching intently the luminous dial of his watch, he realized he had never for a moment believed they would reach the point of action. Even when he had given them the precise information they required of the American Ambassador's movements (he had learned the details from Charley Fortnum over a Long John) and supplied them with the drug they needed, he still didn't believe that anything would really happen. Only when he woke that morning and heard Léon's voice, "The show goes on," did it occur to him that perhaps these amateurs might after all be dangerous. Was it Léon Rivas who was dying now? Or Aquino?

It was two twenty-two when he went outside for the third time. A car swerved round the block and stopped, the engine running. A hand waved to him.

As far as he could tell in the light of the dashboard, he didn't know the man at the wheel, but his companion he was able to guess at in the dark by the line of the thin beard which outlined the jaw. It was in a police station cell that Aquino had grown his beard and had begun to write his poetry, and it was in the cell too that he had developed a hungry passion for *chipá*, those doughy rolls made out of mandioca, that can only be properly appreciated after semistarvation.

"What went wrong, Aquino?"

"The car would not start. Dust in the carburetor. That was it, Diego? And then there was a police patrol."

"I meant who is dying?"

"Nobody, we hope."

"León?"

"He is all right."

"Why did you telephone? You promised not to involve me. León promised."

He would never have consented to help them if it had not been for León whom he had missed almost as much as his father when he and his mother left on the river boat. León was someone whose word he believed that he could always trust, even though his word seemed later to have been broken when Plarr heard that León had become a priest instead of the fearless *abogado* who would defend the poor and the innocent, like Perry Mason. In his school days León had possessed an enormous collection of Perry Masons stiffly translated into classical Spanish prose. He lent them carefully, one at a time, to selected friends. Perry Mason's secretary Della was the first woman to arouse Plarr's sexual appetite.

"Father Rivas told us to fetch you," the man called Diego said.

He continued to call León Father, Doctor Plarr noticed, though he had broken a second vow when he left the Church and married, but that particular broken promise was not one which worried Plarr, who never went to Mass except when he accompanied his mother on one of his rare visits to the capital. León, it seemed to him, was struggling back from a succession of failures toward the primal promise to the poor he had never intended to break. He would end as an *abogado* yet.

They turned into Tucumán and then into San Martín, but Doctor Plarr after that tried to avoid looking out. It was as well not to know where they were going. If the worst happened he wanted to betray as little as possible under interrogation.

They were driving fast enough to attract attention. He asked, "You are not afraid of the police patrols?"

"León has them all mapped out. He has studied them for a month."

"But tonight—surely it's a little bit special."

"The Ambassador's car will have been found in the upper Paraná. They will be searching every house on the border, and they will have warned them in Encarnación across the river. There will be road blocks on the road to Rosario. The patrols here must have been cut. They need the men elsewhere. And this is the last place they will look for him with the Governor waiting at his house to take him to the airport."

"I hope you are right."

For a moment, without meaning to, Doctor Plarr raised his eyes as the car lurched round a turning, and he saw on the pavement a deck chair containing a stout elderly woman whom he knew, as he knew the small open doorway behind her—her name was Señora Sanchez and she never slept before her last customer had gone home. She was the richest woman in town or so it was believed.

Doctor Plarr said, "What happened about the Governor's dinner? How long did they wait?" He could imagine the confusion. One couldn't telephone to a lot of ruins.

"I do not know."

"Surely you had somebody on the watch?"

"We had enough on our hands."

He was back with the amateurs; it seemed to Doctor Plarr that the plot would have been better written by Saavedra. Ingenuity, if not *machismo*, was distinctly lacking.

"I heard a plane. Was it the Ambassador's?"

"If it was, it must have gone back empty."

"You seem to know very little," Doctor Plarr said. "Who is hurt?"

The car drew suddenly and roughly up on the margin of a dirt track. "We get out here," Aquino said. After

Doctor Plarr had left the car he heard it being backed a few yards. He stood still, letting his eyes grow accustomed to the dark, until he was able to see by starlight the kind of place they had brought him to. It was part of the *bidonville* which lay between the city and the bend of the river. The track was almost as wide as a city street, and he could just see a shack made out of dried mud and old petrol cans hidden among the avocados. As his sight cleared he began to make out other huts standing concealed among the trees, like men in ambush. Aquino led him on. The doctor's feet sank more than ankle deep in mud. Even a jeep would have to pass slowly here. There would be plenty of warning if the police made a raid. Perhaps after all they were amateurs of some intelligence.

"Is *he* here?" he asked Aquino.

"Who?"

"Oh, for God's sake, there are no microphones in the trees. The Ambassador, of course."

"Yes, he is here all right. But he has not come round after the injection."

They moved as quickly as they could along the mud track, passing several dark huts. The silence seemed unnatural—not even a child crying. Doctor Plarr paused to recover breath. "These people," he whispered, "they must have heard your car."

"They will not talk. They think we are smugglers. Anyway you can imagine—they are no friends to the police."

Diego led the way down a side turning where the mud was even deeper. It had not rained for two days, but in this *barrio* of the poor the mud lay permanently until the dry season was well advanced. There was nowhere for the water to drain, and yet, as Doctor Plarr knew well, the inhabitants had to walk as much as a mile in order to find a tap which gave water fit for drinking. The children—he had treated many of them—were big-bellied from protein deficiency. Perhaps he had been many times down this very track—it was indistinguishable from all the others; he had always needed a guide when he visited a patient here. For some reason *The Taciturn Heart* came back to his mind. To fight for one's honor with knives over a woman, that belonged to another, an absurdly outdated world, which had ceased to exist except in the romantic imagination of writers like Saavedra. Honor meant nothing to the starving. To them belonged the more serious fight for survival.

"Is that you, Eduardo?" a voice asked.

"Yes, is that you, León?"

Somebody held a candle up long enough for him to reach the threshold. Then the door was closed quickly behind him.

In the light of the candle he saw the man whom they still called Father Rivas; León looked as thin and immature in his T-shirt and jeans as the boy he had known in the country across the border. His brown eyes were too big for his face, the large ears set almost at right angles to his skull made him resemble one of the small mongrel dogs which haunted the *barrio* of the poor. There was the same soft fidelity in the eyes and a vulnerability in the protruding ears. He could have been taken in spite of his age for a shy seminarist.

"You have been a long time, Eduardo," he complained softly.

"Ask your driver Diego about that."

"The Ambassador is still in a coma. We had to give him a second injection. He was thrashing around too much."

"I told you a second shot would be dangerous."

"Everything is dangerous," Father Rivas said gently, as though he were in the confessional warning someone against the temptation of proximity.

While Doctor Plarr unpacked his briefcase Father Rivas went on, "He is breathing very heavily."

"What will you do if he stops breathing altogether?"

"We shall have to change our tactics."

"How?"

"We shall have to announce he was executed. Revolutionary justice," he added with an unhappy grin. "Please, I beg you, do all you can."

"Of course."

"We do not want him to die," Father Rivas said. "Our job is to save lives."

They went into the only other room, in which a bed had been improvised out of a long wooden box—he couldn't see clearly what kind of a box—with a few blankets spread over it. Doctor Plarr heard the deep uneven breathing of the drugged man, like someone struggling awake from a nightmare. He said, "Bring the light closer." He bent down and looked closely at the flushed face. For a long moment he couldn't believe his eyes. Then he laughed from the shock of what he had seen. "Oh León," he said, "you have taken up the wrong profession."

"What do you mean?"

"You would do better to go back to the Church. You are not made to be a kidnapper."

"I do not understand. Is he dying?"

Doctor Plarr said, "You needn't worry, León, he's not going to die, but this isn't the American Ambassador."

"Not . . ."

"This is Charley Fortnum."

"Who is Charley Fortnum?"

"Our Honorary Consul," Doctor Plarr said in the same tone of mockery which Doctor Humphries had employed.

"But that is impossible," Father Rivas exclaimed.

"Charley Fortnum's veins run with alcohol, not blood.

28

The morphine I gave you would have acted more gently on the Ambassador. The Ambassador is afraid of alcohol. They had to provide Coca-Cola for the dinner tonight. So Charley told me. He will be all right in a little while. Leave him to sleep it off," but before he had time to leave the room the man on the wooden box opened his eyes. He stared at Doctor Plarr and Doctor Plarr stared back at him. It was as well to know for certain whether he were recognized.

"Take me home," Fortnum said, "home," and then his body lurched sideways into a deeper sleep.

"Did he recognize you?" Father Rivas asked.

"How would I know?"

"If he recognized you it would complicate matters."

Somebody lit a second candle in the outer room, but no one spoke; it was as though they all waited to catch a suggestion in another man's eyes as to what should be done now. At last Aquino said, "This will not please El Tigre."

"It's really rather comic," Doctor Plarr said, "when you think of it. That must have been the Ambassador's plane I heard, and he was in it. On the way back to Buenos Aires. I wonder how the Governor's dinner went without an interpreter." He looked from one face to another, but no one smiled in return.

There were two men in the room who were unknown to him, and for the first time he noticed a woman who lay asleep on the floor in a dark corner—he had mistaken her for a *poncho* which someone had dropped. One of them was a Negro with a pockmarked face, the other an Indian who spoke up now. He couldn't understand the words—they were not Spanish. "What is he saying, León?"

"Miguel thinks we ought to put him into the river to drown."

"And what did you say?"

"I said the police would be interested in a body found three hundred kilometers away from the car."

"The idea's absurd," Doctor Plarr said. "You can't murder Charley Fortnum."

"I try not to think in those terms, Eduardo."

"Is killing a matter of semantics to you now, León? I remember you were always good at semantics. You used to explain the Trinity to me in the old days, but your explanation was more complicated than the catechism."

"We do not want to kill him," Father Rivas said, "but what can we do? He saw you."

"He won't remember when he wakes. He always forgets things completely when he's drunk." Doctor Plarr added, "How on earth did you make such a mistake?"

"That I must find out," Father Rivas replied, and he began to talk again in Guaraní.

Doctor Plarr took one of the candles and went back to the doorway of the other room. Charley Fortnum looked quite peacefully asleep on the box, just as though he were in his own great brass bedstead at home, where he lay always on the right side near the window. A sense of fastidiousness made the doctor choose the left side, near the door, when he slept in it himself with Clara.

Charley Fortnum's face as long as he had known him had always been a little flushed. His blood pressure was high and he was too fond of whisky. He had passed sixty, but his thin hair retained a soft and mouselike tint like a boy's, and his coloring to the unprofessional eye gave a false impression of health. He looked like an out-of-doors man, a farmer. Indeed he had a camp about fifty kilometers from the city, where he grew a little grain and maté. He liked trundling from field to field in an old Land Rover which he called Fortnum's

Pride. "Off for a gallop," he would say, grinding at the gears, "hi-yup."

Now he suddenly raised his hand and waved it. His eyes were closed. He was dreaming. Perhaps he thought he was waving to his wife and the doctor, as he left them on the verandah to deal with dull medical business. "Women's insides," Charley Fortnum had said once. "Never understood them. One day you must draw me a diagram."

Doctor Plarr went quickly back into the outer room. "He's all right, León. You can dump him safely by the road somewhere for the police to find."

"We cannot do that. He may have recognized you."

"He's fast asleep. Anyway he would say nothing to hurt me. We are old friends."

"I think I know what must have happened," Father Rivas said. "The information you gave us—it was quite correct up to a point. The Ambassador came from Buenos Aires by car, he spent three nights on the road because he wanted to see the country, and the Embassy sent a plane from Buenos Aires to bring him back after his dinner with the Governor. All those details were correct enough, but you never told us your Consul was going with him to the ruins."

"I didn't know. He told me about the dinner—that was all."

"He did not even go in the Ambassador's car. At least we would have grabbed both of them then. He must have taken his own car and then have left while the Ambassador was still lingering around. Our men were only expecting one car to pass. Our outpost flashed the signal when it went by. He had seen the flag."

"The Union Jack, not the Stars and Stripes. He hadn't even the right to fly that."

"In the dark you cannot see clearly and he had been told about the diplomatic number plate."

"It was CC not CD."

"The letters look much the same in the dark on a moving car. You cannot blame him. Alone in the dark —frightened probably. It could have happened to me or you. A fatality."

"The police may not know what has happened to Fortnum yet. If you release him quickly . . ."

Doctor Plarr, in face of their attentive silence, felt as though he were pleading before a tribunal. He said, "Charley Fortnum's no good to you as a hostage."

"He is a member of the diplomatic corps," Aquino said.

"No, he isn't. An Honorary Consul is not a proper Consul."

"The British Ambassador would have to intervene."

"Of course. He would report the affair home. Just as he would for anyone British. If you kidnapped me or old Humphries it would be much the same."

"The British will ask the Americans to bring pressure on the General in Asunción."

"You can be sure the Americans will do nothing of the kind. Why should they? They don't want to anger their friend the General for the sake of Charley Fortnum."

"But he is a British *Consul*."

Doctor Plarr began to despair of ever convincing them of how unimportant Charley Fortnum was. He said, "He had not even the right to put CC on his car. He was in trouble for that."

"You knew him well, I think?" Father Rivas said.

"Yes."

"And you liked him?"

"Yes. In a way." It wasn't a good sign that León already spoke of Fortnum in the past tense.

"I am sorry. I can understand how you feel. It is always much easier to deal with strangers. Like in the confessional box. I used to hate it if I recognized a voice. One can be harsh so much more easily to a stranger."

"What can you gain by holding him, León?"

"We came over the border to do a job. There are a lot of our people who would be discouraged if nothing happened. In our situation something must always happen. Even the kidnapping of a Consul is something."

"An Honorary Consul," Doctor Plarr corrected.

"It will be a warning to people who are more important. Perhaps they will take our next threat seriously. That is a small tactical point gained in a long war."

Doctor Plarr said, "So I suppose you'll be prepared to hear the stranger's confession and give him absolution before you kill him? Charley Fortnum's a Catholic, you know. He'll appreciate having a priest at his deathbed."

Father Rivas said to the Negro, "Give me a cigarette, Pablo."

"He will be even glad of a married priest like you, León," Doctor Plarr said.

"You were willing enough to help us, Eduardo."

"In the case of the Ambassador, yes. His life wouldn't have been in any danger. They would have given way. In any case an American . . . he's a combatant. The Americans have killed plenty of men in South America."

"Your father is among those we are trying to help— if he is still alive."

"I don't know whether he would have liked your method."

"We have not chosen our method. *They* have reduced us to this."

"What on earth can you ask in return for Charley Fortnum? Perhaps a case of real Scotch?"

"For the American Ambassador we would have demanded the release of twenty prisoners. For a British

Consul I think we shall have to halve the bill. That is up to El Tigre."

"Where the hell is your El Tigre?"

"Only those in Rosario are in touch with him until the operation is finished."

"I suppose his schedule did not allow for mistakes. Or for human nature. The General can kill the men you name and say they died years ago."

"We have been through that argument many times. If they kill them our demands will be greater next time."

"León, listen to me. If you can be sure that Charley Fortnum will remember nothing, surely . . . ?"

"How could we ever be certain? You have no drugs to wipe out memory. Does he mean so much to you, Eduardo?"

"He's a voice in the confessional box which I have recognized."

"Ted," a familiar voice called to him from the inner room. "Ted."

"You see," Father Rivas said, "he knows you."

Doctor Plarr turned his back on the tribunal and went through the doorway. "Yes, Charley," he said, "here I am. How do you feel?"

"God awful, Ted. What happened? Where am I?"

"You had an accident with your car. Nothing serious."

"Are you going to take me home?"

"Not yet. You must lie quiet for a while. In the dark. You've got a bit of concussion."

"Clara's going to be anxious."

"Don't worry. I'll deal with Clara."

"You mustn't upset her, Ted. The child . . ."

"I *am* her doctor, Charley."

"Of course, old man, I'm a bloody fool. Will she be able to see me?"

"In a few days you'll be going home."

"A few *days!* Have you a drink with you, Ted?"

"No. I'm going to give you something better—to make you sleep."

"You are a good friend, Ted. Who are those men out there? Why do you have to use a torch?"

"There's a power cut. When you wake up it will be daylight."

"You'll look in and see me?"

"Of course."

Charley Fortnum lay still for a moment and then asked in a voice which must have carried clearly into the other room, "It wasn't really an accident, Ted, was it?"

"Of course it was an accident."

"The sunglasses . . . what happened to the sunglasses?"

"What sunglasses?"

"They were Clara's," Charley Fortnum said. "She liked those sunglasses. I shouldn't have borrowed them. Couldn't find my own." He raised his knees toward his chest and settled on his side with a long sigh. "It's the measure that counts," he said and lay still like an aged embryo which had failed to get born.

In the other room Father Rivas sat with his chin on his crossed fingers and his eyes closed. He might be praying, Doctor Plarr thought as he came back into the room, or perhaps he was only listening carefully to the words of Charley Fortnum as he once used to listen in the confessional to the voice of a stranger in order to decide what penance . . .

"What blunderers you are," Doctor Plarr accused him. "What amateurs!"

"On our side we are all amateurs. The police and the soldiers are the professionals."

"An Honorary Consul, alcoholic at that, in place of an Ambassador."

"Yes. And Che took photographs like a tourist and

left them around. At least no one here has a camera. Or keeps a journal. We learn from our mistakes."

"Your driver will have to take me home," Doctor Plarr said.

"Yes."

"I will come back tomorrow . . ."

"You will not be needed any more, Eduardo."

"Perhaps not by you, but . . ."

"It is better if he does not see you again before we decide . . ."

"León," Doctor Plarr said, "you can't be serious about this. Old Charley Fortnum . . ."

Father Rivas said, "He is not in our hands, Eduardo. He is in the hands of the governments. In the hands of God too, of course. I do not forget my old claptrap, you notice, but I have never yet seen any sign that He interferes in our wars or our politics."

PART
TWO

1

It was easy for Doctor Plarr to remember the first time he met Charley Fortnum. The meeting occurred a few weeks after he had arrived in the city from Buenos Aires. The Honorary Consul was exceedingly drunk, and he had lost the use of both legs. Doctor Plarr was making his way up Bolívar when an elderly gentleman leaned from the window of the Italian Club and called to him for help. "The bloody waiter's gone home," he explained, speaking in English.

When Doctor Plarr entered the club he found a drunk man who seemed perfectly content—the only trouble was he couldn't stand up, but this didn't worry him at all. He said he was quite comfortable on the floor. "I've sat on worse things," he said, "including horses."

"If you'll take one arm," the old man said, "I'll take the other."

"Who is he?"

"The gentleman you see sitting here on the floor and refusing to get up is Mr. Charles Fortnum, our Honorary Consul. You are Doctor Plarr, aren't you? Glad to meet you. I'm Doctor Humphries. Doctor of Letters, not medicine. We three, you may say, are the pillars of the English colony, but one pillar has fallen."

Fortnum said, "The measure was wrong." He added something about the wrong kind of glass. "You have to have the right sort of glass or you get confused."

"Is he celebrating something?" Doctor Plarr asked.

"His new Cadillac arrived safely last week, and to-day he's found a purchaser."

"You've been eating here?"

"He wanted to take me to the Nacional, but he's much too drunk for the Nacional—or even my hotel. Now we've got to get him home somehow, but he insists on going to see Señora Sanchez."

"A friend of his?"

"Of half the men in this town. She runs the only good brothel here—or so they say. I'm not a good judge of that kind of thing myself."

"Surely they are illegal," said Doctor Plarr.

"Not in this city. We are a military headquarters—don't forget that. The military don't allow anyone in B.A. to dictate to them here."

"Why not let him go?"

"You can see why—he can't stand up."

"Surely the point of a brothel is that one can lie down?"

"Something has to stand up," Doctor Humphries said with unexpected coarseness and an expression of distaste.

In the end they lugged Charley Fortnum between them across the street to the little room which Doctor Humphries occupied in the Hotel Bolívar. There were fewer pictures on the walls in those days because there were fewer damp stains, and the shower had not yet begun to drip.

Inanimate objects change at a faster rate than human beings. Doctor Humphries and Charley Fortnum were not noticeably different men that night than they were now; a crack in the plaster of a neglected house grows more quickly than a line on a human face, paint changes color more rapidly than hair, and a room's decay is continuous: it never comes to a temporary halt on that high plateau of old age where a man may live a long time without apparent change. Doctor Humphries had been established on the plateau for many years, and Charley Fortnum, though he was still on one of the lower slopes, had found a reliable weapon in the fight against senility—he had pickled in alcohol some of the high spirits and the naïveté of earlier days. As the years passed, Doctor Plarr could discern little alteration in either of his early acquaintances—perhaps Humphries moved more slowly between the Bolívar and the Italian Club, and sometimes he believed he could detect in Charley Fortnum increasing spots of melancholy, like mold, in his well-bottled bonhomie.

Doctor Plarr left Fortnum with Humphries at the Hotel Bolívar and went to fetch his car. He was living in the same flat in the same block that he inhabited now. Lights were still burning in the port, where laborers worked through the whole night. On a flat barge in the Paraná they had mounted a metal tower from which an iron rod pounded the bottom of the river. Thud, thud, thud, the noise reverberated like tribal drums. From a second barge lengths of pipe were extended, attached to some underwater engine which sucked the gravel out of the riverbed and sent it scuttling and rattling down the waterfront to an inlet half a mile away. The Governor, who had been appointed by the newest President after that year's *coup d'état,* was planning to deepen the port so that it might take ferries of greater draught from the Chaco shore and receive larger passenger boats from the capital. When, after a second military *coup,* this time in Córdoba, he was dismissed from office, the idea was abandoned, to the benefit of Doctor Plarr's sleep. The Governor of the Chaco, it was said, had not been prepared to spend the necessary money to deepen his side of the river, and the passenger boats from the capital were already too large in the dry season to mount beyond the city where passengers had to be transferred anyway to smaller boats for the voyage to the Paraguayan republic in the north. It was difficult to judge who had made the initial mistake, if it was a mistake. The question *Cui bono?* pointed at no individual, since all the contractors had benefited and all undoubtedly had shared their benefits with others. The harbor works before they were abandoned had done a lot of good; they were responsible for a grand piano in one house, a new refrigerator in somebody's kitchen, and perhaps in some small unimportant sub-contractor's cellar, where spirits had hitherto been little known, lay a dozen or two cases of the national Scotch.

When Doctor Plarr returned to the Hotel Bolívar he found Charley Fortnum drinking strong black coffee made on a spirit ring which was installed on a marble-topped washstand, beside the soap dish and Doctor Humphries' tooth glass. He had become a good deal more coherent, and it was all the more difficult to dissuade him from visiting Señora Sanchez. "There's a girl there," he said. "A real girl. Not what you think at all. I've got to see her again. Last time I wasn't in a fit condition . . ."

"You aren't in a fit condition now," Humphries said.

"You don't understand me at all, do you? I only want to talk to her. We aren't all bloody lechers, Humphries. There's a quality about María. She doesn't belong . . ."

"She's a whore like all the rest, I suppose," Doctor Humphries said, clearing his throat. Doctor Plarr was soon to learn that, whenever Humphries disapproved of a subject, his throat clogged with phlegm.

"And that's where you're both of you so bloody wrong," Charley Fortnum said, although Doctor Plarr had not expressed an opinion. "She *is* different from all the others. She's got a sort of refinement. Her family comes from Córdoba. There's good blood in her or else I'm not Charley Fortnum. I know you think I'm a fool, but there's something well . . . almost virginal about that girl."

"And you're the Consul here, honorary or not. You've no business to be seen in a low dive like that."

"I respect the girl," Charley Fortnum said, "I respect her even when I sleep with her."

"It's all you are capable of doing tonight."

After a little more harsh persuasion, Fortnum allowed himself to be assisted to Doctor Plarr's car.

There he brooded in silence for a time, while his chin shook to the movement of the engine. "One grows old I suppose," he said suddenly. "You are young. You don't suffer from memories, regrets . . . Are you married?" he asked abruptly as they drove up San Martín.

"No."

"I was married once," Fortnum said, "twenty-five years ago—it seems a century now. It didn't work out. She was an intellectual if you understand what I mean. She didn't understand human nature." He switched— by an association of ideas Doctor Plarr found it impossible to follow—to his present condition. "I always feel a great deal more human," he said, "when I've drunk just over half a bottle. A little less than half—that's no use at all, but a little more . . . Of course the effect doesn't last, but half an hour of feeling really good is worth some sadness afterward."

"Are you talking of wine?" Doctor Plarr asked with incredulity. He couldn't believe that Fortnum had been so moderate.

"Wine, whisky, gin, it's all the same. It's the measure that counts. There's something psychological in the measure. Less than half a bottle and Charley Fortnum's a poor lonely bastard with only Fortnum's Pride for company."

"Fortnum's Pride?"

"My proud and well-groomed steed. But one glass over the half-bottle—any glass, even a liqueur glass, it's just the measure that counts and Charley Fortnum's quite himself again. Fit for royalty. You know I went on a picnic with some royals once among the ruins. We had two bottles among the three of us, and it was quite a day, I can tell you, but that's another story. Like Captain Izquierdo. Remind me to tell you one day about Captain Izquierdo." It was very hard for a stranger to follow Charley Fortnum's associations.

"Where's the Consulate? Is it the next turning on the left?"

"Yes, but we could take the second or third just as well and make a little turn. I enjoy your company, doctor. What did you say your name was?"

"Plarr."

"Do you know what my name is?"

"Yes."

"Mason."

"I thought . . ."

"That's what they called me at school. Mason. Fortnum and Mason, the inseparable twins. It was the best English school in B.A. My career though was less than distinguished. A good word to get out so distinct . . . so well. The right measure you see. Not too much and not too little. I was never a prefect, and the marble team was the only one I made. Not recognized officially. We were a snobbish school. All the same the headmaster, not the one I knew, that was Arden—we called him Smells—well, this new man wrote me a letter of congratulation when I became Honorary Consul. I wrote to him first, of course, and told him the glad news, so I suppose he couldn't very well ignore me altogether."

"Will you tell me when we get to the Consulate?"

"We've passed it, old man, but never you mind. I've got a clear head. You just take another turn. First to the right and then left again. I'm in the sort of mood when I could drive like this all night. In sympathetic company. No need to pay attention to the one-way signs. Diplomatic privilege. The CC on the car. I can talk to you, doctor, as I can talk to no other man in this city. Spaniards. A proud people but they have no sentiment. Not as we English know it. No sense of Home. Soft slippers, the feet on the table, the friendly glass, the ever-open door. Humphries is not a bad chap

43

—he's as English as you or me, or is he Scotch?—but he has the soul of a—pedagogue. Another good word that. He always tries to correct my morals, and yet I don't do much that's wrong, not really wrong. Tonight, if I'm a little pissed, it was the fault of the glasses. What's your other name, doctor?"

"Eduardo."

"But I thought you were English?"

"My mother's Paraguayan."

"Call me Charley. Would you mind if I called you Ted?"

"Call me what you like, but for God's sake tell me where the Consulate is."

"The next corner. But don't go expecting too much. No marble halls, no chandeliers and potted palms. It's only a bachelor's digs—a bureau, a bedroom—all the usual offices, of course. The best the buggers at home are ready to provide. No sense of national pride. Penny wise, pound foolish. You must come out to my camp— that's where my real home is. Nearly a thousand acres. Eight hundred anyway. Some of the best maté in the country. We could drive there now—it's only three quarters of an hour from here. A good night's sleep and afterward—a hair of the dog. I can give you real Scotch."

"Not tonight. I have patients to see in the morning."

They stopped outside an old colonial house with Corinthian pillars; the white plaster gleamed in the moonlight. On the first floor a flagstaff projected and a shield bore the royal arms. Charley Fortnum swayed a little on the pavement, gazing up. "Is it true?" he asked.

"Is what true?"

"The flagstaff. Isn't it leaning over a bit too much?"

"It looks all right to me."

"I wish we had a simpler flag than the Union Jack. I hung it upside down once on the Queen's birthday. I could see nothing wrong with the bloody thing, but

Humphries was angry—he said he was going to write to the Ambassador. Come up and have a glass."

"I must be getting home—if you can manage by yourself."

"I promise you it's real Scotch. I get Long John from the Embassy. They all prefer Haig there. But Long John gives you a free glass with every bottle. Very nice glasses, too, with the measures marked. Women, Men, and Shipmaster. I count myself, of course, a Shipmaster. I've got dozens of Long John glasses out at the camp. I like that name Shipmaster. Better than Captain which could be a mere military term."

He had the classical difficulty with his key, but succeeded on his third attempt. Swaying on the doorstep he made a speech from under the Corinthian columns to Doctor Plarr who waited impatiently on the pavement for him to finish.

"It's been a very agreeable evening, Ted, even if the goulash was damned awful. Good to speak occasionally the native tongue—gets rusty from unuse—the tongue that Shakespeare spoke. You mustn't think I'm always as happy as this, but it's the measure that counts. Moments of melancholy too when I'm glad of a friend's company. And remember any time you need a Consul, Charley Fortnum's only too happy to be of service. To any Englishman. Or Scotsman or Welshman for that matter. We all have something in common. All belong to the once United bloody Kingdom. Nationality's thicker than water, though that's a nasty term, when you think of it, thicker. Reminds you of things better forgotten and forgiven. Did they give you syrup of figs as a boy? Just walk straight up. Middle door on the first floor, but you can't miss the big brass plate. Wants so much polishing you wouldn't believe the hours of labor a brass plate needs. Grooming Fortnum's Pride is nothing to it." He slipped back into the dark hall behind, disappearing from sight.

Doctor Plarr drove home to the new yellow block and the noise of gravel grating up the pipes and the whine of the rusty cranes. It seemed to him, as he lay in bed and tried to sleep, that in the years to come he was unlikely to find much in common with the Honorary Consul.

Though Doctor Plarr was in no hurry to resume his acquaintance with Charles Fortnum, a month or two after their first encounter he received certain documents which had to be witnessed by a British Consul.

His first attempt to see the Consul was not successful. He arrived at the Consulate about eleven in the morning. The Union Jack fluttered from the dubious pole in the hot dry wind from the Chaco. He wondered why it was flying at all, until he remembered that the day was the anniversary of the armistice of one world war before the last. He rang the bell and soon he felt sure that an eye was watching him through a spyhole in the door. He stood well back in the sunlight to be inspected, and immediately a small dark woman with a big nose snatched the door open. She stared at him with the intense preoccupied gaze of a bird of prey which was accustomed to watch a point from far off for indications of carrion; perhaps she was surprised to find the carrion so close and still alive. No, she said, the Consul was not in. No, she was not expecting him. Tomorrow? . . . Perhaps. She couldn't be sure about that. It hardly seemed to Doctor Plarr the proper way to run a Consulate.

Doctor Plarr took an hour's siesta after lunch and then he returned to the Consulate on his way to some bedridden patients in the *barrio popular*—if you could call what they lay on beds. He was agreeably surprised when the door was opened by Charles Fortnum himself. The Consul had spoken at their first meeting of having moments of melancholy. Perhaps he was suffering from such a moment now. He looked at the doctor with a frown which was defensive and puzzled as though an unpleasant memory stirred somewhere in his unconscious.

"Yes?"

"I'm Doctor Plarr."

"Plarr?"

"We met one night with Humphries."

"Oh yes, did we? Of course. Come in."

Three doors opened off a dark passage. From behind one of them there seeped the smell of unwashed dishes. Perhaps another indicated a bedroom. The third stood open and Fortnum led him in. A desk, two chairs, a filing cabinet, a safe, a colored reproduction of Annigoni's portrait of the Queen with a crack in the glass —that was about all. And the desk was quite bare except for a stand-up calender which advertised an Argentinian tea.

"I'm sorry to disturb you," Doctor Plarr said. "I looked in this morning . . ."

"I can't always be here. I have no assistant. There are a lot of official duties. This morning . . . yes, I was with the Governor. What can I do for you?"

"I've brought some documents I want witnessed."

"Show them to me."

Fortnum sat heavily down and began to open a number of drawers. From one he pulled a blotting pad, from another paper and envelopes, from a third a seal, a ballpoint pen. He began to arrange them on the desk as though they were chessmen. He reversed the position of the seal and the pen—perhaps inadvertently he had put the queen on the wrong side of the king. He read the documents with apparent care, but his eyes betrayed him—the words obviously meant nothing to him —then he waited for Doctor Plarr to sign. Afterward he stamped the papers and added his own signature,

Charles Q. Fortnum. "A thousand pesos," he said. "Don't ask about the Q. I keep it dark." He offered no receipt, but Doctor Plarr paid without question.

The Consul said, "I've got a splitting headache. You know how it is—the heat, the humidity. This is a damnable climate. God knows why my father chose to live in it and die in it. Why didn't he settle in the south? Anywhere but here."

"If you feel that way, why don't you sell up and go?"

"Too late," the Consul said, "I'm sixty-one next year. What's the good of doing anything at sixty-one? Have you any aspirin in that case of yours, Plarr?"

"Yes. Have you some water?"

"Just give it me as it is. I eat the things. They work quicker that way." He chewed up the aspirin and asked for another.

"Don't you find the taste disagreeable?"

"You get accustomed. I don't like the taste of water here either if it comes to that. My God, I do feel like hell today."

"Perhaps I ought to take your blood pressure."

"Why? Do you think there's something wrong?"

"No, but a check is always good at your age."

"It's not my blood pressure that's wrong. It's life."

"Overworked?"

"I wouldn't exactly say that. But there's a new Ambassador—he bothers me."

"What about?"

"He wants a report on the maté industry in this province. Why? Nobody drinks maté in the old country. Never heard of it probably, but I'll have to work for a week, driving around on bad roads, and then those fellows at the Embassy wonder why I have to import a new car every two years. It's my right to have one. My diplomatic right. I pay for it myself and if I choose to sell it again it's my concern not the Ambassador's. Fortnum's Pride is more reliable on these roads. I charge

48

nothing for her, and yet I'm wearing her out in their service. What a lot of mean bastards they are, Plarr, at the Embassy. They even question the rent I pay for this office."

Doctor Plarr unpacked his briefcase.

"What's all that nonsense?"

"I thought we agreed to take your blood pressure."

"Then we'd better go into the bedroom," the Consul said. "It wouldn't look good if my maid came in. The news would be all over the city in no time that I was a dying man. And then the bills would pour in."

The bedroom was almost as bare as the bureau. The bed had been disturbed during the siesta hour, and a pillow lay on the floor beside an empty glass. A photograph of a man with a heavy moustache in riding kit hung above the bed like a substitute for the Queen. The Consul sat on the rumpled coverlet and bared his arm. Doctor Plarr began to inflate the rubber band.

"Do you really think there's something wrong about these headaches?"

Doctor Plarr watched the dial. He said, "I think there's something wrong in drinking so much at your age." He let the air run out.

"Headaches run in the family. My father had terrible headaches. He died suddenly. A stroke. That's him up there. He was a great horseman. He tried to make me one too, but I couldn't bear the stupid brutes."

"I thought you told me you had a horse. Fortnum's Pride, wasn't it?"

"Oh, that's not a horse, that's my Land Rover. You'll never catch me on a horse's back. Tell me the worst, Plarr."

"These contraptions never tell the worst—or the best. All the same your pressure's a bit high. I'll give you some tablets, but couldn't you cut down the drink a little?"

"That's what the doctors were always saying to my

father. He told me once he might have been paying a lot of parrots for squawking the same thing. I suppose I must take after the old bastard—except for the horses. They scare me stiff. He used to be angry about that. He said, 'You've got to conquer fear, Charley, or it will conquer you.' What's your other name, Plarr?"

"Eduardo."

"I'm Charley to my friends. Mind if I call you Ted?"

"If you must."

Charley Fortnum sober had arrived at the same stage of intimacy which he had reached on the last occasion, though by a longer route. Doctor Plarr wondered how often, if their acquaintance continued, they would have to tread the same path before they arrived on the last lap at Charley and Ted.

"You know there's only one other Englishman in this city. A fellow called Humphries, an English teacher. Met him?"

"We were all together one night. Don't you remember? I saw you home."

The Honorary Consul looked at him with an expression of near fear. "No, I don't. Not a thing. Is that a bad sign?"

"Oh, it happens to all of us sometimes if we are drunk enough."

"When I saw you outside the door, I did think for a moment I remembered your face. That's why I asked your name. I thought I might have bought something from you and forgotten to pay. I'll have to go a bit steadier, won't I? For a while, I mean."

"It wouldn't do you any harm."

"I remember some things very well, but I'm like the old man—he used to forget a lot too. Do you know once—I'd fallen off my horse, it got up suddenly on its hind legs—just to test me, the beast I mean. I was only six, it knew I was only a kid, it was right by the house, and my father was sitting there on the verandah.

I was scared in case he might be angry, but what scared me worse was I could see when he looked down at me, where I lay on the ground, that he didn't even remember who I was. He wasn't angry at all, he was puzzled and worried, and he went back to his chair and took up his glass again. So I went round the back to the kitchen (the cook was always a good friend of mine), and I left the bloody horse. Of course I understand now. We had that much in common. He forgot things when he was drunk. Are you married, Ted?"

"No."

"I was once."

"Yes, so you told me."

"I was glad when we split up, but all the same I wish we'd had a child first. When there's no child it's generally the man's fault, isn't't?"

"No. I think the chances are about even."

"I'd be sterile anyway, wouldn't I, by now?"

"Of course not. Age doesn't make you sterile."

"If I had a child I wouldn't try to make him conquer fear like my father did. It's part of human nature, isn't it, fear? If you conquer fear, you conquer your human nature, too. It's a bit like the balance of nature. I read in a book once that, if we killed all the spiders in the world, we would all of us be suffocated under the weight of flies. Have you got a child, Ted?"

The name Ted had an irritating effect on Doctor Eduardo Plarr. He said, "No. If you want to call me by a Christian name I wish you'd call me Eduardo."

"But you are as English as I am."

"I'm only half English and that half is in prison or dead."

"Your father?"

"Yes."

"And your mother?"

"She's living in B.A."

"You're lucky. You have somebody to save for. My mother died when I was born."

"It's not a good reason to kill yourself with drink."

"That's not the reason, Ted. I only mentioned my mother in passing, that's all. What's the good of a friend if one can't talk to him?"

"A friend doesn't make a good psychiatrist."

"You sound a hard man, Ted. Haven't you ever loved anyone?"

"That depends on what you call love."

"You analyze too much," Charley Fortnum said. "It's a young man's fault. Don't turn up too many stones is what I always say. You never know what you'll find underneath."

Doctor Plarr said, "My job is to turn up stones. Guesswork is not much good when you make a diagnosis."

"And what's your diagnosis?"

"I'm going to give you a prescription, but it won't do you any good unless you cut down on your drinking."

He went back into the Consul's office. He was irritated by the sense of time wasted. He could have seen three or four patients in the poor quarter of the city during the time he had spent listening to the self-pity of the Honorary Consul. He walked out of the bedroom and sat down at the desk and wrote his prescription. He felt the same sense of wasted time as when he visited his mother and she complained of headaches and loneliness while she sat before a plate heaped up with éclairs in the best tea shop of Buenos Aires. She always implied that she had been deserted by her husband—because a husband's first duty was to his wife and child and he should have fled with them.

Charley Fortnum put on his jacket in the next room. "You aren't going, are you?" he called.

"Yes. I've left the prescription on the desk."

"What's the hurry? Stay and have a drink."

"I have patients to see."

"Well, I'm your patient too, aren't I?"

"You are not the most important of them," Doctor Plarr said. "The prescription isn't renewable. You'll have enough tablets for a month, and then we'll see."

Doctor Plarr closed the door of the Consulate with a sense of relief, the relief he always felt when he finally left his mother's apartment after a visit to the capital. He hadn't enough time available to waste any of it on the incurable.

2

Nearly two years passed before Doctor Plarr visited for the first time the establishment which was so ably run by Señora Sanchez, and then it was not in the company of the Honorary Consul. He went there with his friend and patient, the novelist, Doctor Jorge Julio Saavedra. Saavedra, as he himself explained over a plate of tough beef at the Nacional, was a man who believed in following a very strict discipline. An observer might have guessed so much from his appearance, which was neat, of a uniform gray, gray hair, gray suit, gray tie. Even in the northern heat he wore the same well-cut double-breasted waistcoat that he used to wear in the coffee houses of the capital. His tailor there, he told Doctor Plarr, was English. "You wouldn't believe it, but I haven't had to buy a new suit in ten years." As for the discipline of work, "I write five hundred words a day after my breakfast. No more no less," he said, not for the first time.

Doctor Plarr was a good listener. He had been trained to listen. Most of his middle-class patients were accustomed to spend at least ten minutes explaining a simple attack of flu. It was only in the *barrio* of the poor that he ever encountered suffering in silence, suffering which had no vocabulary to explain a degree of pain, its position or its nature. In those huts of mud or tin where the patient often lay without covering on the dirt floor he had to make his own interpretation from a shiver of the skin or a nervous shift of the eyes.

"Discipline," Jorge Julio Saavedra was repeating, "is more necessary to me than to other more facile writers. You see I have a demon where others have a talent. Mind you I envy them their talent. A talent is friendly. A demon is destructive. You cannot conceive how much I suffer when I write. I have to force myself day after day to sit down pen in hand and I struggle for expression . . . You will remember in my last book, that character, Castillo, the fisherman, who wages an endless war with the sea for such a small reward. In a way you might say that Castillo is a portrait of the artist. Such daily agony and the result—five hundred words. A very small catch."

"I seem to remember Castillo died from a revolver shot in a bar defending his one-eyed daughter from rape."

"Ah yes, I am glad you noticed the Cyclops symbol," Doctor Saavedra said. "A symbol of the novelist's art. A one-eyed art because one eye concentrates the vision. The diffuse writer is always two-eyed. He includes too much—like a cinema screen. And the violator? Perhaps he represents this melancholy of mine which descends for weeks at a time, when I struggle for hours to do my daily stint."

"I hope you find my tablets give you some help."

"Yes, yes, they help a little, of course, but sometimes I think it is only the daily discipline which saves me from suicide." Doctor Saavedra, with his fork suspended on the way to the mouth, repeated, "Suicide."

"Oh come, surely your faith won't allow you . . . ?"

"In those black moments, doctor, I have no faith, no faith at all. *En una noche oscura.* Shall we open another bottle? This wine from Mendoza is not wholly bad."

After the second bottle the novelist revealed another rule of his self-imposed discipline, his weekly visit to the house of Señora Sanchez. He explained that it was not merely a question of keeping his body calm so as to prevent important desires coming between him and his work; from his weekly visit he learned a great deal about human nature. In the social life of the city there was no contact between the classes. How could dinner with Señora Escobar or Señora Vallejo provide him with any insight into the life of the poor? The character of Carlota, the daughter of Castillo, the heroic fisherman, was based on a girl he had met in the establishment of Señora Sanchez. Of course she had two eyes. She was indeed remarkably pretty, but when he came to write his novel he found her beauty gave her story a false and banal turn; it fitted ill with the bleak severity of the fisherman's life. Even the violator became a conventional character. Pretty girls were being violated all the time everywhere, especially in the books of his contemporaries, those facile writers of undoubted talent.

At the end of dinner Doctor Plarr was easily persuaded to accompany the novelist on his disciplinary visit, though he was tempted more by curiosity than sexual desire. They left their table at midnight and set out on foot. Though Señora Sanchez was protected by the authorities it was better not to leave a car outside in case an inquisitive policeman noted the number. Such an addition to one's police file might one day prove undesirable. Doctor Saavedra wore pointed highly polished shoes and gave the impression of hopping when he walked because he was a little pigeon-toed. One half expected to see bird marks left behind on the dusty pavement.

Señora Sanchez sat in a deck chair outside her house knitting. She was a very stout lady with a dimpled face and a welcoming smile from which kindliness was oddly lacking, as though it had been mislaid accidentally a moment before like a pair of spectacles. The novelist introduced Doctor Plarr.

"I am always glad to welcome a medical gentleman," Señora Sanchez said. "You will appreciate how well my girls are looked after. I employ your colleague Doctor Benevento, a most sympathetic man."

"So I have heard. I have not met him," Doctor Plarr said.

"He comes here on Thursday afternoons and all my girls are very fond of him."

They passed through the narrow lighted doorway. Except for Señora Sanchez in her deck chair there were no exterior signs to differentiate her establishment from the other houses in the respectable street. A good wine, Doctor Plarr thought, needs no bush.

It was a house very different in character from the clandestine brothels he had occasionally visited in the capital where small rooms were darkened by closed shutters and crammed with bourgeois furniture. There was a pleasant country air about this house. An airy patio about the size of a tennis court was surrounded by small cells. Two open doors faced him when he had taken a seat, and he thought the cells looked gayer, cleaner, and in better taste than Doctor Humphries' bedroom at the Hotel Bolívar. Each possessed a little shrine with a lighted candle which gave the tidy interiors the atmosphere of a home rather than of a place of business. A group of girls sat at a table apart, while two talked with young men, leaning against the pillars of the verandah which surrounded the patio. There was no sign of hustling—it was obvious Señora Sanchez was strict about that; here a man might take his time. One man sat alone over a glass, and another, dressed like a *peón,* stood by a pillar, watching the girls with an unhappy, envious expression (perhaps he hadn't the means to buy even a drink).

A girl called Teresa came immediately to take the novelist's order ("Whisky," he advised, "the brandy is not to be trusted"), and afterward sat down with them unasked. "Teresa comes from Salta," Doctor Saavedra explained, leaving his hand in her care like a glove in a cloakroom. She turned it this way and that and examined the fingers as though she were looking for holes. "I am thinking of setting my next novel in Salta."

Doctor Plarr said, "I hope your demon won't insist on giving her one eye."

"You laugh at me," the novelist said, "because you have so little idea of how a writer's imagination works. He has to transform reality. Look at her—those big brown eyes, those plump little breasts, she's pretty isn't she"—the girl gave a gratified smile and scratched his palm with her nail—"but what does she represent? I am not planning a love story for a woman's magazine. My characters must symbolize more than themselves. Now it *has* occurred to me that with perhaps one leg . . ."

"A girl with one leg could be more easily violated."

"There is no violation in my story. But a beauty with one leg—don't you see the significance of that? Think of her halting walk, her moments of despair, the lovers who feel they do her a favor if they stay with her one night. Her stubborn faith in a future which somehow will be better than today's. For the first time," Doctor Saavedra said, "I am proposing to write a political novel."

"Political?" Doctor Plarr asked with some surprise.

A cell door opened and a man came out. He lit a cigarette, went to a table and drank from an unfinished glass. In the glow of light, below the saint's shrine, Doctor Plarr could see a thin girl who was straightening the bed. She arranged the coverlet with care before she came out and joined her companions at their communal table. An unfinished glass of orange juice awaited her. The *peón* by the pillar watched her with his hungry envy.

"Don't you resent that man?" Doctor Plarr asked Teresa.

"What man?"

"The one over there who stands staring, doing nothing."

"Let him stare, he does no harm, poor man. And he has no money."

"I was telling you about my political novel," Doctor Saavedra spoke with irritation. He removed his hand from Teresa's grasp.

"But I don't understand the point of one leg."

"A symbol," Doctor Saavedra said, "of this poor crippled country, where we still hope . . ."

"Will your readers understand? I would have thought something more direct. Those students last year in Rosario . . ."

"If one is to write a political novel of lasting value it must be free from all the petty details that date it. Assassinations, kidnapping, the torture of prisoners—these things belong to our decade. But I do not want to write merely for the seventies."

"The Spaniards tortured their prisoners three hundred years ago," Doctor Plarr murmured, and he looked again for some reason toward the girl at the communal table.

"Are you not coming with me tonight?" Teresa asked Doctor Saavedra.

"Yes, yes, all in good time. I am talking to my friend here on a subject of great importance."

Doctor Plarr noticed on the other girl's forehead, a little below the hairline, a small gray birthmark, in the spot where a Hindu girl wears the scarlet sign of her caste.

Jorge Julio Saavedra said, "A poet—the true novelist must always be in his way a poet—a poet deals in absolutes. Shakespeare avoided the politics of his time, the minutiae of politics. He wasn't concerned with Philip of Spain, with pirates like Drake. He used the history of the past to express what I call the abstraction of politics. A novelist today who wants to represent tyranny should not describe the activities of General Stroessner in Paraguay—that is journalism not literature. Tiberius is a better example for a poet."

Doctor Plarr thought how agreeable it would be to take the girl to her room. He had not slept with a woman for more than a month, and how easily sexual attention can be caught by something superficial, like a birthmark in an unusual position.

"Surely you understand what I mean?" the novelist asked him severely.

"Yes. Yes. Of course."

Doctor Plarr was prevented by a certain fastidiousness from treading quickly in another man's tracks. What interval, he wondered, would he be prepared to accept? Half an hour, an hour—or merely the physical absence of his predecessor, who had already ordered himself another drink?

"I can see the subject has no interest at all for you," Doctor Saavedra said with disappointment.

"The subject . . . forgive me . . . I've drunk rather heavily tonight."

"I was talking of politics."

"But of course politics interest me. I'm a kind of political refugee myself. And my father . . . I don't even know whether my father is alive. Perhaps he died. Perhaps he was murdered. Perhaps he is shut up in a police station somewhere across the border. The General doesn't believe in prisons for political offenders—he leaves them to rot alone in police stations all over the country."

"That is exactly my point, doctor. Of course I sympathize with you, but how can I make art out of a man shut up in a police station?"

"Why not?"

"Because it is a special case. It is a situation which belongs to the nineteen seventies. I hope my books will be read, if only by discriminating readers, in the twenty-first century. My fisherman Castillo I have tried to make timeless."

Doctor Plarr remembered how seldom he had thought of his father, and perhaps it was a sense of guilt because of his own safety and comfort which made him a little angry now. He said, "Your fisherman is timeless because he never existed." He regretted his words immediately. "I am sorry," he said. "Don't you think we ought to have another drink? And your charming companion—we are neglecting her."

"There are more important subjects than Teresa," Saavedra said, but he surrendered his hand again into her keeping. "Isn't there a girl here who pleases you?"

"Yes, there is one, but she has found another customer."

The girl with the birthmark had joined the solitary drinker and they were proceeding together to her cell. She passed her former companion without a glance and he hadn't enough curiosity to look at his successor. There was something clinical in a brothel which appealed to Doctor Plarr. It was as though he were watching a surgeon accompanying a new patient to the operating theater—the previous operation had been successful and was already out of mind. Only in television dramas did emotions of love, anxiety or fear infiltrate into the wards. His first years in Buenos Aires, while his mother complained, dramatized and wept over his missing father's fate, and the later years when she became volubly content with sweet cakes and chocolate ices had given Doctor Plarr a suspicion of any emotion which was curable by means as simple as an orgasm or an éclair. The memory of a conversation—if you could call it that—with Charley Fortnum came back to him. He asked Teresa, "Do you know a girl here called María?"

"There are several Marías," Teresa said.

"She comes from Córdoba."

"Oh, that one. She died a year ago. She was really bad, that one. Somebody killed her with a knife. He went to prison, poor man."

"I suppose I had better go with the girl," Saavedra said. "I am sorry. It is not often I have an opportunity to discuss problems of literature with a cultivated man. In a way I would really much prefer to have another drink and continue our talk." He looked at his captive hand as though it belonged to someone else and he hadn't the right to pick it up.

"There will be other opportunities," Doctor Plarr encouraged him, and the novelist surrendered. "Come, *chica*," he said and rose. "You will wait for me, Doctor? I shall not be long tonight."

"Perhaps you will learn a lot about Salta."

"Yes, but there is always a moment when a writer has to say 'Enough.' One mustn't know too much." Doctor Plarr had the impression that Jorge Julio Saavedra under the influence of drink was beginning to repeat a lecture he had once delivered to some woman's club in the capital.

Teresa pulled him by the hand. He rose reluctantly and followed her to where the candle burned below her statue of the Avila saint. The door closed on them. A novelist's work, he had once said sadly to Doctor Plarr, is never finished.

It was a quiet evening at the establishment of Señora Sanchez. All the doors were open except the two which hid Teresa and the girl with the birthmark. Doctor Plarr finished his drink and left the patio. He was sure the novelist, in spite of his promise, would take his time. After all he had a decision to make—whether the girl should lose her leg at the femur or the knee.

Señora Sanchez was still plying her needles. A friend had joined her. She sat and knitted in a second deck chair. "You found a girl?" Señora Sanchez asked.

"My friend did."

"There was no one who pleased you?"

"Oh, it wasn't that, but I drank too much at dinner."

"You can ask your colleague Doctor Benevento about my girls. They are very clean."

"I am sure they are. I shall certainly return, Señora Sanchez."

But in fact more than a year passed before he did come back. He looked in vain then for the girl with the birthmark on her forehead. He was neither surprised nor disappointed. Perhaps it was the time of her period, but in any case girls in such establishments change frequently. Teresa was the only one he recognized. He stayed with her for an hour, and they talked about Salta.

3

Doctor Plarr's practice prospered. He never regretted leaving the harsh competition of the capital, where there were too many doctors with German, French and English degrees, and he had grown fond of the small city by the great Paraná River. There was a local legend that those who once visited the city always returned, and it had certainly proved true in his case. One glimpse of the little port with its background of colonial houses, seen for an hour one dark night, had drawn him back. Even the climate did not displease him—the heat was less humid than he remembered it in the land of his childhood, and when the summer broke up at last with an enormous eruption of thunder, he liked watching from the window of his apartment the forked flashes dig into the Chaco shore. Nearly every month he gave a dinner to Doctor Humphries, and sometimes now he would take a meal with Charley Fortnum who was always either sober, laconic, and melancholy, or drunk, talkative, and what he liked to term "elevated." Once he went out to Charley Fortnum's camp, but he was no judge of a maté crop and he found the heaving motion of Fortnum's Pride as he was driven around hectare by hectare—Charley called it "farming"—so disagreeable that he refused the next invitation. He preferred a night at the Nacional when Charley would talk unconvincingly of a girl he had found.

Every three months Doctor Plarr flew down to Buenos Aires and spent a weekend with his mother who was growing more and more stout on her daily diet of cream cakes and *alfajores* stuffed with *dulce de leche*. He could not remember the features of the beautiful woman in her early thirties who had said goodbye to his father on the river front and who wept continuously for lost love throughout the three days' voyage to the capital. Since he had no old photograph of her to remind him of the past, he always pictured her as the woman she had become with three chins and heavy dewlaps and a stomach which, outlined in black silk, imitated pregnancy. On the shelves of his apartment the works of Doctor Jorge Julio Saavedra annually increased by one volume, and of all his books Doctor Plarr thought he preferred the story of the one-legged girl of Salta. After the first visit, he had lain with Teresa several times at the Sanchez house and he was amused to observe how far fiction deviated from reality. It was almost a lesson in the higher criticism. He possessed no close friends, though he remained on good terms with two former mistresses whom he had first met as patients; he was also on friendly terms with the latest Governor, and enjoyed his visits to the Governor's big maté plantation in the east, flying there in the Governor's private plane and descending on the lawn between two flower beds in time for an excellent lunch. At Bergman's orange-canning factory closer to the city he was an occasional guest, and sometimes he went fishing in a tributary of the Paraná with the director of the airport.

Twice there were attempted revolutions in the capital which made big headlines in *El Litoral,* but on both occasions when he telephoned to his mother he found she knew nothing of the disturbances; she read no newspaper and never listened to the radio, and Harrods and her favorite teashop remained open through all the troubles. She told him once that she had been satiated forever with politics during their life in Paraguay. "Your father could talk of nothing else. Such undesirable people used to come to the house, sometimes in the middle of the night, dressed in any old clothes. And you know what became of your father." The last was an odd turn of phrase since neither of them knew anything at all—whether he had been killed in the civil war or died of disease or become a political prisoner under the dictatorship of the General. His body was never identified among the corpses which were sometimes washed up on the Argentine side of the river with hands and legs tied with wire, but his might well have been one of those skeletons which remained for years undiscovered after they had been tossed from planes into the Chaco wastes.

Nearly three years after his first meeting with Charley Fortnum Doctor Plarr was drawn into a conversation about him by Sir Henry Belfrage, the British Ambassador—a successor to the man who had given the Honorary Consul so much trouble with the maté report. It was one of the periodic cocktail parties for the British colony, and Doctor Plarr, who happened to be in the capital on a visit to his mother, attended it with her. He knew nobody there by more than sight—at best a nodding acquaintance. There was Buller, the manager of the Bank of London and South America, Fisher, the Secretary of The Anglo-Argentinian Society, and an old gentleman called Forage who spent all his days at the Hurlingham Club. The Representative of the British Council was, of course, there too—his name for some Freudian reason Plarr always forgot—a pale frightened little man with a bald head who came to the party in charge of a visiting poet. The poet had a high-pitched voice and an air of being consciously out of place under the chandeliers. "How soon can we get away?" he was heard to shriek. And again, "Too much water with the whisky." It was the only voice in the room which carried any distance above the low continuous din like that of an aeroplane engine, and one naturally expected it to cry something more relevant, like "Fasten your seatbelts."

Doctor Plarr thought Belfrage was only interested in making polite conversation when they found themselves alone together between a gilt-legged sofa and a Louis Quinze chair. They were far enough away from the hubbub around the buffet to hear themselves speak. He could see his mother firmly wedged in and gesticulating at a priest with a canapé. She was always happy with priests, and so he felt relieved of responsibility.

"I think you know our Consul up there?" Sir Henry Belfrage said. He always referred to the northern province as "up there" as though he wanted to emphasize the vast length of the Paraná River winding its slow way down from those distant frontiers so far from the southern civilization of the Rio de la Plata.

"Charley Fortnum? Oh yes, I do see him occasionally. But I haven't for some months. I've been busy—a lot of sickness."

"You know—in a job like this—one always inherits a few *difficulties* with a new post. Strictly between ourselves the Consul up there is one of them."

"Really?" Doctor Plarr replied with caution, "I would have thought . . . ," though he had no idea how he would finish the sentence if it were required of him.

"There's nothing for him to do up there. I mean as far as we are concerned. Now and then I ask him to make a report on something—for the sake of appearances. I don't want him to think he's forgotten. He *was* useful once to one of my predecessors. Some young fool who got mixed up with the guerrillas and tried to do a Castro against the General in Paraguay. As far as I can see from the files we've paid for half his telephone bills and most of his stationery ever since."

"Didn't he once help with some royals too? Guiding them round the ruins?"

"There was something of that sort," Sir Henry Belfrage said. "Very minor royals as far as I remember. I oughtn't to say it, of course, but royalty can cause us an awful lot of trouble. Once we had to ship a polo pony . . . you have no idea of the complications *that* involved, and it was during the meat embargo too." He meditated a while. "At least Fortnum could try a little harder to get on with the English colony up there."

"As far as I know there are only three of us within fifty miles. The fellows with camps seldom come to the city."

"Then it shouldn't be difficult for him. You know this chap Jeffries?"

"Do you mean Humphries? If you are thinking about

the Union Jack episode—flying it upside down—do *you*
know the right way up?"

"No, but thank God I've got chaps who do. I wasn't
thinking of that—that happened in Callow's time. The
trouble now is that Fortnum seems to have made a
most unsuitable marriage—according to this man Humphries. I wish he'd stop writing to us. Who is he?"

"I hadn't heard about Fortnum's marriage. He's a
bit old for it. Who's the woman?"

"Humphries didn't say. In fact he was a bit ambigu-
ous all round. Fortnum seems to have kept it a great
secret. I don't take the story seriously, of course. There's
no security involved. He's only an Honorary Consul.
We don't have to *investigate* her. I just thought—if you
happened to have heard anything . . . In a way an
Honorary Consul is more difficult to get rid of than a
career man. He can't be transferred. That word honorary . . . it's a bit bogus when you come to think of it.
Fortnum imports a new car every two years and sells it.
He's not entitled to—he's not in the service—but I suppose he's pulled a fast one with the local authorities
there. I wouldn't be surprised if he doesn't make more
than my Consul does here. Poor old Martin has to toe
the line. He can't go buying cars on his salary, nor can
I. Unlike the Ambassador of Panama. My God, my
poor wife's tied up with that poet. What's his name?"

"I don't know."

"I just wanted to say—Plarr isn't it? . . . As you live
up there . . . I've never met this man Humphries . . . oh
well, they send them here in droves."

"Humphries?"

"No, no. Poets. If they are poets. The British Council
always say they are, but I've never heard of any of
them. When you are back up there, Plarr, do what you
can. You're someone I can trust to drop the right word
. . . no scandal, you understand what I'm getting at

. . . This fellow Humphries, he strikes me as the sort of man who might write home. To the F.O. After all it's no concern of ours whom Fortnum marries. If you could somehow tactfully tell this chap Humphries to mind his own business and not bother us. Thank God he's getting old. Fortnum, I mean. We'll retire him the first chance we have. Oh dear, look at my poor wife. She's trapped."

"I'll go and save her if you like."

"My dear chap, will you? I daren't. These poets are touchy brutes. And I always get their names mixed up. They are like this fellow Humphries—they write home —to the Arts Council. I won't forget this, Plarr. Anything I can ever do for you . . . up there . . ."

The doctor found himself with more work than usual on his hands when he returned to the north. He had no time for Humphries, that old troublemaker, and he was not interested in Charles Fortnum's marriage—whether fortunate or unfortunate. Once, when some remark recalled the Ambassador's words to him, he wondered whether Charley might possibly have married his housekeeper, that hawklike woman who had opened the door when he visited the Consulate for the first time. A marriage like that seemed not improbable. Old men, like dissident priests, were frequently known to marry their housekeepers, sometimes as a measure of false economy, sometimes from fear of a lonely death. Death to Doctor Plarr, who was still in his early thirties, appeared in the guise of a fortuitous accident on the road or an unforeseen cancer, but in the mind of an old man it was the inevitable end of a long and incurable sickness. Perhaps Charley Fortnum's alcoholism was a symptom of his fear.

One afternoon, while the doctor was taking an hour's siesta, his bell rang. He opened the door and there was the hawklike woman, bristling yet again in the hope of carrion. He nearly took a chance and addressed her as Señora Fortnum.

The guess would have proved mistaken. Señor Fortnum, she said, had telephoned to her from the camp. His wife was ill. He wanted Doctor Plarr to drive out to the camp and visit her.

"Did he say what was wrong?"

"Señora Fortnum has a pain in the stomach," the woman replied with contempt. The marriage had obviously pleased her no more than it had pleased Doctor Humphries.

Doctor Plarr drove to the camp in the cool of the evening. The small ponds on either side of the highway looked like patches of molten lead in the last lingering light. Fortnum's Pride was standing at the end of a mud road under a grove of avocados, the heavy brown pears the size and shape of cannon balls. On the verandah of the rambling bungalow Charley Fortnum sat before a bottle of whisky, a syphon and, astonishingly, two clean glasses. "I've been waiting for you," he said reproachfully.

"I couldn't come earlier. What's the trouble?"

"Clara's been in a lot of pain."

"I'll go in and see her."

"Have a whisky first. I looked in at her just now and she was asleep."

"Thank you then, I will. I'm thirsty. There's a lot of dust on the road."

"Soda? Say when."

"Right to the top."

"I wanted to have a word with you anyway—before you went in. You've heard about my marriage I suppose?"

"The Ambassador told me."

"Had he anything to say?"

"No. Why?"

69

"There's been a lot of talk. And Humphries cuts me."

"That's lucky for you."

"You see—" Charley Fortnum hesitated. "Well, she is very young," he said. It was not clear whether he was excusing his critics or apologizing for himself.

Doctor Plarr said, "Lucky again."

"She's not twenty, and, you know, I won't see sixty again."

Doctor Plarr wondered if he had been summoned to advise the Consul on a less soluble problem than his wife's stomach-ache. He drank to fill what he thought might be an awkward silence.

"That's not the trouble," Charley Fortnum said. (Doctor Plarr was surprised by his insight.) "I can manage things well enough so far . . . and afterward . . . there's always the bottle, isn't there? An old family friend. The bottle I mean. Helped my father too, the old bastard. I just wanted to explain about her. Otherwise you might be a bit surprised when you see her. She's so very young. And shy too. She's not used to this sort of life. A house like this and servants. And the country. The country's awfully quiet after dark."

"Where does she come from?"

"Tucumán. Real Indian blood. A long way back of course. I ought to warn you—she doesn't much care for doctors. She's had a bad experience of them."

"I'll try to win her confidence," Doctor Plarr said.

"This pain," Charley Fortnum said, "it did occur to me it might be, you know, a child. Or something of the kind."

"She doesn't take the pill?"

"You know what these Spanish Catholics are like. Superstition, of course. Like walking under a ladder. Clara doesn't know who Shakespeare is, but she's heard all about the Pope's what-do-you-call-it. Anyway I'd have to get the pills somehow through the Embassy.

Can you imagine what they'd say? You can't even buy them under the counter here. Of course I always wore a thing until we were really together."

"So you bore the sin for her?" Doctor Plarr teased him.

"Oh well, my conscience has got pretty tough with age. Another little thing won't do it any harm. And if she's happier that way . . . When you've finished your whisky . . ."

He led Doctor Plarr down a corridor hung with Victorian sporting prints: riders falling into a stream, checked at a bullfinch, rebuked by the master. He walked softly on tiptoe. At the end of the corridor he opened a door just a crack and looked in. "I think she's awake," he said. "You'll find me on the verandah, Ted, with the whisky. Don't be long."

One electric candle was alight below the statuette of a saint, a saint whom Doctor Plarr didn't recognize, and he was reminded for a moment of the small cells that stood around the patio at the house of Señora Sanchez, each with a votive candle. "Good evening," he said to the head on the pillow. The face was so covered in dark hair that only the eyes were visible; they peered back at him, like a cat's from a shrubbery.

"I don't want to be examined," the girl told him. "I won't be examined."

"I don't want to examine you. I want to hear about your stomach-ache, that's all."

"It's better now."

"Good. Then I won't stay long. May I turn up the light?"

"If you have to," she said and brushed the hair away from her face. Below the hairline Doctor Plarr saw a small gray birthmark in the spot where a Hindu girl . . .

He said, "Whereabouts do you feel the pain? Show me."

She turned the sheet down and indicated a place on

her naked body. He put his hand out to touch her, but she moved her body away from him. He said, "Don't be afraid. I'm not going to examine you in Doctor Benevento's way," and he heard her catch her breath. Nonetheless she allowed him to press his fingers on her stomach.

"There?"

"Yes."

"Nothing to worry about," he said. "A little inflammation of the intestine, that's all."

"Intestine?" He could see the word was strange to her and frightening.

"I'll leave some bismuth powder for you with your husband. Take it in water. If you mix some sugar with it, it doesn't taste too bad. I wouldn't drink whisky if I were you. You are more used to orange juice, aren't you?"

She looked at him with a startled expression and whispered, "What's your name?"

"Plarr," he said, and added, "Eduardo Plarr." He doubted whether she knew the surname of any man apart from Charley Fortnum.

"Eduardo," she repeated, and this time took a bolder look at him. She asked, "I don't know you, do I?"

"No."

"But you know Doctor Benevento?"

"I've met him once or twice." He stood up. "I don't suppose those Thursday visits were very agreeable." He added, before she could speak, "You aren't ill. You don't have to stay in bed."

"Charley" (she pronounced the name as "Charlee" with an accent on the last syllable) "said I must stay in bed until the doctor came."

"Well, the doctor's come, hasn't he? So there's no longer any need . . ."

When he looked back from the door he saw she was

72

watching him. She had forgotten to draw up the sheet. He said, "I never asked you your name."

"Clara."

He said, "Teresa was the only girl I ever knew there."

Returning down the passage he thought of the stat-uette of Saint Teresa of Avila which had presided over his own exercises and the more literary ones of Doctor Saavedra. Presumably it was the friend of Saint Francis who now looked down on the bed of Charley Fortnum. He remembered the way he had seen the girl first as she straightened the sheets in her cell, bent like a Negress directly from the waist. He was accustomed by now to too many women's bodies. When he first became the lover of one of his patients it was not her body which excited him but a slight stammer and a scent he didn't recognize. There was nothing distinctive about Clara's body except for her unfashionable thinness, the small-ness of her breasts, the immature thighs, the almost im-perceptible mount of Venus. She might be nearly twen-ty, but she didn't look more than sixteen—Mother Sanchez recruited them early.

He stopped before the print of a man in a scarlet coat on a runaway horse which had overridden the hounds; the master, purple in the face, was shaking a fist at the culprit, and beyond the hounds lay a vista of fields and hedgerows and a small stream lined by what he took to be willows, an unfamiliar foreign countryside. He thought with a sense of surprise: I have never seen a little stream like that. In this continent even the smallest tributaries of the great rivers were wider than the Thames in his father's picture book. He tried the word "stream" again on his tongue: a stream must have a strange poetic charm. You couldn't call a stream the shallow inlet where he sometimes went to fish and where you couldn't bathe for fear of sting rays. A stream had to be peaceful, gently running, shaded by willows, without danger. This land, he thought, is really too vast for human beings.

Charley Fortnum was waiting for him with the glasses refilled. He asked with uneasy jocularity, "Well, what's the verdict?"

"Nothing. A little inflammation. There's no reason for her to lie in bed. I'll give you something she can take in water. Before meals. I wouldn't let her drink whisky."

"I didn't want to run any risks, Ted. I don't know much about women. Their insides and all that. My first wife was never ill. She was a Christian Scientist."

"Before you bring me all the way out here another time, do have a word first on the telephone. I'm pretty busy at this time of year."

"I suppose you think me foolish, but she needs an awful lot of protection."

Plarr said, "I should have thought—in that sort of life—she would have learned to look after herself."

"What do you mean?"

"She worked with Mother Sanchez, didn't she?"

Charley Fortnum clenched a fist. A bubble of whisky hung on the corner of his lip. Doctor Plarr thought that he could almost see the blood pressure rise. "What do you know about her?"

"I never went with her if that's what you are afraid of."

"I thought you might be one of those bastards . . ."

"Surely you were one of those yourself. I seem to remember your telling me about a girl called María from Córdoba."

"That was different. That was physical. Do you know I never touched Clara for months? Not until I was sure she loved me a little. We used to talk, that's all. I went to her room, of course, because otherwise she would have been in trouble with Señora Sanchez. Ted, you won't believe me, but I've never talked to anyone about so many things as I have to that girl. She's interested in everything I tell her. Fortnum's Pride. The maté crop. The movies. She knows a lot about the movies. I was never much interested in them myself, but she always knows the latest dope about a woman called Elizabeth Taylor. Have you heard of her—and a fellow called Burton? I always thought Burton was a kind of beer. We even talked about Evelyn—that was my first wife. I can tell you I was pretty lonely before I met Clara. You'll think it nonsense, but I loved her the first moment I saw her. Somehow from the first I didn't want to do anything, not till she wanted it too. She couldn't understand that. She thought there was something wrong with me. But it was real love, not brothel love I wanted. I don't suppose you can understand that either."

"I'm not quite sure what the word love means. My mother loves *dulce de leche*. So she tells me."

"Has no woman ever loved you, Ted?" Fortnum inquired. A kind of paternal anxiety in his voice irritated Doctor Plarr.

"Two or three have told me so, but they had no difficulty in finding someone else after I said goodbye. Only my mother's love of sweet cakes isn't likely to change. She will love them in sickness and in health till death do them part. Perhaps that's the real true love."

"You're too young to be a cynic."

"I'm not a cynic. I'm curious, that's all. I like to know the meaning which people put on the words they use. So much is a question of semantics. That's why in medicine we often prefer to use a dead language. There's no room for misunderstanding with a dead language. How did you get the girl away from Mother Sanchez?"

"I paid."

"And she was happy to leave?"

"She was a bit bewildered at first and frightened too. Señora Sanchez was angry. She didn't like losing her.

She told her she wouldn't have her back when I got tired of her. As if that would ever happen."

"Life's a long time."

"Mine isn't. Be frank, Ted, you wouldn't give me ten more years would you? Even though I've knocked down a bit on the drink since I knew Clara."

"What will happen to her afterward?"

"This isn't a bad little property. She could sell it and go to Buenos Aires. You can get fifteen percent interest now without risk. Even eighteen if you take a chance. And you know I can import a car every two years . . . Perhaps five more cars to sell before I kick the bucket. I calculate that would mean another five hundred pounds a year."

"She could eat sweet cakes with my mother at the Richmond."

"No joking, would your mother consent to meet Clara one day?"

"Why not?"

"You don't know what a difference Clara's made to me."

"You must have made quite a difference to her too," Doctor Plarr said.

"When you get to my age you accumulate a lot of regrets. It's not a bad thing to feel you've made at least one person a little happier."

It was the kind of simple, sentimental and self-confident statement which Doctor Plarr found embarrassing. No reply was possible. It was a statement which it would be rude to question and impossible to confirm. He made his excuses and drove home.

All down the dark country road he thought of the young woman in the great Victorian bed which had belonged, with the sporting prints, to the Honorary Consul's father. She was like a bird which had been bought in the market in a makeshift cage and transferred to one at home more roomy and luxurious, equipped with perches and feeding bowls and a swing to play on.

He was surprised by the amount of thought he was giving the girl, who was only a young prostitute he had noticed once in the establishment of Señora Sanchez because of her odd birthmark. Had Charley really married her? Perhaps Doctor Humphries had misled the Ambassador when he spoke of a marriage. Probably Charley Fortnum had taken a new housekeeper—that was all. If that were the case he would be able to reassure the Ambassador. A wife provided worse material for a scandal than a mistress.

But his thoughts were like the deliberately banal words of a clandestine letter in which the important phrases have been added between the lines in secret ink to be developed in privacy. Those hidden phrases described a girl in a cell leaning down to make her bed, a girl who returned to her table and picked up her glass of orange juice, as though she had been momentarily interrupted by a tradesman at the door, a thin body stretched out on Charley Fortnum's double bed, with immature breasts which had never suckled a child. All three of Doctor Plarr's mistresses had been married women, mature women proud of their lush figures which smelt of expensive bath oils. She must have been a good whore, he thought, to have been taken out by two men in succession with a figure like hers, but that was no reason why he should think of her all the way home. He tried to change the direction of his thoughts. There were two hopeless cases of malnutrition in the *barrio* of the poor, there was a police officer he was attending who would soon be dead of throat cancer, there was Saavedra's melancholy and Doctor Humphries' dripping shower, and yet try as he would his mind returned continually to that small hill of Venus—mount was a misnomer.

He wondered how many men she had known. Doctor

Plarr's last mistress, who was married to a banker called Lopez, had told him with some pride of his four predecessors—perhaps she was trying to arouse a sense of competition. (One of her lovers, he knew from another source, had been her chauffeur.) The fragile body on Charley Fortnum's bed must have known hundreds. Her stomach was like the site of an old country battlefield where pale grass grew which had abolished the scars of war, and a small stream flowed peacefully between the willows: he was back in the passage, outside the bedroom, staring at the sporting prints and resisting the desire to return.

He braked sharply as he approached the road which led to Bergman's orange-canning factory, and for a moment he contemplated reversing the car and driving back to the camp. Instead he lit a cigarette. I will not be the victim of an obsession, he thought. The attraction of a whorehouse is the attraction I sometimes find in trivial shopping—I may see a tie which momentarily attracts me, I wear it once or twice, then I leave it in the drawer and it becomes overlaid with newer ties. Why didn't I try her out when I had the chance? If I had bought her that night at Señora Sanchez' she would be lying safely forgotten at the bottom of the drawer. Is it possible, he wondered, if a man is too rational to fall in love, that he may be reserved for a worse fate, to fall into an obsession? He drove angrily in the direction of the city where the reflection of the light lay flat along the horizon and the Three Marys hung on their broken chain in the sky overhead.

Some weeks later Doctor Plarr woke early. It was a Saturday and he had a few hours free. He decided to spend them in the open air with a book while the morning was still fresh; he preferred somewhere out of sight of his secretary who read only what she called serious books—those of Doctor Saavedra among them.

He chose a collection of stories by Jorge Luis Borges. Borges shared the tastes he had himself inherited from his father—Conan Doyle, Stevenson, Chesterton. *Ficciones* would prove a welcome change from Doctor Saavedra's last novel which he had not been able to finish. He was tired of South American heroics. Now Doctor Plarr, sitting under the statue of an heroic sergeant—*machismo* again—who had saved the life of San Martín—was it a hundred and fifty years ago?—read with a sense of immense relaxation of the Countess de Bagno Regio, of Pittsburgh and Monaco. After a time he grew thirsty. To appreciate Borges properly he had to be taken, like a cheese biscuit, with an apéritif, but in this heat Doctor Plarr wanted a longer drink. He decided to call on his friend Gruber and demand a German beer.

Gruber was one of Doctor Plarr's earliest friends in the city. As a boy he had escaped from Germany in 1936 when the persecution of the Jews was intensified. He was an only child, but his parents had insisted that he escape abroad, if only to save the name of Gruber from becoming extinct, and his mother baked a special cake for his journey in which to hide the few small valuables they were able to send with him—his mother's engagement ring set with inconsiderable diamonds and his father's gold wedding ring. They told him they were too old to make a new life in a strange continent and they pretended to believe that they were too old to be regarded as a danger by the Nazi state. Of course he never heard from them again: they had made their withered little plus two sign to that mathematical formula—the Final Solution. So Gruber like Doctor Plarr was a man without a father. He didn't even possess a family grave. Now he kept a photographic store in the main shopping street of the city, which, with its overlapping signs and slogans stuck out over the sidewalks, had a Chinese look. He was an optician as well. "Germans," he once said to Doctor Plarr, "always inspire confidence as chemists, opticians and photographic specialists. More people have heard of Zeiss and Bayer than of Goebbels and Goering, and even more people here have heard of Gruber."

Gruber left his customer installed in the private section of his shop, where he worked on his lenses. There the doctor could see all that went on without being noticed himself, for Gruber (he had a passion for gadgets) had fitted a small internal television screen on which he was able to watch in miniature, as in a candid camera program, the customers outside in the shop. For some reason, which Gruber had never been able to explain, his shop attracted the prettiest girls in the city (no *boutique* could compete with Gruber), as though pulchritude and the practice of photography were linked. They came in flocks to receive their color prints and they examined them with cries of excitement, chattering like birds. Doctor Plarr watched them while he drank his beer and listened to Gruber's gossip of the province.

"Have you met Charley Fortnum's woman?" Doctor Plarr asked.

"You mean his wife?"

"She can't be his wife, surely? Charley Fortnum's a divorced man. And there's no remarriage here—it's convenient for single men like me."

"Didn't you hear that his wife died?"

"No. I've been away. And when I saw him the other day he didn't mention it."

"He went off with this new girl to Rosario and got married there. So people say. Nobody really knows, of course."

"That was an odd thing for him to do. It couldn't have been necessary. You know where he found her?"

"Yes, but she's a very pretty girl," Gruber said.

"Oh yes, one of the best of Mother Sanchez' lot. But one doesn't necessarily have to marry a pretty girl."

"Girls of that kind often make good wives, especially for old men."

"Why old men?"

"Old men are not very demanding and girls like that are glad of a rest."

The phrase "like that" irritated Doctor Plarr. After seven days he was still obsessed by the unremarkable body which Gruber had classified so easily. Now on the television screen he saw a girl who leaned across the counter to buy a roll of Kodachrome in the same way Clara had leaned across her bed at Señora Sanchez'. She was more beautiful than Charley Fortnum's wife, and he felt no desire for her at all.

"Girls like that are very content to be left alone," Gruber repeated. "You know they count it good luck when they find a caller who is impotent or too drunk to perform. They have a native word for it here—I have forgotten the Spanish, but it means a Lenten visitor."

"Have you been often to the Sanchez place?"

"Why should I? Look at the temptations I have to resist nearer home with all these charming customers of mine. Some of the films they bring me to develop are quite intimate, and when I hand the packet back to one, I can see the amusement in her eyes. He has observed that moment when the bikini slipped, she is thinking—and so I have. By the way, there were two men in here the other day who asked about you. They wanted to know if you could possibly be the Eduardo Plarr they knew years ago in Asunción. They saw your name on those films I sent round to you on Thursday. Of course I said I had no idea."

"Were they police agents?"

"They didn't look like police agents, but of course it doesn't do to take chances. I heard one of them call the other father. He didn't look old enough to be his father and he wasn't dressed like a priest, and that made me suspicious."

"I'm on good terms with the Chief of Police here. Sometimes he calls me in when Doctor Benevento's on holiday. Do you think those men came from across the border? The General's agents perhaps? But why should he be interested in me? I was only a boy when I left . . ."

"Talk of the devil," Gruber said.

Doctor Plarr looked quickly at the television screen expecting to see two strangers reflected there, but all he saw was a thin girl in sunglasses of an exaggerated size —they might have been made for a skin diver. "She buys sunglasses," Gruber said, "as other women buy costume jewelry. I've sold her at least four pairs."

"Who is she?"

"You ought to know. You were talking about her just now. Charley Fortnum's wife. Or girl if you prefer it."

Doctor Plarr put down his beer and went into the shop. The girl was examining a pair of sunglasses and she was too absorbed to notice him. The lenses were colored bright mauve, the rims were of incandescent yellow, and the sidepieces were encrusted with chips of what looked like amethyst. She took her own glasses off and tried the new ones on, and immediately added ten years to her age. Her eyes were quite invisible: all he could see was his own mauve face mirrored back at him.

The assistant said, "We have only just received these from Mar del Plata. They are all the fashion there."

Doctor Plarr knew that Gruber was probably watching him on the television screen, but why should he care? He asked, "Do you like them, Señora Fortnum?"

She said, "Who . . . ? Oh, it is you, Doctor, Doctor . . . ?"

"Plarr. They make you look a lot older, but of course you can afford to add a few years."

"They cost too much. I was only trying them on for fun."

"Wrap them up," he told the assistant. "And a case . . ."

"They have their own case, doctor," she said, beginning to polish the glasses.

"No," Clara said, "I cannot . . ."

"You can with me. I am your husband's friend."

"That makes it all right?"

"Yes."

She gave a jump which he was to learn later was her expression of joy at any present, even a sweet cake. He had never known a woman accept a present so frankly, with less fuss. She said to the assistant, "Please, I will wear them. Put the old ones in the case." In these glasses, he thought, as they left Gruber's shop together, she looks more like my mistress and less like my younger sister.

"It is very kind of you," she said, speaking like a well-brought up schoolgirl.

"Come and sit by the river where we can talk." When she hesitated he added, "Nobody can recognize you in those glasses. Not even your husband."

"You do not like them?"

"No. I don't like them at all."

"I thought they looked very rich and very smart," she said with disappointment.

"They are a good disguise. That was why I wanted you to have them. No one would recognize the young Señora Fortnum with me now."

She said, "Who *would* recognize me? I know no one and Charley is at home. He sent me with the foreman. I said I wanted to buy something."

"What?"

"Oh, just something. I did not know what."

She walked contentedly beside him, following whatever direction he chose to take. He felt disturbed by the easy way that things were happening. He remembered the stupid conflict in his mind when he wanted to turn his car back toward the camp, and the number of occasions, during the last week, when he had lain awake, wondering what was the right move to make in order to see her again. He ought to have known it would be no more difficult than leading her to her cell at Señora Sanchez' house.

She said, "I am not frightened of you today."

"Perhaps because I have given you a present."

She said, "Yes, it could be that. A man would never bother to give a present to someone he did not like, would he? And the other day I thought you did not like me. I thought you were my enemy."

They came to the bank of the Paraná. A small bastion jutted into the river, fringed with white pillars, making a tiny temple for a naked statue of classical innocence which faced the water. The ugly yellow block of flats where he lived was hidden by the trees. The leaves were like the lightest of feathers; they gave an illusion of coolness because they seemed to be always in motion— a breath of air undetectable on the skin was enough to set them waving. A heavy barge moved past them up the river, coughing against the current, and the usual black plume of smoke lay across the Chaco.

She sat and stared at the Paraná; when he looked at her all he could see was his own face reflected in the mirror-glass. He said, "For God's sake take off those spectacles. I don't want to shave."

"Shave?"

"I look at myself like that twice a day—that's quite enough."

She took them off obediently and he saw her eyes, which were brown and expressionless and indistinguishable from all the Spanish women's eyes he had ever known. She said, "I do not understand."

84

"Oh, forget what I said. Is it true that you are married?"

"Yes."

"What does it feel like?"

"I think it's like wearing another girl's dress," she said, "which doesn't fit."

"Why did you do it?"

"He wanted to marry. Something to do with his money when he dies. And if there's a child . . ."

"Have you started one?"

"No."

"Well, it must be better than life at Mother Sanchez'."

"It is different," she said. "I miss the girls."

"And the men?"

"Oh, I am not bothered about them."

They were alone on the long parade beside the Paraná: for men it was the hour of work, for women of shopping. Everything here had its proper hour—the hour for the Paraná was evening, and then it was the time for young true lovers, who held hands and didn't speak. He said, "When do you have to be home?"

"The *capataz* is picking me up at Charley's office at eleven."

"It is nine o'clock now. How will you fill in the time?"

"I will look at the shops and then I will have a coffee."

"Do you never see any of your old friends?"

"The girls are all asleep now."

"You see those flats there beyond the trees?" Doctor Plarr asked. "I live there."

"Yes?"

"If you want coffee I can give you coffee."

"Yes?"

"Or orange juice," he said.

"Oh, I do not really like orange juice. Señora Sanchez said we must keep sober, that was all."

He asked, "Will you come with me?"

"It would not be right, would it?" she asked, as though she were seeking information from someone whom she knew and trusted.

"It was right at Mother Sanchez' . . ."

"But I had my living to earn there. I sent money home to Tucumán."

"What happens now?"

"Oh, I send money to Tucumán just the same. Charley gives it to me."

He stood up and put out his hand. "Come along." He was prepared to be angry if she hesitated, but she took his hand with the same shallow obedience and followed him across the road, as though the distance were no greater than across the little patio at Mother Sanchez'. The lift, however, made her hesitate. She told him she had never been in a lift before—there were few houses in the city which stood more than two stories high. She tightened her hand in excitement or fear, and when they reached the top floor she asked, "Can we do that again, please?"

"When you go."

He led her straight to his bedroom and began to undress her. A catch of her dress stuck, and she took the work out of his hands. All she said, while she lay naked on the bed waiting for him to join her, was, "Those sunglasses cost you much more than a visit to Señora Sanchez," and he wondered whether she thought of them as a payment in advance. He remembered how Teresa would count the peso notes and afterward lay them on a ledge below her saint's statue as though they were the result of a collection in church. They would be divided later in the correct proportion with Señora Sanchez: the personal gift always came later.

As he joined her he thought with relief: this is the

end of my obsession, and when she cried out, he thought: I'm a free man again, I can say goodnight to Señora Sanchez as she knits in her deck chair and I can walk back along the river with a sense of lightness which wasn't mine when I left home. The last number of the *British Medical Journal* lay on his desk—it had remained a whole week in its wrapping, and he was in the mood for reading something in a style even more precise than a story by Borges, and of greater practical value than a novel by Jorge Julio Saavedra. He began to read an article of startling originality—or so it seemed to him—on the treatment of calcium deficiency by a doctor called Caesar Borgia.

"Are you asleep?" the girl asked.

"No," but all the same he was surprised when he opened his eyes and saw the sunlight between the slats of the blind. He had thought it was night and that he was alone.

The girl caressed the inside of his thigh and ran lips down his body. He felt no more than a mild interest, a curiosity to see if she were capable of arousing him a second time. Perhaps that was the secret of her success at Mother Sanchez'—she gave a man double his money's worth. She climbed on to his body and cried out an obscenity, taking his ear between her teeth, but the obsession had died with his desire, and he felt depressed at the void it left behind. For a week he had lived with one idea and now he missed the idea as a mother might miss the crying of an unwanted child. I never really desired her, he thought, I only desired my idea of her. He would have liked to get up and go, leaving her alone to make the bed and afterward find another customer.

"Where is the bathroom?" she asked. There was nothing to distinguish her from the others he had known except that she played her comedy with more spirit and invention.

He had dressed when she returned, and he watched

impatiently while she put on her clothes. He was afraid she would ask him for the coffee he had promised and linger a long time over it. It was his hour for visiting the *barrio popular*. The women by now would have finished their first chores and the children would have returned from carrying water. He asked, "Do you want me to drop you at the Consulate?"

"No," she said. "I had better walk. The *capataz* may be there waiting."

"You have not done much shopping."

"I will show Charley the sunglasses. He will never know how much they cost."

He took a ten-thousand-peso note from his pocket and held it out to her. She turned it over as if to make sure of the amount. She said, "Nobody ever gave me more than five thousand afterward. Generally it was two. Mother Sanchez did not like us taking more. She was afraid it meant we had been hustling. She was wrong. Men are odd that way. If they can do nothing they always give you more."

"As if any of you cared," he said.

"As if we cared."

"A Lenten visitor."

The girl laughed. She said, "It is good to be able to talk free again. I cannot talk free to Charley. I think he wants to forget all about Señora Sanchez." She handed him back the note. "It would not be right," she said, "now I am married. And I do not need it. Charley is generous. And the sunglasses cost a lot." She put them on, so that again he saw his own face staring back at him, in miniature, as though he were a doll looking out of a doll's house window. She asked, "Shall I see you again?"

He wanted to say, "No. It's all finished now," but common politeness—and the relief he felt because she had forgotten the coffee—made him reply formally, like a host to a guest whom he doesn't really want to encourage to call again. "Of course. One day when you come into town . . . I'll give you my telephone number."

"You need not give me a present every time," she assured him.

"And you needn't play a comedy," he said.

"Comedy?"

He said, "I know there are always men who want to believe you are finding the same pleasure that they do. Naturally at Mother Sanchez' you had to play a part to earn your present, but here you see—you need not act any longer. Perhaps you have to act with Charley, but not with me. You don't have to pretend anything at all with me."

"I am sorry," she said. "I did something wrong?"

"It always used to annoy me," Doctor Plarr went on, "in that house of yours. A man is not nearly so stupid as he seems to you. He knows he has come to get a pleasure and not to give it."

She said, "All the same I think I pretended very well because I got bigger presents than the other girls." She wasn't annoyed. He could tell that she was accustomed to this sadness after coition. He didn't differ, even in that, from the other men she had known. And this void, he thought—is she right? is it no more than the temporary *tristitia* most men feel when they leave a brothel behind?

"How long were you there?"

"Two years. I was nearly sixteen," she said, "when I arrived. The girls gave me a cake with candles on my birthday. I had never seen one before. It was very pretty."

"Does Charley Fortnum like you to pretend like that?"

"He likes me to be very quiet," she said, "and very tender. Is that what you would have liked too? I am sorry . . . I thought . . . You are so much younger than Charley, so I thought . . ."

"I would like you to be yourself," he said. "Be as indifferent as you like. How many men have you known?"

"How could I remember that?"

He showed her the way to work the lift, and she asked him to come down with her—she was still a little afraid of it, even though it excited her. When she pressed the button and it began to descend she gave the same jump she had given in Gruber's shop. At the door she admitted to him that she was afraid of the telephone too. "And your name—I have forgotten your name."

"Plarr. Eduardo Plarr." He tried her name for the first time aloud. "You are Clara, aren't you?" He added, "If you are afraid to use the telephone, *I* shall have to telephone to you. But perhaps Charley will answer."

"He usually drives around the camp before nine. And Wednesdays he is nearly always in town—though he likes me to come with him."

"Oh well," Doctor Plarr said, "we shall find a way." He didn't bother to see her into the street or watch her go. He was a free man.

And yet, inexplicably, the same night, while he was trying to sleep, he thought with regret that he had a clearer memory of her stretched out in Charley Fortnum's bed than he had of her in his own. An obsession may sleep awhile, but it doesn't necessarily die, and in less than a week he wanted to see her again. He would have liked to hear her voice, however indifferent it might sound on the telephone, but the telephone never rang with any message of importance.

PART
THREE

1

Doctor Plarr did not arrive home from the hut until nearly three in the morning. Because of police patrols Diego took a circuitous route and dropped him near the house of Señora Sanchez, thus giving him an excuse, if one were needed, for being out on foot in the early morning. There was one awkward moment when he climbed the stairs and a door on the floor below him opened and a voice demanded, "Who is that?" He called down, "Doctor Plarr. Why are children born at unconscionable hours?"

Although he lay down on his bed he hardly slept at all. Nevertheless he got through his morning's work with more than usual expedition and drove out to Charley Fortnum's camp. He had no idea of the kind of situation with which he might have to cope, and he was in a tired, nervous and angry mood, expecting to find a hysterical woman awaiting him. While he lay sleepless in bed he had considered the possibility of disclosing all to the police, but that would be to condemn León and Aquino to almost certain death, probably Fortnum as well.

It was a heavy sun-drenched midday when he arrived at the camp and a police jeep stood beside Fortnum's Pride in the shade of the avocados. He walked into the house without ringing, and in the living room he found the Chief of Police talking to Clara. She was not the hysterical woman he had anticipated but a young girl sitting stiffly on the sofa as though she were receiving orders from a superior. ". . . all we can," Colonel Perez was saying.

"What are you doing here?" Doctor Plarr asked.

"I have come to see Señora Fortnum, doctor, and you?"

"I have come to see the Consul on business."

"The Consul is not here," Colonel Perez said.

Clara gave him no greeting. She seemed to be waiting without a will of her own, as she had often waited in the patio of the establishment, for one of many men to lead her away—hustling being forbidden by Mother Sanchez.

"He is not in town," Doctor Plarr said.

"You have been to his office?"

"No. I telephoned."

He regretted immediately what he had said, for Colonel Perez was no fool. One ought never to volunteer information to a policeman. Doctor Plarr had watched more than once the cool and efficient way Perez went to work. On one occasion a man had been found stabbed on a raft of logs which had been floated down the Paraná from two thousand kilometers away. In Doctor Benevento's absence Doctor Plarr was summoned to a bend of the river near the airport where the logs were waiting for transshipment. At the bottom of a little slippery country path, where snakes rustled in the undergrowth, he reached a small wooden jetty—the so-called port for timber.

A family had been living on the raft for a month. Doctor Plarr, stumbling across the logs behind Perez, admired the easy way in which the police officer balanced: he felt himself in constant danger of slipping when the logs sank underfoot and leaped up again. It must, he thought, be a little like standing on a horse as it cantered round a circus ring.

"You spoke to his housekeeper?" Colonel Perez asked.

Doctor Plarr was again annoyed at himself for his rash lies. He was Clara's doctor. Why had he not simply said that this was a routine medical visit to a pregnant wife? One lie in the presence of a policeman seemed to multiply like bacilli. He said, "No. There was no answer."

Colonel Perez considered his reply through a long silence.

He remembered how rapidly and easily Perez had walked over the heaving trunks as though he were treading a firm city pavement. The logs covered half the width of the river. A group of people, diminished by distance, stood in the very center of the wide horizontal forest. Perez and he had to jump from one raft to another to reach them, and every time he jumped the doctor feared he would fall into the gap between the rafts, though the gap was usually less than a meter. His shoes became waterlogged as the trunks sank beneath his weight and rose again. "I warn you," Perez said, "it's not going to be very pretty. The family have been traveling on the raft for weeks with the body. It would have been much better if they had just pushed it into the water. We would never have known."

"Why didn't they?" Doctor Plarr asked, with his arms stretched out as though he were walking a tightrope.

"The murderer," Perez said, "wanted him to have a Christian burial."

"He has admitted killing him then?" the doctor asked.

"Oh, he admitted it to me," Perez replied. "You see —these are all my own people."

When they reached the group—two men, a woman and a child with two officers—Doctor Plarr noticed that the police had not even bothered to take away the assassin's knife. He sat cross-legged beside the disagreeable corpse as though it were his job to guard it. He had an expression of sadness more than of guilt.

Colonel Perez said, "I came to tell the señora that her husband's car has been found in the Paraná not far from Posadas. There is no sign of a body, so we hope he may have escaped."

"An accident? Of course you know—the señora won't mind my saying it—Fortnum is rather a heavy drinker."

"Yes. But there are other possibilities," Colonel Perez said.

The doctor would have found it easier to play his part to the police officer or to Clara if he had been alone with either of them. He was afraid when he spoke that one or the other would detect something false in his tone. He asked, "What do you think may have happened?"

"Any incident which occurs so close to the border may be political. We always have to remember that. You remember the doctor who was kidnapped in Posadas?"

"Of course. But why on earth Fortnum? There's nothing political about him."

"He is a Consul."

"Only an Honorary Consul." Even the Chief of Police seemed unable to understand that distinction.

Colonel Perez spoke to Clara, "We shall let you know, señora, as soon as there is any news." He put his hand on the doctor's elbow. "There is something I would like to ask you, doctor." The colonel led Doctor Plarr across the verandah, where the dumbwaiter with its Long John glasses seemed to emphasize the remarkable absence of Charley Fortnum (he would certainly have invited them to take "a spot" before they left), and on into the deep shade of the avocado trees. He picked up one of the fallen fruit, examined it for ripeness with an expert's eye and put it in the back of the police car, laying it down carefully where the sun wouldn't strike. "A beauty," he said. "I like to eat them mashed in a little whisky."

"What is it you want?" the doctor asked.

"There is one thing which worries me a little."

95

"You don't really believe that Fortnum has been kidnapped?"

"It is one of the possibilities. It has even occurred to me that he might have been the victim of a silly mistake. He was with the American Ambassador, you see, in the ruins. The Ambassador obviously would be a more likely target. If that is the case the men must be strangers—perhaps from Paraguay. You and I would never make a mistake like that, doctor. I only say 'you' because you are nearly one of us. Of course there is always the possibility you might be indirectly concerned."

"I'm not quite the kidnapping type, colonel."

"I was thinking about your father across the border. You told me once that he was either dead or in prison. You might have a motive. Forgive the way I think aloud, doctor, but I always feel a little at sea when it comes to political crime. In politics crime is often the occupation of a *caballero*. I am more used to crimes which are committed by criminals—or at least by violent or poor men. For money or lust."

"Or *machismo*," the doctor said, venturing to tease him.

"Oh, everything here is *machismo*," Perez said, and he smiled at the doctor's remark in so friendly a way that Plarr felt a little reassured. "Here *machismo* is only another word for living. A word for the air we breathe. When there is no *machismo* a man is dead. Are you coming back to the city, doctor?"

"No. Now that I am here I may as well take a look at Señora Fortnum. She is expecting a baby."

"Yes. She told me that." The Chief of Police had his hand on the door of the car, but at the last moment he turned and said in a low voice as though they were sharing a friendly confidence, "Doctor, why did you tell me you rang up the Consul's office and that there was no reply? I have had a man stationed there all the morning in case a call came."

"You know what the telephone service is like in this city."

"When a telephone is out of order one usually hears an engaged tone, not a ringing tone."

"Not always, colonel. Anyway it may have been the ringing tone. I did not listen very carefully."

"And yet you came all the way out to the camp?"

"It was about time anyway that I visited Señora Fortnum. Why should I lie to you?"

"I have to think of all the possibilities, doctor. Even a crime of passion is possible."

"Passion?" the doctor smiled. "I am an Englishman."

"Yes, it is unlikely—I know that. And in the case of Señora Fortnum . . . one would not suppose a man like you with all your chances would find it necessary . . . yet I have known crimes of passion even in a brothel."

"Charley Fortnum is a friend of mine."

"Oh, a friend . . . It is usually a friend one betrays, isn't it, in these cases?" Colonel Perez put a hand on the doctor's shoulder. "You must forgive me. I know you well enough, doctor, to allow myself a little speculation when I feel myself at a loss. As I do now. I have heard it said your relations with Señora Fortnum have been very close. All the same—I agree—I would not have thought they would require the elimination of her husband. And yet I still keep wondering why you lied to me."

He climbed into the car. His revolver holster creaked as he eased himself down in his seat. He leaned back to make sure that the avocado was not in a position where it would bounce and bruise.

Doctor Plarr said, "I was not thinking, colonel, when I spoke, that was all. Lying to the police is almost an automatic reflex. And I was unaware you knew so much about me."

"This is a small city," Colonel Perez said. "It is always safer to assume common knowledge when you sleep with a married woman."

Doctor Plarr watched the police car out of sight and then went reluctantly back into the house. Secrecy, he thought, is part of the attraction in a sexual affair. An open affair has always a touch of absurdity.

Clara sat exactly where he had left her. He thought: this is the first time we have been together with no sense of hurry, no rendezvous for her to keep at the Consulate, no fear that Charley will return accidentally from farming. She asked, "Do you think he is dead?"

"No."

"Perhaps it would be good for everybody if he were."

"Not for Charley."

"Yes. Even for Charley. He is so afraid," she said, "of getting old."

"All the same I don't suppose he wants to die just yet."

"The baby was kicking hard this morning."

"Yes?"

"Do you want to go to the bedroom?"

"Of course." He waited for her to get up and lead the way.

They never kissed on the mouth (that was part of the brothel training), and he followed her with a slow renewal of excitement. In a real love affair, he thought, you are interested in a woman because she is someone distinct from yourself; then bit by bit she adapts herself to you, she picks up your habits, your ideas, even your turns of phrase, she becomes part of you, and then what interest remains? One cannot love oneself, one cannot live for long close to oneself—everyone has need of a stranger in the bed, and a whore remains a stranger. Her body has been scrawled over by so many men you can never decipher your own signature there.

When they were quiet and her head was lying against his shoulder in the same attitude taken by a peaceful lover, she began a sentence which he mistook for one he had too often heard, "Eduardo, is it true? Do you really . . . ?"

"No," he said firmly.

He thought she was demanding the same answer to a banal question that his mother had constantly forced out of him after they left his father, the answer which each of his mistresses sooner or later had always insisted on—"Do you really love me, Eduardo?" One merit of a brothel is that the word love is seldom if ever employed. He repeated, "No."

"How can you be sure?" she asked. "Just now you sounded so certain he was alive, but even that policeman thinks he is dead."

Doctor Plarr realized he had been mistaken and in his relief he kissed her close to the mouth.

The news came over the radio from the local station while they were at lunch. It was the first meal they had ever taken together, and they were both of them ill at ease. Eating food side by side seemed more intimate to Doctor Plarr than the sexual act. The maid served them and disappeared between each course into the vast untidy regions of the ramshackle house, regions which he had never penetrated. First she served them an omelette, then an excellent steak which was far better than the goulash at the Italian Club or the tough beef at the Nacional. There was a bottle of Charley's Chilean wine which had more body than the cooperative wine from Mendoza. It was odd eating so formally and so well with one of Señora Sanchez' girls. It opened an unexpected vista into quite another sort of life, a domestic life equally strange to both of them. It was as though he had taken a boat down one of the small tributaries of the Paraná and suddenly found himself in some great delta like that of the Amazon, where all sense of direction can be lost. He felt an unaccustomed tenderness toward Clara who had made this strange voyage possible. They picked their words carefully, it was the first time there were words to pick; they had a subject of conversation—Charley Fortnum's disappearance.

Doctor Plarr began to speak of him as though he were, after all, certainly dead—it seemed to him safer that way, for otherwise she might begin to wonder what was the source of his hope. Only when Clara spoke of the future did he change his tack in order to evade a dubious topic. Charley, he assured her, might yet prove to be alive. To navigate in this new Amazonian waste of deeps and shoals proved difficult—it made for a confusion of tenses. "It's quite possible he escaped from the car, and then if he was exhausted he might have been carried a long way by the current . . . He may have landed far from any village . . ."

"But why was his car in the river there?" She added with regret, "It was the new Cadillac. He was going to sell it next week in Buenos Aires."

"Perhaps he had some errand in Posadas. He was a man who might well . . ."

"Oh no, I know he was not going to Posadas. He was coming to see me. He did not want to go to those ruins. He did not even want to go to the Governor's dinner. He was anxious about me and the baby."

"Why? He had no reason. You are a strong girl, Clara."

"I pretended sometimes to be sick so he would ask you to come and see me. It was easier for you that way."

"What a little bitch you are," he exclaimed with pleasure.

"And he took my best sunglasses, the ones you gave me. I shall never see them again now. They were my favorite sunglasses. They were so smart. And they came from Mar del Plata."

"I will go to Gruber's tomorrow," he said, "and get you another pair."

"It was the only one they had."

"They can order another pair."

"He borrowed them once before and nearly broke them."

"He must have looked a bit odd in them," Doctor Plarr said.

"He never cares what he looks like. And he saw very badly when he had been drinking." The tenses, present and past, swung to and fro like the arrow of a barometer moving irregularly between settled and unsettled weather.

"Did he love you, Clara?" It was not a question which had ever troubled him. Charley Fortnum, as Clara's husband, had never meant more to him than a slight inconvenience when he felt the need to have her quickly, but Charley Fortnum, lying drugged on a box in a dirty back room, took on the appearance of a serious rival.

"He was always kind to me."

After the avocado ice had been served he felt desire for her beginning to return. He had no patients to see before the evening; he could take a siesta at the camp without keeping his ear pricked for the rumbling approach of Fortnum's Pride. After the morning climax he would be able to prolong his pleasure through the whole afternoon. She had never, since that first occasion in his flat, attempted to play the comedy of passion, and her indifference had begun to represent a challenge. Sometimes when he was alone he dreamed of surprising her into a genuine cry of excitement.

"Did Charley ever say why he married you?" he asked.

"I told you. It was a question of money when he died. And now he's dead."

"Perhaps."

"Would you like to have more ice? I can call María. There is a bell, but Charley always rings it."

101

"Why?"

"I am not used to bells. All these electric things—they frighten me."

It amused him to watch her sitting upright at the end of the table like a hostess. He thought of his mother in the old days on the *estancia* when he had been brought in by his nurse for the dessert—she too had often served an avocado ice. She had been far more beautiful than Clara—they were not to be compared—but he remembered all the aids which she had bought for beauty in those days; they stood two deep on the long dressing table that stretched from wall to wall. He wondered sometimes whether even in those days his father had not taken second place to Guerlain or Elizabeth Arden.

"What was Charley like as a lover?"

Clara did not bother to answer. She said, "The radio . . . we ought to listen. There may be news."

"News?"

"News of Charley, of course. What are you thinking about?"

"I was thinking of the long afternoon we can spend together."

"He might turn up."

Taken off his guard he said, "He won't turn up."

"Why are you so sure that he is dead?"

"I'm not sure, but if he is alive he will go to a telephone before he does anything else. He will not want to surprise you—and the baby."

"We ought to listen all the same."

After getting Asunción first he found a local station. There was no news. Only a sad Guaraní song came over the air and the music of a harp. She said, "Do you like champagne?"

"Yes."

"Charley has some champagne. He was given it once

in exchange for Long John Whisky—real French champagne, he said."

The music stopped. A voice announced the station and the news bulletin, and news of Charley Fortnum took first place. A British Consul—the speaker left out the qualifying and diminishing adjective—had been kidnapped. There was no mention of the American Ambassador. Somehow León must have communicated with his contacts. The omission lent Charley a certain importance. It made him sound worth kidnapping. The authorities, so the speaker said, believed the kidnappers were Paraguayan. It was thought that the Consul might have been taken across the river and the kidnappers were making their demands through the Argentine government in order to confuse the trail. Apparently they had demanded the release of ten political prisoners who were held in Paraguay. Any police action in Paraguay or Argentina would endanger the life of the Consul. A plane to Havana or Mexico City must be arranged for the prisoners . . . There were the usual detailed conditions. The announcement had been made only an hour ago by a telephone call from Rosario to the *Nación* in Buenos Aires. The announcer said there was no possibility that the Consul was held in the capital, for his car had been found near Posadas more than a thousand kilometers away.

"I do not understand," Clara said.

"Keep quiet and listen." The announcer went on to explain that the kidnappers had chosen their time with some skill, for General Stroessner at the moment was on an unofficial holiday in the south of Argentina. He had been informed of the kidnapping and he was reported to have said, "That is no concern of mine. I am here for fishing." The kidnappers had given the Paraguayan government until Sunday midnight to agree to their terms by an announcement on the radio. When that time expired they would be forced to execute their prisoner.

"But why Charley?"

"It must have been a mistake. There's no other explanation. You mustn't worry. He will be back home in a few days. Tell your maid you wish to see no one— I expect there will be journalists coming out here."

"You will stay?"

"I'll stay for a while."

"I do not think I want to make love."

"No. Of course. I understand."

They moved together down the long passage hung with sporting prints, and Doctor Plarr paused to look again at the narrow stream shaded by willows situated in that small northern island where his father had been born. No general went fishing with his colonels in streams like those. He carried the thought of his father's abandoned home into the bedroom. He asked, "Do you ever want to go back to Tucumán?"

"No," she said, "of course not. Why do you ask me that?"

She lay on the bed without taking off her clothes. It was cool as a sea cave in the shuttered air-conditioned room.

"What does your father do?"

"He cuts cane," she said, "in the season, but he is getting old."

"And out of season?"

"They live on the money I send them. They would starve if I died. I will not die, will I? with the baby?"

"No, of course not. Have you no brother or sister?"

"I had a brother, but he went away—no one knows where." He sat on the edge of the bed and her hand touched his for a moment and withdrew. Perhaps she was afraid he would take her gesture for a comedy of tenderness and resent it. "He went away," she said, "to cut cane one morning at four o'clock and then he never came back. Perhaps he died. Perhaps he just went away."

He was reminded of his father's disappearance. Here they lived on a continent, not on an island. What a vast area of land, with ill-defined frontiers of mountain, river, jungle and swamp, there was to lose oneself in— all the way from Panama to Tierra del Fuego. "Your brother never wrote?"

"How could he? He did not know how to read or write."

"But you can."

"A little. Señora Sanchez taught me. She liked her girls to be educated. And Charley has helped me too."

"You had no sister?" he asked.

"Yes. She had a baby in the fields and strangled it and then she died."

He had never asked about her family before. He could think of no reason for questioning her now, unless perhaps he was seeking to discover what lay behind his obsession. Was there some characteristic in which she differed from the other girls he had seen at Señora Sanchez' house? Perhaps if he discovered the nature of the difference, the obsession would be killed like a trauma at the end of analysis. He would have strangled the obsession as her sister had strangled her child. He said, "I am tired. Let me lie down beside you for a bit. I need to sleep. I was up until three this morning."

"What were you doing?"

"I was seeing a patient," he said. "Will you wake me when it begins to get dark?"

The air conditioner humming by the window sounded like a natural summer sound, and once through his sleep he seemed to hear a bell ringing—the big ship's bell which hung on a rope from the eaves of the verandah. He was half aware that she had got up and left him. He heard distant voices, the sound of a car starting, and then she was back, lying beside him, and he slept again. He dreamt, as he hadn't dreamt for some years, of the *estancia* in Paraguay. He was lying in his child's bunk at the top of a ladder, he listened to the noise of keys which were turned and bolts which were pushed to—his father was making the house secure, but he was afraid all the same. Perhaps someone had been locked in who should have been locked out.

Doctor Plarr opened his eyes. The raised edge of the bunk became Clara's body set against his own. It was dark. He could see nothing. He put his hand out and touched her and he felt the baby move. He put his fingers up to her face. Her eyes were open. He said, "Are you awake?" but she didn't answer. He asked, "Is something wrong?"

She said, "I do not want Charley back, but I do not want him to die either."

He was astonished by this expression of emotion. She had shown none at all, as she sat and listened to Colonel Perez, and, when she had spoken to him after Perez left, it was of the Cadillac and of the lost sunglasses from Gruber's.

She said, "He was good to me. He is a kind man. I do not want him to be hurt. I only want him not to be here."

He began to comfort her with his hand as he would have comforted a frightened dog, and gently, without intention, they came together. He felt no lust, and when she moaned and tightened, he felt no sense of triumph.

He wondered with sadness, why did I ever want this to happen? Why did I think it would be a victory? There seemed to be no point in playing the game since now he knew what moves he had to make to win. The moves were sympathy, tenderness, quiet, the counterfeiting of love. He had been drawn to her by her indifference, even her enmity. She said, "Stay with me tonight."

"How can I? Your maid would know. You can't trust her not to tell Charley."

"I could leave Charley."

"It's too soon to think of that. First we have to save him—somehow."

"Yes, of course, but afterward . . ."

"You were anxious about him just now."

"Not about him," she said. "About me. When he is here I can talk about nothing—only the baby. He wants to forget that Señora Sanchez ever existed, so I can never see my friends because they all work there. What good am I to him? He does not want to make love to me any more because he is afraid it will do something to the baby. Do what? Sometimes I long to tell him—it is not yours anyway, so why do you bother about it?"

"Are you sure it isn't his?"

"Yes. I am sure. Perhaps if he knew about you he would let me go."

"Who were those people who came to the house just now?"

"Two journalists."

"Did you speak to them?"

"They wanted me to make an appeal to the kidnappers—for Charley. I did not know what to say. I knew one of them—he used to have me sometimes when I was with Señora Sanchez. I think he was angry about the baby. Colonel Perez must have told him about the baby. He said the baby was news. He always thought I liked him more than the other men. So I think his *machismo* was hurt. These men always believe you when you pretend. It suits their pride. He wanted to show his friend, the photographer, that there was something special between us, but there was nothing. Nothing. I was angry and I began to cry, and they took a picture. He said 'Fine. O.K. Fine. That's what we want. The sorrowing wife and mother-to-be,' he said, and they drove away."

It was not easy to interpret her tears correctly. Were they tears for Charley, tears of anger, tears for herself?

"What a funny beast you are, Clara," he said.

"Is something wrong?"

"You were acting again just now, weren't you?"

"What do you mean? Acting?"

"When we made love."

"Yes," she said. "Of course I was acting. I always try to do what you like. I always try to say what you like. Yes. Just like at Señora Sanchez. Why not? You have your *machismo* too."

He half believed her. He wanted to believe her. If she were speaking the truth there might be something still to discover, the game was not over yet.

"Where are you going?" she asked.

"I have been wasting a lot of time here, Clara. There must be something I can do to help Charley."

"And me? What about me?"

"You had better take a bath," he said, "or your maid might smell the sex."

2

Doctor Plarr drove back to the city. He told himself it was necessary to do something about Charley Fortnum immediately, but he had no idea what. Perhaps if he stayed quiet everything might be put in order in the accustomed way—the British and American Ambassadors would bring the right diplomatic pressure to bear, Charley Fortnum would be found deposited some early morning in a church and go home—home?—and

ten prisoners in Paraguay would be given their liberty—
it was even possible his father might be among them.
What else could he do but leave things to sort themselves out? He had already lied to Colonel Perez, he
was implicated.

Of course, to salve his conscience, he might make an
emotional appeal to León Rivas to let Charley Fortnum
go—"in the name of our old friendship." But León was
a man under orders and in any case Doctor Plarr had
no clear idea of where to find him. In the *barrio* of the
poor all the marshy tracks resembled one another, there
were the same avocado trees everywhere, the same huts
of mud or tin, and the same potbellied children carrying
petrol tins of water. They would look at him with their
blank eyes which were already infected by trachoma
and reply nothing to any question. It might take him
hours, even days, to find the hut where Charley Fortnum was hidden, and what good would his appeal do
in any case? He tried unsuccessfully to reassure himself
that León was not a man to commit murder, nor was
Aquino, but they were only instruments—there remained El Tigre, whoever he might be.

He had heard of El Tigre for the first time one evening when he had passed León and Aquino sitting side
by side in his waiting room. They were just two strangers among the other patients and he hadn't given them
a second look. All who waited there were the responsibility of his secretary.

His secretary was a pretty young woman called Ana.
She was dauntingly efficient and the daughter of an
influential official in the public health department. Doctor Plarr sometimes wondered why he had never been
tempted to make love to her. Perhaps he hesitated because of the white starched uniform which she had
adopted of her own wish—it would creak or crackle if
one touched her: she might have been connected to a
burglar alarm. Or perhaps it was the importance of her

father, or her piety, real or apparent, which deterred him. She always wore a small gold cross round her neck, and once, when he had been driving through the square by the cathedral, he had seen her emerge with her family from Sunday Mass carrying a missal bound in white vellum—it might have been a first Communion present, for it closely resembled the sugar almonds which are distributed on such occasions.

The evening when León and Aquino came to see him, he had dealt with all the other patients before it became the turn of the two strangers. He had not remembered them because there were always new faces waiting his attention. Patience and patients were words closely allied. His secretary came with a crackle to his side and put a slip of paper on the desk. "They want to see you together," she said. He put back on the shelf a medical book he had been consulting in front of a patient—for some reason patients gained confidence if they could see a colored picture, an aspect of human psychology which American publishers knew well. When he looked back the two men were standing side by side in front of his desk. The smaller, who had protruding ears, said, "It *is* Eduardo surely?"

"León," Plarr exclaimed, "it is León, León Rivas?" They embraced with a certain shyness. Plarr asked, "How many years . . . ? I haven't heard from you since you sent me that Ordination card. I was sorry I could not come to the ceremony—it would have been unsafe for me."

"That is all over anyway."

"Why? Have they thrown you out?"

"I am married for one thing. The Archbishop did not like that."

Doctor Plarr hesitated.

León Rivas said, "I am very lucky. She is a fine woman."

"Congratulations. Who in all Paraguay did you find willing to celebrate the marriage?"

"We made our vows to each other. You know a priest at a marriage is never more than a witness. In an emergency . . . this was an emergency."

"I had forgotten things were so easy."

"Oh, I can assure you not so easy. It needs a lot of thought. That sort of marriage is more irrevocable than in a church. Don't you recognize my friend?"

"No . . . I don't think so . . . no . . ." Doctor Plarr tried to strip away the thin beard and identify some schoolboy face which he might have known years ago in Asunción.

"Aquino."

"Aquino? Why of course it's Aquino." Another embrace: it was like a military ceremony, a kiss on the cheek and a decoration awarded for a dead past in a devastated land. He asked, "What are you doing now? You were going to be a writer, weren't you? Are you a writer?"

"There are no writers left in Paraguay."

"We saw your name on a parcel in Gruber's shop," León said.

"So he told me, but I thought you were police agents from over there."

"Why? Are you watched?"

"I don't think so."

"We have come from over there."

"Are you in trouble?"

"Aquino has been in prison," León said.

"They let you out?"

"The authorities did not exactly invite me to go," Aquino said.

"We were lucky," León explained. "They were transferring him from one police station to another, there was a little shooting, but the only man who was killed was the policeman we were going to pay. He was shot by his own side, by accident. We had given him only half the money in advance, so we got Aquino cheap."

"Are you going to settle here?"

"Not settle," León said. "We are here to do a job. Afterward we shall go back."

"You are not patients then?"

"No, we are not patients."

Doctor Plarr appreciated the dangers of a frontier. He got up and opened the door. His secretary was standing beside the filing cabinet in the outer office. She inserted a card here, a card there. Her cross swung to and fro as she moved, like a priest's censer. He closed the door. He said, "You know, León, I'm not interested in politics. Only medicine. I am not like my father."

"Why are you here and not in Buenos Aires?"

"I was not doing very well in Buenos Aires."

"We thought you might want to know what had happened to your father."

"Do *you* know?"

"I think we may soon be in a position to find out."

Doctor Plarr said, "I had better make notes about your condition. I'll put down low blood pressure for you, León, a suspicion of anemia . . . Aquino—perhaps your gall bladder . . . I will put you down for x-rays. You understand my secretary will expect to see what diagnosis I make."

"We believe your father may be alive still," León said. "So naturally we thought of you . . ."

There was a knock on the door and the secretary came in. She said, "I have finished all the cards. If you would let me go now . . ."

"A lover waiting?"

She said, "Today is Saturday," as though that ought to explain everything.

"I know that."

"I want to go to Confession."

"Oh," Doctor Plarr said, "of course, I am sorry, Ana.

112

I forgot. Of course you must go." His lack of desire for her irritated him, so he deliberately found an occasion to vex her. "Pray for me," he said.

She ignored his flippancy. "If you will leave those two cards on my desk when you have finished . . ." Her dress crepitated, as she went out, like a nocturnal insect.

Doctor Plarr said, "I doubt if her Confession will take very long."

"Those who have nothing to confess always take the longest," León Rivas said. "They want to please the priest and give him something to do. A murderer has only one thing on his mind, so he forgets all the rest— perhaps worse things. One can deal with him very quickly."

"You still talk like a priest, León. What made you marry?"

"I married when I lost faith. A man must have something to guard."

"I can't imagine you without your faith."

"I only mean my faith in the Church. Or in what they have made of it. Of course I know one day things may be better. But I was ordained when John was Pope. I am not patient enough to wait for another John."

"You were going to be an *abogado* before you became a priest. What are you now?"

"A criminal," León said.

"You are joking."

"No. That is why I have come to you. We need your help."

"To rob a bank?" Doctor Plarr asked. He couldn't take León seriously, when he looked at those familiar protruding ears and remembered so much . . .

"To rob an Embassy—you might call it that."

"But I'm no criminal, León." He added deliberately, "Except for an abortion or two," to see if the priestly eyes would flinch a little, but they stared back at him with indifference.

"In a wrong society," León Rivas said, "the criminals are the honest men." The phrase came a bit too glibly. It was probably a well-known quotation. Doctor Plarr remembered how first there had been the law books León studied—he had once explained to him the meaning of tort. Then there had been all the works of theology—León was able to make even the Trinity seem plausible by a sort of higher mathematics. He supposed there must be other primers to read in the new life. Perhaps he was quoting Marx.

"The new American Ambassador," León said, "is planning to visit the north in November. You have contacts here, Eduardo. All we need are the exact details of his program."

"I'm not going to be an accomplice in murder, León."

"There will be no murder. A murder would be of very little use to us. Aquino, tell him about the treatment they gave you."

"It was simple," Aquino said. "Not at all up-to-date. Nothing electric. Like the *conquistadores* they managed with a knife . . ."

Doctor Plarr listened with nausea. He had been present at many unpleasant deaths which had affected him less. In those cases there had been something to do, some means of helping in however small a degree. He felt sickness at this narrative in the past tense, just as years ago, when he was a young student, he had been upset by the dissection of a cadaver for educational purposes. When it came to a living body there was always curiosity and hope. He asked, "And you didn't talk?"

"Of course I talked," Aquino said. "They have it all in the files now. The counterinsurgency section of the CIA was pleased with me. Two of their agents were there, and they gave me three packets of Lucky Strike. A packet for each man I had betrayed."

"Show him your hand, Aquino," León said.

Aquino laid his right hand on the desk like a patient seeking advice. Three fingers were missing: the hand without them looked like something drawn up in a fish net from the river where eels were active. Aquino said, "That was why I began to write poetry. Verse was less tiring than prose with only a left hand. I could learn it by heart. I was allowed a visitor every three months (that was another reward they gave me) and I would recite her the verses I had made."

"They were good verses," León said, "for a beginner. A kind of Purgatorio in *villancico.*"

"How many of you are there?" Doctor Plarr asked.

"A dozen of us crossed the border, not counting El Tigre. He was already in Argentina."

"Who is El Tigre?"

"The one who gives the orders. We call him that, but it is a term of affection. He likes to wear striped shirts."

"The scheme sounds mad, León."

"It has been done before."

"Why kidnap the American Ambassador here instead of the one you have in Asunción?"

"That was our first plan. But the General takes great precautions. Here, you must know it yourself, they have much less fear of guerrillas since the failure in Salta."

"All the same you are in a foreign country."

"South America is our country, Eduardo. Not Paraguay. Not Argentina. You know what Che said, 'The whole continent is my country.' What are you? English or South American?"

Doctor Plarr remembered the question, but he still could not answer it as he drove into the city past the white Gothic prison which always reminded him of a sugar decoration for a wedding cake. He told himself that León Rivas was a priest, and not a murderer. And

Aquino? Aquino was a poet. It would have been easier to discount the danger to Charley Fortnum if he had never seen him lying unconscious on a box, a box so oddly shaped that it might have been a coffin.

3

Charley Fortnum woke with the worst head he could ever remember having. His eyes were aching and his vision was blurred. He whispered, "Clara," putting out his hand to touch her side, but all he touched was a mud wall. Then an image came to his mind of Doctor Plarr standing over him during the night with an electric torch. The doctor had told him some implausible story of an accident.

It was daylight now. The sunlight seeped across the floor under the door of the next room, and he could tell, even through his bruised eyes, that this was no hospital. Nor was the hard box on which he lay a hospital bed. He swung his legs over the side and tried to stand up. He was giddy and nearly fell. Clutching the side of the box, he saw that he had been lying all night upon a coffin. It gave him, as he would have put it, a nasty turn.

"Ted?" he called. He didn't associate Doctor Plarr with practical jokes, but there had to be some sort of explanation, and he was anxious to be back with Clara. Clara would be frightened, Clara wouldn't know what to do. Why, she was afraid even to use the telephone. "Ted?" he called again in a dry croak. Whisky had never treated him like this before, not even the local brand. Whom the bloody hell had he been drinking with and where? Mason, he told himself, you've got to pull yourself together. It was always to Mason he attributed his worst errors and his worst failings. In his boyhood when he still practiced confession it was always Mason who knelt in the box and muttered abstract phrases concerning sins against purity, though it was Charley Fortnum who would leave the box, his face ashine with beneficence after Mason's absolution. "Mason, Mason," he whispered now, "you snotty little beast, Mason, what were you up to last night?" He knew that when he exceeded the proper measure he was apt to forget things, but never before had he forgotten to quite this extent . . . He took a stumbling step toward the door and for the third time called out to Doctor Plarr.

The door was pushed open and a stranger stood there waving a sub-machine gun at him. He had the narrow eyes and jet black hair of an Indian and he shouted at Fortnum in Guaraní. Fortnum, in spite of his father's angry insistence, had never learned more than a few words of Guaraní, but it was clear enough that the man was telling him to get back onto the so-called bed. "All right, all right," Fortnum said, speaking English so that the man would no more understand him than he understood Guaraní. "Keep your shirt on, old man." He sat down on the coffin and said, "Piss off," with a sense of relief.

Another stranger in blue jeans, naked to the waist, came in and ordered the Indian away. He carried a cup of coffee. The coffee smelled like home, and Charley Fortnum was a little comforted. The man had protruding ears and for a moment Charley was reminded of a boy at school whom Mason had unmercifully teased, though Fortnum repented afterward and shared a bar of chocolate with the victim. This memory gave him a sense of reassurance. He asked, "Where am I?"

"You do not need to worry," the man replied. He held out the coffee.

"I have to go home. My wife will be anxious."

117

"Tomorrow. I hope you will be able to go tomorrow."

"Who was that man with a gun?"

"Miguel. A good man. Drink your coffee, please. You will feel much better then."

"What's your name?" Charley Fortnum asked.

"León," the man said.

"I mean your family name?"

"None of us here have families," the man said, "so we are nameless."

Charley Fortnum turned this statement over in his mind like a difficult phrase in a book; it made no more sense to him at the second reading.

"Doctor Plarr was here last night," he said.

"Plarr? Plarr? I do not think I know anyone called Plarr."

"He told me I had been in an accident."

"It was I who told you that," the man said.

"It was not you. I saw him. He carried an electric torch."

"You dreamt him. You have had a shock . . . Your car was badly damaged. Please drink your coffee. You will remember things better perhaps afterward."

Charley Fortnum obeyed. It was very strong coffee, and it was true that his head began to clear. He asked, "Where is the Ambassador?"

"I do not know of any Ambassador."

"I left him in the ruins. I wanted to see my wife before dinner. I wanted to see that she was all right. I don't like leaving her for long. She is expecting a baby."

"Yes? That must make you very happy. It is a fine thing to be the father of a child."

"I remember now. There was a car across the road. I had to stop. There was no accident. I'm quite sure there was no accident. And why the gun?" His hand shook a little as he drank his coffee. He said, "I want to go home now."

118

"It is much too far to walk from here," the man said. "You are not fit yet. And the way—you do not know the way."

"I will find a road. I can stop a car."

"Better to rest today. After the shock. Tomorrow perhaps we can find you some transport. Today it is not possible."

Fortnum threw what was left of his coffee in the man's face and charged into the other room. Then he stopped. The Indian stood twelve feet away in front of the outer door, pointing his gun at Charley Fortnum's stomach. His dark eyes shone with pleasure, as he moved the gun a little this way, a little that, as though he were deciding his target, between the navel and the appendix. He said something which amused him in Guaraní.

The man called León came from the inner room. He said, "You see. I told you. You cannot go today." One cheek was flushed red from the hot coffee, but he spoke gently, without anger. He had the patience of someone who was more used to enduring pain than inflicting it. He said, "You must be hungry, Señor Fortnum. If you would like some eggs . . ."

"You know who I am?"

"Yes, yes, of course. You are the British Consul."

"What are you going to do with me?"

"You will have to stay with us for a little while. Believe me, we are not your enemies, Señor Fortnum. You will be helping us to save innocent men from imprisonment and torture. By this time our man in Rosario will have telephoned to the *Nación* to tell them you are in our care."

Charley Fortnum began to understand. "You got the wrong man, is that it? You were after the American Ambassador?"

"Yes, it was an unfortunate mistake."

"A very bad mistake. No one is going to bother about Charley Fortnum. What will you do then?"

The man said, "I am sure you are wrong. You will see. Everything will be arranged. The British Ambassador will talk to the President. The President will speak to the General. He is here in Argentina on a holiday. The American Ambassador will intervene too. We are only asking the General to release a few men. Everything would have been quite easy if one of our men had not made a mistake."

"You were not very well-informed, were you? The Ambassador had two police officers with him. And his secretary. That was why there was no room for me in his car."

"We could have dealt with them."

"All right. Give me your eggs," Charley Fortnum said, "but tell that man Miguel to put away his gun. It spoils my appetite."

The man called León knelt before a small spirit stove on the earth floor and busied himself with matches, a frying pan, a bit of lard.

"I could do with some whisky if you have it."

"I am sorry. We have no spirits."

The lard began to bubble in the pan.

"Your name is León, eh?"

"Yes." The man broke two eggs one after the other on the edge of the pan. As he held two half shells over the pan there was something in the position of the fingers which reminded Fortnum of that moment at the altar when a priest breaks the Host over the chalice.

"What will you do if they refuse?"

"I pray they will accept," the kneeling man said, "I am sure they will accept."

"Then I hope to God God hears you," Charley Fortnum said. "Don't fry the eggs too hard."

*　　*　　*

It was not until the afternoon that Charley Fortnum heard the official news about himself. The man León turned on a pocket radio at noon, but the battery failed in the middle of some Guaraní music and he had no spares. The young man with a beard whom León called Aquino went into town to buy more batteries. He was a long time gone. A woman came in from the market with food and cooked their lunch, a vegetable soup with a few scraps of meat. She made a great show too of cleaning the hut, raising the dust in one part so that it settled in another. She had a lot of untidy black hair and a wart on her face and she treated León with a mixture of possessiveness and servility. He called her Marta.

Once Charley Fortnum, with embarrassment because of the woman's presence, said he wanted to use a lavatory. León gave an order to the Indian who led him to a cabin in the yard at the back of the hut. The door had lost one of its hinges and wouldn't close, and inside there was only a deep hole dug in the earth with a couple of boards across it. When he came out the Guaraní was sitting a few feet away playing with his gun, sighting it on a tree, a bird flying past, at a stray mongrel dog. Through the trees Charley Fortnum could see another hut, even poorer than the one to which he was returning. He thought of running to it for help, but he felt sure the Indian would welcome the chance to try his gun. When he got back he said to León, "If you can get a couple of bottles of whisky I'll pay you for them." No one had stolen his wallet, he had noticed that, and he took out the necessary notes.

León gave the money to Marta. He said, "You will have to be patient, Señor Fortnum. Aquino is not back. No one can go till he returns. And it is a long walk into the town."

"I will pay for a taxi."

"I am afraid that is not possible. There are no taxis here."

The Indian squatted down again by the door. Charley Fortnum said, "I'm going off to sleep a bit. That drug you gave me was pretty strong." He went back into the inner room and stretched out on the coffin. He tried to sleep, but he was kept awake by his thoughts. He wondered how Clara was managing in his absence. He had never left her alone for a whole night before. He knew nothing about childbirth, but he had an idea that shock or anxiety could affect the unborn child. He had even tried to cut down his drinking after he married Clara—except for that first married night of whisky and champagne when for the first time they made love properly, without impediment, in the Hotel Italia in Rosario—an old-fashioned hotel which smelled agreeably of undisturbed dust like an ancient library.

They had gone there because he thought she would be a little scared of the Riviera Hotel which was new, expensive, and air conditioned. There were papers he had to collect at the Consulate at Santa Fe 939 (he remembered the number because it represented the month and year of his first marriage), the papers which if inquiries were made would show that there was no impediment to his second marriage—it had taken weeks to get a copy of Evelyn's death certificate from a small town in Idaho. He was able at the same time to leave his will in a sealed envelope in the Consulate safe. The Consul was a pleasant middle-aged man. He and Charley Fortnum had hit it off right away when for some reason the subject of horses came up. He invited them back after the civil and religious ceremonies and opened a bottle of genuine French champagne. That little drinking ceremony among the file boxes compared very favorably with the reception in Idaho after his first marriage. He remembered with horror the white cake and the relations-in-law who wore dark suits and even hard collars, although it was a civil marriage which was not acceptable in Argentina. They had been prudent and not spoken of it when they returned. His wife had refused a Catholic marriage—it was against her conscience as she had become a Christian Scientist. Of course the civil marriage made her inheritance unsafe —which was also an indignity. He wanted very much to arrange things more safely for Clara; to ensure there were no cracks in the walls of this second marriage. He intended to leave her, when he came to die, in a security which was impregnable.

After a while he slid into a deep dreamless sleep; he was only awakened when the radio in the next room began to repeat his own name—Señor Carlos Fortnum. The police—the announcer said—believed he might have been brought to Rosario because the telephone call to the *Nación* had been traced to that city. A city of more than half a million inhabitants couldn't be searched very thoroughly, and the authorities had been given only four days in which to agree to the kidnappers' terms. One of these four days had already passed. Charley Fortnum thought: Clara will be listening to the broadcast, and he thanked God Ted would be around to reassure her. Ted would know what had happened. Ted would go to see her. Ted would do something to keep her calm. Ted would tell her that, even if they killed him, she would be all right. She had so much fear of the past—he could tell that from the way she never spoke of it. It was one of his reasons for marrying her, to prove she would never under any circumstances have to return to Mother Sanchez. He took exaggerated care of her happiness like a clumsy man entrusted with something of great fragility which didn't belong to him. He was always afraid of dropping her happiness. Someone was talking now about the Argentine football team which was touring Europe. He called, "León!"

The small head with the bat ears and the attentive

eyes of a good servant peered round the door. León said, "You have slept a long time, Señor Fortnum. That is good."

"I heard the radio, León."

"Ah, yes." León was carrying a glass in one hand and a bottle of whisky was tucked under each arm. He said, "My wife has brought two bottles from the town." He showed the whisky proudly (it was an Argentine brand) and counted out the change with care. "You must not worry. Everything will be over in a few days."

"Everything will be over with me, you mean? Give me that whisky." He poured out a third of a glass and drank it down.

"I am sure tonight we shall hear them announce that they have accepted our terms. And then by tomorrow evening you can go home."

Charley Fortnum poured out another dose.

"You are drinking too much," the man called León said with friendly anxiety.

"No, no. I know the right measure. And it's the measure that counts. What's your other name, León?"

"I told you I have no other name."

"But you have a title, haven't you? Tell me what you are doing in this setup, Father León."

He could almost believe the ears twitched, like a dog's, at a familiar intonation—"Father" taking the place of "walk" or perhaps "cat."

"You are mistaken. You saw my wife just now. Marta. She brought you the whisky."

"But once a priest always a priest, Father. I spotted you when you broke those eggs over the dish. I could see you at the altar, Father."

"You are imagining things, Señor Fortnum."

"And what are *you* imagining? You might have made a good bargain for the Ambassador, but you can't get anything in return for me. I'm not worth a peso to a human soul—except my wife. It seems an odd thing for a priest to become a murderer, but I suppose you'll get someone else to do the thing."

"No," the other said with great seriousness, "if it should ever come to that, which God forbid, I will be the one. I do not want to shift the guilt."

"Then I'd better leave you some of this whisky. You'll need a swig of it—in how many days did they say—three was it?"

The other man's eyes shifted. He had a frightened air. He shuffled two steps toward the door as though he were leaving the altar and was afraid of treading on the skirt of a soutane which was too long for him.

"You might stay and talk a bit," Charley Fortnum said. "I feel more scared when I'm alone. I don't mind telling *you* that. If one can't talk to a priest who can one talk to? That Indian now . . . he sits there and stares at me and smiles. He *wants* to kill."

"You are wrong, Señor Fortnum. Miguel is a good man. He has no Spanish, that is all, and so he smiles just to show he is a friend. Try to sleep again."

"I've had enough sleep. I want to talk to you."

The man made a gesture with his hands, and Charley Fortnum could imagine him in church, making his formal passes. "I have so many things to do."

"I can always keep you here if I try."

"No, no. I *must* go."

"I can keep you here easily. I know the way."

"I will come back presently, I promise."

"All I have to say to keep you is—Father, please hear my confession."

The man stayed stuck in the doorway with his back turned. His protruding ears stood out like little hands raised over an offering.

"Since my last confession, Father . . ."

The man swung around and said angrily, "You must not joke about things like that. I will not listen to you if you joke . . ."

"But that's no joke, Father. I'm not in a position to joke about anything at all. Surely every man has a lot to confess when it comes to dying."

"My faculties have been taken away," the other said in a stubborn voice. "You must know what that means if you are really a Catholic."

"I seem to know the rules better than you, Father. You do not need faculties, not in an emergency—if there is no other priest available . . . there isn't, is there? Your men would never let you bring one here . . ."

"There is no emergency—not yet."

"All the same time is short . . . if I ask . . ."

The man reminded him again of a dog, a dog who has been reproved for a fault which he does not clearly understand. He began to plead, "Señor Fortnum, I assure you there never will be an emergency . . . it will never be necessary . . ."

" 'I am sorry and beg pardon'—that's how I begin, isn't it? It's been the hell of a long time . . . I've been once to church in the last forty years . . . a while ago when I got married. I was damned if I'd go to confession though. It would have taken too long and I couldn't keep the lady waiting."

"Please, Señor Fortnum, do not mock me."

"I'm not mocking *you*, Father. Perhaps I'm mocking myself a bit. I can do that as long as the whisky lasts." He added, "It really is a funny thing when you come to think of it. 'I ask forgiveness of God through you, Father.' That *is* the formula, isn't it—and all the time you'll have the gun ready. Don't you think we ought to begin now? Before the gun is loaded. There are plenty of things I have on my mind."

"I will not listen to you." He made the gesture of putting his hands against the protruding ears. They flattened and sprang back.

Charley Fortnum said, "Oh, don't worry, forget it.

I was only half serious. What difference does it make anyway?"

"What do you mean?"

"I don't believe a thing, Father. I would never have bothered to marry in a church if the law hadn't forced me to. There was the question of money. For my wife, I mean. What was your intention, Father, when *you* married?" He added quickly, "Forgive me. I had no business to ask that."

But the little man, it seemed, was not angry. The question even appeared to have an attraction for him. He came slowly across the floor with his mouth ajar, as though he were a starving man drawn irresistibly by the offer of bread. A little saliva hung at the corner of his mouth. He came and crouched down on the floor beside the coffin. He said in a low voice (he might have been kneeling in the confessional box himself), "I think it was anger and loneliness, Señor Fortnum. I never meant any harm to her, poor woman."

"I can understand the loneliness," Charley Fortnum said, "I've suffered from that too. But why the anger? Who were you angry with?"

"The Church," the man said and added with irony, "my Mother the Church."

"I used to be angry with my father. He didn't understand me, I thought, or care a nickel about me. I hated him. All the same I was bloody lonely when he died. And now"—he lifted his glass—"I even imitate him. Though he drank more than I do. All the same a father's a father—I don't see how you can be angry with Mother Church. I could never get angry with a fucking institution."

"She is a sort of person too," the man said, "they claim she is Christ on earth—I still half believe it even now. Someone like you—*un Inglés*—you are not able to understand how ashamed I felt of the things they made me read to people. I was a priest in the poor part of Asunción near the river. Have you noticed how the poor always cling close to the river? They do it here too, as though they plan one day to swim away, but they have no idea how to swim and there is nowhere to swim to for any of them. On Sunday I had to read to them out of the Gospels."

Charley Fortnum listened with a little sympathy and a good deal of cunning. His life depended on this man, and it was vitally important for him to know what moved him. There might be some chord he could touch of fellow feeling. The man was speaking immoderately as a thirsty man drinks. Perhaps he had been unable to speak freely for a long time: perhaps this was the only way he could unburden himself to a man who was safely dying and would remember no more what he said than a priest in the confessional. Charley Fortnum asked, "What's wrong with the Gospels, Father?"

"They make no sense," the ex-priest said, "anyway not in Paraguay. 'Sell all and give to the poor'—I had to read that out to them while the old Archbishop we had in those days was eating a fine fish from Iguazú and drinking a French wine with the General. Of course the people were not actually starving—you can keep them from starving on mandioca, and malnutrition is much safer for the rich than starvation. Starvation makes a man desperate. Malnutrition makes him too tired to raise a fist. The Americans understand that well —the aid they give us makes just that amount of difference. Our people do not starve—they wilt. The words used to stick on my lips—'Suffer little children,' and there the children sat in the front rows with their pot bellies and their navels sticking out like doorknobs. 'It were better that a millstone were hung around his neck,' 'He who gives to one of the least of these.' Gives what? gives mandioca? and then I distributed the Host —it's not so nourishing as a good *chipá*—and then I drank the wine. Wine! Which of these poor souls had ever tasted wine? Why could we not use water in the sacrament? He used it at Cana. Wasn't there a beaker of water at the Last Supper He could have used instead?" To Charley Fortnum's astonishment the doglike eyes were swollen with unshed tears.

The man said, "Oh, you must not think we are all of us bad Christians as I am. The Jesuits do what they can. But they are watched by the police. Their telephones are tapped. If anyone seems dangerous he is quickly pushed across the river. They do not kill him. The Yankees would not like a priest to be killed, and anyway we are not dangerous enough. I spoke in a sermon once about Father Torres who was shot with the guerrillas in Colombia. I only said that unlike Sodom the Church did sometimes produce one just man, so perhaps she would not be destroyed like Sodom. The police reported me to the Archbishop and the Archbishop forbade me to preach any more. Oh well, poor man, he was very old and the General liked him, and he thought he was doing right, rendering to Caesar . . ."

"These things are a bit above my head, Father," Charley Fortnum said, lying propped on his elbow on the coffin and looking down at the dark head which still showed the faint trace of a tonsure through the hair, like a prehistoric camp in a field seen from a plane. He interjected "Father" as often as he could: it was somehow reassuring. A father didn't usually kill his son, although of course it had been a near miss in the case of Abraham. "I am not to blame, Father."

"I am not blaming you, Señor Fortnum, God forbid."

"I can see how the American Ambassador from your point of view—well, he was a legitimate objective. But me—I'm not even a proper Consul and the English are not in *this* fight, Father."

The priest muttered a cliché absentmindedly, "They say one man has to die for the people."

"But that was what the crucifiers said, not the Christians."

The priest looked up. "Yes, you are right," he said, "I was not thinking when I spoke. You know your Testament."

"I have not read it since I was a boy. But that's the kind of scene which sticks in the mind. Like Struwelpeter."

"Struwelpeter?"

"He had his thumbs cut off."

"I never heard of him. Is he one of your martyrs?"

"No, no, it's a nursery story, Father."

"Have you children?" the priest asked sharply.

"No, but I told you. In a few months there should be one around. He kicks hard already."

"Yes, I remember now." He added, "Don't worry, you will be home soon." It was as though the sentence were framed in question marks and he wanted the prisoner to reassure him by agreeing, "Yes, of course. It goes without saying," but Charley Fortnum refused to play that game.

"Why this coffin, Father? It seems a bit morbid to me."

"The earth is too damp for sleeping on, even with a cloth under you. We did not want you to catch rheumatism."

"Well, that was a kindly thought, Father."

"We are not barbarians. There is a man near here in the *barrio* who makes coffins. We bought one from him. It was much safer than buying a bed . . . There is a greater demand in the *barrio* for coffins than beds. Nobody asks questions about a coffin."

"And I suppose you thought it might be handy later on for stowing away a body."

"That was not in our minds, I swear. To ask for a bed would have been dangerous."

"Oh well, I think I *will* have another whisky, Father. Have one with me."

"No, You see—I am on duty. I have to guard you." He gave a timid smile.

"You would not be difficult to overpower, would you? Even for an old man like me."

"There are always two of us on duty," the priest said. "Miguel is out there now with his gun. Those are El Tigre's orders. There is another reason for that too. One man might be talked around. Or even bribed. We are all of us human beings. This is not the sort of life any of us would have chosen."

"The Indian does not speak Spanish?"

"Yes, that too is a good thing."

"Do you mind if I stretch my legs a little?"

"Of course you may."

Charley Fortnum went to the doorway and checked the truth of what the priest had said. The Indian was squatting by the door with the gun on his lap. He smiled at Fortnum confidentially, as though they shared a secret joke. Almost imperceptibly he moved the position of his gun.

"You speak Guaraní, Father?"

"Yes. I used to preach in Guaraní once."

A few minutes ago there had been a moment of closeness, of sympathy, even of friendship between them, but that moment had passed. When a Confession is finished, the priest and the penitent are each alone. They pretend not to recognize each other if they pass in the church. It was as though it were the penitent who stood now by the coffin looking at his watch. Charley Fortnum thought: he is checking to see how many hours are left.

"Change your mind and have a whisky with me, Father."

"No. No, thank you. One day perhaps when all this is over." He added, "He is late. I should have been gone long before now."

"Who is late?"

The priest answered angrily, "I have told you before that people like us have no names."

The darkness was falling and in the shuttered outer room one of them had lit a candle. They had left his door open and he could see the Indian sitting close beside the door nursing his gun. Charley Fortnum wondered when his turn would come to sleep. The man called León had been gone a long while. There was a Negro he had not noticed before . . . If I had a knife, he wondered, could I make a hole to escape by?

The man called Aquino brought in a candle, carrying it in his left hand. Charley Fortnum noticed that he kept his right hand always concealed in his jeans. Perhaps it held a gun—or a knife—and his thoughts went back to the rather hopeless idea of cutting a hole through the dried mud of the wall. In an impossible situation one had to try the impossible. He asked, "Where is the Father?"

"He has things to do in the town, Señor Fortnum."

They always treated him with great courtesy, he noticed, as though they were trying to reassure him, "There is nothing personal in this affair. Once it is over we can meet as friends." Or was it perhaps the habitual courtesy which a prison warder is said to show even the most brutal murderer before his execution? People have the same awed respect for death as they have for a distinguished stranger, however unwelcome he may be, who visits their town.

He said, "I'm hungry. I could eat an ox." It wasn't true, but perhaps they would be foolish enough to let him have a knife with his food. He had an impression he was in the hands of amateurs, not professionals.

"Soon," Aquino said, "be a little patient, Señor Fortnum. We are waiting for Marta. She has promised to make us a stew. She is not a very good cook, but if you had been in prison like me . . ."

He thought: stew. That means I'll be given only a spoon again. "There is still some whisky left," he said. "Will you have a drink with me?"

Aquino said, "We are none of us supposed to drink."

"A small one—to keep me company."

"A very small one then. I will eat one of the onions Marta has brought for the stew. It will take away the smell. I do not want to disappoint León. For him it comes naturally to be strict, but we are not all priests, thank God. That is a very large whisky," he protested.

"Large? Why, it is only half as big as mine. *Salud.*"

"*Salud.*"

He noticed Aquino still kept his right hand in his pocket.

"What are you, Aquino?"

"What do you mean, what am I?"

"Are you a worker?"

"I am a criminal," Aquino said with pride. "We are all criminals."

"Is that a full-time occupation?" Fortnum raised his glass and Aquino followed suit. "You must have begun somewhere."

"Oh, I went to school like all the world. It was run by priests. They were good men, and it was a good school. León was there too—he wanted to be an *abogado*. As for me, I wanted to be a writer, but even a writer has to live, so I went into the tobacco business. I made money selling American cigarettes in the street. Smuggled cigarettes from Panama. Good money too . . . I mean I was able to share a room with three others and we had enough to buy *chipás*. You get quite fat on *chipás*. They are better than mandioca."

"I have a camp outside the city," Charley Fortnum

said, "I could do with a new *capataz*. You are an educated man. You could easily learn the job."

"Oh, I have another job now," Aquino said with pride. "I told you—I am a criminal. I am also a poet."

"A poet?"

"At school León helped me to write. He said I had talent, but once I sent an article to the paper in Asunción criticizing the Yankees. In our country it is forbidden by the General to publish anything against the Yankees, and afterward they would not even read any of the articles I sent in. They thought I was writing something between the lines which would get them into trouble. They thought I was a *político,* and so naturally —what else could I do? I became a *político.* So then they sent me to prison. It happens always that way, if you are a *político* and you are not a Colorado, one of the General's party."

"Was it bad in prison?"

"Pretty bad," Aquino said. He pulled out his right hand and showed it to Charley Fortnum. "That is when I started to make poetry. It takes a long time to learn to write anything with the left hand, and it is very slow work. I hate things which are slow. I would rather be a mouse than a tortoise, even though the tortoise lives a longer time." He had become voluble after his second gulp of whisky. "I admire the eagle which drops on its victim like a rock out of the sky, but not the vulture which flaps slowly down, looking as it goes to see if the carrion moves. That is why I took to poetry. Prose moves too slowly, poetry drops like an eagle and stabs before you know. Of course in prison they would not give me paper or a pen, but I did not have to write the poetry. I could learn it by heart."

"Was it good poetry?" Charley Fortnum asked. "Not that I'd know the difference."

Aquino said, "I think some of it was good." He finished his whisky. "León said some of it was good. He told me it was like a man called Villon. He was a criminal like me."

"Never heard of him," Charley Fortnum said.

"The first poem I wrote in prison," Aquino said, "was about the first prison of all—the one we all of us know. Do you know what Trotsky said when they showed him his new home in Mexico? They had made it secure from assassins, or so they thought. He said, 'This reminds me of my first prison. The doors make the same sound.' My poem had a refrain, 'I see my father only through the bars.' I was thinking, you see, of the pens in which they put children in bourgeois houses. In my poem the father went on following the child all through his life—he was the schoolmaster, and then he was the priest, the police officer, the prison warder, and last he was General Stroessner himself. I saw the General once when he was touring the country-side. He came to the police station I was in and I saw him through the bars."

"I have a child on the way," Charley Fortnum said. "I would like to see the little bastard, if only for a short time. But not through bars, you know. I would like to live long enough to know if it's a boy or a girl."

"When will it be born?"

"In five months I think or thereabouts. I'm not quite sure. I'm a bit hazy about all that sort of thing."

"Don't worry. You will be home, señor, long before then."

"Not if you kill me," Charley Fortnum replied, hoping against hope to receive the usual reassuring response, however false it might sound. He was not surprised when none was forthcoming. He was beginning to live in the region of truth.

"I have written a good many poems about death," Aquino said cheerfully, with satisfaction, as he held the last drop of his whisky up to catch the light of the candle. "The one I like best has the refrain, 'Death is a common weed: requires no rain.' León disagrees with me—he says I am writing there like a farmer—I wanted to be a farmer once. He likes better the one that goes, 'Whatever the crime, the same meal's served to all.' And there is another I am pleased with, though I do not really know what exactly I mean by it, but it sounds fine, when you recite it properly, 'When death is on the tongue, the live man speaks.' "

"You seem to have written the hell of a lot about death."

"Yes. I think about half my poems are about death," Aquino said. "It is one of the two proper subjects for a man—love and death."

"I don't want to die before my child is born."

"I wish you all the luck in the world, Señor Fortnum. But none of us has a choice. Perhaps tomorrow I will be killed by a car or a fever. And a bullet is one of the quickest and most honorable of deaths."

"I suppose that's the way you are going to kill me."

"Naturally . . . What other way is there? We are not cruel men, Señor Fortnum. We shall not cut off your fingers."

"And yet one can go on living without a few fingers. You haven't found them so important, have you?"

"Oh, I understand your fear of pain—I know what pain can do to a man—what it did to me—but I cannot understand why you are so afraid of death. Death will come in any case, and there is a long afterward if the priests are right and nothing to fear if they are wrong."

"Did you believe in that 'afterward' when they tortured you?"

"No," Aquino admitted. "But I did not think of death either. There was only the pain."

"We have an expression in English—a bird in the hand is worth two in the bush. I don't know anything about that 'afterward.' I only know I would like to live another ten years, at my camp, watching the little bastard grow."

"But, Señor Fortnum, think what might happen in those ten years. Your child might die, children die so easily here, your wife might betray you, you might be tortured by a long cancer. A bullet is simple and quick."

"Are you sure of that?"

"Perhaps a little more whisky would do me no harm," Aquino said.

"I'm thirsty myself. You know the old saying—An Englishman is always two whiskies below par."

He poured it out very carefully: there was hardly more than a quarter of a bottle left, and he thought with sadness of his camp, of the dumbwaiter on the verandah and the fresh bottle which had always stood ready at hand. He asked, "Are you married?"

"Not exactly," Aquino replied.

"I have been married twice. The first time it didn't take. The second time—I don't know why—I felt different. Would you like to see a photograph?"

He found one in his pocketbook—a square Kodachrome print. Clara was sitting at the wheel of Fortnum's Pride, staring sideways at the camera with an expression of fear as though it might go off like a revolver.

"A pretty girl," Aquino commented politely.

"Of course you know she can't really drive," Fortnum said, "and there's a lot too much blue in the print. You can see that from the color of the avocados. It wasn't one of Gruber's best efforts." He looked at the photograph with an expression of regret. "It's a bit out of focus too," he said, "it doesn't do her proper justice, but I had taken one over the measure and I suppose my hand must have shaken a bit." He looked anxiously at what remained in the bottle.

"As a rule," he said, "there is nothing better to steady the hand. What about finishing the bottle?"

"A very little for me," Aquino said.

"Every man has his own proper measure. I'd never criticize anyone for not sharing mine. A measure's sort of built into a man's system, like a lift in a block of flats." He was watching Aquino carefully. He had judged correctly that their measures were very different. He said, "I liked that poem of yours about death."

"Which one?"

"I have such a shocking memory. What will you do with the body?"

"Body?"

"My body."

"Señor Fortnum, why talk about disagreeable subjects? I write about death, yes, but only death the great abstraction. I do not write about the death of friends."

"Those people, you know, in London—they've never even heard of me. What do they care? I don't belong to the right club."

"'Death is a common weed: requires no rain.' Was that the poem you meant?"

"Yes, of course, that was the one. I remember now. All the same, Aquino, even if it's as common as all that, one ought to die with a bit of dignity. You will agree to that? *Salud.*"

"*Salud,* Señor Fortnum."

"Call me Charley, Aquino."

"*Salud,* Charley."

"I wouldn't like people to find me like this—dirty, unshaven . . ."

"You can have a bowl of water if you like, Charley."

"And a razor?"

"No."

"Only a Gillette. I can't do much harm with a Gillette."

It was the measure which counted all right. Everything seemed possible to him now. For instance, even

138

with a pair of scissors—he could moisten the baked earth of the wall first.

"A pair of scissors then just for a trim?"

"I would have to ask León first, Charley."

A pointed stick?—he searched for a suitable euphemism. He felt sure, now he had drunk the right measure and he had his wits about him, that it was possible to escape. He said, "I want to write to Clara—she's my wife. The girl in the photo. You can keep the letter until it's all over and you are safe. I just want her to know that I thought of her at the end. A pencil—a sharp pencil," he added incautiously, taking a look at the wall and wondering whether after all he was a bit overoptimistic. There was one point where the wall had crumbled a little: he could see wisps of straw which had been mixed with the mud.

"I have a ballpoint," Aquino said, "but I had better ask León, Charley." He took it out of his pocket and looked at it carefully.

"What harm can there be, Aquino? I would ask your friend myself, but you know how it is, I never feel at ease with priests."

Aquino said, "You must give us anything you write. And we shall have to read it."

"Of course. Shall we open the other bottle?"

"You are not trying to make me drunk? I can drink any man under the table."

"No, no. It's only I haven't had the proper measure myself yet. It's one over the half that counts with me, and you've drunk half my measure yourself."

"It may be a long time before we can buy you more."

"Let tomorrow look after tomorrow. That sounds like something from the Bible. I'm getting the literary touch too. The whisky helps. You see I'm not much used to letter-writing. This is the first time I've been separated from Clara—since we were really together."

"You will need some paper, Charley."

"Yes, I'd forgotten that."

Aquino brought him five sheets of paper pulled off a pad. "I have counted them," he said. "You must return all the sheets to me, used or not."

"And some water to wash in. I don't want to leave dirty marks all over my letter."

Aquino obeyed, but he grumbled a little this time. "This is not a hotel, Charley," he said, planking the basin down and splashing the water on the earth floor.

"If it was, I would be able to hang a notice 'Not to be disturbed' on the door. Take a little more whisky with you, Aquino."

"No. I have drunk enough."

"Be a friend and shut the door. I can't bear that Indian staring at me."

When he was alone Charley Fortnum chose the worn spot on the wall, rubbed water in and attacked it with the ballpoint. After a quarter of an hour there was a little wormcast of dirt on the floor, and a tiny indentation in the wall. If it had not been for the whisky he would have despaired. He propped himself on the floor to hide the mark, washed the ballpoint, and began a letter. He had to justify the time he had spent. "My dear little Clara," he began and hesitated a long while. For his official reports he used a typewriter which always seemed to find the right bureaucratic phrase, "In reply to your letter of August 10," "I have received yours of December 22." "How I miss you," he wrote now. It was the only important thing he had to write; anything he added would be only a repetition or a paraphrase of that. "It seems years since I drove away from the camp. You had a headache that morning. Is it better now? Please do not take too many aspirins. They are bad for the stomach and they must be bad for the baby too. You will see, won't you, that a tarpaulin is kept over Fortnum's Pride in case the rains come."

The letter, he thought, would not be delivered until he was home again or until he was dead, and the sense of an immense distance grew up between the mud hut and the camp, between the coffin and the jeep waiting under the avocados, Clara lying late in the double bed, the dumbwaiter standing idle on the verandah. Tears pricked at his eyes, and he remembered how his father would rebuke him: "Be a man, Charley, not a coward. You cry too easily. I can't bear self-pity. You should be ashamed. Ashamed. Ashamed." The word rang like the knell for all hope. Sometimes, but not often, he would defend himself. "But I'm not crying for me. I squashed a lizard this morning in the shutters. I didn't mean to. I was trying to let it out. I'm crying for the lizard, not for me." He was not crying now for himself. The tears were for Clara and a few of them for Fortnum's Pride, both left alone and defenseless. All he was suffering was a little fear and a little discomfort. Loneliness, as he knew from experience, was a worse thing to suffer.

He abandoned the letter, took another swallow of whisky, and started to dig again with the ballpoint pen. The wall absorbed the water and was soon as dry again as a bone. After half an hour he gave up. He had made a hole as large as a mouse-hole, but not an inch deep. He took up his letter again and wrote defiantly, "I can tell you Charley Fortnum's on his mettle. I'm not the poor chap they think I am. I'm your husband, and I love you far too much to let any bastards like these stand between you and me. I'm going to think up something and I'm going to put this letter in your hands myself, and we'll laugh at it together and we'll drink some of that good French champagne I've been saving for a special occasion. Champagne never did a baby any harm, or so I'm told." He stopped writing and laid the letter aside because an idea was really beginning to form in however hazy a way. He wiped the sweat off his forehead and for a moment he had the impression that he was wiping away the whisky too, leaving his mind clear.

"Aquino," he called, "Aquino."

Aquino came reluctantly and suspiciously in. "No more whisky," he said.

"I want to use the lavatory, Aquino."

"I will tell Miguel to go with you."

"No, please, Aquino . . . I'll never get a proper shit with that Indian sitting outside waving his gun at me. He's longing to use it, Aquino."

"Miguel means no harm. He is interested in the gun —that's all. He has never had one before."

"He frightens me just the same. Why not take the gun yourself and guard me, Aquino? I know you wouldn't shoot unless you had to."

"He would not like anyone else to hold his gun."

"Then I'll damn well shit in here."

"I will speak to him," Aquino said.

It's difficult for most men to shoot a friendly man in cold blood—Charley Fortnum's plan was as simple as that.

When Aquino returned he was holding the sub-machine gun. "All right," he said, "go ahead. I know I have only my left hand, but remember no one needs to be a marksman with one of these. One bullet will always go home."

"Even a poet's bullet," Charley Fortnum said, raking up a smile. "I wish you would give me a copy of that poem. I'd like to keep it as a souvenir."

"Which poem?"

"You know the one I mean. The one about death."

He walked through the outer room. The Indian did not look at him. He was watching the gun with anxiety as though something very dear had been put in untrustworthy hands.

Charley Fortnum talked all the way to the shed among the avocados. His watch had stopped during his coma and he had no idea of the time, but he could see how long the shadows were. Under the trees heavy with dark-brown fruit it was already night. He said, "I've nearly finished that letter. It's a damned difficult one to write." When he got to the door of the shed he turned and tried a smile out on Aquino. If Aquino smiled back it would be a good sign, but Aquino didn't smile. Perhaps he was only preoccupied. Perhaps he had drunk the wrong measure.

Charley Fortnum waited in the hut for a reasonable time, screwing his courage up. Then he came quickly out and turned sharp right to put the hut between them. It was only a matter of yards and under the trees the darkness waited. He heard a short burst of fire, a shout, an answering shout, he felt nothing. He cried out, "Don't shoot, Aquino." At the second burst he fell on the very edge of the dark.

PART
FOUR

1

The day began badly for Sir Henry Belfrage at breakfast. For the third time running the cook had fried his egg on both sides. He said, "Did you forget to tell Pedro, dear?"

"No," Lady Belfrage said, "I swear I didn't. I remember distinctly . . ."

"He must have picked the habit up from the Yankees. It's a Yankee custom. Don't you remember the trouble we had once at the Plaza in New York? They've got a name for 'fried on one side.' Can you remember it? Pedro might understand."

"No, dear . . . I don't think I ever heard it."

"Sometimes I sympathize with those chaps who write about Yankee imperialism. Why should we have to eat our fried eggs like this? Soon he'll be giving us maple syrup with our sausages. That was a terrible wine we had last night at the American Embassy, darling. Californian, I suppose."

"No, dear. It was Argentine."

"Ah, he was trying to curry favor with the Minister of the Interior. But the Minister would have preferred a good French table wine like we serve here."

"Not a very good wine all the same."

"The best we can afford with our miserable expense allowance. Did you notice that he served *Argentine* Scotch?"

"The trouble is, dear, he doesn't drink anything himself. Do you know he was quite shocked because Mr. . . . poor Mr. C . . . you know our Consul, Mason isn't it?"

146

"No, no, the other chap. Fortnum."

"Well, poor Mr. Fortnum apparently brought two bottles of Scotch with him when they went to the ruins."

"I don't blame him for that. Do you know the Ambassador travels with an icebox full of Coca-Cola? I wouldn't have drunk so much of that bloody wine if he hadn't watched me with those New England eyes of his. I felt like that girl in the book who had a scarlet letter A on her dress. A for Alcoholism."

"I think it was Adultery, dear."

"I daresay. I only saw the film. Years ago. They didn't make it clear."

The day which had begun miserably enough with the badly fried eggs got steadily worse. Crichton, the Press Attaché, came to see him to protest that he was being driven up the wall by telephone calls from the press. He complained to Sir Henry, "I keep telling them that Fortnum was only an Honorary Consul. The reporter on *La Prensa* can't understand the difference between Honorary and Honorable. I wouldn't be surprised if they make him the son of a peer."

Sir Henry said soothingly, "I doubt if they know enough about our titles for that."

"They seem to think the whole affair is so very important."

"Only because it's the silly season, Crichton. They have no Loch Ness monster here, and the flying saucers go on all through the year."

"I wish we had some tranquillizing statement we could make, sir."

"So do I, Crichton, so do I. Of course you can say I spent several hours last night with the American Ambassador—you needn't say I have a damn bad head as a consequence."

"The *Nación* has had another anonymous telephone call—from Córdoba this time. Only four days left."

"Thank God it's no longer," the Ambassador said. "Next week it will all be over. He'll be either dead or freed."

"The police think that Córdoba is a blind and he may be in Rosario—or even here by this time."

"We ought to have retired him six months ago and then none of this would have happened."

"The police say the kidnapping was a mistake, sir. They wanted the American Ambassador. If that's right surely the Americans ought to be grateful to us and do something."

"Wilbur," Sir Henry Belfrage said, "—the Ambassador insists that I call him Wilbur—refuses to admit he was the intended victim. He says the U.S.A. is very popular in Paraguay—Nelson Rockefeller's tour proved that. No one threw stones in Paraguay or set fire to any offices. It was as quiet as it was in Haiti. He calls Rockefeller Nelson—it had me confused for a moment. Do you know I really thought for a moment he was going to invite me to call Rockefeller Nelson too?"

"I can't help being sorry for the poor devil."

"I don't think Wilbur needs any of our sympathy, Crichton."

"I didn't mean him—I meant—"

"Oh, Mason? Damnation, my wife has started calling him Mason and now I'm doing the same. If Mason gets into an official telegram, God knows where it will end up in London. They'll think it has something to do with the Mason-Dixon line. I shall have to say to myself Fortnum, Fortnum, Fortnum, like that raven which said Nevermore."

"You don't think they will really kill him, sir?"

"Of course I don't, Crichton. They didn't even kill that Paraguayan Consul they took a few years back. The General said he wasn't interested, and they let the fellow go. This isn't Uruguay or Colombia—or Brazil, for that matter. Or Bolivia. Or Venezuela. Or even

148

Peru," he added apprehensively as the field of hope narrowed.

"We are in South America, though, aren't we?" Crichton said with incontestable logic.

A few tiresome telegrams came in during the morning. Somebody had started another Falkland Islands scare: the islands cropped up, like Gibraltar, whenever there was nothing else to worry about. The Foreign Secretary wanted to know as a consequence how Argentina was likely to vote in the latest African issue before the United Nations. The Chief Clerk had issued a new directive about entertainment expenses, and Sir Henry Belfrage could see the time rapidly approaching when he too might have to serve Argentinian wine. There was also a question about the British entry at the Mar del Plata film festival—a Conservative member of Parliament had described the British entry by some man called Russell as pornographic. There had been no directive at all about Fortnum since the previous day when Belfrage had been ordered to see the Foreign Minister and afterward to act in concert with the American Ambassador—the British Ambassador in Asunción had received the same instruction, and Sir Henry hoped he had an American to deal with who was a little more dynamic than Wilbur.

After lunch his secretary told him that a Doctor Plarr was asking to see him.

"Who's Plarr?"

"He comes from the north. I think he wants to see you about the Fortnum case."

"Oh bring him in, bring him in," Sir Henry Belfrage said, "let them all come." He was vexed at losing his siesta—it was the only time of day when he could feel a private person. There was a new Agatha Christie waiting by his bed, fresh from his bookshop in Curzon Street.

"We've met before somewhere," he said to Doctor

Plarr, and he looked at Plarr with suspicion—everyone in B.A. except the Army people seemed to have the title of Doctor. A thin lawyer's face, he thought; he never felt at ease with lawyers; he found himself shocked by the heartlessness of legal jokes—a convicted murderer was no more to them than a patient with incurable cancer to a surgeon.

"Yes—here at the Embassy," Doctor Plarr reminded him. "A cocktail party. I rescued your wife from a poet."

"Of course, of course, I remember now, my dear chap. You live up there. We talked about Fortnum, didn't we?"

"That's right. I'm looking after his wife. She's having a baby, you know."

"Oh, you *are* that kind of doctor, are you?"

"Yes."

"Thank God! One never knows here, does one? And you really are British too. Not like the O'Briens and the Higginses. Well, well, it must be an awful anxiety for poor Mrs. Fortnum. You must tell her we are doing everything in our power . . ."

"Yes," Doctor Plarr said, "of course, she realizes that, but I thought I'd like to know a little of how things are going. I flew down to B.A. this morning, because I felt I had to see you and learn a little, and I'm flying back tonight. If there were some definite news I could take back with me . . . to comfort Mrs. Fortnum . . ."

"It's an awfully difficult situation, Plarr. You see, something which is everybody's responsibility is always nobody's responsibility. The General is down here in the south fishing and refuses to discuss the matter while he's on holiday. The Foreign Minister says it's a purely Paraguayan affair, and the President can't be expected to bring pressure on the General, when he's a guest of the nation. Of course the police are doing their best, but they've probably been told to act as discreetly as possible. For Fortnum's own sake."

"But the Americans . . . Surely they can bring pressure on the General. He wouldn't exist twenty-four hours in Paraguay without their help."

"I know all that, but it makes it the more awkward, Plarr. You see the Americans take the sensible view that these kidnappings have to be discouraged—even if it means, well, how shall I put it? a certain danger to life. Like that German Ambassador they killed—where was it? Guatemala? In this case, to be quite frank . . . well, an Honorary Consul is not an Ambassador. They feel it would be a bad principle if they interfered. The English are not very popular with the General. Of course if Fortnum were an American he would probably take a different view."

"The kidnappers thought he was. So the police say. They think the kidnappers were looking for a diplomatic car in the dark and CC is awfully like CD."

"Yes, how often we've told the damned fool not to fly a flag or show CC plates. An Honorary Consul hasn't the right to use them."

"Still a death sentence seems a bit severe."

"What more can I do, Plarr? I've been twice to the Foreign Ministry. Last night I spoke unofficially to the Minister of the Interior. He was having dinner with Wilbur—I mean the American Ambassador. I can't do a thing more without instructions from London, and London has a remarkable sense of—well—unurgency. By the way how is your mother? It all comes back to me now. You are *that* Plarr. Your mother often has tea with my wife. They both like sweet cakes and those things with *dulce de leche*."

"*Alfajores.*"

"That's the name. Can't stand them myself."

Doctor Plarr said, "I know what a nuisance I must seem to you, Sir Henry, but my father is in one of the

General's jails if he's still alive. Perhaps this kidnapping is his last chance. That makes me suspect to the police, so I feel personally concerned. And besides there's Fortnum. I can't help feeling responsible a bit for him. He's not a patient of mine, but Mrs. Fortnum is."

"Wasn't there something odd about that marriage? I got a letter from up there, from some old busybody called Jeffries."

"Humphries."

"Yes. That was the name. He wrote to me that Fortnum had married an 'undesirable' woman. Lucky man! I've reached the age when I never meet anyone of that sort."

"It did occur to me," Doctor Plarr said, "that I might be able to make contact with the kidnappers. They may telephone Mrs. Fortnum if they find they are getting nowhere with the authorities."

"A bit improbable, my dear chap."

"But not impossible, sir. If something like that did happen and I had some hope to offer them . . . Perhaps I could persuade them to extend their time limit—say for a week. In that case surely there might be a chance to negotiate?"

"If you want my honest opinion you would only be extending the agony—for Fortnum and Mrs. Fortnum. If I were Fortnum I'd prefer a quick death."

"But surely something could be done?"

"I'm sure of this, Plarr, I've seen Wilbur twice and the Americans won't budge. If they can discourage kidnapping by letting an Honorary British Consul, in an obscure province, take the rap, they'll be very satisfied. Wilbur says Fortnum is an alcoholic—he brought two bottles of whisky to their picnic at the ruins and the Ambassador only drinks Coca-Cola. I looked up our file on him, but there wasn't anything very definite about alcoholism, though one or two of his reports . . . well, they did sort of ramble. There was a letter too from that man—Humphries?—saying he had flown the Union Jack upside down. But you don't need to be an alcoholic to do that."

"All the same, Sir Henry, if the kidnappers could be persuaded to delay only a little . . ."

Sir Henry Belfrage knew the time for his siesta was irrevocably lost—the new Agatha Christie would have to wait. He was a kind man and a conscientious one, and he was modest into the bargain. He told himself that in Doctor Plarr's situation he would have been unlikely to fly in the November heat to Buenos Aires to help the husband of a patient. He said, "There is something you might try to do. I very much doubt if you would be successful, but all the same . . ."

He hesitated. With a pen in his hand he was a master of compression: his reports were admirably short and lucid, and a telegram never presented him with the least difficulty. He was at home in his Embassy as he had been at home in his nursery. The chandeliers glittered like the glass fruit on a Christmas tree. In the nursery he could remember building neatly and quickly with his colored bricks. "Master Henry is a clever boy," his nurse always said, but sometimes when he was let out on the vast green spaces of Kensington Gardens he strayed wildly. There were moments with strangers— just as there still were at his annual cocktail party— when he nearly panicked.

"Yes, Sir Henry?"

"I'm so sorry, my dear chap. My mind was wandering. I've got a terrible head this morning. That wine from Mendoza . . . Cooperatives! What can a Cooperative know about wine?"

"You were saying . . ."

"Yes, yes." He put his hand into his breast pocket and touched his ballpoint pen. It was like a talisman. He said, "A delay would be only useful if we could get people sufficiently interested . . . I've been doing all I can, but nobody at home knows Fortnum. Nobody cares about an Honorary Consul. He doesn't belong to the Service. And to tell you the truth I advised getting rid of him six months ago. *That* letter will certainly be on the files. So everyone at home will be relieved when the dateline is passed and there are no more minutes to write—and he's released as I believe."

"And if he's killed?"

"I'm afraid the F.O. will take the credit for that too. It will be a sign of firmness; it will show they won't treat with blackmailers. You know the kind of words they'll use in the Commons. Law and order. No Danegeld. They'll quote Kipling. Even the Opposition will applaud."

"It's not only Charles Fortnum. There's his wife . . . she's having a baby. Suppose the press took it up . . ."

"Yes. I see what you mean. The woman who waits, etcetera. But from what that man Humphries wrote I don't think the kind of wife Fortnum has married will arouse the right sort of sentiment in the English press. Not family reading. *The Sun* might use the real story of course or the *News of the World,* but it would hardly have the effect we want."

"What *do* you suggest, Sir Henry?"

"You must never, never quote me on this, Plarr. The F.O. would put me out to grass if they knew I had suggested anything of the kind. And I don't suppose for a moment my idea would do any good. Mason is not the right material."

"Mason?"

"I'm sorry. I meant Fortnum."

"You haven't suggested anything yet, Sir Henry."

"Well, what I was getting at . . . There's nothing a civil servant hates more than a yelp in *respectable* papers. Sometimes the only way to get action is the right publicity. If you could organize some reaction in your city . . . Even a telegraphed appeal from the

English Club to *The Times.* Tribute to his . . ." He touched his pen again as though he might draw from it the correct official jargon. ". . . . his untiring pursuit of British interests."

"But there is no English Club, sir. I don't think there are any other English in the city except Humphries and me."

Sir Henry Belfrage took a quick look at his finger-nails (he had mislaid his nail brush). He said something so rapidly that Doctor Plarr couldn't catch a word.

"I'm sorry. I didn't hear . . ."

"My dear chap, I don't have to spell it out to *you.* Form an English Club immediately and telegraph your tribute to *The Times* and *Telegraph.*"

"Do you think it would do any good?"

"No, I don't, but there's no harm in trying. There's always some Opposition M.P. who will take it up whatever his leaders say. At least it might give the Parliamentary Secretary *un mauvais quart d'heure.* And then there are the American papers. It's just possible they might copy. *The New York Times* can be quite virulent. 'Fighting Latin-American independence to the last Englishman.' You know the kind of line the antiwar chaps might take. It's rather a forlorn hope, of course. If he'd been a business tycoon everybody would be a great deal more interested. The trouble is, Plarr, Fortnum is such pitiably small beer."

There was no plane by which he could return north before the evening, and Doctor Plarr could think of no excuse with which to ease his conscience if he failed to meet his mother. He knew very well what would please her most, and he made a rendezvous by telephone for tea at the Richmond in the Calle Florida—she had no liking for inescapable family conversations in her apartment which she kept almost as airless as the dome over the wax flowers she had bought at an antique shop near Harrods. He always had the impression in her flat that there were secrets from him lying about everywhere, on shelves and on tables, even pushed away under the sofa, secrets she didn't want him to see— perhaps only tiny extravagances on which she had spent the money he sent her. Cream cakes were food, but a china parrot was an extravagance.

He had to move at a snail's pace through the crowd that filled the narrow *calle* every afternoon when it was closed to traffic. He was not displeased, for every minute he lost before meeting his mother was pure gain.

He saw her at the far end of the crowded tea room, sitting in unrelieved black before a plate of sweet cakes. She said, "You are ten minutes late, Eduardo." From his early childhood they had always spoken Spanish together. Only with his father had he spoken English, and his father was a man of few words.

"I am sorry, mother. You should have begun." When he bent to kiss her cheek he could smell the hot chocolate in her cup like a sweet breath from a tomb.

"Call the waiter, dear, if there is not a cake here that pleases you."

"I don't really want to eat anything, mother. I'll just have a cup of coffee."

She had heavy pouches below her eyes, but they were not, Doctor Plarr knew, the pouches of grief, but of constipation. He had an impression that if they were squeezed they would squirt cream like an éclair. It is terrible what time can do to a beautiful woman. A man's looks often improve with age, seldom a woman's. He thought: a man should never love a woman less than twenty years younger than himself. In that way he can die before the vision fades. Had Fortnum insured himself against disillusion when he married Clara, who was more than forty years younger than himself? Doctor Plarr thought, I'm not so wise, I shall outlive her attraction by many years.

"Why the mourning, mother?" he asked. "I have never seen you in black before."

"I am mourning for your father," Señora Plarr said and wiped the chocolate off her fingers with a paper napkin.

"Have you had news then?"

"No, but Father Galvão has been speaking to me very seriously. He says that for the sake of my health I must give up vain hopes. Do you know what day it is, Eduardo?"

He searched his mind without success—he was even uncertain of the day of the month. "The fourteenth?" he asked.

"It is the day we said goodbye to your father in the port of Asunción."

He wondered whether his father, if he were to walk into the tea room now, could possibly recognize the stout and pouchy woman who had a smear of cream at the corner of the mouth. In our memories people we no longer see age gracefully. Señora Plarr said, "Father Galvão held a Mass this morning for the repose of his soul." She scrutinized the plate of cakes and picked a particular éclair, not noticeably different from the others. Yet when he searched his memory he could still just remember a lovely woman who lay and wept in her cabin. Tears at the age she had been then enhanced the brilliance of her eyes. There were no pouches to mar them.

He said, "I still have hope, mother. You know the kidnappers have named him on the list of prisoners they want released?"

"What kidnappers?" He had forgotten she never read the papers.

"Oh well," he said, "it's too long a story to tell you now." He added politely, "What a very nice black dress."

"I am glad you like it. I had it made specially for the

157

Mass this morning. The material was quite inexpensive, and I had it run up by a little woman . . . You must not think I am extravagant."

"No, of course not, mother."

"If only your father had been less obstinate . . . What was the use of staying on the *estancia* to be murdered? He could have sold it for a good price, and we could have been happy here together."

"He was an idealist," Doctor Plarr said.

"Ideals are all very well, but it was very wrong of him and very selfish of him not to put his family first."

He wondered what kind of bitter and reproachful prayers she had muttered that morning at Father Galvão's Mass. Father Galvão was a Portuguese Jesuit who for some reason had been transferred from Rio de Janeiro. He was very popular with women—perhaps they were more ready to confide in him because he had come from a long way off.

All around him in the Richmond he heard the chatter of women's voices. He could hardly distinguish a single phrase. He might have been in an aviary, listening to a babel of birds from many different regions. There were those who twittered in English, others in German, he even heard a French phrase which his mother would appreciate, *"George est très coupable."* He looked at her as she tipped her mouth toward the chocolate. Had she ever felt any love for his father or himself, or had she just played the comedy of love like Clara? He had grown up, during the years he spent alone with his mother in Buenos Aires, to despise comedy. There were no sentimental relics in his apartment—not even a photograph. It was as bare and truthful—almost—as a police station cell. Even during his affairs with women he had always tried to avoid that phrase of the theater, "I love you." He had been accused often enough of cruelty, though he preferred to think of himself as a painstaking and accurate diagnostician. If for once he had been aware of a sickness he could describe in no other terms, he would have unhesitatingly used the phrase "I love," but he had always been able to attribute the emotion he felt to a quite different malady —to loneliness, pride, physical desire, or even a simple sense of curiosity.

Señora Plarr said, "He never loved either of us. He was a man who never knew what love meant."

He wanted to ask her seriously, "Do we?" but he knew she would take it as a reproach, and he had no desire to reproach her. With more justice he could reproach himself for equal ignorance. Perhaps, he thought, she is in the right and I resemble my father. He said, "I do not remember him at all clearly, except that, when he said goodbye, I noticed how gray his hair had become. I remember too how he would go round locking all the doors at night. The noise always woke me up. I do not even know how old he would be if he were alive now."

"He would have been seventy-one today."

"Today? Then was it on his birthday . . . ?"

"He told me the best present he could receive from me was to watch the two of us go off down the river. It was very cruel of him to say that."

"But, mother, I don't think he could have meant it cruelly."

"He had not even told me beforehand. I had no time to pack properly. I forgot some of my jewels. There was a little watch with diamonds which I used to wear with a black dress. You remember the black dress? But of course you would not remember. You were always such an unobservant boy. He said he was afraid I would tell my friends and they would gossip and the police would stop us. I had prepared a very nice birthday dinner for him, with a cheese savory—he always liked savories better than a dessert. That is what it is like to marry a foreigner. Our tastes were never the same. This morning I prayed very hard he might not be suffering too much."

"I thought you believed he was dead."

"Suffering in purgatory of course I mean. Father Galvão says that the worst pain in purgatory is when people see the consequence of their actions and the suffering they have caused to those they love." She picked out another éclair.

"But you said he loved neither of us."

"Oh, I suppose he did feel a certain affection. And duty. He was very English. He preferred the company of other men. I have no doubt he went to the Club after the boat left."

"What club?" For years they had not spoken so much of his father.

"It was not a safe club for him to belong to. It was called the Constitutional, but the police closed it. Afterward the members met in secret—once even at our *estancia*. He would not listen to me when I protested. I said, 'You have a wife and child.' He said, 'Every member of the club has a wife and child.' I said, 'In that case they should have more important things to talk about than politics.' Oh well," she added with a little sigh, "those are old quarrels. Of course I have forgiven him. Tell me a little about yourself, dear," and her eyes glazed over with lack of interest.

"Oh," he said, "there is nothing really to tell."

The evening plane to the north represented a hazard for a man like Doctor Plarr who liked to remain alone. Few strangers or tourists traveled by it. Among the passengers were usually local politicians returning from a visit to the capital, or expensive wives whom he had sometimes examined (they would have gone to Buenos Aires for a shopping expedition or a party, even for a hairdo because they didn't trust their local hairdresser).

They would form a noisy group of familiars in the small two-engined plane.

There was only the smallest chance of an undisturbed flight, and his spirits sank when, from just across the gangway, Señora Escobar greeted him, before he even saw her, with a parrot cry of pleasure. "Eduardo!"

"Margarita!"

He began resignedly to unbuckle his safety belt, so as to take the empty seat beside her.

"No," she told him in a quick whisper, "Gustavo is with me. He is at the back talking to Colonel Perez."

"Colonel Perez is here too?"

"They are talking about the kidnapping. Do you know what I believe?"

"No?"

"I think the man Fortnum has run away from his wife."

"Why would he do that?"

"You must know the story, Eduardo. She is a *putain*. She comes from that horrible house in Calle . . . but you are a man. You know very well the one I mean."

He remembered that Margarita had always, when she wished to be a little coarse, employed a French term. He could hear her crying, in the carefully measured shadows of her room, made by the *persianas* two thirds closed, *"Baise-moi, baise-moi!"* Never would she have allowed herself to use the equivalent Spanish phrase. She said, "I have not seen you for such a long time, Eduardo," with a sigh as carefully adjusted for the occasion as the shutters of her bedroom. He wondered what had happened to her new lover—Gaspar Vallejo of the financial department. He hoped that there had been no quarrel.

The roar of the engines saved him from the need to reply, and by the time the overhead warnings had been switched off and they were high above the khaki-colored Plata, which turned black as the evening darkened, he had a vague phrase ready on the tongue. "You know what it is like to be a doctor, Margarita."

"Yes," she said, "I know—who better? Do you still see Señora Vega?"

"No. I think she must have changed her doctor."

"I would never do that, Eduardo—there are not so many good doctors as that. If I have not asked you to come to see me it is only that I have been disgustingly well. Why, here is my husband at last. Look whom we have here, Gustavo! Do not pretend you have forgotten Doctor Plarr."

"How could I forget him? Where have you been all this long time, Eduardo?" Gustavo Escobar laid his hand heavily on Doctor Plarr's shoulder and kneaded it gently—he had the Latin-American desire to touch any man to whom he spoke. Even the knife-thrust in one of Jorge Julio Saavedra's stories could be interpreted as a way of touching. "We have missed you," he went on in the loud voice of a deaf man. "How often my wife has said 'I wonder why Eduardo never calls on us now?' "

Gustavo Escobar had a large black moustache and abundant sideburns: his face, brick-red as laterite, resembled a clearing which has been hacked out of the bush, and his nose reared like the horse of a *conquistador*. Escobar said, "I have missed you as much as my wife has. All those friendly little dinners we used to have . . ."

Doctor Plarr, during the whole time that he had been Margarita's lover, had never been able to distinguish with certainty between his rough playfulness and his irony. Margarita had always assured him that her husband was a man of the most passionate jealousy—it would have hurt her pride to feel he did not really care. Perhaps indeed he did care, for she was at least one of his women, even though he had a great many. Doctor Plarr on one occasion had encountered him at Mother

Sanchez' house where he was entertaining four girls at once. The girls, against all the rules of the house, were drinking champagne, good French champagne which he must have brought with him. No rules of the house were likely to be enforced against Gustavo Escobar. Doctor Plarr sometimes wondered whether he had ever been a client of Clara's. What sort of comedy would she have played for him? Perhaps abasement?

"What have you been up to, my dear Eduardo, in Buenos Aires?"

"I have been to the Embassy," Doctor Plarr shouted back at him, "and I have seen my mother. And you?"

"My wife has been shopping. As for myself I had lunch at the Hurlingham." He continued to finger Doctor Plarr's shoulder almost as though he were considering whether to buy him for breeding purposes (he had a big *estancia* on the Chaco side of the Paraná).

"Gustavo is deserting me again for a whole week," Margarita said. "He always allows me to go shopping just before he deserts me."

Doctor Plarr would have liked to turn the conversation to his successor, Gaspar Vallejo, to whom the information she had given him ought more properly to have been addressed. It would have been reassuring to know that Vallejo was still a friend of the family.

"What about joining me on the *estancia,* Eduardo? I can give you some good shooting."

"A doctor is tied to his patients," Doctor Plarr said.

The plane dipped in an air pocket and Escobar had to grasp the back of Plarr's seat.

"Be careful, *caro*. You will hurt your precious self. Better sit down."

Perhaps it was the mechanical expression of his wife's solicitude which irritated Escobar. Or perhaps he took the warning as a reflection on his *machismo*. He said with quite unmistakable irony, "You are tied to a very favorite patient at the moment, I believe, Eduardo?"

"All my patients are favorite ones."

"Señora Fortnum is having a baby, I believe?"

"Yes. And so, I expect you know, is Señora Vega, but she doesn't trust me with a childbirth. She goes to Doctor Benevento now."

"A discreet man Eduardo," Escobar said. He fumbled past his wife to the seat by the window and sat down. Almost as soon as he closed his eyes he appeared to be asleep, sitting bolt upright. He looked as one of his ancestors might have looked, asleep on the saddle, crossing the Andes; he rocked gently with the stride of the plane across the snowy summits of the clouds.

"What did he mean, Eduardo?" his wife asked in a whisper.

"How do I know?"

He remembered that Escobar had always been a very heavy sleeper. Once, very early in their relationship, Margarita had told him, "Nothing ever wakes him except a sudden silence. Just go on talking."

"What about?" he had asked.

"Anything. Why not tell me how much you love me?" They had been sitting together on a sofa and her husband was sleeping in an armchair at the opposite end of the room, the back of the chair turned to them. Doctor Plarr couldn't even tell whether his eyes were closed. He said cautiously, "I want you."

"Yes?"

"I want you."

"Don't sound so staccato," she said as she touched him. "He needs to hear the steady murmur of conversation."

It is difficult to keep a monologue going while a woman makes love to you. In desperation Doctor Plarr had begun to recount the story of the Three Bears, beginning it in the middle, while all the time he watched with anxiety the powerful statuesque head above the chair back.

"And then the third bear said in his gruff voice, 'Who has been eating up my porridge?' "

Señora Escobar sat astride him as though she were a child playing ponies. "And so all three bears went upstairs and the little bear said, 'Who has been sleeping in my bed?' " He clutched Señora Escobar's shoulders, and lost the thread of the story, so that he had to continue with the first phrase which came into his head, "This is the way the postboy rides. Gallopy, gallopy, gallopy." When they were relaxed again on the sofa side by side, Señora Escobar—he had not been given enough time to think of her yet as Margarita—said, "You were speaking in English. What were you saying?"

"I was telling you how much I wanted you," Doctor Plarr said warily. The postboy had been a game he had played with his father: his mother had no repertoire. Perhaps Spanish children had no games—or no childish ones.

"What did Gustavo mean about Señora Fortnum?" Margarita asked again, bringing him back to the present and the plane which lurched in the wind currents above the Paraná.

"I have no idea."

"You would disappoint me terribly, Eduardo, if you really had anything to do with that little *putain*. I am still very fond of you."

"Excuse me, Margarita," he said. "I want to have a word with Colonel Perez." The lights of La Paz blinked below them—there was a white ruled line of lamps along the river with complete darkness on the other side, as though the lamps marked the edge of a flat world. Perez was sitting at the far end of the plane near the lavatory and the seat beside him was empty.

"Any news, Colonel?" Doctor Plarr asked.

"News of what?"

"Of Fortnum."

"No. Why? Were you expecting any?"

"I thought perhaps the police might have some . . . Didn't the radio say you were looking for him in Rosario?"

"If he had been really in Rosario they could easily have brought him into Buenos Aires by this time."

"And what about the call from Córdoba?"

"That was probably a stupid attempt to confuse us. Córdoba is out of the question. I doubt if they could have even reached Rosario by the time of the call. It would have taken fifteen hours in the fastest car."

"Then where do you suppose he is?" Doctor Plarr asked.

"He is probably dead in the river or else he is hidden nearer home. What were you doing in Buenos Aires?"

It was a polite question, not a police question. He was no more interested than Escobar.

"I wanted to see the Ambassador about Fortnum."

"Yes. What did he have to say?"

"I interrupted his siesta, poor man. He said the trouble is that no one's really interested."

Colonel Perez said, "I assure you I am. Yesterday I wanted to organize a thorough search of the *barrio popular,* but the Governor thought it too dangerous. He does not want shooting if possible. Ours has been a very quiet province up till now except for a little trouble from those third world priests. He sent me off to Buenos Aires today to talk to the Minister of the Interior. I think the Governor hopes to delay matters. If he can postpone action long enough and we are lucky Fortnum's body may be found outside the province. No one can complain then that we acted imprudently. The blackmail will have failed. Everyone will be happy. Except myself. Even your government will be happy. I hope they will pay a pension to the widow?"

"I doubt it. He was only an Honorary Consul. What did the Minister say?"

"He is not afraid of shooting, that man. We could do with more like him. He advises the Governor to go ahead whatever happens and to use troops if necessary. The President wants everything settled before the General finishes his fishing. What else did your Ambassador say?"

"He said if the papers made enough fuss . . ."

"Why should they? Have you heard the afternoon radio? A BOAC plane has crashed. A hijacker let off his grenade this time. There are a hundred and sixty-seven deaths—a hundred and sixty-seven Fortnums, and one of them a film star. No, Doctor Plarr, we have to admit that ours is a very small affair."

"Do you want to give up then?"

"Oh no—I have dealt all my life in small affairs, and I have always preferred to see them settled. Unfinished dossiers take up a lot of room. A smuggler was shot yesterday on the river, so we have been able to close his file. Somebody has stolen a hundred thousand pesos from a bedroom in the Nacional—but we have our eyes on the man. And early this morning there was a small bomb found in the church of La Cruz. A very small bomb—for we are a very quiet province—and it was set to go off at midnight when the church was empty. If it had exploded, though, it might have destroyed the miraculous cross—and that would have been real news in *El Litoral,* even if not in the *Nación.* Perhaps it may become news in any case. There are rumors already that Our Lady herself got down off her altar and defused the bomb with her own hands and the Archbishop has visited the scene. You know the cross was first saved—years before Buenos Aires even existed—when lightning killed the Indians who were going to burn it." The door of the lavatory opened. "You know my colleague Captain Velardo, doctor? I was telling the doctor about our new miracle, Rubén."

"You may laugh, colonel, but the bomb did not go off."

"You see, doctor, Rubén half believes."

"I keep an open mind. Like the Archbishop. The Archbishop is an educated man."

"I think the fuse was badly set."

"And why was the fuse badly set? One has to go back to the source, colonel. A miracle is very much like a crime. You say the fuse was badly set, but how can we be sure that it was not Our Lady who guided the hand which set the fuse?"

"All the same I prefer to believe we are kept in the air now by the engines—even though they are not Rolls Royce—rather than by divine intervention."

The plane dropped again in a pocket of air and the warning lights went on, telling them to fasten seat-belts. Doctor Plarr thought that Colonel Perez looked a little uneasy. He went back to his seat.

2

Having sent out invitations by telephone from the airport Doctor Plarr waited for his two guests on the terrace of the Nacional. On a sheet of hotel notepaper he drafted a careful letter which he believed the Ambassador would have found sober and convincing. The city was beginning to wake up for the evening hours after the long siesta of the afternoon. A chain of cars drove by along the riverside. The white naked statue in the belvedere shone under the lamplight, and the Coca-Cola sign glowed in scarlet letters like the shrine of a saint. Through the darkness the ferry boat was screaming a warning from the Chaco shore. It was a few min-

utes past nine—far too early for most people to dine—
and Doctor Plarr was alone on the terrace except for
Doctor Benevento and his wife. Doctor Benevento sat
taking little sips at an apéritif, as though he were suspiciously testing the tonic of a rival, while his wife, a
severe and middle-aged woman who wore a large gold
cross like some order of distinction, ostentatiously took
nothing and watched the disappearance of her husband's
apéritif with a false air of patience. It was a Thursday,
Doctor Plarr remembered, and perhaps Doctor Benevento had come straight to the hotel from his weekly
inspection of Mother Sanchez' girls. The two doctors
ignored each other: after all the years which had passed
since he arrived from Buenos Aires Doctor Plarr was
still in the eyes of Doctor Benevento a foreign inter-
loper.

Humphries was the first of his guests to arrive. He
was tightly buttoned in a dark suit and his forehead
was wet in the humid night. His temper was not improved when a bold mosquito, immediately he sat
down, attacked his ankle through a thick gray woolen
sock. The professor of English struck angrily out and
complained, "I was just leaving for the Italian Club
when I got your message," as if he resented being
deprived of his usual goulash. He looked at the third
place at table and asked, "Who's coming?"

"Doctor Saavedra."

"In God's name why? I can't understand what you
see in that fellow. A pompous ass."

"I thought his advice might be useful. I want to draft
a letter to the papers from the Anglo-Argentinian Club
on behalf of Fortnum."

"You are fooling me. What club? It doesn't exist."

"You and I are going to found the club tonight.
Saavedra, I hope, will be the president, I will be the
chairman. I thought you wouldn't mind taking on the

job of honorary secretary. There won't be very much to do."

"This is sheer madness," Humphries said. "As far as I know there's only one other Englishman in the city. Or there was. I'm convinced Fortnum's absconded. That woman of his must have been costing him a great deal of money. Sooner or later we shall hear that the accounts at the Consulate are in the red. Or more likely we shall hear nothing at all. Those Embassy fellows in B.A. are sure to hush things up. For the honor of their so-called service. One never gets at the truth of anything." It was his perpetual and quite genuine complaint. Truth was like a difficult sentence which his pupils never succeeded in getting grammatically right.

Doctor Plarr said, "At least there's no doubt about the kidnapping. That's true enough. I've talked to Perez."

"Do you trust what a policeman says?"

"This policeman, yes. Look, Humphries, be reasonable. We have to do *something* for Fortnum. Even if he did fly the Union Jack upside down. The poor devil has only three days left to live. The Ambassador today —he doesn't want it known—suggested we ought to write some sort of tribute to the papers. Anything to stir up a little interest. From the English Club here. Oh, yes, yes, you've already said it. Of course there's no such club. Coming back on the plane I thought it would be better to call the club the Anglo-Argentinian. In that way we can use Saavedra's name and we have more chance of making the B.A. papers. We can talk about the good influence Fortnum has always had on our relations with Argentina. We can speak of his cultural activities."

"Cultural activities! His father was a notorious drunkard and so is Charley Fortnum. Don't you remember the night we had to haul him back to the Bolívar? He

couldn't even stand up. All he has done for our relations with Argentina is to marry a local whore."

"All the same we can't just let him die."

"I wouldn't raise my little finger," Humphries said,
"for that man."

Something was going on inside the Nacional. The
maître d'hôtel, who had come out on the terrace to
breathe the air before the night's activities began, was
hurrying back to the dining room. A waiter, who was
halfway to Doctor Benevento's table, turned tail in
response to a signal. Through the French window of
the restaurant Doctor Plarr saw the pearl-gray gleam
of Jorge Julio Saavedra's suit as the author paused to
exchange a few words with the staff. A woman from
the cloakroom took his hat, the waiter took his cane,
the manager came hurrying from his office to join the
maître d'hôtel. Doctor Saavedra was explaining something, pointing here and there; when he came out on
the terrace, they escorted him in a phalanx toward
Doctor Plarr's table. Even Doctor Benevento rose a
few inches in his seat, as Doctor Saavedra pigeon-toed
by in his gleaming pointed shoes.

"Here comes the great novelist," Humphries sneered.
"I bet none of them has read a word he ever wrote."

"You are probably right, but his great-grandfather
was Governor here," Doctor Plarr said. "In Argentina
they have a strong sense of history."

The manager wanted to know whether the table was
placed in a position satisfactory to Doctor Saavedra;
the *maître d'hôtel* whispered in Doctor Plarr's ear news
of a special dish which was not marked on the menu—
some salmon had arrived that day fresh from Iguazú;
there was also a *dorado* if Doctor Plarr's guests would
prefer that.

When the staff had departed one by one, Doctor
Saavedra said, "They make a ridiculous fuss of me. I
was only telling them I was going to set a scene in my

171

new novel in the restaurant of the Nacional. I wanted to explain where I wanted my character to be seated. I had to see exactly what would lie in his view at the moment when Fuerabbia, his assailant, enters armed from the terrace."

"Is it a detective story?" Humphries asked with malice. "I like a good detective story."

"I trust I shall never write a detective story, Doctor Humphries, if by a detective story you mean one of those absurd puzzles, which are the literary equivalent of a jigsaw. In my new book I am concerned with the psychology of violence."

"Gauchos again?"

"No, not gauchos. This is a contemporary novel— my second venture into politics. It is set in the time of the dictator Rosas."

"I thought you said it was contemporary."

"The ideas are contemporary. If you were a writer, Doctor Humphries, instead of a teacher of literature, you would know a novelist has to stand at a distance from his subject. Nothing dates more quickly than the immediately contemporary. You might as well expect me to write a story about the kidnapping of Señor Fortnum." He turned to Doctor Plarr. "I had some difficulty in getting away tonight, something unpleasant happened, but when my doctor calls I have to obey. What is it all about?"

"Doctor Humphries and I have decided to found an Anglo-Argentina Club."

"An excellent idea. What activities . . . ?"

"Cultural of course. Literary, archaeological. We want you to be president."

"I am honored," Doctor Saavedra said.

"One of the first things I would like the club to do is to make an appeal to the press on the subject of Fortnum's kidnapping. If he had been here he would certainly have been a member."

"How can I help you?" Doctor Saavedra asked. "I have hardly spoken to Señor Fortnum. Just once at Señora Sanchez' . . ."

"I have brought a rough draft—a very rough draft. I am no writer—except of prescriptions."

Humphries said, "The man has absconded. That is all there is to it. He probably arranged the whole affair himself. Personally I refuse to sign."

"Then we shall have to do without you, Humphries. Only your friends—if you have any—may wonder, when the letter's published, why you are not a member of the Anglo-Argentinian Club. They may even think you were blackballed."

"You know there's no such club."

"Oh yes, there is, and Doctor Saavedra has agreed to be our president. This is the first club dinner. And we have a very good salmon from Iguazú. If you don't wish to be a member, go away and have some goulash at your Italian joint."

"Are you trying to blackmail me?"

"In a good cause."

"Morally you are no better than the kidnappers."

"No better—all the same I would rather they didn't kill Charley Fortnum."

"Charley Fortnum's a disgrace to his country."

"No signature. No salmon."

"You give me no alternative," Doctor Humphries said, undoing his napkin.

Doctor Saavedra read the letter with care. He laid it down beside his plate. "If I might take this home and work on it," he said. "It lacks—you must not mind my criticism, it comes from a professional conscience—it lacks the sense of urgency. It reads as coldly as a company report. If you would leave the letter in my hands I will write you something with color and dramatic effect. Something the press would have to print on its own merits."

173

"I want to cable it tonight to *The Times* in London and get it into tomorrow's papers in Buenos Aires."

"A letter like this cannot be hurried, Doctor Plarr, and I am a slow writer. Give me till tomorrow and I promise you the result will be worth waiting for."

"The poor devil may have only about three days to live. I'd rather cable my rough draft tonight than wait till tomorrow. Over in England it's already tomorrow."

"Then you will have to do without my signature. I'm sorry, doctor, it would be wrong for me to put my name to the letter as it stands now. No one in Buenos Aires would believe I had a hand in it. It contains— forgive me—some terrible clichés. Just listen to this . . ."

"That is why I wanted you to rewrite the letter. Surely you can do it now. At the table."

"Do you believe writing is as easy as that? Would you do a delicate operation, on the spur of the moment, on this table? I will sit up all night if necessary. The quality of the letter I write you will more than make up for the delay, even in translation. By the way who is going to translate it—you or Doctor Humphries? I would like to check the translation before you send it abroad. I trust your accuracy, of course, but it is a question of style. In a letter like this we have to move the reader, to bring home to him the character of this poor man . . ."

"The less you bring home his character the better," Humphries said.

"As I see it, Señor Fortnum is a simple man—not very wise or intelligent—and suddenly he finds himself close to violent death. Perhaps he has never even thought of death before. It is a situation in which such a man either succumbs to fear or he grows in stature. Consider the case of Señor Fortnum. He is married to a young wife, a child is on the way . . ."

"We have no time to write a novel on the subject," Doctor Plarr said.

"When I met him, he had drunk a little too much. I found his company embarrassing until I saw, behind the superficial gaiety, a profound melancholy."

"You are not far wrong there," Doctor Plarr said with surprise.

"He was drinking, I think, for the same reason that I write—to escape the darkness of his own spirit. He confided to me that he was in love."

"In love at sixty!" Humphries exclaimed. "He ought to have got beyond all that nonsense."

"I have not got beyond it," Doctor Saavedra said. "If I were beyond it, I would no longer be able to write. The sexual instinct and the creative instinct live and die together. Youth, Doctor Humphries, lasts longer in some men than you, from your personal experience, may suppose."

"He just wanted to keep a whore handy. Do you call that love?"

"If we could get back to the letter . . ." Doctor Plarr said.

"And what do you call love, Doctor Humphries? An arranged marriage in the Spanish tradition? A large family of children? Let me tell you I have loved a whore myself. A whore can have more generosity of spirit than you will find in the bourgeoisie of Buenos Aires. As a poet I have been helped better by a whore than by any critic—or professor of literature."

"I thought you were a novelist, not a poet."

"In Spanish we do not confine the term poet to those who write metrically."

"The letter," Doctor Plarr interrupted. "Let us try to finish the letter before we finish the salmon."

"You must let me think quietly—the opening sentence is the key to the rest. One has to strike the right tone, even the right rhythm. The right rhythm in prose is every bit as important as the right meter in a poem.

This is a very good salmon. May I have another glass of wine?"

"You can drink the whole bottle if you will write the letter."

"What a fuss to make about Charley Fortnum," Doctor Humphries said. He had finished his salmon, he had drained his glass, he had nothing to fear. "You know there's another possible motive for his disappearance—he doesn't want to stand father to another man's child."

"I want to begin the letter with a character study of the victim," Doctor Saavedra said, ballpoint in hand, a little salmon shaking on his upper lip, "but somehow Señor Fortnum refuses to come alive. I have had to cross out almost every other word. In a novel I could have created him in a few sentences. It is his reality which defeats me. I am hamstrung by his reality. When I write down a phrase it is as though Fortnum himself put a hand on my wrist and said, 'But this is not how I am at all.' "

"Let me pour you another glass."

"There is another thing he says to me which makes me hesitate. 'Why are you trying to send me back to the kind of life I used to lead, a life sad and without honor?' "

"Charley Fortnum never worried much about honor," Doctor Humphries said, "so long as there was enough whisky around."

"If you could look deep enough into anyone's character, even perhaps your own, you would find the sense of *machismo*."

It was past ten o'clock and guests were beginning to drift across the terrace for dinner. They moved along separate routes, passing on either side of Doctor Plarr's table, like migrating tribes passing a rock in the desert, and they carried their children with them. A baby, which might have been an idol of wax, sat upright in a pram: a pale-faced child of three staggered from fatigue across the marble desert dressed in a blue party dress, her little ears pierced for gold rings; a boy of six drummed his way, yawning at every step, along the terrace wall. One had the impression that they had crossed a whole continent to arrive here. No doubt at dawn, the grazing exhausted, they would pack up and move to another camping ground. Doctor Plarr said impatiently, "Give me back my letter. I want to send it as it is."

"In that case I cannot put my name to it."

"And you, Humphries?"

"I won't sign. You can't threaten me now. I've finished my salmon."

Doctor Plarr took the letter and tore it in two. He put some money on the table and rose.

"Doctor Plarr, I am sorry to anger you. Your style is not bad, it is workmanlike, but nobody would believe that I had written the letter."

Doctor Plarr went to the lavatory. As he washed his hands he thought: I am like Pilate, a cliché of which Doctor Saavedra would not approve. He washed his hands scrupulously as though he were about to examine a patient. Raising them from the water he looked into the glass and threw a question at the worried image there—if they kill Fortnum will I marry Clara? It would not be a necessary consequence; she would never expect him to marry her. If she inherited the camp she could sell it and move elsewhere—home to Tucumán? Or perhaps she would take a flat in B.A. and eat sweet cakes like his mother? It would be more satisfactory for all of them if Fortnum lived. Fortnum would make a better father for the child than he would—a child needed love.

As he dried his hands he heard the voice of Doctor Saavedra behind him. "You think I have failed you, doctor, but you are not aware of all the circumstances."

The novelist was urinating. He had turned up the right sleeve of his pearl-gray jacket; he was a fastidious man.

Doctor Plarr said, "I thought it was not too much to ask you to sign a letter, however badly written, and perhaps save a man's life."

"I think I had better tell you the real reason. I need more than one of your pills tonight. Doctor, I have been deeply wounded." Doctor Saavedra buttoned up his trousers and turned. "I have spoken to you already about Montez?"

"Montez? No, I can't remember the name."

"He is a young novelist in Buenos Aires—not so young now, I suppose, older than you, the years pass quickly. I helped him to get his first novel published. A very strange novel. Surrealist but excellently written. Emece turned it down, Sur would not accept it, and I only persuaded my own publisher to take it by promising that I would write a favorable criticism. In those days I was writing a weekly column in the *Nación* which had a lot of influence. I was fond of Montez. I felt myself to be a sort of father to him. Even though, during my last years in Buenos Aires, I saw very little of him. He had made his own friends after his success. All the same I never failed to praise his work when I had the chance. Now see what he has written about me." He took from his pocket a folded page of print.

It was a long and well-written article. The subject was the bad effect of the epic poem, *Martín Fierro,* on the Argentine novel. Borges the author excepted from his criticism. He had a few words of praise for Mallea and Sabato, but he made cruel fun of Jorge Julio Saavedra's novels. The word mediocre appeared frequently, the word *machismo* rang mockingly out from nearly every paragraph. Was he revenging the patronage which Saavedra had once shown him, all the boring counsel to which he had probably been forced to listen? Doctor Plarr said, "Yes, it is a betrayal, Saavedra."

"Not only of myself. Of his country. *Martín Fierro* is Argentina. Why, my own grandfather died in a duel. He fought with bare hands against a drunken gaucho who insulted him. Where would we be now"—his hands waved from basin to *urinoir*—"if our fathers had not reverenced *machismo*? You see what he writes about the girl from Salta. He has not even understood the symbolism of her one leg. If I had signed your letter imagine how he would have sneered at the style. 'Poor Jorge Julio—that is what happens to a writer who runs away from his peers and hides in the provinces. He writes like a clerk of the *intendente*.' I wish Montez were here now so that I could teach him the meaning of *machismo*. Here on these tiles."

"Have you a knife handy?" Doctor Plarr asked, hoping in vain to raise a smile.

"I would fight him as my grandfather did with my bare hands."

Doctor Plarr said, "Your grandfather was killed."

"I am not afraid of death," Doctor Saavedra said.

"Charley Fortnum is. It's a very small thing to do —to sign a letter."

"A small thing? To sign a piece of prose like that? It would be much easier to give my life. Oh, I know it's impossible for someone who is not a writer to understand."

"I am trying to," Doctor Plarr said.

"Your purpose is to draw attention to Señor Fortnum's case? Is that right?"

"Yes."

"Then this is what I suggest. Inform the newspapers and your government that I have offered myself as a hostage in his place."

"Are you serious?"

"I am quite serious."

It might work, Doctor Plarr thought, there is just a faint possibility that in this crazy country it might work. He was moved to say, "It's brave of you, Saavedra."

"At least I will show young Montez that *machismo* is not an invention of the author of *Martín Fierro*."

"You realize," Doctor Plarr said, "they might accept your offer? And then there would be no more novels by Jorge Julio Saavedra—unless perhaps the General reads you and you have a big public in Paraguay."

"You will cable Buenos Aires and *The Times* of London too? You will not forget *The Times*? Two of my novels were published in England. And *El Litoral*. You must telephone them. The kidnappers are sure to read *El Litoral*."

They went together to the manager's office which was empty and Doctor Plarr wrote out the cables. When he turned he saw the eyes of Doctor Saavedra red with unshed tears. Saavedra said, "Montez was like a son to me. I admired his books. They were so different from my own, and they had quality—I could see they had quality. Yet all the time he must have been despising me. I am an old man, Doctor Plarr, so death is not very far off from me in any case. That story I was describing to the hotel manager—the story of the intruder—I was going to call the novel *The Intruder*—it would probably never have been finished. Even while I was planning it I knew it belonged to *his* region of literature and not to mine. I used to give him advice and see me now—planning to imitate him. It is the privilege of the young to imitate. I would prefer to die in a way that even Montez would have to respect."

"He will say that you were killed too in the end by *Martín Fierro*."

"In Argentina we are most of us killed by *Martín Fierro*. But a man has the right to choose the moment of death."

"Charley Fortnum has not been allowed to choose."

"Señor Fortnum is caught up in a contingency. I agree that is not a dignified way to die. It is like a street accident or a case of *gripe*."

Doctor Plarr offered to drive Saavedra home. He had never yet been invited to visit the novelist and he had imagined him in occupation of some old colonial house with barred windows looking out on a shady street, with a few orange trees and *lapachos* in the garden, a house as dignified and out of fashion as his clothes. Perhaps there would be portraits on the wall of the great-grand-father who had been Governor of the province and of the grandfather who had been killed by the gaucho.

"It is not far. I can easily walk," Saavedra said.

"I think we ought to talk a little more about your offer and how it can be carried through."

"All that is out of my hands now."

"Not entirely."

As he drove Doctor Plarr pointed out to the novelist that from the moment his offer was published in *El Litoral* he would be watched by the police. "The kid-nappers will have to communicate with you and suggest some way of making the exchange. It would be easier if you left the town tonight before the police know. You could stay out of sight with some friend in the country."

"How would the kidnappers find me?"

"Perhaps through me. They probably know I am a friend of Señor Fortnum."

"I cannot run away and hide like a criminal."

"Then it will be difficult for them to take your offer up."

"Besides," Doctor Saavedra said, "there is my work."

"Surely you can take it with you."

"That is easy for you to say. You can go and attend a patient anywhere, you carry your experience with you. But my work is tied to the room where I work. When I came here from Buenos Aires it was nearly a year before I could put a pen to paper. My room was like a hotel room. To write one must have a home."

A home: Doctor Plarr was surprised to find the novelist lived in a block even more modern and shabby than his own in a quarter close by the prison wall. The gray apartment houses stood in squares as though they formed an extension of the prison. One expected them to be lettered A, B and C and to be reserved for different categories of criminal. Doctor Saavedra's apartment was on the third floor and there was no lift. Children played a kind of bowls with tin cans in front of the entrance, and the smell of cooking pursued them up the stairs. Perhaps Doctor Saavedra felt that an explanation was required. He spoke a little breathlessly after his climb as he paused on the second floor. "You know a novelist does not pay visits like a doctor. He has to live with his subject. I could not live comfortably in a bourgeois setting because I write about the people. The good woman who cleans for me here is the wife of a warder at the prison. I feel myself in the right *milieu*. I put her in my last book. Do you remember? She was called Caterina and was the widow of a sergeant. I think I caught her way of thinking." He opened his door and said with a note of defiance, "Here you are at the heart of what my critics call the world of Saavedra."

It was indeed a very small world. Doctor Plarr had an impression that the long pursuit of literature had brought the novelist little material reward beyond his tidy suit and his polished shoes and the respect of the hotel manager. The living room was narrow and long like a railway compartment. One shelf of books (most of them were Saavedra's own), a folding table which would have almost spanned the room if it had been opened, a nineteenth-century painting of a gaucho on a horse, one easy chair and two upright chairs—that was all the furnishing there was, apart from a huge antique mahogany cupboard which must have once belonged in more spacious quarters, for the baroque curlicues above the pediment had been cut to fit under the ceiling. Two open doors, which Doctor Saavedra quickly shut, gave Plarr glimpses of a monastic bedstead and the chipped enamel of a cooking stove. Through the window, which was veined by a rusty mesh against mosquitoes, came the clatter of tins from the children playing below.

"May I give you a whisky?"

"A small one, please."

Doctor Saavedra opened the cupboard; it was like an enormous chest in which the possessions of a lifetime had been packed for an impending departure. Two suits hung there. Shirts and underwear and books had been stacked indiscriminately on the shelves: an umbrella leaned among obscure shapes at the back: four ties dangled from a rod: a little pile of photographs in old-fashioned frames shared the floor with two pairs of shoes and some books for which there had been no room elsewhere. On a ledge over the suits stood a whisky bottle, a half-finished bottle of wine and a few glasses—one of them chipped—a pile of cutlery and a bowl of bread. Doctor Saavedra said defiantly, "I am a little cramped for room, but I want the smallest possible space around me when I write. Space distracts." He looked anxiously at Doctor Plarr and attempted a smile. "This is the womb of my characters, doctor, and there is room for little else. You must forgive me if I cannot offer you any ice, but this morning my refrigerator failed and the electrician has not yet come."

"I prefer my whisky neat after dinner," Doctor Plarr said.

He had to stand on the points of his small gleaming shoes to reach the top of the wardrobe. A cheap plastic shade painted with pink flowers, which were beginning to brown from the heat, hardly dimmed the harshness of the central light. Watching Doctor Saavedra reach for the glass with his white hair, in his pearl-gray suit and his brightly polished shoes, Doctor Plarr felt much the same astonishment that he had felt in the *barrio* of the poor when he saw a young girl emerge in an immaculate white dress from a waterless hovel of mud and tin. He felt a new respect for Doctor Saavedra. His obsession with literature was not absurd whatever the quality of his books. He was willing to suffer poverty for its sake, and a disguised poverty was far worse to endure than an open one. The effort needed to polish his shoes, to press the suit . . . He couldn't, like the young, let things go. Even his hair must be cut regularly. A missing button would reveal too much. Perhaps he would be remembered in the history of Argentine literature only in a footnote, but he would have deserved his footnote. The bareness of the room could be compared to the inextinguishable hunger of his literary obsession.

Doctor Saavedra tripped toward him holding two glasses. He asked, "How long do you think we shall have to wait for a response?"

"It may never come."

"Your father's name, I believe, is on the list of those they want released?"

"Yes."

"It would be strange for you, I imagine, to see your father again after all this time. How happy your mother will be if . . ."

"I think she would prefer him dead. He wouldn't fit in with her life now."

"And perhaps if Señor Fortnum returned he would not be welcomed by his wife either?"

"How can I tell?"

"Oh come, Doctor Plarr, I have friends at the house of Señora Sanchez."

"So she has been back there?" Doctor Plarr asked.

"I was there early this evening and so was she. They were making a great fuss of her—even Señora Sanchez. Perhaps she hopes to have her back. When Doctor Benevento came to see the other girls I took her to the Consulate."

"She told you about me?"

He was a little irritated by her indiscretion, but nonetheless he felt a sense of relief. He was escaping from secrecy. There had not been one soul in the city to whom he could talk of Clara, and what better confidant could he hope to have than his own patient? There were secrets which Doctor Saavedra too would not want known.

"She told me how very kind you had been to her."

"Is that all she said?"

"It was all that was necessary between old friends."

"Was she one of your girls?" Doctor Plarr asked.

"I was with her only once, I think."

Doctor Plarr felt no jealousy. To think of Clara waiting naked in her cell in the candlelight while Doctor Saavedra hung up his pearl-gray suit was like watching on the stage a scene, both sad and comic, from a remote seat at the back of the gallery. Distance removed the characters so far from him that he could be touched only by a formal compassion. He asked, "Didn't you like her enough to try again?"

Doctor Saavedra said, "It was not a question of liking. She was a good young woman, I am sure, quite attractive too, but she had nothing *special* for my purpose. She never struck me as a character—a character —forgive me if I speak like the critics—in the world of Jorge Julio Saavedra. Montez claims that world has no real existence. What does he know in Buenos Aires? Doesn't Teresa exist—you remember the evening when you met her? Before we had been together five minutes Teresa was the girl from Salta. There was something she said—I can't even remember the words now. I went with her four times and then I had to drop her, because she was saying too many things which were unsuitable. They confused my idea."

"Clara comes from Tucumán. You got nothing from her?"

"Tucumán is not a suitable region for me. My region is the region of extremes. Montez does not understand that. Trelew . . . Salta. Tucumán is an elegant city, and it is surrounded by half a million hectares of sugar. What *ennui!* Her father was a cane-cutter, wasn't he? And her brother disappeared."

"I would have thought that might have made a good subject for you, Saavedra."

"Not for me. She never came alive. It was all dull poverty with no *machismo* in half a million hectares." He added bravely as though the night were not noisy with the tins rolling back and forth in the cement yard below, "You do not realize how quiet and dull bare poverty can be. Let me give you a little more whisky. It is a genuine Johnny Walker."

"No, no, thank you. I must go home." All the same he lingered. Novelists were supposed to have acquired a certain wisdom . . . He asked, "What do you suppose will become of Clara if Fortnum dies?"

"Perhaps you might marry her?"

"How can I? I would have to go away from here."

"You could easily find a better living somewhere else. Rosario?"

Doctor Plarr said, "This is my home too—or the nearest I have ever come to a home since I left Paraguay."

"And you feel your father not so far away?"

"You *are* a perceptive man, Saavedra. Yes, it may have been my father's nearness which brought me here. In the *barrio* of the poor I am aware of doing something he would have liked to see me do, but when I am with my rich patients, I feel as though I had left his friends to help his enemies. I even sleep with them sometimes, and when I wake up I look at the face on the pillow through his eyes. I suppose that's one reason why my affairs never last long, and when I have tea with my mother in the Calle Florida among all the other ladies of B.A. . . . he sits there too and criticizes me with his blue English eyes. I think my father might have cared for Clara. She is one of his poor."

"Do you love the girl?"

"Love, love, I wish I knew what you and all the others mean by the word. I want her, yes. From time to time. Sexual desire has its rhythms as you well know." He added, "She has lasted longer than I thought possible. Teresa was your one-legged girl from Salta. Perhaps Clara is—my poor. But I never want her to be my victim. Was that what Charley Fortnum felt when he married her?"

Doctor Saavedra said, "I may not see you again. I have come to you for pills against melancholy, but at least I have my work. I wonder whether you do not need those pills more than I do."

Doctor Plarr looked at him without understanding. His thoughts were elsewhere.

When he got into the lift to his flat Doctor Plarr remembered the excitement with which Clara had made her first ascent in it. Perhaps, he thought, I will telephone to the Consulate and tell her to join me. The bed at the Consulate was too narrow for both of them, and, if he joined her there, he would be forced to leave before the hawklike woman came in the morning.

He let himself in and went first to his consulting room to see whether his secretary Ana had left a note on his desk, but there was nothing there. He drew the curtains and looked down on the port: three policemen were standing by the Coca-Cola stall, perhaps because the weekly boat to Asunción lay at the jetty. It was like the scene of his boyhood, but he looked at it in reverse from his fourth-floor window above the river.

He said, "God help you, father, wherever you are," speaking aloud. It was easier to believe in a god with a human sense of hearing than in some omniscient force which could read his unuttered thoughts. Strangely the face he conjured up when he spoke was not his father's but Charley Fortnum's. The Honorary Consul lay stretched out on the coffin and whispered, "Ted." Doctor Plarr's father had called him Eduardo as though in compliment to his wife. When he tried to substitute Henry Plarr's face for Charley Fortnum's he found his father's features had been almost eliminated by the years. As with an ancient coin that has been buried a long time in the ground he could only distinguish a faint unevenness of surface which might once have been the outline of a cheek or a lip. It was Charley Fortnum's voice which appealed to him again, "Ted."

He turned away—hadn't he done all in his power to help?—and opened the bedroom door. He saw by the light from the study the body of Fortnum's wife outlined under the sheets. "Clara!" he said. She woke immediately and sat up. He noticed her clothes had been folded carefully on a chair, for she possessed the neatness of her former profession. For a woman who has to take off her clothes many times in a night it is essential to arrange them carefully or a dress would be hopelessly crumpled after two or three clients. She had told him once that Señora Sanchez insisted on each girl paying for her own laundry—it made for tidyness.

"How did you get in?"

"I asked the porter."

"He opened the door for you?"

"He knows me."

"He has seen you here?"

"Yes. And there too."

So I have shared her with the porter as well, he

thought. How many more of the unknown warriors of her battlefield would take form sooner or later? Nothing was more alien to the life of the Calle Florida and the tinkle of teacups and the cakes of *dulce de leche,* white as snow. He had shared Margarita for a while with Señor Vallejo—most affairs overlap at the beginning or the end—and he preferred the porter to Señor Vallejo, the smell of whose shaving lotion during those last dilatory months he had sometimes detected on Margarita's skin.

"I told him you would give him money. You will?"

"Of course. How much? Five hundred pesos?"

"A thousand would be better."

He sat on the edge of the bed and pulled the sheet back. He was not yet tired of her thin body and the small breasts which barely yet, any more than her belly, indicated pregnancy. He said, "I am very glad you are here. I was going to call you up, though it wouldn't have been very wise. The police think I had something to do with the kidnapping. They suspect my motive may be jealousy," he added, smiling at the idea of it.

"They would not dare do anything to you. You look after the finance secretary's wife."

"They might start watching me all the same."

"What would that matter? They watch me."

"Did they follow you here?"

"Oh, I know how to deal with men like that. It is not the police I worry about, but that swine of a journalist. He was back at the camp just after it got dark. He offered me money."

"What for? A story?"

"He wanted to sleep with me."

"What did you say?"

"I told him I did not need his money any more, and then he got angry. He really believed I liked him for himself when I was with Señora Sanchez. He thought he was a great lover. Oh, how I hurt his pride," she went on with pleasure, "when I told him that Charley was twice the man he was."

"How did you get rid of him?"

"I called the policeman (they have left one at the camp—they say he is there to protect me, but he watches me all the time), and while the two of them were arguing I drove away."

"But you don't know how to drive, Clara."

"I watched Charley often enough. It is not so difficult. I knew the things to push and the things to pull. I got them mixed up at first, but all was right in the end. It went in jerks as far as the road, and then I found how to do things properly and I drove faster than Charley."

"Poor Fortnum's Pride," Plarr said.

"I think I drove a little too fast because I did not see the *camión* coming."

"What happened?"

"There was an accident."

"Were you hurt?"

"The jeep was hurt but not me."

Her eyes gleamed up at him from the pillows; they were bright with the excitement of strange events. Never before had he known her to talk so much. She had for him still the attraction of a stranger—like some unknown girl at a cocktail party. He said, "I like you," lightly, without thought, as he might have said it over the cocktails, neither of them believing the words meant any more than "Come and sleep with me."

"The driver gave me a lift," she said. "Of course he wanted to make love, and I said I would when we got to the town at a house he goes to in San José, but I got out at the first traffic lights, before he could stop me, and I went to Señora Sanchez. Oh, she was glad to see me I can tell you, really glad, not angry with me at all, and she put on a bandage herself."

"Then you *were* hurt?"

"I told her I knew a good doctor," she said and smiled and pulled the sheet off to show the bandage round her left knee.

"Clara, I must take it off and see . . ."

"Oh, it can wait," she said. "You love me a little?" She corrected herself quickly, "Do you want to make love to me?"

"Plenty of time for that. Lie still and let me take the bandage off."

He tried to be as gentle as possible, but he knew he must be hurting her. She lay quiet without complaint, and he thought of some of his bourgeois patients who would have persuaded themselves that the pain was unbearable; they might even have fainted from fear or to win his attention. "Good peasant stock," he said with admiration.

"What do you mean?"

"You are a brave girl."

"But that cut is nothing. You should see what men do to themselves in the fields when they cut cane. I have seen a boy with half his foot cut off." She asked casually, as though she were making polite conversation about a relative whom they had in common, "Is there any news yet of Charley?"

"No."

"Do you still think he may be alive?"

"I am pretty sure of it," he said.

"Then you *have* had news?"

"I have talked to Colonel Perez again. And I have been to Buenos Aires today to see the Ambassador."

"But what shall we do if he comes back?"

"Do? I suppose what we are doing now. What else?" He finished retying the bandage. "We shall go on just as we always did. I shall come to see you at the camp, and Charley will go farming." It was as though he were describing some life which had been pleasant enough once, but in which he no longer quite believed.

"It was good seeing the girls again at Señora Sanchez'. I told them I had a lover. Of course I did not tell them who."

"I'm surprised they didn't know. Everybody in this town seems to know except poor Charley."

"Why do you call him poor Charley? He was happy. I always did what he wanted me to do."

"What did he want?"

"Not very much. Not very often. It was boring, Eduardo. I have not the words to tell you how boring it was. He was kind and careful of me. He never hurt me like you hurt me. Sometimes I say thank you to Our Lord and Our Blessed Lady that it is your child which is stuck in me here, not his. What sort of child would have come out if it had belonged to Charley? The child of an old man. I would have wanted to strangle it at birth."

"Charley would make a better father than I could ever be."

"He cannot do one thing better than you can."

Oh yes, he can, Doctor Plarr thought, he can die better, and that is quite something.

She put out a hand and touched him on the cheek —he could feel the nerves through her fingertips. She had never caressed him like that before. A face was part of the forbidden territory of tenderness, and the purity of the gesture shocked him as much as though a young girl had touched his sex. He withdrew quickly. She said, "Do you remember that time at the camp when I told you I was pretending? But, *caro,* I was not pretending. Now when you make love to me I pretend. I pretend I feel nothing. I bite my lip so as to pretend. Is it because I love you, Eduardo? Do you think I love you?" She added with a humility which put him on his guard as much as a demand, "I am sorry. I did not really mean that . . . It makes no difference, does it?"

No difference? How could he begin to explain to her the vast extent of the difference? "Love" was a claim which he wouldn't meet, a responsibility he would refuse to accept, a demand . . . So many times his mother had used the word when he was a child; it was like the threat of an armed robber, "Put up your hands or else . . ." Something was always asked in return: obedience, an apology, a kiss which one had no desire to give. Perhaps he had loved his father all the more because he had never used the word or asked for anything. He could remember only a single kiss on the quay at Asunción and that was the kind of kiss one man can give to another. It was like the formal kiss he had seen French generals give in photographs after they have presented a decoration. It claimed nothing. His father would sometimes pull at his hair or tap him on his cheek. The English phrase "Old fellow" was the nearest that he ever came to an endearment. He remembered his mother, as she wept in the cabin while the ship pulled into the current, telling him, "I have only you to love me now"; she had reached at him from her bunk, repeating "Darling, my darling boy," as Margarita had reached at him years later from her bed, before Señor Vallejo had come to take his place, and he remembered how Margarita had called him "the love of my life" as his mother had sometimes called him "My only boy." He felt no belief at all in sexual love, but lying awake in the overcrowded flat in Buenos Aires he had sometimes recalled, as his mother's footsteps creaked toward the privy, the illicit nocturnal sounds which he had heard on the *estancia* in Paraguay —the tiny reverberations of a muffled knock, strange tiptoes on the floor below, whispers from the cellar, a gunshot which rang out an urgent warning from far away across the fields—those had been the signals of a genuine tenderness, a compassion deep enough for

his father to be prepared to die for it. Was that love?
Did León feel love? Even Aquino?

"Eduardo," he came back from far away to hear her
imploring him, "I will say anything you want. I did
not mean to make you angry. What do you want,
Eduardo? Tell me. Please. What do you want? I want
to know what you want, but how can I know if I do
not understand?"

"Charley is simpler, isn't he?"

"Eduardo, will you always be angry if I love you?
I swear it won't make any difference. I will stay with
Charley. I will come only when you want me just like
at the house."

He was startled by the doorbell which rang and
stopped and rang again. He hesitated to go. Why
hesitate? Hardly a week passed without a telephone
call or a ring at the door during the night. "Lie quiet,"
he said, "it is only a patient." He went into the hall
and looked through the spyhole in the door, but no
one was visible in the darkness of the stairhead. He felt
he was back in the Paraguay of his childhood. How
often his father must have called out before a bolted
door as he called now, "Who is it?" trying to make the
intonation sound firm.

"The police."

He unlocked the door and found himself face to face
with Colonel Perez. "May I come in?"

"When you say 'Police' how can I refuse?" Doctor
Plarr asked. "If you had said 'Perez' I might have told
you, since you are a friend, to call tomorrow morning,
at a better time."

"It was because we are good friends that I said
'Police' to warn you this is an official call."

"Too official for a drink?"

"No, it has not reached that point yet."

Doctor Plarr led Colonel Perez to his consulting
room and brought out two whiskies of the Argentinian

mark. He said, "I keep the little genuine Scotch I have for social visits."

"Yes, I understand. And your meeting with Doctor Saavedra tonight, that I suppose was purely social?"

"Are you having me watched?"

"Not until now. Perhaps I ought to have done so earlier. Someone on *El Litoral* told me of your telephone call tonight, and of course the cables you left at the hotel interested me when they showed them to me. There is no such thing in this city as an Anglo-Argentinian Club, is there?"

"No. Did the cables go off?"

"Why not? There was no harm in them. But then there was the lie you told me yesterday . . . You seem to be very mixed up in this affair, doctor."

"You are right of course, if you mean I'm doing my best to have Fortnum released, but surely both of us are working for that."

"There is quite a difference, doctor. I am not really interested in Fortnum, only in his kidnappers. I would prefer the blackmail to be unsuccessful, because it would discourage others. You on the other hand want the blackmail to succeed. Of course—it is only natural —I would like to win the game both ways, to save Señor Fortnum. Are you alone here?"

"Yes. Why?"

"I was looking out of the window and I thought I saw a light go off in the next room."

"It was a car passing by the river road."

"Yes. Perhaps." He drank his whisky slowly. Doctor Plarr had an odd impression that he was at a loss for words. "Do you really believe, doctor, these men can get your father released?"

"Well, prisoners have been released by the same method."

"Not in return for a mere Honorary Consul."

"Even an Honorary Consul is human—he has the

right to live. The British Government would not want him murdered."

"It does not depend on the British Government, it depends on the General, and I doubt if the General worries much about any human life. Except his own, of course."

"He depends on American aid. If they insist . . ."

"Yes, but he already gives the Yankees something in return which they value a great deal more than an English Honorary Consul. The General has one great quality, like Papa Doc used to have in Haiti. He is anti-communist. Are you quite sure you are alone, doctor?"

"Of course."

"It was only . . . I thought I heard . . . well, never mind. Are *you* a communist, doctor?"

"No. I have always found Marx unreadable. Like most economics. But you really believe these kidnappers are communist? It is not only communists who are against tyranny and torture."

"Some of the men they want released are communist—or so the General claims."

"My father is not."

"Then you do really believe he is still alive?"

The telephone rang out at Doctor Plarr's elbow. He lifted the receiver unwillingly. A voice which he recognized as León's said, "Something has happened. We need you urgently. We have been trying all day . . ."

"It is so very urgent? I have a friend drinking with me."

"Are you under arrest?" the voice whispered up the line.

"Not for the moment."

Colonel Perez leaned forward, watching him, trying to hear.

"It is too late to telephone me. Yes, yes, I know. A little fear is quite natural under the circumstances, but the temperature of a child always runs high. Give her two more aspirin."

"I will call you again in fifteen minutes."

"I hope you will not find it necessary. Ring me up tomorrow morning but not too early. I have had a long day, I have been to Buenos Aires." He added with his eye on Colonel Perez, "I want to get to bed."

"In fifteen minutes," the voice of León repeated. Doctor Plarr put down the receiver.

"Who was that?" Perez asked. "Oh, forgive me, I get into the habit of asking questions. It is a police vice."

"Only a worried parent," Doctor Plarr said.

"I thought I heard a man's voice."

"Yes. The father. Men are always much more worried about their children than women. The mother is in Buenos Aires shopping. What were we talking about, colonel?"

"Your father. It is strange that these men included his name in their list. There are so many others who would be much more useful to them. Younger men. Your father must be quite an old man now. It almost looks as though they were paying for some help you could give them . . ." He finished his sentence with a vague gesture.

"What could I do for them?"

"All the publicity you are trying to arrange—it's useful to them. It is something they cannot do for themselves. They do not want to kill the man. His death would be a sort of defeat. And then—it occurred to me only today, I am a slow thinker—they knew what the papers never printed—the real program the Governor had made for the Ambassador's visit. It is funny how something so obvious escaped me for so long. They must have received information, confidential information."

"Perhaps. But not from me. I am not in the Governor's confidence."

"No, but Señor Fortnum knew and he might have told you. Or Señora Fortnum. It is not an unusual thing for a woman to mention to her lover when her husband is going to be away."

"You make me out a Don Juan with my patients, colonel. I might be afraid of a husband in England, but here the General Medical Council does not operate. I hope you have not been bothering Señora Fortnum?"

"I wanted to have a word with her, but she was not at the camp. This evening she visited the Sanchez house. Then she went to the Consulate, but she is not there now. I was a little anxious at first because Señor Fortnum's Land Rover was found by the road damaged —poor man, he has had two cars smashed in two days. I was glad to hear she had been with Señora Sanchez and that her injuries were only small ones. You have been attending a patient, doctor, I think? Your right sleeve is turned up."

Doctor Plarr pushed the telephone away from him. He was afraid it might speak to him again too soon. He said, "How observant you are, colonel. I did not trust Señora Sanchez as a doctor. Clara is with me here."

"And I was right too about your lies yesterday."

"An affair always involves a few lies."

"I am sorry to have interrupted you, doctor, but it was the lies which bothered me. After all we are old friends. We have even shared a few adventures in our time. Señora Escobar, for example."

"Yes, I remember. I told you I was leaving her and the coast was—nearly—clear. I never understood why in the end she preferred Vallejo to you."

"She did not trust my motives. The common fate of a policeman. You see Señor Escobar has a landing strip on his *estancia* in the Chaco. Probably whisky and cigarettes come out of Paraguay by that route."

"A public benefactor."

"Yes, of course I would never have interfered with him. I hope those aspirins work. You will not want to be interrupted again." Colonel Perez drained his whisky and stood up. "You have relieved my mind a great deal. Of course I understand now why you would want Señor Fortnum released. A husband is of great importance in a love affair. He is a way of escape when an affair begins to get boring. No one would wish to leave a woman quite alone. Well, we shall have to try and save Señor Fortnum for you—and capture his kidnappers too. They will know what to do with them on the other side of the river."

Doctor Plarr went with him to the door. "I am glad you are feeling happier about me."

"Secrets always smell bad to a policeman, even innocent secrets. We are trained, like a dog with cannabis, to scent them out. Take my advice, doctor, you have really done enough now, so please do not interfere any more. We have always been friendly, but if you meddle in this affair, you must look out for yourself. I will shoot first and send a wreath later."

"You sound a bit like Al Capone."

"Yes. Capone too supported order in his own way." He opened the door and hesitated for a moment on the dark landing, as though something important had slipped his memory. "There is one more thing I ought perhaps to have told you earlier. I *do* have news of your father. From the Chief of Police in Asunción. Naturally we checked with him all the names that the kidnappers put on their list. Your father was killed more than a year ago. He tried to escape with another man—a man called Aquino Ribera—but he was too old and too slow. He could not make it and he was abandoned. You see—it is no good thinking there is anything you can do to help him now. Goodnight, doctor. I am sorry to bring you bad news, but at any rate I leave you with a woman. A woman is the best comforter a man can have."

The telephone began to sound again, almost as soon as the door closed.

Doctor Plarr thought: León cheated me. He has been lying to me all along in order to get my help. I won't answer the telephone. Let them get out of their own mess in their own way. Not for a moment did it occur to him that it might be Colonel Perez who had lied. The police were strong enough to speak the truth.

The bell rang and rang as he stood stubbornly in the hall, and then whoever was calling him gave it up. For all he knew this time it might have been one of his patients, and in the accusing silence he began to feel guilt for his egoism: it was like the silence after a suicide's cry for help. There was silence in the bedroom too. From Clara a little while ago had come an appeal. He had walked away from that too.

The small patch of marble floor on which he stood seemed like the edge of an abyss; he could not move one step in either direction without falling deeper into the darkness of involvement or guilt. He stood and listened to the silence—in the flat where Clara lay, in the midnight street outside where a police car would now be moving home, in the *barrio popular* where something must have happened among the huts of mud and tin. Silence, like a thin rain, blew across the great river into the world-abandoned republic where his father was lying dead in the deepest silence of all— "He was too old and slow. He couldn't make it and they abandoned him." He felt giddy on his ledge of marble parquet. He couldn't stand motionless for ever. Again the telephone rang and he moved back into his office.

León's voice spoke. "What has happened?"

"I had a visitor."

"The police?"

"Yes."

"You are alone now?"

"Yes. Alone."

"Where have you been all day?"

"In Buenos Aires."

"But we tried to get you last night."

"I was called out."

"And this morning at six."

"I couldn't sleep. I took a walk by the river. You said you wouldn't need me any more."

"Your patient needs you now. Go down to the river and stand near the Coca-Cola stall. We can see if anyone is watching. If the road is clear we will pick you up."

"I have just had news of my father. From Colonel Perez. Is it true?"

"What news?"

"That he made a break, but he was too slow, and you abandoned him."

He thought: if I detect one lie over the telephone—even a hesitation—I will put the receiver down, and I will never answer again.

León said, "Yes. I am sorry. It is true. I could not tell you before. We needed your help."

"And my father is dead?"

"Yes. They shot him at once. As he lay on the ground."

"You could have told me."

"Perhaps, but we could not take the risk."

León's voice reached him as though across an immeasurable distance, "Will you come?"

"Oh yes," Doctor Plarr said, "I'll come." He put down the receiver and went into the bedroom. He turned on the light and saw Clara, her eyes wide open, watching him.

"Who was it came?"

"Colonel Perez."

"Are you in trouble?"

"Not from him."

"And the telephone?"

"A patient. I have to go out for a while, Clara."

He remembered there was some question which had been left hanging unanswered between them, but he couldn't remember now what it was. He said, "My father is dead."

"Oh, Eduardo. I am sorry. Did you love him?" She couldn't take love for granted any more than he could, even between a father and son.

"Perhaps I did."

He had once known a man in Buenos Aires who was illegitimate. The man's mother died without telling him the name of his father. He searched through his mother's letters, he asked questions of her friends. He even examined bank records—his mother had an income which must have come from somewhere. He was not angry, nor shocked, but the desire to know who his father was vexed him like an itch. He explained to Doctor Plarr, "It is like one of those little picture puzzles with quicksilver. I cannot get the eyes in the right place, and yet I cannot put the puzzle down." Then one day he learned his father's name: that of an international banker who had been dead a long time. He said to Plarr, "You cannot imagine how empty I feel now. What is there left to interest me?" It is that kind of emptiness, Doctor Plarr thought, which I am experiencing now.

"Come and lie down, Eduardo."

"No. I must go out."

"Where?"

"I am not sure. It is something to do with Charley."

"Have they found his body?" she asked.

"No, no, nothing like that." She had half thrown the

sheet off and he tucked it around her. He said, "You will catch cold from the air-conditioner."

"I will go back to the Consulate."

"No, stay here. I shall not be very long."

In solitude, one welcomes any living thing—a mouse, a bird on the sill, Robert Bruce's spider. In complete loneliness even a certain tenderness can be born. He said, "I am sorry, Clara. When I come back—" but he could not think of anything which was really worthwhile to promise her. He put his hand over her stomach and said, "Look after it. Sleep well." He turned the light out so that he could no longer see her eyes watching him—puzzled, as though his actions were too complicated for any girl from the establishment of Señora Sanchez to understand. On the stairs (the lift might have been heard by his neighbors) he tried to remember what that question of hers had been which he had never answered. It could not have been very important. The only questions of importance were those which a man asked himself.

PART
FIVE

1

Doctor Plarr came back from the inner room and said to Father Rivas, "He will do well enough. Your man couldn't have aimed better if he had intended it. He hit the Achilles tendon. Of course, it will take time to mend. If you give him time. What happened?"

"He tried to escape. Aquino fired at the ground first and then at his legs."

"It would be better if he could be taken to hospital."

"You know that is impossible."

"All I can do is to strap him up. His ankle ought to be put in plaster. Why don't you give up the whole affair, León? I can keep him in my car for three or four hours to give you the time to disappear, and I'll tell the police I found him by the road."

Father Rivas did not trouble to reply. Doctor Plarr said, "It is always the same when one thing goes wrong —it is like an error in an equation . . . Your first error was mistaking him for the Ambassador and now this follows. Your equation will never work out."

"You may be right, but unless we receive orders from El Tigre . . ."

"Get your orders then."

"Impossible. After we announced the kidnapping all contact was broken. We are on our own here. In that way if we are captured, we cannot talk."

"I have to go. I must get some sleep."

"You will stay here with us," Father Rivas said.

"That's not possible. If I'm seen leaving in daylight . . ."

"If your telephone is tapped they will know you are

206

an accomplice of ours already. If you go back they may arrest you and your friend Fortnum will be left without a doctor."

"I have other patients to consider, León."

"But *they* can find other doctors."

"If you get your way . . . or you kill him . . . what happens to me?"

Father Rivas indicated the Negro called Pablo in the doorway. "You were abducted and kept here by force. It is the simple truth. We cannot allow you to leave now."

"Suppose I just walk through that door?"

"I will tell him to shoot. Be reasonable, Eduardo. How can we trust you not to lead the police here?"

"I'm no police informer, León, in spite of the trick you played on me."

"I wonder. A man's conscience is not a simple thing. I believe in your friendship. But how do I know you would not persuade yourself you had to return for the sake of your patient? The police would follow you, and your Hippocratic oath would condemn us all to die. And then there is that sense of guilt I think you feel. They say you sleep with Fortnum's wife. If it is true, trying to atone for that might demand all our deaths."

"I am not a Christian any longer, León. I don't think in those terms. I have no conscience. I am a simple man."

"I have never met a simple man. Not even in the confessional, though I used to sit there for hours on end. Man was not created simple. When I was a young priest, I used to try to unravel what motives a man or woman had, what temptations and self-delusions. But I soon learned to give all that up, because there was never a straight answer. No one was simple enough for me to understand. In the end I would just say, 'Three Our Fathers, Three Hail Marys. Go in peace.' "

Doctor Plarr moved impatiently away. He looked once again at his patient. Charley Fortnum was sleeping quietly enough—a drugged contented sleep. They had collected some extra blankets from somewhere to make the coffin bed more comfortable. Doctor Plarr came back into the outer room and stretched on the floor. It seemed to him he had passed a very long day. It was difficult to believe he had taken tea only the afternoon before at the Richmond in the Calle Florida and watched his mother eat her éclairs.

The image of his mother remained with him when he fell asleep and she talked to him in her usual vein of complaint, telling him how his father would not rest like a respectable man of property in the interior of his coffin. They had constantly to shuffle him back inside, and that was no way for a *caballero* to enjoy his eternal peace. Father Galvão was on the way from Rio de Janeiro to see what he could do to persuade him to rest tranquil.

Doctor Plarr opened his eyes. The Indian Miguel lay asleep on the floor beside him, and Father Rivas had taken Pablo's place in the doorway with a gun across his lap. A candle stuck in a saucer cast a shadow of his ears on the wall behind. Doctor Plarr was reminded of the dogs his father would make for him on the nursery wall. For a while he lay awake looking at his old schoolmate. León, León dog ears, Father dog ears. He remembered León saying, in one of those long serious conversations which they used to have at fourteen, that there existed only half a dozen careers worth a man's while to follow: a man should be a doctor, a priest, a lawyer (always, of course, on the right side), a poet (if he wrote well enough), or a manual worker. He couldn't remember now what the sixth career was, but it certainly wasn't a kidnapper's or an assassin's.

He whispered across the floor, "Where are Aquino and the others?"

"This is a military operation," León said. "We have been trained by El Tigre. We set our outposts, and we keep our watches at night."

"And your wife?"

"She is in the town with Pablo. This hut belongs to him, and he is known there. It is safer that way. You need not whisper. An Indian falls asleep, at any moment, whenever he is not required. The only sound which can wake him is hearing his name—or a noise that may be dangerous. Look at him, lying quietly there while we talk. I envy him. That is real peace. Sleep is meant to be like that for all of us, but we have lost the animal touch."

"Tell me about my father, León. I want the truth." He had no sooner said it than he remembered how Doctor Humphries always demanded the real truth, even from the Neapolitan waiter, and got only a dusty answer.

"Your father and Aquino were in the same police station a hundred kilometers southeast of Asunción. Near Villarica. He had been there fifteen years, and Aquino only ten months. We did our best, but he was old and sick. El Tigre was against our trying to save your father, but we outvoted him. We were wrong. Perhaps your father would be alive now if we had listened to El Tigre."

"Yes. Perhaps. In a police station. Dying slowly."

"It was a question of seconds. A quick dash. He could have done it easily in the days when you knew him, but fifteen years in a police station—you decay there more quickly than in a prison. The General knows there is comradeship in a prison. And so he plants his victims out in separate pots with insufficient earth, and they wither with despair."

"Did you see my father?"

"No, I was sitting in the escape car with a grenade ready in my lap. Praying."

"Do you still believe in prayer?"

Father Rivas made no reply and Doctor Plarr fell asleep.

It was daylight when he woke and he went at once into the inner room to look at his patient. Charley Fortnum watched him come in. "So you really *are* one of them," he said.

"Yes."

"I don't understand you, Ted. What has all this got to do with you?"

"I've told you often about my father. I thought these men might help him."

"You were my friend—and Clara's."

"I'm not responsible for their mistake. How does your ankle feel?"

"I've suffered much worse from toothache. You've got to get me out of here, Ted. For Clara's sake."

Doctor Plarr told Fortnum of his visit to the Ambassador. He realized, as he spoke, that it was an encouraging story. Charley Fortnum took the details slowly in. "You really got to the old man himself?"

"Yes. He's doing his best."

"Oh, they'll be relieved in B.A. when I'm dead. I know that well enough. They won't have to sack me then. An ungentlemanly act. They are all such bloody gentlemen there."

"Colonel Perez too is doing all he can. It won't be long before they find this place."

"It will come to the same thing if they do. Do you suppose these fellows will ever let me get out of here alive? Have you spoken to Clara?"

"Yes. She's all right."

"And the baby?"

"Nothing to worry about."

"I tried to write her a letter yesterday. I wanted her to have something she could look at afterward, though I doubt if she would be able to make much out of it.

She still finds reading pretty difficult. I thought that somebody might read it aloud to her—perhaps you, Ted. Of course that meant I couldn't say all I felt for her, but I thought if the worst happens you would let her know."

"Know what?"

"How I feel. I know you are a cold fish, Ted. I've often called you that. I sound sentimental to you, but I've come to think about a lot of things lying here—I've had the hell of a time to fill in. It seems to me that all the prime of life—well, they were pretty empty years, without any purpose, just growing that bloody weed maté to earn some cash—cash for what, for who? I wanted someone I could do something for—not just make a living for myself. There are people who fall back on cats and dogs, but I never cared much for them. Nor horses either. Horses! I could never stand the bloody brutes. All I had to fall back on was Fortnum's Pride. I used to pretend to myself she was alive. I'd give her gas and oil and listen to her innards, but I know she was less real than one of those dolls which make wee-wee. Of course there was my wife for a while, only she was always so damned superior—there wasn't anything I could ever do for her which she couldn't do better for herself. I'm sorry. I'm talking too much, but you seem closer to me than anyone else because you've met Clara."

"Talk all you want. There's nothing else we can do in the situation we are in. I'm as much a prisoner here as you are."

"They won't let you go?"

"No."

"Then Clara—she's got no one?"

Doctor Plarr said with irritation, "She can look after herself for a day or two. It's a lot easier for her than for you or me."

"They won't kill *you*."

"No, they won't kill me if they can help it."

"You know there was a time before I met Clara when I thought I'd found somebody I could love. She was a girl at Mother Sanchez' too. She was called María, but she was bad, that one."

"Somebody knifed her."

"Yes. Fancy you knowing. Well, it was a little while after that when I saw Clara. I don't know why I hadn't noticed her before. I'm not a good judge of women, I suppose, and María—well, she sort of dazzled me. Clara wasn't beautiful in that way, but she was honest. I could trust her. To make someone like Clara happy is a kind of success, isn't it?"

"A modest sort of success."

"Yes, *you* can say that, but I'm used to failing, and I can't set my sights very high. If things had gone better, who knows . . . I quit drinking for nearly a week when they made me an Honorary Consul, but of course that didn't last. I've still got the letter they sent me from the Embassy. I'd like you to give it to Clara if I don't get out of here. It's in the top left-hand drawer of my desk in the Consulate. You can pick it out easily because of the Royal Arms on the flap. She can keep it to show the child one day." He tried to shift his position on the coffin and winced.

"Did that hurt?"

"Only a stab." He gave a low laugh. "When I think of my wife and Clara—my God, how different two women can be. My wife told me once she'd married me out of pity. Pity for what? She was like a man in the house—knew every damn thing about electricity. She could even fix a washer on a tap. And if I ever had a little one over the right measure she had no sympathy at all. Of course it wasn't reasonable to expect much from her. She was a Christian Scientist and even cancer didn't exist in her eyes, though her father died of it, so you could hardly expect her to believe in a hangover. All the same she needn't have talked so bloody loud when I had one. Her voice went through my head like a drill. Now Clara—Clara's a real woman, she knows when to be silent, God bless her. I'd like to keep her happy till the end."

"That ought to be easy. She doesn't strike me as a difficult woman."

"No. But I suppose sooner or later a test always comes. Like those bloody examinations we used to have at school. I'm not exactly insured against failing."

They might have been talking, Doctor Plarr thought, about two different women—one was the woman whom Charley Fortnum loved—the other was a prostitute from Mother Sanchez' house who had waited in his bed the night before. She had asked him something. And then Colonel Perez had rung the bell. It was no use trying to remember now what it was she had asked him.

Toward the end of the morning Marta came back from the city with a copy of *El Litoral*—the Buenos Aires papers had not yet arrived. The editor had given headlines to Doctor Saavedra's offer—larger headlines, Doctor Plarr considered, than the story was likely to receive elsewhere. He waited to see León's reaction, but he made no comment when he passed the paper without a word to Aquino. Aquino said, "Who is this Saavedra?"

"A novelist."

"Why should he think we want a novelist in place of a Consul? What good is a novelist? Anyway he is an Argentinian. Who cares if an Argentinian dies? Not the General. Not even our own President. Nor the world either. One less of the underdeveloped to spend money on."

At one o'clock Father Rivas turned on the radio and got a news-bulletin from Buenos Aires. Doctor Saavedra's offer was not even mentioned. Was he listening, Doctor Plarr wondered, in that little room near the prison, listening to a silence which must seem to him more humiliating than a rejection? The kidnapping had already ceased to interest the Argentinian public. There were other more exciting events which clamored for attention. A man had killed the lover of his wife (in a fight with knives of course)—that was a story which never lost appeal to a Latin American; the usual flying saucers had been reported from the south, there had been an army *coup* in Bolivia, and there was a detailed account of the activities of the Argentina football team in Europe (someone had cut up the referee). At the close of the broadcast the announcer said: "There is still no news of the kidnapped British Consul. The time to fulfill the conditions set by the kidnappers expires on Sunday at midnight."

Someone tapped on the outer door. The Indian who was back on guard stood flattened against the wall with his gun held out of sight. There were all six of them in the room at the moment—Father Rivas, Diego, the driver of the car, the pockmarked Negro Pablo, Marta and Aquino. Two of them should have been on duty outside, but now in the broad daylight, when everything was quiet, León had allowed them to come in to listen to the news on the radio, a mistake which he was probably regretting. The knock came a second time, and Aquino turned off the radio.

"Pablo," Father Rivas said.

Unwillingly Pablo approached the door. He pulled a revolver from his pocket, but the priest told him sharply, "Put it back."

Doctor Plarr wondered with a sense of resignation, even of relief, whether this was going to be the climax of the whole absurd affair. Would there be a burst of firing when the door opened?

Father Rivas may have had the same thought, for

214

he moved to the center of the room as though, if this were indeed the end, he wanted to be the first one to die. Pablo pulled the door back.

An old man stood outside. He wavered in the speckled sunlight and stared silently at them with what seemed an unnatural curiosity, until Doctor Plarr realized he was blind from cataract. The old man felt the edge of the door with a hand paper-thin, veined like an old leaf.

"José, what are you doing here?" the Negro exclaimed.

"I came to find the Father."

"There is no Father here, José."

"Oh yes, there is, Pablo. I was sitting by the water tap yesterday and I heard someone say, 'The Father who lives with Pablo is a good Father.' "

"What do you want a Father for? Anyway, he has gone."

The old man moved his head from one side to the other as though he were listening with each ear in turn, distinguishing the different breaths that sounded in the room, heavy breaths and muted breaths, one of them hurried, another—Diego's—with an asthmatic whistle.

"My wife has died," he told them. "When I woke this morning and put my hand out to wake her she was cold as a wet stone. She was all right last night. She made my soup, and it was very good soup. She never told me she was going to die."

"You must get the priest of the *barrio,* José."

"He is not a good priest," the old man said. "He is the Archbishop's priest. You know that very well, Pablo."

"The Father who came here was only a visitor. A relation of my cousin in Rosario. He has gone away again."

"Who are all the people in the room, Pablo?"

"My friends. What do you suppose? We were listening to the radio when you came."

"My goodness, have you a radio, Pablo? How rich you have become all of a sudden."

"It is not mine. It belongs to a friend."

"What a rich friend you have. I need a coffin for my wife, Pablo, and I have no money."

"You know that will all be arranged, José. We in the *barrio* will see to that."

"Juan says you bought a coffin from him. You have no wife, Pablo. Let me have your coffin."

"I need the coffin for myself, José. The doctor has told me I am a very sick man. Juan will make you a coffin and all of us in the *barrio* will pay him."

"But there is the Mass. I want the Father to say the Mass. I do not want the Archbishop's priest." The old man took a step into the room, feeling toward them with his hands, palms up.

"There is no Father here. I told you. He has gone back to Rosario."

Pablo stood between the old man and Father Rivas as though he feared that even in his blindness he could pick a priest out.

"How did you find your way here, José?" Diego asked. "Your wife was the only eyes you had."

"Is that Diego? I can see well enough with my hands." He held them out, fingers pointed first at Diego, then at where the doctor stood, and afterward he turned them toward Father Rivas. They were like eyes on stalks, of some strange insect. He didn't even look at Pablo. Pablo he took for granted. It was the others, the strangers, whom his hands and ears sought. He gave the impression that he was numbering them like a prison warder, while they stood in silence for his inspection. "There are four strangers here, Pablo." He took a step toward Aquino and Aquino shuffled back.

"They are all friends of mine, José."

"I never knew what a lot of friends you have, Pablo. They are not of this *barrio*."

"No."

"They will be welcome all the same to come and see my wife."

"They will come later, but I must lead you home now, José."

"Let me hear the radio speak, Pablo. I have never heard a radio speak."

"Ted!" the voice of Charley Fortnum called from the next room, "Ted!"

"Who is that calling, Pablo?"

"A sick man."

"Ted! Where are you, Ted?"

"A gringo!" The old man added with awe, "I have never known a gringo in the *barrio* before. And a radio. You have become a big man, Pablo."

Aquino turned the sound of the radio full on to drown the voice of Charley Fortnum and a woman's voice spoke loudly of the outstanding merits of Kellogg's Rice Krispies. "Popping with life and vigor," the voice said. "Golden and Honey Sweet."

Doctor Plarr went quickly into the back room. He whispered, "What do you want, Charley?"

"I dreamed someone was in the room. He was going to cut my throat. I was damn scared. I wanted to be sure you were still here."

"Don't speak again. There's a stranger here. If you speak you will put all our lives in danger. I'll come back to you when he's gone."

In the other room, as he returned, a woman's tinned voice was saying, "She will love the scented smoothness of your cheek."

The old man said, "It is like a miracle. To think a box is able to say beautiful things like that."

Then someone began to sing a romantic ballad of love and death.

"Here, José, touch the radio. Hold it in your hands." They all felt easier when the old man's hands were occupied—not turning to look at them. He held the radio close to his ears as though he were afraid to miss a single one of the beautiful words it spoke.

Father Rivas took Pablo aside. He whispered, "I will go with him if you think it will do any good."

"No," Pablo said, "all the *barrio* will be gathered at his hut to see the body of his wife. They will know he has gone to fetch a priest. If the Archbishop's priest comes, he will want to know who you are. He will want to see your papers. He might send for the police."

Aquino said, "An accident should happen to the old one before he gets back."

"No," Pablo said, "I will not agree to that. I have known him since I was a child."

"Anyway," the driver Diego gave his opinion in a sullen voice, "to stop his mouth would be too late now. How did the woman at the water tap know a priest was here?"

Pablo said, "I have told no one."

"There are never any secrets for long in a *barrio*," Father Rivas said.

"He knows of the radio and the gringo," Diego said. "That is the worst of all. We ought to move from here quickly."

"You would have to carry Fortnum on a stretcher," Doctor Plarr said.

The old man shook the radio. He complained, "It does not rattle."

"Why should it rattle?" Pablo asked.

"There is a voice in it."

"Come, José," Pablo said, "it is time for you to go back to your poor wife."

"But the Father," José said, "I want the Father to anoint her."

"I tell you, José, there is no Father here. The Archbishop's priest will do that."

"He never comes when we send for him. He is always busy at a meeting. It will be many hours before he comes, and where will the soul of my poor wife be wandering all that while?"

Father Rivas said, "She will come to no harm, old man. God does not wait for the Archbishop's priest."

The man's hands turned quickly toward him. He said, "You—you there who spoke—you have a priest's voice."

"No, no, I am not a priest. If you had your sight you would see my wife is here beside me. Speak to him, Marta."

She said in a low voice, "Yes. This is my husband, old one."

Pablo said, "Come. I will take you home."

The old man clung obstinately to the radio. The music was loud, but not loud enough for him. He pressed it against his ear.

"He told us he came here alone," Diego whispered. "How could he? Suppose someone led him here on purpose and left him at the door . . ."

"He has been here twice before with his wife. The blind remember a path well. Anyway if I take him home I can tell if someone is waiting for him or watching."

"If you do not return in two hours," Aquino said, "if they stop you . . . then we shall kill the Consul. You can tell them that." He added, "If only I had aimed at his back yesterday, we would be far away by now."

"I have heard a radio," the old man said with astonishment. He laid it down gently like a fragile thing. "If only I could tell my wife . . ."

"She knows," Marta said, "she knows everything."

"Come, José." The Negro took the old man's right hand and pulled him toward the door, but he was stubborn. He twisted round, and with his free hand he seemed to be counting them over again. He said, "What a big party you have here, Pablo. Give me something to drink. Give me some *caña*."

"We have nothing to drink here, José." He pulled the blind man out and the Indian closed the door quickly behind them. For a moment they felt relief like a breath of wind cooling the thunder-heavy day.

"What do you think, León?" Doctor Plarr asked. "Was he a spy?"

"How can I tell?"

"I think you should have gone with the poor man, Father," Marta said. "His wife is dead and there is no priest to help him."

"If I had gone I would have endangered all of us."

"You heard what he said. The Archbishop's priest cares nothing for the poor."

"And do you think I care nothing for them? I am risking my life for them, Marta."

"I know that, Father. I was not accusing you. You are a good man."

"She has been dead for hours. What difference can a little oil make now? Ask the doctor."

"Oh, I deal only with the living," Doctor Plarr said.

The woman touched her husband's hand. "I did not want to offend you, Father. I am your woman."

"You are not my woman. You are my wife," Father Rivas said with angry impatience.

"If you say so."

"I have explained to you how it is over and over again."

"I am a stupid woman, Father. I do not always understand. Does it matter so much? A woman, a wife . . ."

"It does matter. Human dignity matters, Marta. A man who feels lust takes a woman for the period of his desire, but I have taken you for life. That is marriage."

"If you say so, Father."

Father Rivas said in a voice which sounded tired with having eternally to teach the same thing, "Not if I say so, Marta. It is the truth."

"Yes, Father. I would feel better if sometimes I could hear you pray . . ."

"Perhaps I pray more often than you know."

"Please do not be angry, Father. I am very proud that you chose me."

She turned on the others who were in the room. "He could have slept with any woman he liked in our *barrio* in Asunción. He is a good man. If he did not go back with the old one, he must have had a good reason. Only, please, Father . . ."

"I wish you would not call me Father all the time. I am your husband, Marta. Your husband."

"Yes, but I would be so proud if just once I could see you as you used to be . . . all dressed at the altar . . . turning to bless us, Father."

The word slipped out again; she put her hand to her mouth too late to stop it.

"You know I cannot do that."

"If I could see you like I saw you in Asunción . . . in white for Easter . . ."

"You will never see me again like that."

León Rivas turned away. "Aquino," he said, "Diego, go back to your posts. We will relieve you in two hours. You, Marta, go back to the town and see if the newspapers have come yet from Buenos Aires."

"You had better buy more whisky for Fortnum," Doctor Plarr said. "His sort of measure soon empties a bottle."

"This time," Father Rivas said, "no one is to share it."

"What are you hinting at?" Aquino asked.

"I am not hinting at anything. Do you think I could not smell your breath yesterday?"

At four it was Aquino who turned on the radio, but this time there was not a single reference to the kidnapping. It was as though they had been wiped off the world's memory. "They do not even mention *your* disappearance," Aquino said to Doctor Plarr.

"They may not know of it yet," Doctor Plarr said. "I am losing count of the days. Is it Thursday? I remember I gave my secretary a long weekend off. She will be busy somewhere gathering indulgences. For the souls in purgatory. I hope we shall not have the benefit of them."

An hour later Pablo returned. No one had shown any suspicion, but he had stayed away longer than he intended because he was bound to join the queue which was waiting to pay the last respects to the dead woman. When he left, the Archbishop's priest had still not arrived. The only anxiety he had felt was when José chatted to everyone about the radio. The old man was immensely proud because he was the only one there who had ever listened to a radio and he had actually held one in his hands. For the time being he seemed to have forgotten about the gringo.

"He will remember soon enough," Diego said. "We ought to get away from here."

Pablo said, "How can we go? With a wounded man."

"El Tigre would say 'Kill him now.' " Aquino argued.

"You had your chance," Diego said.

"Where is Father Rivas?" Pablo asked.

"On guard."

"There should be two of you out there."

"A man must have a drink. My maté was finished. It was Marta's job to bring more, but Father Rivas sent her into the town to buy whisky for the gringo. He must never be left thirsty."

"Aquino, you go."

"I take no orders from you, Pablo."

If this inaction goes on much longer, Doctor Plarr thought, they will be fighting each other.

It was evening by the time Marta returned. The papers from Buenos Aires had arrived and in the *Nación* a few lines were devoted to Doctor Saavedra, though the reporter found it necessary to remind his readers who Saavedra was. "The novelist," he wrote, "who is best known by his first book, *The Silent Heart*," getting the title wrong.

The evening seemed interminably drawn out. It was as though, sitting there for hours in silence, they formed part of a universal silence all around them, the silence of the radio, the silence of the authorities, even the silence of nature. No dogs barked. The birds had ceased to sing, and when rain began to fall it was in heavy spaced drops, as infrequent as their words— the silence seemed all the deeper between the drops. Somewhere far off there was a storm, but the storm was happening across the river in another country.

Whenever any of them spoke, the danger of a quarrel arose even over the most innocent remark. The Indian alone was unaffected. He sat and smiled with gentle content as he oiled his gun. He cleaned the crevices of the bolt with tenderness and with sensuous pleasure like a woman attending to her first baby. When Marta gave them soup, Aquino complained of a lack of salt, and Doctor Plarr thought for a moment she was going to throw a plate full of the despised soup in his face. He left them and went into the inner room.

Charley Fortnum said, "If only I had something to read . . ."

Doctor Plarr said, "There's not enough light to see by." Only one candle lit the room.

"Surely they could give me a few more candles."

"They don't want any light to show outside. Most people in this *barrio* sleep as soon as it's dark . . . or make love."

"Thank God there's still plenty of whisky. Have a glass. It's an odd relationship, isn't it? They shoot me down like a dog and then they give me whisky. This time I didn't even pay for it. Is there any news? When they put the radio on they turn it so damn low I can't hear a thing."

"There's no news at all. How are you feeling?"

"Pretty awful. Do you think I'll live to see the end of this bottle?"

"Of course."

"Then be an optimist and give yourself a bigger dose."

They drank together in the silence which they had only momentarily broken. Doctor Plarr wondered where Clara was. At the camp? at the Consulate? At last he said, "What made you marry Clara, Charley?"

"I told you—I wanted to help her."

"You needn't have married her to do that."

"If I hadn't she'd have lost a lot in taxes when I died. Besides I wanted a child. I love her, Ted. I want her to feel secure. I wish you knew her a bit better. A doctor sees only the outside—oh, and the inside too, I suppose, but you know what I mean. To me she's like . . . like . . ." He couldn't find the word he wanted and Doctor Plarr was tempted to supply it. She's like a looking glass, he thought, a looking glass which has been manufactured by Mother Sanchez to reflect any man who looks at her—to reflect Charley's fumbling tenderness with her own imitation of it and my . . . my . . . but the right word failed him too. It certainly wasn't "passion." What was the question she had asked him just before he left her? She reflected even one's suspicion of her. He was angry with her as though in some obscure way she had done him an injury. One could use her to shave in, he thought, remembering Gruber's sunglasses.

"You'll laugh at me," Charley Fortnum rambled on, "but she reminds me a bit of Mary Pickford in those old silent movies . . . I don't mean her face, of course, but, well, a sort of . . . I suppose you might call it innocence."

"Then I hope the child turns out to be a girl. A boy like Mary Pickford would hardly make his way in the world."

"I don't mind which it is, but Clara seems to want a boy." He added with self-mockery, "Perhaps she wants him to take after me."

Doctor Plarr had a savage desire to tell him the whole truth. It was only the wounded body which stopped him, stretched helplessly out on the coffin lid. To disturb a patient would be unprofessional. Charley Fortnum raised his glass of whisky and added, "Not as I am now, of course. Cheers."

Doctor Plarr heard the voices rise higher in the next room.

"What's happening out there?" Charley Fortnum asked.

"They are quarreling among themselves."

"What about?"

"Probably about you."

2

Just after nine o'clock on Friday morning a helicopter came flying low down over the *barrio*. It went back and forth in regular lines, like a pencil along a ruler, up and down every muddy track, just above the trees, tireless and probing. Doctor Plarr was reminded of the way his own fingers had to make tracks sometimes along a patient's body, seeking the exact spot of pain.

Father Rivas told Pablo to join Diego and Marta who were on guard outside. "The whole *barrio* will be watching," he said. "They will notice if in this one hut people show indifference." He told Aquino to keep watch on Fortnum in the inner room. Though there was no possible way for Fortnum to signal his presence there, Father Rivas was taking no chances.

Doctor Plarr and the priest sat in silence and watched the roof of the room as though the machine at any moment might come crashing through on top of them. After the helicopter had passed, they could hear the rustle of the leaves falling like rain. When that sound ceased they stayed dumb, waiting for the chopper to return.

Pablo and Diego came in. Pablo reported, "They were taking photographs."

"Of this hut?"

"Of the whole *barrio*."

"Then they have seen your car," Doctor Plarr said. "They will wonder what a car is doing here."

"We have it well hidden," Father Rivas said. "We can only hope . . ."

226

"They were making a very careful search," Pablo told them.

"It would be better to shoot Fortnum now," Diego said.

"Our ultimatum does not expire till Sunday midnight."

"They have rejected it already. The helicopter shows that."

Doctor Plarr said, "Extend your ultimatum a few days. You have to give time for my publicity to work. You are in no immediate danger. The police dare not attack you."

"El Tigre set the time limit," Father Rivas said.

"You *must* have some way of communicating with him, whatever you say."

"We have none."

"You sent news of the Fortnum capture."

"That line was cut immediately."

"Then act yourself. Have someone telephone *El Litoral*. Give them another week."

"Another week for the police to find us," Diego said.

"Perez dare not search too closely. He does not want to find a dead man."

The chopper became audible again. They heard it from a long way off, hardly louder than a man humming. The first time it had traveled from east to west. Now it tracked above the trees going from north to south and back again. Pablo and Diego returned into the yard, and their long wait was resumed to the sound of the dropping leaves. At last silence came back.

The two men returned. "They must have taken a picture of every path and hut in the *barrio*."

"More than the city council ever did," the Negro said. "Perhaps after this they will realize we need more water taps."

Father Rivas called Marta in from the yard and whispered instructions to her. Doctor Plarr tried to hear what he was saying, but he could hear nothing until the voices rose.

"No," Marta said, "no, I will not leave you, Father."

"Those are my orders."

"Did you tell me I was your wife or your woman?"

"Of course you are my wife."

"Oh yes, you say that, it's easy to say that, yet you treat me like your woman. You say 'Go away' because you have finished with me. I know very well now I am only your woman. No priest would marry us. They all refused you. Even your friend, Father Antonio."

"I have explained a dozen times to you a priest is not necessary for a marriage. A priest is only a witness. People marry each other. Our vow is all that counts. Our intention."

"How can *I* tell what your intention was? Perhaps you just wanted a woman to sleep with. Perhaps I am your whore. You treat me like a whore when you tell me to go away and leave you."

Father Rivas raised his hand as though he wanted to strike her and then he turned away.

"If I am not your sin, Father, why is it you will not say Mass for us? We are all in danger of death, Father. We need a Mass. And that poor woman in the *barrio* who died . . . Even the gringo in there . . . He needs your prayers too."

The old schoolboy desire to mock at León came back to Doctor Plarr. "It's a pity you ever left the Church," he said. "You see—they are losing confidence in you."

Father Rivas looked up at him with the inflamed eyes of a dog who defends a bone. "I never told you I had left the Church. How can I leave the Church? The Church is the world. The Church is this *barrio*, this room. There is only one way any of us can leave the Church and that is to die." He made the gesture of a man who is tired of useless discussion. "Not even then, if what we sometimes believe is true."

"She only asked you to pray. Have you forgotten how to pray? I certainly have. I can never get further than Hail Mary, and then.I mix the words up with an English nursery rhyme, 'Mary, Mary, quite contrary.' "

Father Rivas said, "I never knew how to pray."

"What are you saying, Father? He does not know what he is saying," Marta told them, as though she were defending a child who had used some foul expression, picked up in the street.

"A prayer for the sick. A prayer for rain. Do you want those? Oh, I know all those by heart, but those are not prayers. Call them petitions if you want to give that mumbo-jumbo a name. You might just as well write them down in a letter and get your neighbors to sign it too and stick it in a postbox addressed to the Lord Almighty. Nobody will ever deliver your letter. Nobody will ever read it. Oh, of course, now and then there may be a coincidence. For once a doctor will give the right medicine and a child recovers. Or a storm comes when you want it. Or the wind changes."

"All the same," Aquino told them from the doorway of the other room, "I used to pray in the police station. I prayed I would have a girl in bed with me again. You are not going to tell me that was not a real prayer. And it worked too. The first day I was out I had a girl. It was in a field while you were off buying food in a village. My prayer was answered, Father. Even if it was in a field and not in a bed."

Like me, Doctor Plarr thought, he is a picador. He pricks the bull's hide to make the beast more active before he dies. The repetitions of the word "Father" were like darts inserted to pierce the skin. Why do we so want to destroy him—or are we hoping to destroy ourselves?—it's a cruel sport.

"What are you doing out here, Aquino? I told you to stay and watch the prisoner."

"The helicopter has gone. What can he do? He is only writing a letter to his woman."

"You gave him a pen? I took away his pen myself when he was brought in."

"What harm can a letter do?"

"They were my orders. If you all start disobeying orders there is no safety for any of us. Diego, Pablo, get outside again. If El Tigre were here . . ."

"But he is not here, Father," Aquino said. "He is somewhere in safety eating well and drinking well. He was not at the police station either when you rescued me. Is he never going to risk his own life like he risks ours?"

Father Rivas pushed him to one side and went on into the inner room. Doctor Plarr found it hard to recognize the boy who had explained the Trinity to him. In the innumerable lines of premature age which criss-crossed the face he thought he could detect a tangle of agonies, like a tangle of fighting snakes.

Charley Fortnum was propped on his left elbow. His bandaged leg stuck out over the side of the coffin, and he wrote slowly, painfully; he didn't look up. Father Rivas said, "Whom are you writing to?"

"My wife."

"It must be difficult to write like that."

"It's taken me a quarter of an hour to do two sentences. I asked your man Aquino to write for me. But he refused. He's been angry with me ever since he shot me. He won't talk to me any more. Why? You would think I'd done him an injury."

"Perhaps you have."

"What injury?"

"Perhaps he feels betrayed. He did not believe you had the courage to trick him."

"Courage? Me? I haven't the courage of a mouse, Father. I wanted to see my wife again, that's all."

"Who is going to give her this letter?"

"Doctor Plarr, perhaps. If you let him go after I am dead. He can read it aloud to her. She doesn't read very well and my handwriting is bad at the best of times."

"If you like I will write the letter for you."

"Thank you a lot. I'd be grateful if you would. I'd rather it was you than anyone else. A letter like this is a sort of secret. Like a confession. And after all you *are* a priest."

Father Rivas took the letter and sat down on the floor beside the coffin.

"I've forgotten what I wrote last."

Father Rivas read, " 'Do not worry, my darling, about being alone with a child. It is better for him to be alone with a mother than with a father. I know that well. I was left alone with my father and it was never any fun. Always horses, horses . . .' That is all. You have written nothing after 'horses.' "

"In the situation I'm in," Charley Fortnum said, "I suppose you think I ought to find some way to forgive. Even my father. Perhaps he wasn't such a bad chap after all. Children hate too easily. Better leave out that stuff about the horses, Father."

Father Rivas drew a line through the words.

"Put instead—but what? I'm damned unused to writing anything personal, that's the trouble. Give me a drop of whisky, Father. It may help the brain to tick, what there is left of it—my brain, I mean."

Father Rivas poured him out a drink.

"I prefer Long John," Charley Fortnum said, "but this stuff you've brought me is not all that bad. If I stay here long enough I'll get quite a taste for Argentinian whisky, but it's more tricky than real Scotch to know the right measure. You wouldn't understand what

I mean, Father, but every drink has its right measure
—not water, of course. Water's not meant for drinking. It rusts the inside or gives you typhoid. It's not
good for man or beast except those bloody horses. Is it
any good asking you to have a small one with me?"

"No. I am, as you would say, on duty. Do you want
to go on with your letter?"

"Yes, of course. I was just waiting a while to let the
whisky work. You've cut out that bit about the horses,
haven't you? What ought I to say next? You see I
want to talk to her quite simply, as if we were alone
together, on the verandah, at the camp, but words
never come easily to me—not on paper, I mean. I
expect you understand. After all you are married too
in a way, Father."

"Yes, I am married too," Father Rivas said.

"But where I'm going there's no marriage, or so
you priests always tell us. It seems a bit of a waste
when I've found the right girl so bloody late in the
day. There ought to be visiting days in heaven, so as
to give us something to look forward to from time to
time. Like they have in prison. If there's nothing to
look forward to, it can't be much of a heaven. You
see I even get theological with the right measure of
whisky. Where *had* I got to? Oh, the horses. You are
quite sure we left out the old bastard's horses?"

Doctor Plarr came in from the outer room; his feet
made no sound on the earth floor, and neither man
looked up. They were busy over the letter. He stood
watching them in silence by the door. They looked to
him like old friends.

" 'Let the child go to the local school,' " Charley
Fortnum dictated. " 'But if he's a boy don't send him
on to that grand English school in B.A. where I went.
I was never happy there. Let him be a real Argentinian
like you are—not a half and half like me.' Have you
got that down, Father?"

"Yes. Had you not better say something to her about the change in the writing? She may wonder . . ."

"I doubt if she'd notice a thing like that. And Plarr can always explain to her how it was. My God, writing a letter is a bit like getting Fortnum's Pride started on a rainy morning. One jerk after another. You begin to think the engine's beginning to run and then it cuts again. Oh well, Father, write—'Lying here, I think of you most of the time, and the baby too. At home you are always on my right side, and I can put my right hand on your stomach and feel the little bastard kick, but there's no right side here. The bed's too narrow. Quite comfortable, of course. I've nothing really to complain about. I'm luckier than most men.' " He paused, " 'Luckier . . .' " and took the bit between his teeth. " 'Before I knew you, my darling, I was a finished man. A man has to have some sort of ambition to live by. Even a millionaire wants to make another million. But before you lived with me there was nothing I could look forward to, except the right measure, of course. My maté was never exactly an exhibition crop. Then I found you and I had something I really wanted to do. I wanted to make you content and safe, and suddenly there was this child of ours. We were in business together. I didn't expect to live long. All I wanted was to make sure that those first years were all right— the first years are important to the child, they sort of set a pattern. You mustn't think though I've given up hope—I will find a way out of here yet in spite of them.' " He paused. "Of course that's only a joke, Father. How can I escape? But I don't want her to think I'm depressed. My God, Fortnum's Pride did begin to work for a while, we nearly got out of that ditch, but I can't manage any more now. Just write, 'My darling girl, all my love.' "

"Are you sure you have finished?"

"Yes. I think so. It's damned hard work writing

letters. To think sometimes on a library shelf you see 'Collected Letters' of somebody or other. Poor bugger. Two volumes of them perhaps. There *is* something I forgot. Just put it at the end. With a P.S. You see, Father, this is the first child she's had. She hasn't any experience. People say a woman knows by instinct. I doubt it though. Write this—'Please don't give the child sweets. They are bad for the teeth, they pretty well ruined mine, and if you are in doubt about anything at all ask Doctor Plarr. He's a good doctor and a good friend.' That's all I can think of, Father." He closed his eyes. "Perhaps I will manage something more later on. I'd like to add a word or two just before you kill me, the famous last words, but I'm too damned tired to think of any more now."

"You must not give up hope, Señor Fortnum."

"What hope? Since I married Clara, I've always been afraid of dying. There's only one happy way to die and that's together, and even if you hadn't interfered, I'd have been too old for it to happen that way. I can hardly bear it when I think she will be alone and frightened when her turn comes to die. I want to be there holding her hand and telling her it's all right, Clara, I'm dying too, don't be scared—it's not all that bad dying. I'm crying now, you can see for yourself that I'm not a brave man. All the same it's not self-pity, Father. I just don't want her to be alone when she dies."

Father Rivas made a gesture—it might have been an attempt to sketch a blessing in the air which he had forgotten how to give. "God will be there," he said without conviction.

"Oh, you can have your God. Sorry, Father, but I don't see any sign of Him around, do you?"

Doctor Plarr had walked back into the outer room in a state of unreasoning rage. It seemed to him that every word of the letter he had heard Fortnum dictate was a reproach aimed unjustly at himself. He was so absorbed in his anger that he strode straight toward the outer door until he felt the Indian's gun pressing into his stomach and stopped. The child, always the child, he thought, a good friend, don't give the child sweets, feel him kicking. He stood there with the gun stuck against his stomach and spat his bile upon the ground.

"What is the matter, Eduardo?" Aquino asked.

"I'm tired to death of being cooped up here. Why the hell can't you trust me and let me go?"

"We need a doctor for Fortnum. If you went away from here you could not come back."

"There's no more I can do for Fortnum, and I'm in a bloody prison here."

"You would not feel that way if you had been in a real prison. This is liberty to me."

"A hundred square meters of dirt floor."

"I was used to nine. So the world has grown a lot larger for me."

"I suppose you can write your poems in any bloody hole, but I have nothing, nothing, to do. I'm a doctor. One patient is not enough."

"I never write poems now. They were just part of the prison life. I wrote verses because they were easy to memorize. It was a way of communicating, that was all. Now I have all the paper I want and a pen and I cannot write a line. Who cares? I live instead."

"You call this life? You can't even walk as far as the town."

"I never cared very much for walking. I have always been a lazy man."

Father Rivas came in. "Where are Pablo and Diego?" he asked.

"On guard," Aquino said. "You sent them out yourself."

"Marta, take one of them with you and go into the
235

town. It may be the last chance we shall have. Buy as many provisions as you can. Enough for three days. Easily portable."

"What is worrying you?" Aquino asked. "You look as if you had heard bad news."

"I am worried about the helicopter—about the blind man too. The ultimatum ends on Sunday night, and the police may be here long before then."

"And afterward?" asked Doctor Plarr.

"We kill him and we make a run for it. We must have food to take with us. We shall have to keep away from towns."

"Do you play chess, Eduardo?" Aquino asked.

"Yes. Why?"

"I have a pocket set."

"Then for God's sake let's have a game."

They sat on the dirt floor with the tiny board between them. Setting out the pieces Doctor Plarr said, "I used to play nearly every week at the Bolívar with an old man called Humphries. I was playing with him there the night you caught the wrong fish."

"A good player?"

"He was better than me that night."

Aquino was a slapdash player, moving too rapidly, and when Doctor Plarr hesitated over a move, he began to hum. "Do be quiet," Doctor Plarr appealed.

"Ha ha. I have got you, have I?"

"On the contrary. Check."

"I can soon cure that."

"Check again. And mate."

He won two games in succession.

"You are too good for me," Aquino said. "I ought to take on Señor Fortnum."

"I have never seen him play."

"You are a great friend of his?"

"In a way."

"And of his wife?"

236

"Yes."

Aquino lowered his voice. "That baby he is always talking about—is it yours?"

Doctor Plarr said, "I am sick to death of hearing about that baby. Do you want another game?"

As they were putting out their pieces they heard the sound of a rifle shot, very far off. Aquino seized his gun, but there was no repetition. Doctor Plarr sat on the floor with a black rook in his hand. It grew damp with sweat. Nobody spoke. At last Father Rivas said, "Only someone shooting at a wild duck. We begin to think everything has to do with our affair."

"Yes," Aquino said, "even the helicopter might have belonged to the city council if you can forget the military markings."

"How long is it before the next radio news?"

"Another two hours. There might be a special announcement though."

"We cannot leave the radio on all the time. It is the only radio in the *barrio*. Too many people know about it already."

"Then Aquino and I might as well have our game," Doctor Plarr said. "I will give you a rook."

"I do not want your rook. I will beat you in a straight match. I am out of practice, that is all."

Over Aquino's shoulder Doctor Plarr could see Father Rivas. A small and dusty object, he looked rather like a shrunken mummy dug out of the ground, together with a few treasured possessions which had been buried with him—a revolver, a tattered paper volume. Was it a missal? Doctor Plarr wondered. A book of prayers? With a sense of extreme boredom he repeated his old refrain, "Check and mate."

"You play too well for me," Aquino said.

"What are you reading, León?" Doctor Plarr asked. "Do you still read your breviary?"

"I gave that up years ago."

"What have you got there?"

"Only a detective story. An English detective story."

"A good one?"

"I am no judge of that. The translation is not very good, and with this sort of book I can always guess the end."

"Then where is the interest?"

"Oh, there is a sort of comfort in reading a story where one knows what the end will be. The story of a dream world where justice is always done. There were no detective stories in the age of faith—an interesting point when you think of it. God used to be the only detective when people believed in Him. He was law. He was order. He was good. Like your Sherlock Holmes. It was He who pursued the wicked man for punishment and discovered all. But now people like the General make law and order. Electric shocks on the genitals. Aquino's fingers. Keep the poor ill-fed, and they do not have the energy to revolt. I prefer the detective. I prefer God."

"Do you still believe in Him?"

"In a way. Sometimes. It is not so easy as all that to answer yes or no. Certainly he is not the same God as the one they taught us at school or in the seminary."

"Your personal God," Doctor Plarr said, teasing again. "I thought that was a Protestant heresy."

"Why not? Is it any worse for that? Is it any less likely to be true? We no longer kill heretics—only political prisoners."

"Charley Fortnum is your political prisoner."

"Yes."

"So you are a bit like the General yourself, León."

"I do not torture him."

"Are you sure of that?"

Marta returned from the town alone. She asked, "Is Diego here?"

238

"No," Father Rivas said, "surely he went with you—or did you take Pablo?"

"He stayed behind in the town. He said he would catch me up. He had to collect petrol. The car is nearly dry, he said, and there is no reserve."

Aquino said, "That is not true."

Marta said, "He was very frightened by the helicopter. By the old man too."

"Do you think he has gone to the police?" Doctor Plarr asked.

"No," Father Rivas said, "I will never believe that."

"Then where is he?" Aquino demanded.

"He may have been arrested on suspicion. He may have gone with a woman. Who knows? Anyway there is nothing for us to do. We can only wait. How long now before the news comes on?"

"Twenty-two minutes," Aquino said.

"Tell Pablo to come in. If they have spotted us, there is no point in leaving him outside to be picked off alone. Better to keep together at the end."

Father Rivas took up his detective story again. He said, "The only thing we can do is hope." He added, "What a wonderful peaceful world this one is. Everything is so well ordered. There are no problems. There is an answer to every question."

"What are you talking about?" Doctor Plarr asked.

"The world in this detective story. Can you tell me what Bradshaw means?"

"Bradshaw?"

It seemed to Doctor Plarr that this was the first time he had seen León so relaxed since the long arguments they used to have when they were schoolboys together. Had he, as the situation grew darker, lost the sense of responsibility, like a roulette player who abandons his chart and no longer bothers even to watch the ball? He should never have tried to be a man of action: as a priest at a bedside he would have been most at his ease waiting passively for the end. "It's an English family name," Doctor Plarr said. "My father had a friend Bradshaw who used to write to him from a town called Chester."

"This one seems to be a man who knows all the trains in England by heart. The trains never take more than a few hours to go anywhere. And they always arrive on time. The detective only has to consult Bradshaw to know exactly when . . . What a strange world your father came from. Here we are little more than eight hundred kilometers from Buenos Aires and the train is supposed to take a day and a half to make the journey, but it is often two or three days late. This English detective is a very impatient man. He is pacing the platform of the station in London, waiting for the train from Edinburgh—that is nearly as far as Buenos Aires surely?—and the train is half an hour late, according to this man Bradshaw, and yet the detective thinks something must be wrong. Half an hour late!" Father Rivas exclaimed. "It is like when I was a child and I would be late in coming home from school and my mother would worry and my father used to say, 'But what could happen to the child between here and the school house?' "

Aquino said with impatience, "And Diego? Diego is late too, and I tell you I worry."

Pablo came into the hut. Aquino told him at once, "Diego has gone."

"Where to?"

"To the police perhaps."

Marta said, "All the way into town he talked about the helicopter. And when we came to the river—oh, he did not say anything, but it was the way he looked. At the ferry landing he said to me, 'That is strange. There are no police controlling the passengers.' I said to him, 'And the other side—can you see all the way across

240

there? And can you tell a policeman when he is out of uniform?' "

Pablo said, "What do you think, Father? I introduced him to you. I feel ashamed. I told you he was a good man to drive the car. And a brave man."

Father Rivas said, "There is no reason to start worrying yet."

"I have to worry. He was my countryman. All you others come from across the border. You can trust each other. I feel as though I were Diego's brother and my brother had betrayed you. You should not have come to me for help."

"What could we have done without you, Pablo? There is nowhere in Paraguay where we could have hidden the Ambassador. Even taking him across the river would have been too dangerous. Perhaps it was a mistake to include any of your countrymen in our group, but El Tigre never thought of us as foreigners here in Argentina. He does not think in terms of Paraguayans, Peruvians, Bolivians, Argentinians. I think he would like to call us all Americans, if it were not for that place up there in the north."

Pablo said, "Diego asked me once why there were only Paraguayans on your list of prisoners to be released. I told him—these are the most urgent cases. Men who have been in prison more than ten years. The next time we strike together perhaps it will be for our own people, like the time in Salta. There were Paraguayans who helped us then. I do not believe he will go to the police, Father."

"Nor do I, Pablo."

"We have only a little time to wait," Aquino said. "They must surrender—or we leave a dead Consul in the river."

"How long before the news?"

"Ten minutes," Doctor Plarr said.

Father Rivas picked up his detective story, but to

241

Doctor Plarr, watching him closely, he seemed to be reading with unnatural slowness. He had fastened his eyes on one passage and he kept them there a long time before he turned the leaf. His lips moved a little. He might have been praying—in secrecy perhaps, because prayers by a priest at a deathbed are the last resort and the patient must not be allowed to hear them. All of us are his patients, Doctor Plarr thought, we are all about to die.

The doctor had no belief that things would turn out well. From a false equation you get only a chain of errors. His own death might be one of the errors, for afterward people would say he had followed in his father's steps, but they would be wrong—that had not been his intention.

He wondered with an unpleasant itch of anxiety and curiosity about his child. The child too was the result of an error, a carelessness on his part, but he had never before felt any responsibility. He had considered the child to be a useless part of Clara like her appendix, perhaps a diseased appendix which ought to be removed. He had suggested an abortion, but the idea had frightened her—perhaps there had been too many unprofessional abortions in the house of Mother Sanchez. Now, waiting for the news bulletin on the radio, he said to himself: the poor little bastard, if only I could have made some sort of arrangement for it. What sort of a mother was Clara likely to prove? Would she go back to Mother Sanchez and have the child brought up as the spoiled brat of a brothel? That would probably be better than life with his mother in B.A. stuffed with *dulce de leche* in the Calle Florida among the international voices of the well-to-do. He thought of the tangle of its ancestry, and for the first time in the complexity of that tangle the child became real to him—it was no longer just one more wet piece of flesh like any other torn out of the body with a cord which had to be cut. This cord could never be cut. It joined the child to two very different grandfathers—a cane-cutter in Tucumán and an old English liberal who had been shot dead in the yard of a police station in Paraguay. The cord joined it to a father who was a provincial doctor, to a mother from a brothel, to an uncle who had walked away one day from the cane fields to disappear into the waste of a continent, to two grandmothers . . . There was no end to the tangle which must constrict the tiny form like the swaddling bandages with which in old days they used to bind the limbs of a newborn child. A cold fish, Charley Fortnum had called him. What effect did it have on a child to have a cold fish for a father? It might have been better if they could have exchanged fathers. A cold fish would have been his own proper parentage rather than a father who had cared enough to die. He would have liked the little bastard to believe in something, but he was not the kind of father who could transmit belief in a good or a cause. He called across the dirt floor, "Do you really believe in God the Father Almighty, León?"

"What? I am sorry. I did not hear. This detective is a very cunning man, so there must be a good reason why the train from Edinburgh is half an hour late."

"I asked if you believed sometimes in God the Father?"

"You have asked me that before. You do not really want to know. You are only mocking me, Eduardo. All the same I will give you my answer when there is no more hope. You will not be ready to laugh then. Excuse me a moment—the story has become more interesting—the Edinburgh express is steaming into a station called King's Cross. King's Cross. Would that be symbolic?"

"No. Just the name of a station in London."

"Be quiet, both of you." Aquino turned the radio up and they listened to the international news which was

243

beamed at that hour from Buenos Aires. The announcer described the visit by the Secretary General of the United Nations to West Africa; fifty hippies had been expelled with violence from Majorca; there was yet another rise in taxes on cars imported to Argentina; a retired general had died in Córdoba at the age of eighty; a few bombs had exploded in Bogotá, and of course the Argentine football team was continuing its violent progress through Europe.

"They have forgotten us," Aquino said.

"If only we could believe that," Father Rivas said. "To stay here . . . forgotten . . . forever. It would not be so bad a fate, would it?"

3

On Saturday at midday the news came for which they had been waiting so long, but they had to listen patiently until the end of the bulletin. It was the policy of all the governments concerned to play down the importance of the Fortnum affair. Buenos Aires quoted moderate expressions of British opinion. *The Times* of London, for instance, had stated that an Argentinian novelist (whose name was not given) had offered himself in exchange for the Consul, and a BBC broadcast put the affair, as the Argentinian commentator remarked, in proper perspective. A Junior Minister had referred to the matter briefly when questioned in a television discussion on political violence occasioned by the tragic death of more than a hundred and sixty BOAC passengers. "I know no more about this affair in Argentina than any of our listeners. I do not have time to read many novels, but before I came out this evening I did ask my wife's bookseller about Mr. Savindra, and I'm afraid he was no better informed than me." The Minister added, "Much as I sympathize with Mr. Fortnum, I want to emphasize that we cannot treat a kidnapping like this as an attack on the British diplomatic service with all that would imply. Mr. Fortnum has never at any time been a member of the diplomatic service. He was born in Argentina, and so far as I know he has not even visited this country. When the unfortunate affair occurred we were about to terminate his engagement as Honorary Consul since he had passed the normal age for retirement and there was really no occasion to replace him as the number of British residents in that particular province has been very much reduced in the last ten years. I am sure you are aware that this Government is making every effort to economize in the Foreign Service."

Asked whether the Government's attitude would have been the same if the victim had been a member of the diplomatic service the Minister said, "Certainly it would have been the same. We don't intend to give in to this kind of blackmail anywhere, under any circumstances. In this particular case we have every confidence that Mr. Fortnum will be released when these desperate men realize the complete futility of their action. It is for the President of Argentina in that case to decide whether he will treat these criminals with clemency. Now, if the chairman will allow me, I would like to return to the real subject of tonight's broadcast. I can assure you that there were no security men on the plane and so no question of an armed struggle . . ."

Pablo turned off the radio.

"What did all that mean?" Father Rivas asked.

Doctor Plarr said, "They have left Fortnum's case in your hands."

"If they have rejected the ultimatum," Aquino said, "the sooner we kill him the better."

"Our ultimatum was not made to the British Government," Father Rivas said.

"Of course," Doctor Plarr hastily corrected himself, "they have to say all that in public. We can't tell what pressures they may be exerting in Buenos Aires and Asunción privately." Even to himself his words lacked confidence.

They all, taking turns with those on guard, spent the afternoon drinking maté, with the exception of Doctor Plarr who had inherited from his father a taste for tea. He played another game with Aquino and, by pretending a slip which lost him his queen, he allowed Aquino a victory, but there was a sullen lack of belief in the way Aquino pronounced "Checkmate."

Doctor Plarr visited his patient twice and found him sleeping on both occasions. He regarded with resentment the peaceful expression on the condemned man's face. He was even smiling a little—perhaps he was dreaming of Clara or the child, or perhaps only of the "proper measure." Doctor Plarr wondered what the years ahead might be like—in the unlikely event of there being any years ahead. He was not worried about Clara: that affair—if you could call it an affair—would have been finished soon in any case. It was the child's image, as he grew up under Charley Fortnum's care, which worried him. For no rational reason he pictured the child as a boy, a boy who resembled two early photographs of himself, one taken at four years and one at eight. His mother preserved them still in the overcrowded apartment, the silver frames tarnished from lack of care, among the china cockatoos and the junk of antique shops.

Charley, he was certain, would have the child brought up as a Catholic—he would be all the more strict about that because he had once broken the laws of the Church himself—and he could imagine Charley listening with sentimental pleasure beside the boy's bunk while the child stumbled through an Our Father. Afterward he would join Clara beside the dumbwaiter on the verandah. Charley would be a very kind father. He would never make his son ride a horse. It was even possible that he would give up drink or at least severely reduce the proper measure. Charley would call the boy "old fellow" and pat his cheek and turn over the pages of *London Panorama* before tucking him up firmly in bed. Doctor Plarr suddenly saw the boy sitting up in his bunk, as he had done, listening to the distant locking of doors, to the low voices downstairs, the stealthy footsteps. There was one night he remembered when he had crept for reassurance to his father's room, and he was looking down now at the bearded face of his father stretched on the coffin—four days' stubble had begun to resemble a beard.

Doctor Plarr returned abruptly to the company of Charley Fortnum's future murderers.

Guard duty had been resumed. Aquino was outside, while Pablo took the place of the Indian at the door. The Guaraní slept quietly on the floor, and Marta was clattering dishes noisily in the yard behind. Father Rivas sat with his back to the wall. He played with some dried beans which he tossed from hand to hand, like the beads of a broken rosary.

"Did you finish your book?" Doctor Plarr asked.

"Oh yes," Father Rivas said. "The end was exactly what I thought. You can always tell. The murderer went and committed suicide on the Edinburgh express. That was why it was half an hour late and why the man Bradshaw was wrong. How is the consul?"

"Sleeping."

"And his wound?"

"Doing all right. But will he live long enough to see it heal?"

"I thought you believed in those secret pressures?"

247

"I thought you believed in something too, León. Things like mercy and charity. Once a priest always a priest—that's the theory, isn't it? Don't start telling me about Father Torres or the bishops who went to war in the Middle Ages. This isn't the Middle Ages and this isn't war. This is the murder of a man who has done you no harm at all—a man old enough to be my father—or yours. Where *is* your father, León?"

"Under a marble monument in Asunción almost as big as this hut."

"We all of us seem to live with dead fathers, don't we? Fortnum hated his. I think I may have loved mine. Perhaps. How can I possibly tell? That word love has such a slick sound. We take credit for loving as though we had passed an examination with more than the average marks. What was your father like? I can't remember even seeing him."

"He was what you would expect, one of the richest of the bourgeoisie in Paraguay. You must remember our house in Asunción with the great portico and the white columns and the marble bathrooms and all the orange and lemon trees in the garden? And the *lapachos* covering the paths with their rose petals. Probably you never saw inside the house, but I am sure you came once to a birthday party in the garden. Friends of mine were never allowed inside the house—there were so many things they might break or soil. We had six servants. I liked them much better than my parents. And there was a gardener called Pedro—he was always busy sweeping up the petals—they were so untidy my mother said. I was very fond of Pedro, but my father threw him out because he stole a few pesos which had been left on a garden seat. My father paid a lot of money every year to the Colorado Party, so there was no trouble for him when the General came to power after the civil war. He was a good *abogado,* but he never worked for a poor client. He served the rich faithfully until he died, and everyone said he was a good father because he left plenty of cash behind him. Oh well, I suppose he was, in that way. It is one of the duties of a father to provide."

"And God the Father, León? He doesn't seem to provide much. I asked last night if you still believed in Him. To me He has always seemed a bit of a swine. I would rather believe in Apollo. At least he was beautiful."

"The trouble is we have lost the power to believe in Apollo," Father Rivas said. "We have Jehovah in our blood. We can't help it. After all these centuries Jehovah lives in our darkness like a worm in the intestines."

"You should never have been a priest, León."

"Perhaps you are right, but it's too late to change now. What time is it? How tired to death I am of this radio, but we have to listen to the news—it is still possible they may give in."

"My watch has stopped. I forgot to wind it."

"Then we had better keep the radio on, however dangerous, as long as there is a chance . . ." He turned the sound as low as he could, but all the same they ceased to be alone. Someone was playing a harp almost inaudibly, someone sang in a whisper. They might have been sitting in a vast hall where they couldn't even see or hear the performers.

There was nothing to do but talk, talk about anything under the sun except about Sunday midnight.

"I've often noticed," Doctor Plarr said, "when a man leaves a woman he begins to hate her. Or is it that he hates his own failure? Perhaps we want to destroy the only witness who knows exactly what we are like when we drop the comedy. I suppose I shall hate Clara when I leave her."

"Clara?"

"Fortnum's wife."

"It *is* true what they say?"

"There's not much point in lying about anything, León, in the position we are in now. Dying is a wonderfully effective truth drug, better than pentothal. You priests have always known that. When the priest arrives I always leave a dying man so that he's free to talk. They most of them want to talk, if they have the strength."

"Are you planning to desert this woman?"

"I'm planning nothing. But it will happen. If I live. I am certain of that. Nothing is for keeps in this world, León. When you entered the Church, weren't you sure in your heart that one day even your priesthood would come to an end?"

"No. I never believed that. Not for a moment. I thought the Church and I wanted the same thing. You see I had been very happy in my seminary. You might say that was the period of my honeymoon. Only there were occasions . . . I suppose it happens the same way in all honeymoons . . . there *was* a hint that something might be wrong . . . I remember one old priest . . . he was the professor in the moral theology course. I've never known a man so cut and dried and sure of the truth. Of course moral theology is the bugbear in every seminary. You learn the rules and find they don't apply to any human case . . . Oh well, I used to think, a little difference of opinion, what does it matter? In the end a man and wife grow together. The Church will grow nearer to me as I grow nearer to her."

"But when you left the Church you began to hate it, didn't you?"

"I have told you—I never left the Church. Mine is only a separation, Eduardo, a separation by mutual consent, not a divorce. I shall never belong wholly to anyone else. Not even to Marta."

"Even a separation brings hate often enough," Doctor Plarr said. "I have seen it happen many times among my patients in this damned country where no one is allowed a divorce."

"It will never happen in my case. Even if I cannot love, I see no reason to hate. I can never forget that long honeymoon in the seminary when I was so happy. Now, if I feel any emotion for the Church, it is regret, not hate. I think she could have used me easily for a good purpose if she had understood a little better. I mean about the world as it is."

The radio murmured on, and they listened with ears alert for the time signal. In the room of mud, which might well have been some primitive aboveground tomb prepared for a whole family, Doctor Plarr no longer felt the least desire to torment León Rivas. If there was anyone he wanted to torment, it was himself. He thought: whatever we may pretend to each other, we have both given up hope. That is why we can talk like the friends we used to be. I have reached a premature old age when I can no longer mock a man for his beliefs, however absurd. I can only envy them.

Curiosity after a while drove him to speak. He remembered how at his first Communion in Asunción, dressed like a diminutive monk with a rope round his waist, he had believed—something, though now he could not remember what.

"It's a long time," he told León, "since I listened to a priest. I thought you taught that the Church was infallible like Christ."

"Christ was a man," Father Rivas said, "even if some of us believe that he was God as well. It was not the God the Romans killed, but a man. A carpenter from Nazareth. Some of the rules He laid down were only the rules of a good man. A man who lived in his own province, in his own particular day. He had no idea of the kind of world we would be living in now. Render unto Caesar, but when *our* Caesar uses napalm and fragmentation bombs . . . The Church lives in time too. Only sometimes, for a short while, for some people—I am not one of them—I am not a man of vision—I think perhaps—but how can I explain to you when I believe so little myself?—I think sometimes the memory of that man, that carpenter, can lift a few people out of the temporary Church of these terrible years, when the Archbishop sits down to dinner with the General, into the great Church beyond our time and place, and then . . . those lucky ones . . . they have no words to describe the beauty of that Church."

"I don't understand a word you say, León. You used to explain things more clearly. Even the Trinity."

"Forgive me. It is such a very long time since I read the right sort of books."

"You haven't the right audience either. I feel no more interested in the Church now than I feel in Marxism. The Bible is as unreadable to me as *Das Kapital.* Only sometimes, like a bad habit, I find myself using that crude word God. Last night . . ."

"Any word one uses from habit means nothing at all."

"All the same, when you shoot Fortnum in the back of the head, are you sure you won't have a moment's fear of old Jehovah and His anger? 'Thou shalt not commit murder.' "

"If I kill him it will be God's fault as much as mine."

"God's fault?"

"He made me what I am now. He will have loaded the gun and steadied my hand."

"I thought the Church teaches that He's love?"

"Was it love which sent six million Jews to the gas ovens? You are a doctor, you must often have seen intolerable pain—a child dying of meningitis. Is that love? It was not love which cut off Aquino's fingers. The police stations where such things happen . . . He created them."

"I have never heard a priest blame God for things like that before."

"I don't blame Him. I pity Him," Father Rivas said, and the time signal struck faintly in the dark.

"Pity God?"

The priest put his fingers on the dial. For a moment he hesitated to turn it. Yes, Doctor Plarr thought, there is always something to be said for remaining ignorant of the worst. I have never told a cancer patient yet that there is no hope any longer.

A voice said as indifferently as if it were reading out a list of prices on the stock exchange, "The following communiqué has been issued from police headquarters. 'At seventeen hours yesterday a man who refused to give his name was arrested while attempting to board the ferry to the Chaco shore. He attempted to escape by plunging into the river, but he was shot by police officers. His body was recovered. It proved to be that of a lorry driver employed at the Bergman orange-canning factory. He had been absent from work since last Monday, the day before the kidnapping of the British Consul. His name was Diego Corredo and his age was thirty-five. Unmarried. His identification is believed to be an important step toward tracing the other members of the gang. It is thought that the kidnappers have not left the province, and an intensive search is now in progress. The commander of the 9th Infantry Brigade has put a parachute company at the disposal of the police.' "

Doctor Plarr said, "Lucky for you he was not interrogated. I doubt if Perez would have many scruples at this stage."

It was Pablo who answered. "They will discover soon enough who his friends were. I was employed at the same factory until a year ago. Everyone knew we were good friends." The man on the radio was talking again about the Argentinian football team. There had been a riot with twenty injured when they played in Barcelona.

Father Rivas woke Miguel and sent him out to relieve Aquino, and when Aquino returned, the old arguments broke out anew. Marta had cooked the anonymous stew which she had served for two days now. Doctor Plarr wondered whether Father Rivas had endured the same meal every day of his married life, but probably it was no worse than he had been accustomed to eat in the poor *barrio* of Asunción.

Aquino waved his spoon and demanded the instant death of Charley Fortnum. "They have killed Diego."

To get away from them awhile Doctor Plarr carried a plate of stew into the other room. Charley Fortnum looked at it with distaste. "I could do with a nice grilled chop," he said, "but I suppose they are afraid I would use a knife to escape."

"We are all eating the same thing," Doctor Plarr said. "I only wish Humphries was here. It might give him an even greater appetite for the goulash at the Italian Club."

" 'Whatever the crime, the same meal's served to all.' "

"A quotation?"

"One of that fellow Aquino's poems. Is there any news?"

"The man called Diego tried to escape to the Chaco, but the police shot him."

"Ten little nigger boys and then there were nine. Will I be the next to go?"

"I don't think so. You are the only card they have left to gamble with. Even if the police discover this hideout they'll be afraid to attack it while you are alive."

"I doubt if they would bother much about me."

"Colonel Perez will bother about his career."

"Are you as scared as I am, Ted?"

"I don't know. Perhaps I have a bit more hope. Or perhaps I have less to lose."

"Yes. That's true. You're lucky. You haven't Clara and the baby to worry about."

"No."

"You know about these things, Ted. Will there be much pain?"

"They say when the wound's serious people feel very little."

"And my wound will be the most serious of all."

"Yes."

"Clara will feel the pain longer than me. I wish it could be the other way round."

They were still arguing in the outer room when Doctor Plarr returned. Aquino was saying, "But what does he know of the situation? He is safe in Córdoba or . . ." He checked himself and looked up at Doctor Plarr.

"Don't worry," Doctor Plarr said, "I am not likely to survive you. Unless you give up this insane idea. You still have time to escape."

"And admit failure," Aquino said, "to all the world."

"You used to be a poet. Were you afraid to admit it when a poem failed?"

"My poems were never published," Aquino said. "No one knew when I failed. My poems were never read out on the radio. There were no questions asked about them in the British Parliament."

"It's your damn *machismo* again, isn't it? Who invented *machismo*? A gang of ruffians like Pizarro and Cortés. Can't any of you for a moment escape your bloody history? You haven't learned a thing, have you, from Cervantes? He had his fill of *machismo* at Lepanto."

Father Rivas said, "Aquino is right. We cannot afford to fail. Once before our people released a man rather than kill him—he was a Paraguayan Consul, the General cared no more about his life than Fortnum's, and when it came to the point we were not prepared to kill. If we are weak again like that, no threat of death will be of any use on this continent. Until more ruthless men than we are begin to kill a great many more. I do not want to be responsible for the deaths which will follow our failure."

"You have a complicated conscience," Doctor Plarr said. "Will you pity God for those murders too?"

"You have no idea, have you, what I meant?"

"No. I was never taught anything about pitying God by the Jesuits in Asunción. Not that I remember."

"Perhaps you would have more faith now if you had remembered a little more."

"Mine's a busy life, León, trying to cure the sick. I can't leave that to God."

"Oh, you may be right. I have always had far too much time. Two Masses on a Sunday. A few feast days. Confessions twice a week. It was mostly the old women who came—and of course the children. The children were forced to come. They were beaten if they did not come, and anyway I gave them sweets. Not as a reward. The bad child received just as many sweets as the good one. I only wanted to make them feel happy while they knelt in that stuffy box. And when I gave them a penance I tried to make it a game we played together, a reward not a punishment. And they sucked their sweets while they said a Hail Mary. I could be happy too, for as long as I was with them. I was never happy with their fathers—or their mothers. I don't know why. Perhaps if I had had a child myself . . ."

"It's a long journey you've made, León, since you left Asunción."

"It was not such an innocent life there as you think. Once a child of eight told me he had drowned his baby sister in the Paraná. People thought she had slipped off the cliff. He told me she used to eat too much and there was less for him. Less mandioca!"

"Did you give him a sweet?"

"Yes. And three Hail Marys for a penance."

Pablo went out on guard in his turn, taking Miguel's place. Marta served the Guaraní with stew and cleaned the other plates. She said, "Father, tomorrow is Sunday. Surely you could say a Mass for us on that day?"

"It is more than three years since I last said a Mass. I doubt if I can even remember the words."

"I have a missal, Father."

"Read the Mass to yourself then, Marta. It will serve just as well."

"You heard what they said on the radio. The soldiers are searching for us now. It may be the last Mass we shall ever hear. And there is Diego—you must say a Mass for him."

"I have no right to say a Mass. When I married you, Marta, I excommunicated myself."

"No one knows you married me."

"*I* know."

"Father Pedro used to sleep with women. Everyone in Asunción knew that. And he said Mass every Sunday."

"He did not marry, Marta. He could go to confession and sin again and go to confession. I am not responsible for his conscience."

"You seem to suffer from an odd lot of scruples, León," Doctor Plarr said, "for a man who plans to murder."

"Yes. Perhaps they are not scruples—only superstitions. You see if I took the Host I would still half believe I was taking His body. Anyway it's a useless argument. There is no wine."

"Oh but there is, Father," Marta said. "I found an

empty medicine bottle in the rubbish dump and when I was in the town I filled it at a *cantina*."

"You think of everything," Father Rivas said sadly.

"Father, you know I have wanted all these years to hear you say Mass again and to see the people praying with you. Of course it will not be the same without the beautiful vestments. If only you had kept them with you."

"They did not belong to me, Marta. Anyway vestments are not the Mass. Do you think the Apostles wore vestments? How I hated wearing them when the people in front of me were all in rags. I was glad to turn my back on them and forget them and see only the altar and the candles—but the money for the candles would have fed half the people there."

"You are wrong, Father. We were all glad to see you in those vestments. They were so beautiful, all the scarlet and the gold embroidery."

"Yes. I suppose they helped you escape from everything for a little while, but to me they were the clothes of a convict."

"But, Father, you won't listen to the Archbishop's rules? You *will* say a Mass for us tomorrow?"

"Suppose what they say is true and I am damning myself?"

"The good God would never damn a man like you, Father. But poor Diego, José's wife . . . all of us . . . we need you to speak to God for us."

Father Rivas said, "All right. I will say Mass. For your sake, Marta. I have done very little for you in these years. You have given me love and all I have given you has been a great deal of danger and a dirt floor to lie on. I will say Mass as soon as it is light if the soldiers give us enough time. Have we any bread left?"

"Yes, Father."

A sense of some obscure grievance moved Doctor

Plarr. He said, "You don't believe yourself in all this mumbojumbo, León. You are fooling them like you fooled that child who killed his sister. You want to hand them sweets at Communion to comfort them before you murder Charley Fortnum. I've seen with my own eyes things just as bad as any you've listened to in the confessional, but I can't be pacified with sweets. I have seen a child born without hands and feet. I would have killed it if I had been left alone with it, but the parents watched me too closely—they wanted to keep that bloody broken torso alive. The Jesuits used to tell us it was our duty to love God. A duty to love a God who produces that abortion? It's like the duty of a German to love Hitler. Isn't it better not to believe in that horror up there sitting in the clouds of heaven than pretend to love him?"

"It may be better not to breathe, but all the same I cannot help breathing. Some men, I think, are condemned to belief by a judge just as they are condemned to prison. They have no choice. No escape. They have been put behind the bars for life."

" 'I see my father only through the bars,' " Aquino quoted with a sort of glum self-satisfaction.

"So here I sit on the floor of my prison cell," Father Rivas said, "and I try to make some sense of things. I am no theologian, I was bottom in most of my classes, but I have always wanted to understand what you call the horror and why I cannot stop loving it. Just like the parents who loved that poor bloody torso. Oh, He seems ugly enough I grant you, but then I am ugly too and yet Marta loves me. In my first prison—I mean in the seminary—there were lots of books in which I could read all about the love of God, but they were of no help to me. Not one of the Fathers was of any use to me. Because they never touched on the horror—you are quite right to call it that. They saw no problem. They just sat comfortably down in the presence of the horror like the old Archbishop at the General's table and they talked about man's responsibility and Free Will. Free Will was the excuse for everything. It was God's alibi. They had never read Freud. Evil was made by man or Satan. It was simple that way. But I could never believe in Satan. It was much easier to believe that God was evil."

Marta exclaimed, "Father, you do not know what you are saying."

"I am not talking as a priest now, Marta. A man has the right to think aloud to his wife. Even a madman, and perhaps I am a little mad. Perhaps those years in Asunción in the *barrio* have turned my brain, so here I am waiting to kill an innocent man . . ."

"You are not mad, León," Aquino said. "You have come to your senses. We will make a good Marxist of you yet. Of course God is evil, God is capitalism. Lay up treasures in heaven—they will bring you a hundred percent interest for eternity."

"I believe in the evil of God," Father Rivas said, "but I believe in His goodness too. He made us in His image—that is the old legend. Eduardo, you know well how many truths in medicine lay in old legends. It was not a modern laboratory which first discovered the use of a snake's venom. And old women used the mold on overripe oranges long before penicillin. So I too believe in an old legend which is almost forgotten. He made us in His image—and so our evil is His evil too. How could I love God if He were not like me? Divided like me. Tempted like me. If I love a dog it is only because I can see something human in a dog. I can feel his fear and his gratitude and even his treachery. He dreams in his sleep like I do. I doubt if I could ever love a toad— though sometimes, when I have touched a toad's skin, I am reminded of the skin of an old man who has spent a rough poor life in the fields, and I wonder . . ."

"I find my disbelief a lot easier to understand than your kind of belief. If your God is evil . . ."

"I have had more than two years in hiding," Father Rivas said, "and we have to travel light. There is no room in our packs for books of theology. Only Marta has kept a missal. I have lost mine. Sometimes I have been able to find a paperback novel—like the one I have been reading. A detective story. That sort of life leaves a lot of time to think and perhaps Marta may be right and my thoughts are turning wild. But I can see no other way to believe in God. The God I believe in must be responsible for all the evil as well as for all the saints. He has to be a God made in our image with a night side as well as a day side. When you speak of the horror, Eduardo, you are speaking of the night side of God. I believe the time will come when the night side will wither away, like your communist state, Aquino, and we shall see only the simple daylight of the good God. You believe in evolution, Eduardo, even though sometimes whole generations of men slip backward to the beasts. It is a long struggle and a long suffering, evolution, and I believe God is suffering the same evolution that we are, but perhaps with more pain."

"I am not so sure of evolution," Doctor Plarr said, "not since we managed to produce Hitler and Stalin in one generation. Suppose the night side of God swallows up the day side altogether? Suppose it is the good side which withers away. If I believed what you believe, I would sometimes think that had happened already."

"But I believe in Christ," Father Rivas said, "I believe in the Cross and the Redemption. The Redemption of God as well as of Man. I believe that the day side of God, in one moment of happy creation, produced perfect goodness, as a man might paint one perfect picture. God's intention for once was completely fulfilled so that the night side can never win more than a little victory here and there. With our help. Because the evolution of God depends on our evolution. Every evil act of ours strengthens His night side, and every good one helps His day side. We belong to Him and He belongs to us. But now at least we can be sure where evolution will end one day—it will end in a goodness like Christ's. It is a terrible process all the same and the God I believe in suffers as we suffer while He struggles against Himself—against His evil side."

"Is killing Charley Fortnum going to help his evolution?"

"No. I pray all the time I shall not have to kill him."

"And yet you will kill him if they don't give in?"

"Yes. Just as you lie with another man's wife. There are ten men dying slowly in prison, and I tell myself I am fighting for them and that I love them. But my sort of love I know is a poor excuse. A saint would only have to pray, but I have to carry a revolver. I slow evolution down."

"Then why . . . ?"

"Saint Paul answered that question, 'What I do is not that which I wish to do, but something which I hate.' He knew all about the night side of God. He had been one of those who stoned Stephen."

"Do you still call yourself a Catholic, believing all that?"

"Yes. I call myself a Catholic whatever the bishops may say. Or the Pope."

Marta said, "Father, you frighten me. All that is not in the catechism, is it?"

"No, not in the catechism, but the catechism is not the faith, Marta. It is a sort of times two table. There is nothing I have said which your catechism denies. You learned when you were a child about Abraham and Isaac, and how Jacob cheated his brother, and Sodom was destroyed like that village last year in the Andes. God when He is evil demands evil things; He can create monsters like Hitler; He destroys children and cities. But one day with our help He will be able to tear His evil mask off forever. How often the saints have worn an evil mask for a time, even Paul. God is joined to us in a sort of blood transfusion. His good is in our veins, and our tainted blood runs through His. Oh, I know I may be sick or mad. But it is the only way I can believe in the goodness of God."

"It's much easier not to believe in a God at all."

"Are you sure?"

"Well, perhaps the Jesuits left one germ of the disease in me, but I have isolated it. I keep it under control."

"I have never spoken aloud like this before—I don't know why I do now."

"Perhaps because you think there is no more hope?"

"Ted," the voice which Doctor Plarr was beginning to hate called from the inner room, "Ted."

Doctor Plarr made no motion to rise.

"Your patient," Father Rivas reminded him.

"I've done all I can for him. What's the good of mending his ankle if you are going to put a bullet through his head?"

"Ted," the voice came again.

"He probably wants to ask me what vitamins Clara ought to give his baby. Or when he ought to be weaned. His baby! The dark side of God must be having a hearty laugh about that. I never wanted a child. I would have got rid of it if she had let me."

"Speak lower," Father Rivas said, "even if you are jealous of the poor man."

"Jealous of Charley Fortnum? Why should I be jealous?" He couldn't control his voice. "Jealous because of the child?—but the child's mine. Jealous because of his wife? She's mine as well. For as long as I want her."

"Jealous because he loves."

263

He was aware of the way Marta looked at him. Even Aquino's silence seemed a criticism.

"Oh love! That's not a word in my vocabulary."

Marta said, "Give me your shirt, Father. I want to wash it ready for the Mass."

"A little dirt will not matter."

"You have slept in it for three weeks, Father. It is not good to go up to the altar smelling like a dog."

"There is no altar."

"Give it to me, Father."

Obediently he stripped off his shirt; the blue was faded by the sun and stained with the marks of food and the whitewash of many walls. "Do what you want," the priest said. "All the same it is a pity to waste our water. We may need all we have of it before the end."

It was too dark to see and the Negro lit three candles. He carried one into the inner room, but brought it back and nipped out the flame. He said, "He is asleep."

Father Rivas turned on the radio and the sad notes of Guaraní music came over the air—the music of a people who are doomed to die. There was a lot of static; it crackled like the machine guns of extinction. Up in the mountains beyond the river the summer was beginning to break up and the lightning quivered on the walls.

"Put out all the pans and pails you have," Father Rivas told Pablo.

The wind came in a sudden blast, the leaves of the avocados swept across the tin roof, and then again the wind dropped. "I shall have to wear a wet shirt at Mass," Father Rivas said, "unless I can persuade Marta that God does not mind a man's naked skin."

Suddenly, as though someone were standing close at their elbow within the hut, a voice spoke to them, "We have been asked by police headquarters to read the following statement." There was a pause while the man found the right place. They could even hear the rustle of the papers he was carrying.

"It is now known where the gang of kidnappers are holding the British Consul captive. They have been located in a certain quarter in the *barrio popular* which . . ." The rain came sweeping down from Paraguay, beating on the roof, and drowned the announcer's words. Marta ran in, holding out a piece of damp cloth, the shirt of Father Rivas. She cried, "Father, what can I do? The rain . . ."

"Hush," the priest said, and he turned the radio louder. The rain passed over them toward the city, and the lightning lit the room almost continuously. Across the Paraná in the Chaco the thunder became audible, like a barrage which has lifted and moved on before an attack.

"You have no longer any hope of escape," the voice continued slowly and ponderously, in an interval of static, speaking with extreme clarity like a teacher explaining a problem of mathematics to a class of children; Doctor Plarr recognized the voice of Colonel Perez. "We know exactly where you are. You are surrounded by men from the 9th Brigade. Before eight tomorrow morning you must send the British Consul out of the hut. He must come alone and walk unmolested into the cover of the trees. Five minutes afterward you must come out yourselves, one by one with arms raised over the head. The Governor guarantees that your lives will be spared and you will not be returned to Paraguay. Do not attempt to escape. If any man leaves the hut before the Consul has been delivered unharmed he will be shot down. No white flag will be respected. You are completely surrounded. I warn you that if any harm . . ." After that the static whined and shrieked through his words, making them unintelligible.

"Bluff!" Aquino said, "only bluff! If they were out there Miguel would have warned us. That man can see an ant in the dark. Kill Fortnum and afterward we will draw lots to see who leaves first. How can they tell on a night like this who it is that leaves the hut—the Consul or another?" He threw the door open and called out to the Indian "Miguel!" Like an answer to his question a semicircle of floodlights flashed on—they flared from between the trees in an arc nearly a hundred yards across. Through the open door Doctor Plarr could see moths crowding away from him towards the lights to beat and shrivel against the reflectors. The Indian lay flattened on the ground, and the doctor's own shadow shot back into the hut and lay stretched there like a dead man on the floor. The doctor moved aside. He wondered whether Perez had seen him and identified him.

"They do not dare shoot into the hut," Aquino said, "for fear of killing Fortnum."

The lights went out again. In the silence between the thunderclaps they heard a rustle no louder than the movements of a rat. Aquino stood at the edge of the doorway and turned his gun toward the darkness. "No," Father Rivas said, "it's Miguel." Another wave of water swept the roof and in the yard a pail was overturned and sent rattling away before the wind.

The darkness did not last. Perhaps the lightning had blown a fuse which was now repaired. The men watching from inside the hut saw the Indian rise to his feet to run, but the lights blinded him. He began to turn in a circle with a hand over his eyes. A single shot was fired and he fell to his knees. It was as though the men of the 9th Brigade had no intention of wasting ammunition on someone of so little importance. The Guaraní knelt with his head bent, like a pious man at the elevation of the Host. He swayed from side to side—he might have been enacting part of a primitive rite. Then with immense effort he began to raise his gun in the wrong direction until it pointed at the open door of the hut. It seemed to Doctor Plarr, who watched flattened against the wall, that the parachutists were waiting with a cruel and patient curiosity to see what happened next. They were not going to waste another bullet. The Indian was no danger to them, for how could he possibly see to shoot in the glare of the lights? Whether he were dying or not was immaterial to them. He could lie there till morning came. Then the gun sailed a few feet through the air toward the hut. It fell out of reach and Miguel was still on the ground.

Aquino said, "We must pull him in."

"He is dead," Doctor Plarr assured him.

"How can you tell?"

The lights went out again. It was as though the men hidden in the trees were playing a cruel game with them.

"This is your chance, doctor," Aquino said.

"What can I do?"

"You are right," Father Rivas said. "They are trying to tempt one of us to go out."

"Your friend Perez might not shoot if *you* went out."

Doctor Plarr said, "My patient is here."

Aquino edged the door further open. The automatic rifle lay just out of reach. He put a hand out toward it. The lights flashed on, and a bullet struck the edge of the door as he banged it shut. The man in charge of the lights must have heard the squeak of the hinge.

"Close the shutters, Pablo."

"Yes, Father."

With the glare of the lights shut out, they felt a sense of protection.

"What shall we do now, Father?" the Negro asked.

"Kill Fortnum at once," Aquino said, "and if the lights go out again we can make a run for it."

Pablo said, "Two of us are dead already. It might be better, Father, if we surrendered. And there is Marta here."

"But the Mass, Father?"

"It seems to me I shall have to make it a Mass for the dead," Father Rivas said.

"Say any sort of Mass you like," Aquino said, "but kill the Consul first."

"How could I say the Mass after I had killed him?"

"Why not if you can say a Mass when you intend to kill him?" Doctor Plarr said.

"Ah, Eduardo, you are still enough of a Catholic to know how to turn the knife in the wound. You will be my confessor yet."

"May I prepare the table, Father? I have the wine. I have the bread."

"I will say it at the first light. I have to prepare myself, Marta, and that takes longer than laying a table."

"Let me kill him while you say your prayers," Aquino said. "Do your work and leave me to do mine."

"I thought your work was writing poems," Doctor Plarr said.

"My poems have all been about death, so I am well qualified."

"It is madness to go on," Pablo said. "Forgive me, Father, but Diego was right to try to escape. It is madness to kill one man and make sure that five of us die. Father . . ."

"Take a vote," Aquino interrupted with impatience. "Let the vote decide."

"Are you turning into a Parliamentarian, Aquino?" Doctor Plarr said.

"Keep to a subject you know, doctor. Trotsky believed in a free vote inside the Party."

"I vote for surrender," Pablo said. He put his hands over his face. The movements of his shoulders showed he was weeping. For himself? For the dead? For shame?

Doctor Plarr thought: the desperadoes! That is what the papers would call them. A failed poet, an excommunicated priest, a pious woman, a man who weeps.

For heaven's sake let this comedy end in comedy. None of us are suited to tragedy.

Pablo said, "I love this house. I had nothing else but the house left when my wife and child died."

Yet another father, Doctor Plarr told himself, are we never going to finish with fathers?

"I vote for killing Fortnum now," Aquino said.

"You told us they were bluffing," Father Rivas said. "Perhaps you are right. Suppose eight o'clock comes and we have done nothing—they still cannot attack us. So long as he is alive."

"Then what do you vote for?" Aquino asked.

"For delay. We gave them till midnight tomorrow."

"And you, Marta?"

"I vote with my husband," she said with pride.

A loudspeaker—so close that it must have been set up among the trees outside—spoke to them, again in the voice of Perez. "The United States Government and the British Government have refused to intervene. If you have been listening to your radio you will know I am telling you the truth. Your blackmail has failed. You have nothing to gain by holding the Consul any longer. Send him out of the hut before 08.00 hours if you wish to save your own lives."

"They insist too much," Father Rivas said.

Somebody was whispering beside the microphone. It was unintelligible—a sound which grated like pebbles drawn back under a wave. Then Perez continued. "There is a dying man outside your door. Send the Consul out to us now, and we will try to save your friend. Are you going to leave one of your own people to die slowly?"

No Hippocratic oath demands suicide, Doctor Plarr told himself. In his childhood his father had read him stories of heroism, of wounded men rescued under fire, of Captain Oates walking out into the snow. "Shoot if

you must this old gray head" was one of his favorite
poems in those days.

He went abruptly into the inner room. He could see
nothing in the darkness there. He whispered, "Are you
awake?"

"Yes."

"How does your ankle feel?"

"It's all right."

"I will bring a light and change the bandages."

"No."

Doctor Plarr said, "The soldiers have us surrounded.
You mustn't give up hope."

"Hope of what?"

"There's only one man who really wants your death."

"Yes?" the indifferent voice replied.

"Aquino."

"And you," Charley Fortnum said, "you! You want
it."

"Why should I?"

"You talk too loud, Plarr. I don't suppose you ever
talked so loud at the camp, even when I was out farming a mile away. You were always so damned discreet,
weren't you, in case the servants heard. But the time
always comes when even a husband has his ears open."
There was a sound of scrabbling in the darkness as
though he were trying to pull himself upright. "I always
thought there was some code of honor for doctors,
Plarr, but of course that's an English notion, and you're
only half English, and as for the other half . . ."

"I don't know what you heard," Doctor Plarr said.
"You must have dreamt it or misunderstood."

"I suppose you thought to yourself what the hell does
it matter, she's only a little tart from Mother Sanchez'
house. How much did she cost you? What did you offer
her, Plarr?"

"If you want to know," Doctor Plarr said in a spurt
of rage, "I gave her a pair of sunglasses from Gruber's."

"Those glasses? She was fond of those glasses. She thought they were smart, and now they've been smashed to bits by your friends. What a swine you are, Plarr. It was like raping a child."

"It came more easily."

Doctor Plarr had not realized how close he was to the coffin bed. A fist struck at him through the dark. It caught him on the neck and made him choke. He stepped back and heard the coffin creak.

"Oh God," Charley Fortnum said, "I've knocked the bottle over." He added, "There was still a measure left. I'd kept it for . . ." A hand groped across the floor, touched Doctor Plarr's shoes and recoiled.

"I'll bring a light."

"Oh no, you won't. I don't want to see your fucking face ever again, Plarr."

"You are taking it too hard. These things happen, Fortnum."

"You don't even pretend to love her, do you?"

"No."

"I suppose you'd had her at the brothel, and so you thought . . ."

"I've told you before—I saw her there, but I never had her."

"I'd saved her from that place and you've begun to push her back."

"I never intended this, Fortnum."

"You never intended to be found out. It was cheaper for you, wasn't it, not having to pay for your fucks."

"What good do scenes like this do? I thought it would be all over quickly and you'd never know. It's not as if she or I really cared for each other. Caring is the only dangerous thing, Fortnum."

"I cared."

"You'd have had her back. You would never have known."

"When did it begin, Plarr?"

"The second time I saw her. At Gruber's. When I gave her the sunglasses."

"Where did you take her? Back to Mother Sanchez?" The persistent questions reminded Doctor Plarr of fingers pressing the pus out of a boil.

"I took her to my flat. I asked her in to have coffee, but she knew very well what I meant by coffee, Fortnum. If it hadn't been me, it would have been someone else sooner or later. She even knew the porter at my flat."

"Thank God," Fortnum said.

"What do you mean?"

"I've found the bottle. It's not spilt."

He could hear the sound of Fortnum drinking. He said, "You'd better save a little for later in case . . ."

"I know you think I'm a coward, Plarr, but I'm not much afraid of dying now. It's a lot easier than going back and waiting at the camp for a child to be born with your face, Plarr."

"It's not how I intended things," Doctor Plarr repeated. He had no anger left with which to defend himself. "Nothing is ever what we intend. They didn't mean to kidnap you. I didn't mean to start the child. You would almost think there was a great joker somewhere who likes to give a twist to things. Perhaps the dark side of God has a sense of humor."

"What dark side?"

"Some crazy notion of León's. You should have heard that—not the things you did hear."

"I wasn't trying to hear—I was trying to get off this damn box and join you. I was lonely, and your drugs don't work any more. I'd nearly got to the door when I heard the priest say you were jealous. Jealous, I thought, jealous of what? And then I heard and I got back on to the box."

In a distant village Doctor Plarr had once been forced to perform an emergency operation for which he was not qualified. He had the choice of risking the operation or letting the woman die. Afterward he felt the same fatigue as he felt now, and the woman had died just the same. He had sat down on the floor in his exhaustion. He thought: I've said all I can. What more can I say? The woman was a long time dying or it seemed so to him then.

Fortnum said, "To think I wrote to Clara telling her you would look after her and the baby."

"I know."

"How the hell do you know?"

"You aren't the only one who overhears things. The joker again. I overheard you dictating to León. It made me angry."

"You angry? Why?"

"I suppose León was right—I *am* jealous."

"Jealous of what?"

"That would be another comic twist, wouldn't it?"

He could hear the sound of Charley Fortnum drinking again. Doctor Plarr said, "Even one of your measures won't last forever."

"I haven't got forever. Why can't I hate you, Plarr? Is it the whisky? I'm not drunk yet."

"Perhaps you are. A little."

"It's an awful thing, Plarr, but there's no one else I can leave them with. I can't trust Humphries . . ."

"I'll give you a jab of morphine if you want to sleep."

"I'd rather stay awake. I've the hell of a lot of things to think about and not much time. I want to be left alone, Plarr. Alone. I have to get used to that, haven't I?"

It seemed to Doctor Plarr that they had all been left completely alone. Their enemies had abandoned them: the loudspeaker had fallen silent, the rain had stopped, and in spite of his thoughts Doctor Plarr slept, though fitfully. The first time he opened his eyes it was the voice of Father Rivas that woke him. The priest was kneeling by the door with his lips pressed to a crack in the wood. He seemed to be speaking to the dead or dying man outside. Words of comfort, a prayer, the formula of conditional absolution? Doctor Plarr turned on his other side and slept again. When he woke a second time, Charley Fortnum was snoring in the other room—a dry-throated grating whisky snore. Perhaps he was dreaming of security in the big bed at home after he had finished the bottle on the dumbwaiter. Was Clara patient with him when he snored like that? When she was forced to lie awake beside him what had her thoughts been? Had she regretted her cell at Mother Sanchez'? There, with the dawn, she could sleep peacefully alone. Did she regret the simplicity of her life there? He had no idea. He could no more imagine her thoughts than he could imagine the thoughts of a strange animal.

The light from the projectors shining under the door lost brilliance. The last day had begun. He remembered an occasion years ago when he sat with his mother at a *son-et-lumière* performance outside Buenos Aires. The searchlights came and went like a professor's white chalk, picking out a tree, under which someone—San Martín was it?—had sat—an old stable where another figure of history had tethered his horse, the windows of a room where a treaty or a constitution—he couldn't remember what—had been signed. A voice explained the story in a prose touched with the dignity of the un-recallable past. He was tired from his medical studies and he fell asleep. When he woke for the third time it was to see Marta busy at the table laying a cloth, while daylight seeped through the interstices of window and door. There were two unlit candles on the table stuck in saucers. "They are all we have left, Father," Marta said.

Father Rivas was still asleep, curled up like an embryo.

Marta repeated, "Father."

One by one, as she spoke, the others began to wake to the new day, León, Pablo, Aquino.

"What time is it?"

"What?"

"What did you say?"

"There are not enough candles, Father."

"The candles do not matter, Marta. You fuss too much."

"Your shirt is still wet. You will catch your death from cold."

"I doubt that," Father Rivas said.

She grumbled her disappointments as she laid out on the table in turn a medicine bottle full of wine, a maté gourd which had to serve as a chalice, a torn dishcloth for a napkin. "It is not how I wanted it to be," she complained. "It is not how I dreamed of it." She put a pocket missal which had lost half its binding open on the table. "What Sunday is it, Father?" she asked, as she fumbled with the leaves. "Is it the twenty-fifth Sunday after Pentecost or the twenty-sixth? Or can it be Advent, Father?"

"I have no idea," Father Rivas said.

"Then how can I find you the right Gospel and the right Epistle?"

"I will take what comes. Pot luck," he said.

Pablo said, "It would be a good thing to release Fortnum now. It must be nearly six, and in two hours . . ."

"No," Aquino said, "we have voted to wait."

"He hasn't voted," Pablo said, indicating Doctor Plarr.

"He has no vote. He is not one of us."

"He will die with us."

Father Rivas took his wet shirt from Marta. He said, "We have no time to argue now. I am going to say Mass. Help Señor Fortnum in if he wants to hear it. I shall be saying Mass for Diego, for Miguel, for all of us who may be going to die today."

"Not for me," Aquino said.

"You cannot dictate to me whom I pray for. I know well enough you believe in nothing. All right. Believe in nothing. Stay in the corner there and believe in nothing. Who cares whether you believe or not? Even Marx cannot guarantee what is true or false any more than I can."

"I hate to see time wasted. We have not so much of it left."

"What would you prefer to do with your time?"

Aquino laughed. "Oh, of course, I would waste it like you. 'When death is on the tongue, the live man speaks.' If I still had a wish to write I would make that verse a little clearer—I almost begin to understand it myself."

"Will you hear my confession, Father?" the Negro asked.

"Of course. In a moment. If you come into the yard. And you, Marta?"

"How can I confess, Father?"

"Why not? You are near enough to death to promise anything. Even to leave me."

"I will never . . ."

"The parachutists will see to that."

"But you, Father?"

"Oh, I will have to take my chance. There are not many people lucky enough to die with a priest handy. I am glad to be one of the majority. I have been one of the privileged too long."

Doctor Plarr left them and went in to the inner room. He said, "León's going to say Mass. Do you want to be there?"

"What time is it?"

"I don't know. Some time after six, I think. The sun has risen."

"What will they do now?"

"Perez has given them till eight to release you."

"They are not going to?"

"I don't think so."

"Then they'll kill me and Perez will kill them. You've got the best chance, haven't you?"

"Perhaps. It's not a big chance."

"My letter to Clara . . . you'd better keep it for me all the same."

"If you want me to."

Charley Fortnum took a wad of papers from his pocket. "Most of these are bills. Unpaid. The tradesmen all cheat except Gruber. Where in hell did I put it?" At last he found the letter in another pocket. "No," he said, "there's not much point in sending it to her now. Why should she care to hear a lot of loving words from me if she has you?" He tore the letter into small pieces. "Anyway I wouldn't want the police to read it. There's a photo too," he said, searching in his wallet. "The only one I've got of Fortnum's Pride, but she's in

277

it as well." He took a quick look and then he tore it also into minute pieces.

"Promise you won't tell her that I knew about you. I wouldn't want her to feel any guilt. If she's capable of it."

"I promise," Doctor Plarr said.

"These bills—you'd better look after them," Charley Fortnum said. He handed them to Doctor Plarr. "There may be enough in my current account to meet them. If not—the buggers have swindled me enough. I'm clearing the decks," he added, "but I don't want the crew to suffer."

"Father Rivas will be starting Mass by now. If you want to hear it, I'll give you an arm in there."

"No, I've never been what you'd call a religious man. I think I'll stay out here with the whisky." He carefully measured what was left in the bottle. "Perhaps one small one now—that leaves a real measure at the last. Bigger than a shipmaster's."

A low voice was speaking in the other room. Charley Fortnum said, "I know people are supposed to get a bit of comfort at the end—by believing in all that. Do you believe in anything at all?"

"No."

Now that the personal truth was out between them Doctor Plarr felt a curious need to speak with complete accuracy. He added, "I don't think so."

"Nor do I—except . . . It's a damn silly thing to feel, but when I'm with that fellow out there, I mean the priest . . . the one who's going to murder me . . . I feel . . . Do you know there was even a moment when I thought he was going to confess to me. To me, Charley Fortnum? Can you beat that? And by God I'd have given him absolution. When are they going to kill me, Plarr?"

"I don't know what the time is. I have no watch.

Some time around eight I suppose. Perez will send in the paras then. What happens afterward, God knows."

"God again! You can't get away from the bloody word, can you? Perhaps I'll go and listen awhile after all. It won't do any harm. It'll please him. I mean the priest. And there's nothing else to do. If you'll help me."

He put his arm around Doctor Plarr's shoulder. He weighed surprisingly light for his bulk—like a body filled only with air. He's an old man, Doctor Plarr thought, he wouldn't have had long to live anyway, and he remembered the night he had met him first, when he and Humphries lugged him protesting across the road to the Bolívar. He had weighed a lot heavier then. They made only two steps toward the door and then Charley Fortnum stopped dead in his tracks. "I can't make it," he said. "Why should I anyway? I wouldn't want to curry favor at the last moment. Take me back to the whisky. That's my sacrament."

Doctor Plarr returned to the other room. He took up his stand near Aquino who sat on the ground, watching the motions of the priest with a look of suspicion. It was as though he feared that Father Rivas was laying some trap, planning a betrayal, as he moved to and fro by the table and made the secret signals with his hands. All Aquino's poems were of death, Doctor Plarr remembered. He wasn't going to be robbed of it now.

Father Rivas was reading the Gospel. He read it in Latin not in Spanish, and Doctor Plarr had long forgotten the little Latin he had once known. He kept his eye on Aquino while the voice ran rapidly on in the dead tongue. Perhaps they thought he was praying with his eyes lowered and a kind of prayer did enter his mind—or at least a wish, heavy with self-distrust, that if the moment came he would have the skill and determination to act quickly. If I had been with them over the border, he wondered, what would I have done when my father called for help in the police-station yard? Would I have gone back to him or escaped as they did?

Father Rivas reached the Canon of the Mass and the consecration of the bread. Marta was watching her man with an expression of pride. The priest lifted up the maté gourd and spoke the only phrases of the Mass which Doctor Plarr had for some reason never forgotten. "As often as you do these things you shall do them in memory of Me." How many acts in a lifetime had he done in memory of something forgotten or almost forgotten?

The priest lowered the gourd. He knelt and rose quickly. He seemed to be whipping the Mass to its conclusion with impatience. He was like a herdsman driving his cattle toward the byre before a storm burst, but he had started home too late. The loudspeaker blared its message in the voice of Colonel Perez. "You have exactly one hour left to send the Consul out to us and save your lives." Doctor Plarr saw Aquino's left hand tighten on his gun. The voice went on, "I repeat you have one hour left. Send the Consul out and save your lives."

". . . who takes away the sins of the world, grant them eternal rest."

Father Rivas began *"Domine, non sum dignus."* Marta's was the only voice which joined his. Doctor Plarr looked around seeking Pablo. The Negro knelt with bowed head by the back wall. Would it be possible, he wondered, before the Mass ended, while they were distracted by the ceremony, to seize Aquino's gun and hold them up for long enough to enable Charley Fortnum to escape? I'd be saving all their lives, he thought, not only Charley's. He looked back toward Aquino, and as though Aquino knew what was in his mind he shook his head.

280

Father Rivas took the kitchen cloth and began to clean the gourd, as punctiliously as though he were back in the parish church at Asunción.

"Ite missa est."

The voice on the loudspeaker answered like a liturgical response, "You have fifty minutes left."

"Father," Pablo said. "The Mass is over. Better surrender now. Or let us vote again."

"My vote is the same," Aquino said.

"You are a priest, Father, you cannot kill," Marta said.

Father Rivas held out the dishcloth. "Go into the yard and burn this. It will not be needed again."

"It would be a mortal sin for you to kill him now, Father. After the Mass."

"It is a mortal sin for anyone at any time. The best I can do is to ask for God's mercy like anyone else."

"Was that what you were doing up at the altar?" Doctor Plarr asked. He felt wearied out by all the arguments, by the slowness with which the short time left them dragged by.

"I was praying I would not have to kill him."

"Posting a letter," Doctor Plarr said. "I thought you didn't believe in any reply to letters like that."

"Perhaps I was hoping for a coincidence."

The loudspeaker announced: "You have forty-five minutes left."

"If they would leave us alone . . ." Pablo complained.

"They want to break our nerve," Aquino said.

Father Rivas left them abruptly. He carried his revolver with him.

Charley Fortnum lay on the coffin. His eyes were open and he stared up at the mud roof. "Have you come to liquidate me, Father?" he asked.

Father Rivas had a look of shyness or perhaps shame. He moved a few steps into the room. He said,

"No. No. Not that. Not yet. I thought there might be something you needed."

"I still have some whisky left."

"You heard their loudspeaker. They will be coming for you soon."

"And then you will kill me?"

"Those are my orders, Señor Fortnum."

"I thought a priest took his orders from the Church, Father. Oh, I forgot. You don't belong any more, do you? All the same you were saying a Mass. I'm not much of a Catholic, but I didn't feel inclined to attend it. It's not exactly a holiday of obligation. Not for me."

"I remembered you at the altar, Señor Fortnum," Father Rivas said with awkward formality, as though he were addressing a bourgeois parishioner. The phrase came from a language which had grown rusty during the last years.

"I'd rather you forgot me, Father."

"I shall never be allowed to do that," Father Rivas said.

Charley Fortnum noticed with surprise that the man was close to tears. He said, "What's the matter, Father?"

"I never believed it would come to this. You see— if it had been the American Ambassador—they would have given way. And I would have saved ten men's lives. I never believed I would have to take a life."

"Why did they ever choose you as a leader?"

"El Tigre thought he could trust me."

"Well, he can, can't he?"

"I don't know now. I don't know."

Does a condemned man always have to comfort his executioner? Charley Fortnum wondered. He said, "Is there anything I can do for you, Father?"

The man looked at him with an expression of hope, like a dog who thinks he has heard the word "walk." He shuffled a step nearer. Charley Fortnum remembered the boy at school with protuberant ears whom Mason used to bully. He said, "I am sorry . . ." Sorry for what? For failing to be the American Ambassador?

The man said, "I know how hard it must be for you. Lying there. Waiting. Perhaps if you could prepare yourself a little . . . that might take your mind off . . ."

"You mean confess?"

"Yes." He explained, "In an emergency . . . even I . . ."

"But I'm no good as a penitent, Father. I haven't confessed in thirty years. Not since my first marriage anyway—which wasn't a marriage. You'd better look to the others."

"I have done all I can for them."

"After such a long time . . . it's impossible . . . I haven't enough belief. I would be ashamed to speak all those pious words, Father, even if I remembered them."

"You would feel no shame now if you had no belief. And you need not say them to me aloud, Señor Fortnum. Only make an act of contrition. In silence. To yourself. That is enough. We have so little time. Just an act of contrition," he pleaded as though he were asking for the price of a meal.

"But I've told you, I've forgotten the words."

The man came two steps nearer, as if he were gathering a bit of courage or hope. Perhaps he hoped to be offered enough cash for a piece of bread.

"Just say you are sorry and try to mean it."

"Oh, I'm sorry for a lot of things, Father. Not the whisky though." He picked the bottle up, scrutinized what was left and put it down again. "It's a difficult life. A man has to have one sort of drug or another."

"Forget the whisky. There must be other things. I only ask you to say—I am sorry for breaking a rule."

"I don't even remember what rules I've broken. There are so many damned rules."

"I have broken the rules too, Señor Fortnum. But I

283

am not sorry I took Marta. I am not sorry I am here with these men. This revolver—one cannot always swing a censer up and down or sprinkle holy water. But if there was another priest here I would say to him, yes I *am* sorry. I am sorry I did not live in an age when the rules of the Church seemed more easy to keep—or in some future when perhaps they will be changed or not seem so hard. There is one thing I can easily say. Perhaps you could say it too. I am sorry not to have had more patience. Failures like ours are often just failures of hope. Please—cannot you say you are sorry you did not have more hope?"

The man obviously needed comfort and Charley Fortnum gave him all he could. "Yes, I suppose I could go about as far as that, Father."

Father, Father, Father. The word repeated itself in his mind. He had a vision of his father sitting bewildered, not understanding, not recognizing him, by the dumbwaiter, while he lay on the ground and the horse stood over him. Poor bugger, he thought.

Father Rivas finished the words of absolution. He said, "Perhaps I will have a drink with you now—a small one."

"Thank you, Father," Charley Fortnum said. "I'm a lot luckier than you are. There's no one to give *you* absolution."

"I only saw your father for a few minutes once a day," Aquino said, "when we walked around the yard. Sometimes . . ." He broke off to listen to the loudspeaker from the trees outside. The voice said, "You have only fifteen minutes left."

"The last quarter of an hour has gone a bit too quickly for my taste," Doctor Plarr commented.

"Will they begin to count out the minutes now? I wish they would let us die quietly."

"Tell me a little more about my father."

"He was a fine old man."

"During the few minutes you had with him," Doctor Plarr asked, "what did you talk about?"

"We never had time to talk of anything much. A guard was always there. He walked beside us. He would greet me—very formally and affectionately like a father greeting his son—and I—well, I had a great respect for him, you understand. There would always be a spell of silence—you know how it is with a *caballero* like that. I would wait for him to speak first. Then the guard would shout at us and push us apart."

"Did they torture him?"

"No. Not in the way they did to me. The CIA men would not have approved. He was an Anglo-Saxon. All the same fifteen years in a police station is a long torture. It is easier to lose a few fingers."

"What did he look like?"

"An old man. What else can I say? You must know what he looked like better than I do."

"He wasn't an old man the last time I saw him. I wish I had even a police snap of him lying dead. You know the kind of thing they take for the records."

"It would not be a pleasant sight."

"It would fill a gap. Perhaps we wouldn't have recognized each other if he had escaped. If he had been here with you now."

"He had very white hair."

"Not when I knew him."

"And he stooped badly. He suffered very much from rheumatism in his right leg. You might say it was the rheumatism which killed him."

"I remember someone quite different. Someone tall and thin and straight. Walking fast away from the quay at Asunción. Turning once to wave."

"Strange. To me he seemed a small fat man who limped."

"I'm glad they didn't torture him—in your way."

"With the guards always around I never had a proper chance to warn him about our plan. When the moment came—he did not even know the guard had been bribed—I shouted to him 'Run' and he looked bewildered. He hesitated. That hesitation and the rheumatism . . ."

"You did your best, Aquino. It was no one's fault."

Aquino said, "Once I recited a poem to him, but I do not think he cared much for poetry. It was a good poem all the same. About death of course. It began, 'Death has the taste of salt.' Do you know what he said to me once? It was as if he were angry—I do not know who with—he said, 'I am not unhappy here, I am bored. Bored. If God would only give me a little pain.' It was an odd thing to say."

"I think I understand," Doctor Plarr said.

"In the end, he must have got his pain."

"Yes. He was lucky at the end."

"As for me I have never known boredom," Aquino said. "Pain yes. Fear. I am frightened now. But not boredom."

Doctor Plarr said, "Perhaps you have not come to the end of yourself. It's a good thing when that happens only when you are old, like my father was." He thought of his mother among the porcelain parrots in Buenos Aires or eating éclairs in the Calle Florida, of Margarita fallen asleep in the carefully shaded room while he lay wide awake watching her unloved face, of Clara, and the child, and the long impossible future beside the Paraná. It seemed to him he was already his father's age, that he had spent as long in prison as his father had, and that it was his father who had escaped.

"You have ten minutes left," the loudspeaker said. "Send the Consul out immediately and afterward one at a time with your hands raised . . ."

It was still giving careful instructions, when Father Rivas came back into the room. Aquino said, "The time is almost up. Better let me kill him now. It is not the job for a priest."

"They may still be bluffing."

"By the time we know for sure it may be too late. These paras are well trained by the Yankees in Panama. They move quick."

Doctor Plarr said, "I am going out to talk to Perez."

"No, no, Eduardo. That would be suicide. You heard what Perez said. He will not even respect a white flag. You agree, Aquino?"

Pablo said, "We are beaten. Let the Consul go."

"If that man passes through the room," Aquino said, "I shall shoot him—and anyone who helps him—even you, Pablo."

"Then they will kill us all," Marta said. "If he dies we shall all die."

"At any rate it will be a memorable occasion."

"Machismo," Doctor Plarr said, "your damned stupid *machismo*. León, I've got to do something for the poor devil in there. If I talk to Perez . . ."

"What can you offer him?"

"If he agrees to extend his time limit, will you extend yours?"

"What would be the good?"

"He *is* the British Consul. The British Government . . ."

"Only an Honorary Consul, Eduardo. You have explained more than once what that means."

"Will you agree if Perez . . ."

"Yes, I will agree, but I doubt if Perez . . . He may not even give you time to talk."

"I think he will. We have been good friends."

A memory came back to Doctor Plarr of the back reach of the river, of the great horizontal forest, of Perez moving without hesitation from dipping log to dipping log toward the little group where the murderer awaited him. "They are all my people," Perez had said.

"Perez is not a bad man as policemen go."

"I am afraid for you, Eduardo."

"The doctor is suffering from *machismo* too," Aquino said. "Go on . . . get out there and talk . . . but take a gun with you . . ."

"It's not *machismo* I'm suffering from. You told me the truth, León. I *am* jealous. Jealous of Charley Fortnum."

"If a man is jealous," Aquino said, "he kills the other man—or gets killed. It's a simple thing, jealousy."

"Mine is not that kind of jealousy."

"What other sort of jealousy is there? You sleep with a man's wife . . . And when he does the same . . ."

"He loves her . . . that's the trouble."

"You have five minutes left," the loudspeaker announced.

"I'm jealous because he loves her. That stupid banal word love. It's never meant anything to me. Like the word God. I know how to fuck—I don't know how to love. Poor drunken Charley Fortnum wins the game."

"One doesn't surrender a mistress so easily," Aquino said. "They cost a lot of trouble to win."

"Clara?" Doctor Plarr laughed. "I paid her with a pair of sunglasses." Memories continued to return. They were like tiresome obstacles which he had to work around, a blindfold game with bottles, before he reached the door. He said, "There was something she asked me before I left home . . . I didn't bother to listen."

"Stay here, Eduardo. You cannot trust Perez . . ."

For a moment after he opened the door Doctor Plarr was dazzled by the sunlight, and then the world came back into sharp focus. Twenty yards of mud stretched before him. The Indian Miguel lay like a bundle of old clothes thrown to one side sodden with the night's rain. Beyond the body the trees and the deep shade began.

There was no sign of anyone alive. The police had probably cleared the people from the neighboring huts. About thirty yards away something gleamed among the trees. It might have been a drawn bayonet which had caught the sun, but as he walked a little nearer and looked more closely, he saw it was only a piece of petrol tin that formed part of a hut hidden among the trees. A dog barked a long distance away.

Doctor Plarr walked slowly and hesitatingly on. No one moved, no one spoke, not a shot was fired. He raised his hands a short distance above his waist, like a conjuror who wants to show that they are empty. He called, "Perez! Colonel Perez!" He felt absurd. After all there was no danger. They had exaggerated the whole situation. He had felt more insecure on the occasion when he followed Perez from raft to raft.

He didn't hear the shot which struck him from behind in the back of the right leg. He fell forward full length, as though he had been tackled in a rugby game, with his face only a few yards from the shadow of the trees. He was unaware of any pain, and though for a while he lost consciousness, it was as peaceful as falling asleep over a book on a hot day.

When he opened his eyes again the shadow of the trees had hardly moved. He felt very sleepy. He wanted to crawl on into the shade and sleep again. The morning sun here was too violent. He was vaguely aware that there was something he had to discuss with someone, but it could wait until his siesta was over. Thank God, he thought, I am alone. He was too tired to make love, and the day was too hot. He had forgotten to draw the curtains.

He heard the sound of breathing; it came from behind him, and he didn't understand how that could be. A voice whispered, "Eduardo." He did not at first

289

recognize it, but when he heard his name repeated, he exclaimed, "León?" He couldn't understand what León could be doing there. He tried to turn round, but a stiffness in his leg prevented him.

The voice said, "I think they have shot me in the stomach."

Doctor Plarr woke sharply up. The trees in front of him were the trees of the *barrio*. The sun was shining on his head because he had not had time to reach the trees. He knew that he would not be safe until he reached the trees.

The voice which he now knew must be León's said, "I heard the shot. I had to come."

Doctor Plarr again tried to turn, but it was no use— he gave up the attempt.

The voice behind him said, "Are you badly hurt?"

"I don't think so. What about you?"

"Oh, I am safe now," the voice said.

"Safe?"

"Quite safe. I could not kill a mouse."

Doctor Plarr said, "We must get you to a hospital."

"You were right, Eduardo," the voice said. "I was never made to be a killer."

"I don't understand what's happened . . . I have to talk to Perez . . . You have no business to be here, León. You should have waited with the others."

"I thought you might need me."

"Why? What for?"

There was a long silence until Doctor Plarr asked rather absurdly, "Are you still there?"

A whisper came from behind him.

Doctor Plarr said, "I can't hear you."

The voice said a word which sounded like "Father." Nothing in their situation seemed to make any sense whatever.

"Lie still," Doctor Plarr said. "If they see either of us move they may shoot again. Don't even speak."

"I am sorry . . . I beg pardon . . ."

"Ego te absolvo," Doctor Plarr whispered in a flash of memory. He intended to laugh, to show León he was only joking—they had often joked when they were boys at the unmeaning formulas the priests taught them to use—but he was too tired and the laugh shriveled in his throat.

Three paras came out of the shade. In their camouflage they were like trees walking. They carried their automatic rifles at the ready. Two of them moved toward the hut. The third approached Doctor Plarr, who lay doggo, holding what little breath he had.

5

In the cemetery were a great number of people whom Charley Fortnum did not know from Adam. One woman in a long old-fashioned dress of black he assumed to be Señora Plarr. She held tightly to the arm of a thin priest whose dark brown eyes turned here and there, to left and right as though he were afraid of missing an important member of the congregation. Charley Fortnum heard her introduce him several times —"This is my friend Father Galvão from Rio." Two other ladies wiped their eyes prominently near the graveside. They might have been hired for the occasion like the undertakers. Neither of them spoke to Señora Plarr, or even to one another, but of course that might have been a matter of professional etiquette. After the Mass in the cathedral they had come separately up to Charley Fortnum and introduced themselves.

"You are Señor Fortnum, the Consul? I was such a

great friend of poor Eduardo. This is my husband, Señor Escobar."

"My name is Señora Vallejo. My husband was unable to come, but I could not bear to fail Eduardo, so I brought with me my friend Señor Duran. Miguel, this is Señor Fortnum, the British Consul whom those scoundrels . . ."

The name Miguel called up immediately in Charley Fortnum's mind the image of the Guaraní as he squatted in the doorway of the hut, tending his gun with a smile, and then he thought of the bundle of rain-soaked clothes past which the parachutists carried him on a stretcher. One of his hands in passing had dangled down and touched a piece of wet material. He began to say, "May I introduce my wife . . . ?" but Señora Vallejo and her friend were already moving on. She held her handkerchief under her eyes—so that it looked rather like a yashmak—until her next social encounter. At least, Charley Fortnum thought, Clara does not pretend grief. It's a kind of honesty.

The funeral, he thought, very much resembled two diplomatic cocktail parties he had attended in Buenos Aires. They were part of a series given for the departing British Ambassador. It was soon after his own appointment as Honorary Consul when he was still regarded with interest because he had picnicked with royalty among the ruins. People wanted to hear what the royals had talked about. This time the second party, with the same guests whom he had seen in the church, was held in the open air of the cemetery.

"My name is Doctor Saavedra," a voice said. "You may remember we met once with Doctor Plarr—"

Charley Fortnum wanted to reply, Surely it was at the house of Mother Sanchez. I remember you well with a girl. I was with María, the one whom somebody stabbed.

"This is my wife," he said, and Doctor Saavedra

bowed with courtesy over her hand; her face must have been familiar to him, if only because of the birthmark on her forehead. He wondered how many of these people knew that Clara had been Plarr's mistress.

"I must go now," Doctor Saavedra said. "I have been asked to say a few words in honor of our poor friend."

He moved toward the coffin, pausing on the way to shake hands and exchange a few words with Colonel Perez. Colonel Perez was in uniform and carried his cap in the crook of his arm. He had the air of being the most serious person present. Perhaps he was wondering how the doctor's death would affect his career. A lot depended, of course, on the attitude of the British Embassy. A young man, Crichton, who was a new face to Charley Fortnum, had flown up from B.A. to represent the Ambassador (the First Secretary being in bed with flu). He stood beside Perez close to the coffin. You could estimate the social importance of a mourner by his closeness to the coffin, for the coffin represented the guest of honor. The Escobars were worming their way toward it, and Señora Vallejo was almost near enough to put out a hand. Charley Fortnum with a crutch under his right arm stayed on the periphery of the smart company. He felt it was absurd to be there at all. He was an imposter. He only owed his position there because he had been mistaken for the American Ambassador.

Also on the periphery, but far removed from Charley Fortnum, stood Doctor Humphries. He too had the air of being out of place and knowing it. His proper habitat was the Italian Club, his proper neighbor the waiter from Naples, who feared he had the evil eye. When he first noticed Humphries Charley Fortnum had taken a step in his direction, but Humphries had backed hastily away. Charley Fortnum remembered telling Doctor Plarr, in some long distant past, that Humphries had cut him. "Lucky you," Plarr had exclaimed. Those had been happy days, and yet all the while Plarr had been sleeping with Clara and Plarr's child was growing in her body. He had loved Clara and Clara had been gentle and tender to him. All that was over. He had owed his happiness to Doctor Plarr. He took a furtive look at Clara. She was watching Saavedra who had begun to speak. She looked bored as though the subject of the eulogy was a stranger who did not interest her at all. Poor Plarr, he thought, he was deceived by her too.

"You were more than a doctor who healed our bodies," Doctor Saavedra said, addressing his words directly to the coffin which was wrapped in a Union Jack that had been lent on request by Charley Fortnum. "You were a friend to each of your patients—even to the poorest among them. All of us know how unsparingly you worked in the *barrio* of the poor without recompense—from a sense of love and justice. What a tragic fate then it was that you, who had toiled so hard for the destitute, died at the hands of their so-called defenders."

Good God, Charley Fortnum thought, can that be the story Colonel Perez is putting out?

"Your mother was born in Paraguay, once our heroic enemy, and it was with a *machismo* worthy of your maternal ancestors who gave their hearts' blood for Lopez—not seeking whether his cause were good or ill—that you walked out to your death from the hut, where these false champions of the poor were gathered, in a last attempt to save their lives as well as your friend's. You were shot down without mercy by a fanatic priest, but you won the day—your friend survived."

Charley Fortnum looked across the open grave at Colonel Perez. His uncovered head was bowed; his hands were pressed to his sides; his feet were at the correct military angle of attention. He looked like a nineteenth-century monument of soldierly grief while Doctor Saavedra continued to establish by his eulogy —was it about that they had spoken together?—the official version of Plarr's death. Who would think to question it now? The speech would be printed verbatim in *El Litoral* and a resumé would surely appear even in the *Nación*.

"Except for your murderers and their prisoner I was the last, Eduardo, to see you alive. Your enthusiasms were so much wider than your professional interests, and it was your love of literature which enriched our friendship. The last time we were together you had called me to your side—a strange reversal of the usual rôle of doctor and patient—to discuss the formation in this city of an Anglo-Argentinian cultural club, and with your usual modesty you invited me to be the first president. My friend, you spoke that night of how best to deepen the ties between the English and the South American communities. How little either of us knew that in a matter of days you would give your own life in that cause. You surrendered everything—your medical career, your appreciation of art, your capacity for friendship, the love you had grown to have for your adopted land, in the attempt to save those misguided men and your fellow countryman. I promise you with my hand on your coffin that the Anglo-Argentinian Club will live, baptized with the blood of a brave man."

Señora Plarr was weeping, and so, more decoratively, were Señora Vallejo and Señora Escobar. "I am tired," Charley Fortnum said, "it's time to go home."

"Yes, Charley," Clara said.

They began a slow walk toward their hired car.

Somebody touched Fortnum's arm. It was Herr Gruber.

Herr Gruber said, "Señor Fortnum . . . I am so glad you are here . . . safe and . . ."

"Nearly sound," Charley Fortnum said. He won-

dered how much Gruber knew. He wanted to get back
to the shelter of the car. He said, "How is the shop?
Doing well?"

"I shall have a lot of photographs to develop. Of the
hut where they held you. Everyone is going out there
to see it. I don't think they always photograph the right
hut. Señora Fortnum, you must have had an anxious
time." He explained to Charley Fortnum, "Señora Fortnum has always bought her sunglasses at my shop. I
have some new designs in from Buenos Aires if she
would care . . ."

"Yes. Yes. Next time we are in town. You must forgive us, Herr Gruber. The sun is very hot and I have
stood too long."

His ankle itched almost unbearably in its plaster
case. They had told him at the hospital that Doctor
Plarr had done a good job. In a matter of weeks he
would be driving Fortnum's Pride again. He had found
the Land Rover standing in its old place under the
avocados, a little battered, with one headlight gone and
the radiator bent. Clara explained it had been borrowed
by one of the police officers. "I shall complain to
Perez," he had said, supporting himself against the car
while he pressed his hands tenderly upon a wounded
plate.

"No, you must not do that, Charley. The poor man
would be in trouble. I told him he could take it." It
wasn't worth an argument on his first day home.

They had driven him straight back from the hospital
through a landscape which seemed like the memory of
a country he had left forever—the byroad which went
to the Bergman orange-canning factory, the disused rail
track of an abandoned camp which had once belonged
to a Czech with an unpronounceable name. He counted
the ponds as he passed—there ought to be four of
them—he wondered how he ought to greet Clara.

There was no real greeting apart from a kiss on the

cheek. He refused to go and lie down on the excuse that he had been on his back too long. He couldn't bear the thought of the large double bed which Clara must so often have shared with Plarr when he was out farming (because of the servants they would have been afraid to disarrange the bed in a guest room). He had sat with his foot propped up on the verandah beside the dumbwaiter. He had been away less than a week, but it seemed a long slow year of separation, long enough for two characters to grow apart—he poured himself out a shipmaster's measure of Long John. Looking up at Clara over the right measure, he said, "Of course they have told you?"

"Told me what, Charley?"

"Doctor Plarr is dead."

"Yes. Colonel Perez came here. He told me."

"The doctor was a good friend to you."

"Yes, Charley. Are you comfortable like that? May I fetch you a pillow?" He thought that after all their love-making and deception it was hard Plarr had not earned a single tear. The Long John had an unfamiliar taste, he had become so accustomed to Argentinian whisky. He began to explain to Clara that it would be best if for the next few weeks he slept alone in one of the guest rooms. The plaster round his ankle made him restless, he said, and she must sleep well—because of the child. She said yes, of course, she understood. It would be arranged.

Now as he shunted on his crutch away from the cemetery toward the hired car, a voice said to him, "Excuse me, Mr. Fortnum . . ." It was the young fellow Crichton from the Embassy. He said, "I wondered if I could come out to your camp this afternoon. The Ambassador has asked me . . . there are certain things he wants me to talk over with you . . ."

"You can have lunch with us," Charley Fortnum said. "You will be very welcome," he added, thinking that anyone, even a man from the Embassy, would help to preserve him from the solitude he would otherwise have to share with Clara.

"I am afraid . . . I would very much like to . . . but I have promised Señora Plarr . . . and Father Galvão. If I could come about four o'clock. I am catching the evening plane to B.A."

When he got back to the camp Charley Fortnum told Clara that he was too tired to eat. He would sleep a bit before Crichton came. Clara made him comfortable—she had been trained to make men comfortable as much as any hospital nurse. He tried not to show that the touch of her hand irritated him when she arranged the pillows. He felt his skin tighten when she kissed his cheek and he wanted to tell her not to trouble. A kiss was worth nothing from someone who was incapable of loving even her lover. And yet, he asked himself, what fault was it of hers? You don't learn about love from a customer in a brothel. And because it was not her fault he must be careful never to show her what he felt. It would have been a lot simpler, he thought, if she had really loved Plarr. He could so easily picture how it would have been if he had found her heartbroken, the gentle way in which he would have comforted her. Phrases from romantic novels came to his head like "Dear, there is nothing to forgive." But as he played with the fancy he remembered she had sold herself for a gaudy pair of sunglasses from Gruber's.

The sun through the jalousies striped the floor of the guest room. One of his father's hunting prints hung on the wall. A huntsman held a fox above the ravening hounds. He looked at the picture with disgust and turned his face away—he had never killed anything in his life, not even a rat.

The bed was comfortable enough, but after all the

coffin with the blankets had not really been very hard
—better than the bed in his nursery when he was a
child. There was a deep quiet here, broken only by an
occasional footstep from the kitchen region or the creak
of a chair out on the verandah. There was no radio to
announce the latest news, no quarreling voices from an
inner room. To be free, he discovered, was a very
lonely thing. He could almost have wished the door to
open, to have seen the priest come shyly in, carrying a
bottle of Argentine whisky. He had felt an odd kinship
with that priest.

There had been no ceremony at the priest's funeral.
He had been shoveled quickly away in unconsecrated
ground, and Charley Fortnum resented that. If he had
known about it in time he would have stood by the
grave and said a few words like Doctor Saavedra,
though he could not remember ever having made a
speech in his life: all the same he could have found the
courage in the heat of his indignation. He would have
told them all, "The Father was a good man. I know he
didn't kill Plarr." But his only audience, he supposed,
would have been a couple of gravediggers and the
driver of the police truck. He thought: at least I'll find
out where they stowed him and I'll lay a few flowers
there. Then he fell into a deep sleep of exhaustion.

Clara woke him because Crichton had arrived. She
found his crutch and helped him on with his dressing
gown, and he went out on to the verandah. He lowered
himself down beside the dumbwaiter and said, "Have
a Scotch."

"It's a bit early, isn't it?" Crichton asked.

"It's never too early for a drink."

"Well, a very small one then. I was saying to Mrs.
Fortnum what a terribly anxious time she must have
had." He put the glass down on a small table without
taking any.

"Cheers," Charley Fortnum said.

"Cheers." Crichton took his glass up again with reluctance. Perhaps he had hoped to leave it untouched on the table until the canonical hour. "There are things the Ambassador wanted me to talk over with you, Mr. Fortnum. Of course I needn't tell you how very very worried we have all been."

"I was a bit worried myself," Charley Fortnum said.

"The Ambassador wants you to know we did everything in our power . . ."

"Yes. Yes. Of course."

"Thank God things turned out all right."

"Not everything. Doctor Plarr's dead."

"Yes. I didn't mean . . ."

"And the priest too."

"Well, he deserved what he got. He murdered Plarr."

"Oh no, he didn't."

"You haven't seen Colonel Perez's report?"

"Colonel Perez is a bloody liar. It was the paras who shot Plarr."

"There was a postmortem, Mr. Fortnum. They checked the bullets. One in the leg. Two in the head. They were not army bullets."

"You mean the surgeon of the 9th Brigade checked them. You can tell the Ambassador this, Crichton, from me. I was in the next room when Plarr went out. I heard all that happened. Plarr went out to try to talk to Perez—he thought he might save all our lives. Father Rivas came to me. He said he had agreed to postpone the ultimatum. Then we heard a shot. He said, 'They have shot Eduardo.' He ran out."

"And gave him the *coup de grâce*," Crichton said.

"Oh no, he didn't. He left his gun where I was."

"With his prisoner?"

"It was out of my reach. He had an argument with Aquino in the other room—and with his wife. I heard Aquino say, 'Kill him first.' And I heard his reply . . ."

"Yes?"

"He laughed. I heard him laugh. It surprised me because he wasn't a man who laughed. A shy sort of giggle sometimes. Not what you'd call a laugh. He said, 'Aquino, for a priest there are always priorities.' I don't know why, but I started to say an 'Our Father,' and I'm not a man who prays. I only got as far as 'thy Kingdom' when there was another shot. No. He didn't kill Plarr. He hadn't even reached him. They carried me past the bodies. They were ten feet apart. I suppose if Perez had been there he would have thought of rearranging them. To make the distance right for a *coup de grâce*. Please tell the Ambassador that."

"Of course I'll tell him what your theory is."

"It's not a theory. The paras scored all three deaths —Plarr, the priest and Aquino. It's what they call good shooting."

"They saved your life."

"Oh yes. Or Aquino's bad aim. You see he had only his left hand. He came nearly up to the coffin I was on before he fired. He said, 'They've shot León.' He was too excited to keep the gun steady, but I don't suppose he would have missed a second time. Even with his left hand."

"Why didn't Perez get your story?"

"He didn't ask me for it. Plarr said once that Perez always has to think about his career."

"I'm glad they got Aquino anyway. He was a murderer—or wanted to be."

"He'd seen his friend shot. You have to remember that. They'd been through a lot together. And he was angry with me. I made friends with him and then I tried to escape. You know he fancied himself as a poet. He used to recite me bits of his poems and I pretended to like them, though they didn't make much sense to me. Anyway, I'm glad the paras were satisfied with three deaths. Those other two—Pablo and Marta—

they were only poor people who got caught up in things."

"They had more luck than they deserved. They needn't have been caught up in things."

"Perhaps it was love of a kind. People do get caught up by love, Crichton. Sooner or later."

"It's not a very good excuse."

"No, I suppose not. Not in the Foreign Service anyway."

Crichton looked at his watch. Perhaps he was satisfied now that the proper hour had been reached. He raised his glass. He said, "I suppose you'll be out of action for quite a while."

"I haven't much to do here anyway," Charley Fortnum said.

"Exactly." Crichton took another drink.

"Don't tell me the Ambassador wants another report on the maté?"

"No, no. We just want you to get well in your own good time. As a matter of fact the Ambassador is writing to you officially at the end of the week, but he wanted me to have a word with you first. After all you've been through, official letters always seem—well, so official. You know how it is. They are written to go on the files. Top copy to London. You have to be so—cautious. Someone at home might possibly look at the files one day."

"What's the Ambassador got to be cautious about?"

"Well, for more than a year, London has been pressing us for economies. Do you know they are cutting us down ten percent on official entertainment and we have to show chits now for the least expenditure? And yet these damn MPs keep on coming out and expect to be invited to lunch at least. Some of them even think they rate a cocktail party. Now you, you know, you've had a pretty long inning. If you were in the Service you would have passed the retiring age quite a while ago. In a way the office forgot about you—until this kidnapping came along. You'll be much safer—out of the front line."

"I see. That's it. It's a bit of a blow, Crichton."

"It's not as if you ever got more than your expenses."

"I could import a car every two years."

"That's another thing—as an Honorary Consul you hadn't really the right."

"The Customs here don't distinguish. And everyone does it. The Paraguayan, the Bolivian, the Uruguayan—"

"Not everyone, Fortnum. We try to keep our hands clean at the British Embassy."

"Perhaps that's why you'll never understand South America."

"I don't want to bear only bad news," Crichton said. "There was something the Ambassador asked me to tell you—in strictest confidence. Have I your promise?"

"Of course. Who would I tell?" There isn't even Plarr, he thought.

"The Ambassador proposes to recommend you for an honor in the List next New Year."

"An honor," Charley Fortnum repeated incredulously.

"An O.B.E."

"Why, that's really kind of him, Crichton," Charley Fortnum said. "I never thought he liked me . . ."

"You won't tell anyone, will you? In theory you know all these things have to be approved by the Queen."

"The Queen? Yes. I understand. I hope it won't make me too proud," Charley Fortnum said. "You know I guided some members of the Royal family once —round the ruins. They were a very nice couple. We had a picnic like I had with the American Ambassador, but they didn't expect me to drink Coca-Cola. I like that family. They do a wonderful job."

"And you'll tell no one—except your wife, of course. You can trust her."

"I don't think she'd understand anyway," Charley Fortnum said.

During the night he dreamt he was walking up a very long straight road with Doctor Plarr. On either side the *lagunas* lay like pewter plates which grew more gray every moment in the evening light. Fortnum's Pride had broken down and they had to reach the camp before it was dark. He was anxious. He wanted to run, but he had hurt his leg. He said, "I don't want to keep the Queen waiting."

"What's the Queen doing at the camp?" Doctor Plarr asked.

"She's going to give me the O.B.E."

Doctor Plarr laughed. "Order of the Bad Egg," he said.

Charley Fortnum woke with a sense of desolation, and the images wound themselves quickly up like a strip of Scotch tape, so that all he could remember was the long road and Plarr laughing.

He lay on his back in the narrow guest-room bed, and he felt his age weigh heavily on his body like a blanket. He wondered how many more years he would have to lie alone like that—it seemed a waste of time. A lamp passed the window. He knew it was carried by the *capataz* going to work; in that case it must be nearly dawn. The lamplight moved along the wall and lit his crutch which looked like a big carved initial letter against the wall, and then dimmed and passed away. He knew exactly what the lamp would be lighting now —first the avocados, then the sheds and afterward the irrigation ditches; from here and there the men would be gathering for work in the gunmetal light.

He swung his good leg out of the bed and reached for the crutch. After Crichton had gone he had told Clara the bad news of his retirement. He could see it meant nothing to her. In the eyes of a girl from Mother Sanchez' house he would seem always to be a rich man. He had said nothing about the O.B.E. As he had told Crichton, she wouldn't understand, and he feared that her indifference might make it seem less important even to himself. And yet he wished he could have told her. He wanted to break the wall of silence which was growing up between them. "The Queen is going to give me an honor," he could hear himself saying to her, for the words "the Queen" would surely mean something even to her. He had often told her about his picnic with royalty among the ruins.

He moved on his crutch diagonally like a crab down the passage between the sporting prints, then put his hand out in the dark to open the door of the bedroom, but the door wasn't there and he moved forward into what he felt certain was an empty room. There wasn't even the faintest sound of breathing to break the silence. He might have been walking alone through another ruin. To make sure he passed his hand back and forth over the pillow, and he felt the coldness and cleanness of a bed which had not been slept in. He sat down on the edge of the bed and thought: she's gone away. Right away. Who with? The *capataz* perhaps?— or one of the workmen? why not? They were more her own kind than he was. She could talk to them as she couldn't talk to him. He had been alone a great many years before he found her and there was no reason to be afraid of the few years likely to be left. He had managed then, he assured himself, and he could manage again. Perhaps Humphries would no longer cut him in the street after his name had appeared among the New Year Honors. They would eat goulash again at the Italian Club and he would invite Humphries to the camp; they would sit together by the dumbwaiter, but Humphries was not a drinking man. He felt a pang of pain because Plarr was dead. By her absence she seemed to be betraying Plarr as well as himself. He felt a little angry with her for Plarr's sake. Surely she could have been faithful for a short while to a dead man—it would have been like wearing something black for a week or two.

He didn't hear her come in, and he was startled when she spoke. She said, "Charley, what are you doing here?"

He said, "It's my room, isn't it? Where have you been?"

"I was afraid of being alone. I went to sleep with María." (María was the maid.)

"What were you afraid of? Ghosts?"

"I was afraid for the child. I dreamed I was strangling the child."

So she cares for something, he thought. It was like a glimmer of light at the end of his darkness. If she is capable of that . . . If she isn't all deception . . .

She said, "I had a friend at Señora Sanchez' house who strangled her baby."

"Sit here, Clara." He took her hand and pulled her gently down beside him.

"I thought you did not want me to be near you." She said the sad truth like a fact of no importance, as another woman might say, "I thought you preferred me in red."

"I have no one else, Clara."

"Shall I put on the light?"

"No. It will be daylight soon. Just now I saw the *capataz* going by to work. How is the baby, Clara?" He knew he had hardly mentioned the baby since he came home. He felt as though he were relearning a language he hadn't spoken since a childhood in another country.

"I think he is all right. But sometimes he is so quiet I feel afraid."

"We shall have to find you a good doctor," he said, speaking mechanically without thought. She made a sound like a dog does when you tread on its paw, an exclamation of shock—or was it pain?

"I am sorry . . . I didn't mean . . ." It was still too dark to see her. He raised his hand and found her face. She was crying. "Clara . . ."

"I am sorry, Charley. I am tired."

"Did you love him, Clara?"

"No . . . no . . . I love you, Charley."

"There's nothing wrong in love, Clara. It happens. It doesn't much matter who with. We get caught up," he told her, and remembering what he had said to young Crichton, he added, "we get kidnapped," attempting a feeble joke to reassure her, "by mistake."

"He never loved me," she said. "To him I was only a girl from Señora Sanchez'. "

"You are wrong." It was like pleading a cause; he might have been attempting to bring two young people to a closer understanding.

"He wanted me to kill the baby."

"You mean in your dream?"

"No. No. He wanted it killed. He really wanted it. I knew then he could never love me."

"Perhaps he'd begun, Clara. Some of us . . . we are a bit slow . . . it's not so easy to love . . . we make a lot of mistakes." He went on for the sake of saying something, "I hated my father . . . I did not much like my wife . . . But they were not really bad people . . . that was only one of my mistakes. Some of us learn to read quicker than others . . . Ted and I were both bad at the alphabet. I am not so good at it even now. When I think of all the mistakes there must be on those files in London," he rambled on, making a little human noise in the darkness in the hope that it might reassure her.

307

"I had a brother I loved, Charley. One day he wasn't there any more. He got up to go cane-cutting, but no one in the fields saw him. He went away just like that. Sometimes at Señora Sanchez' house I used to think, Perhaps he will come here looking for a girl and then he will find me and we will go away together."

There seemed at last to be a sort of communication between them and he tried hard to keep the thin thread intact. "What shall we call the child, Clara?"

"If he is a boy—would you like Charley?"

"One Charley's enough in the family. I think we will call him Eduardo. You see I loved Eduardo in a way. He was young enough to be my son."

He put his hand tentatively on her shoulder and he felt her body shaken with tears. He wanted to comfort her, but he had no idea how to do it. He said, "He really loved you in his way, Clara. I don't mean anything wrong . . ."

"It is not true, Charley."

"Once I heard him say he was jealous of me."

"I never loved him, Charley."

Her lie meant nothing to him now at all. It was contradicted too plainly by her tears. In an affair of this kind it was the right thing to lie. He felt a sense of immense relief. It was as though, after what seemed an interminable time of anxious waiting in the anteroom of death, someone came to him with the good news that he had never expected to hear. Someone he loved would survive. He realized that never before had she been so close to him as she was now.

ABOUT THE AUTHOR

Graham Greene was born in 1904 and educated at Berkhamsted School, where his father was the headmaster. On coming down from Balliol College, Oxford, where he published a book of verse, he worked for four years as a sub-editor on *The Times.* He established his reputation with his fourth novel, *Stamboul Train,* which he classed as an "entertainment" in order to distinguish it from more serious work. In 1935 he made a journey across Liberia, described in *Journey Without Maps,* and on his return was appointed film critic of the *Spectator.* In 1926 he had been received into the Roman Catholic Church and was commissioned to visit Mexico in 1938 and report on the religious persecution there. As a result he wrote *The Lawless Roads* and, later, *The Power and the Glory.*

Brighton Rock was published in 1938 and in 1940 he became literary editor of the *Spectator.* The next year he undertook work for the Foreign Office and was sent out to Sierra Leone in 1941–43. One of his major postwar novels, *The Heart of the Matter,* is set in West Africa and is considered by many to be his finest book. This was followed by *The End of the Affair, The Quiet American,* a story set in Vietnam, *Our Man in Havana,* and *A Burnt-Out Case.* His most recent novels are *The Comedians, Travels with My Aunt,* and *The Honorary Consul.* In 1967 he published a collection of short stories under the title: *May We Borrow Your Husband?* His autobiography, *A Sort of Life,* was published in 1971.

In all, Graham Greene has written some thirty novels, "entertainments," plays, children's books, travel books, and collections of essays and short stories. He was made a Companion of Honour in 1966.